THE DECEPTION

THE SECRET TALES, BOOK 2

SANNA BRAND

**Afterworld
Publishing**

EPIGRAPH

"Oh, what a tangled web we weave...when first we practice to deceive."
—Sir Walter Scott

DEDICATION

To my Shaina Maidelas
Robin, Amy, Abby, Laura, Franny, Deborah, and Kresse

Thank you for your friendship, light, and laughter!

CHAPTER
ONE

1818

The Duke of Devonshire's glittering ball was in full cry. Lord Patrick Lansdowne—naval captain, a marquess' brother, and a newly minted viscount—had little use for it; his attendance for another purpose—to purchase a painting by the illustrious Reginald Pheland, the late Baron Halafair.

Patrick stood on the balcony, checking his watch every few minutes. The baron was long dead and paintings by his hand seldom came up for sale. They went for a hefty price. While Patrick admired the artist's landscapes, his seascapes drew him like no other artist. The movement of the waves, the singular scent of the sea, the colors of dawn and sunset—Halafair's work put Patrick back on deck, the sea beneath him, the place he always wished to be.

His purchase this evening had come about through a circuitous route via factor and letters exchanged, the factor sending a study and sketches by Pheland of the work in question.

He'd learned of the painting through word of mouth and found it odd the seller was not using an auction house, a far more typical venue.

Patrick was well acquainted with the late Pheland's baroness,

Beatrice, and their two daughters through his sister-in-law, Rose. He never mentioned his passion for the baron's work, as the family was endlessly assaulted by Pheland's admirers, some fanatical in their devotion.

The factor had planned to deliver the painting yesterday, but a late note said the seller would be standing in for him this evening, the ball the venue for the transfer, and the man's insistence on wearing a mask. He had used the alias "Kauffman."

The whole procedure felt dodgy, the seller's *nom de plume* referencing Angelica Kauffman, a famed artist and a founder of the Royal Academy of Arts. Which was why he had tucked a pocket pistol into his boot.

Why choose a woman artist's name? Perhaps the seller *was* a woman. Interesting.

He had used the name Signor Ricci, after an Italian friend, having no intention of revealing his true one, the price undoubtedly rising to staggering heights. Patrick had told the factor their meeting *must* be tonight, for he sailed on the morrow. He'd used strong words, for his purchase was no trifling business. Kauffman indeed.

The reply to his missive had intrigued him. "Kauffman" had written, "*Life* is a serious business, sir. This is commerce, and one should not give a transaction too much weight."

The seller had a point.

Patrick played along by wearing a domino. Behind him, through the French doors, dancers pranced and whirled. The night was clear, stars spangling the sky, the same ones he charted at sea.

Patrick checked his pocket watch yet again. The meeting time neared. He made his way downstairs to the second floor and into Devonshire's library, as noted in the missive. The vast room held stacks upon stacks of books, two sliding ladders, and a spiral staircase that wound upward to a second level.

Before him, a large hearth flickered, with two wing chairs placed at angles before its flames.

Patrick paced, early by fifteen minutes, as he intended to arrive before the seller. His nerves were aquiver, his adrenaline high, much as when he stood on deck facing an enemy's brace of cannon.

The mantel clock chimed midnight and behind him, a rustle.

Patrick whirled to see a woman enveloped in a large cloak, the cobalt blue of her gown flashing beneath as she emerged from a wing chair. His shock yielded to an appreciation of her elegant form and carriage, her glittering owl-shaped mask shading her eyes, much of her face, and her bound hair.

"Have you brought the funds, sir?" the seller said.

Patrick froze, stunned, and then he chuckled softly.

That laugh, smokey and warm as velvet. Charlotte Pheland would recognize it anywhere—Lord Patrick Lansdowne, now Lord Hawthorne, if she recalled. *Devil have it!* Her nerves aquiver since the ball's start, prickled.

Patrick wore a mask, as instructed, his tall form hinting at muscle beneath his elegant clothes. He carried himself like the military man he was, one who knew his place in the world.

Charlotte understood at some point she would sell a painting to a friend. So be it.

Though wary, she could not renege. Her mother and sister's well-being, along with Halafair's maintenance, depended upon it. As it was, they'd spent a small fortune on her dress to impress the buyer. While their dear papa had been a warm and cheerful man and an exceptional artist, he had been unwise when it came to funds. Upon her father's death, they had been destitute until her mother married Earl Fielding, a man whose name was never voiced by Mama, herself, or Claire, not if they could help it. A despicable man, and with Fielding's passing, their financial support suffered another shocking reversal.

"Good sir, I repeat, have you brought the funds?" she said.

The man nodded, bristling with energy as if mere flesh and bone could not contain him.

"Sir?" she repeated.

He reached into his tailcoat's inner pocket and withdrew a pouch.

Charlotte crossed her arms. She might know Patrick Lansdowne, but she would not release the painting to a mute, his silence suggesting mischief.

The absurdity of their face-off nearly tickled her fancy. She lifted the wrapped painting from behind the chair. "I am afraid we shall not commence the sale, my good man, unless you speak." Charlotte turned to leave.

He laughed again, soft and low, the sound always charming her. Charlotte stepped toward the door. "If you do not speak, you will neither see nor leave with the Pheland painting you desired so very much."

She brushed a hand over the paperweight in her pocket—a clever addition courtesy of Rose—the glass bauble insurance against nefarious doings. Not that she would cosh Patrick on the head. Would she? Tension tightened her belly. "Well?"

"What do you wish me to say, Madame Kauffman?"

"You can be an ass, Patrick." She tossed her mask onto a chair and approached him.

He removed his domino, as well. "I see your hearing is in good order, Lady Charlotte," he said with sarcasm. "It is obviously I."

Unbelievable. She'd seen him only last week at Woodbine, a brother-in-law after her stepsister, Rose, had married Patrick's brother, Rhys. The naval captain, a charmer, was also a nuisance who tweaked her and others with his sarcasm and quips.

"You admire my father's work?" she said.

The man's stiff posture relaxed a fraction. "Admire is too faint a word, Charlotte. His seascapes take me to the place I love most in this world."

Patrick could not have surprised her more, having expected a set down, rather than enthusiasm. "That pleases me, for all this cloak-and-dagger wears on a person."

He let out a chuckle. "I agree. Yet your factor insisted upon it."

Charlotte's cheeks heated. "I admit that was my doing. My agent contracted the influenza, and it is quite awkward selling one's father's paintings."

"Why not use an auction house, for heaven's sake?" He leaned against a wing chair's back, crossing a leg, relaxed, devilishly handsome, and utterly proud, his black hair agleam in the candlelight.

Charlotte could not reveal she feared an auction house's scrutiny. "I had an unpleasant issue with Sotheby's, and Christie's proved no better, thus I have taken the sales in hand myself."

"Why sell them?" he said.

"Shall we get on with it?"

He moved closer and laid a hand on her shoulder, his brows drawn together with concern. "Charlotte, why sell your father's work? You are part of our family now. If you need funds, we can help."

"I appreciate your kindness, Patrick, very much. But—"

With a rattle, the double doors swung wide, to reveal the Duke of Devonshire leading a throng into the library, expounding, "And here we have our newest library, which is dedicated to..."

Devonshire spotted them and went silent.

That gossip Lady Ablethorp was with him, too. Curse it. Mama and Claire, Rose and Rhys, and his sisters. And there was the Duke of Wellington, for all that was holy. *Heavens!*

Patrick dropped his hand from her shoulder, but not soon enough.

Lady Ablethorp plowed forward. "What do we have here? An assignation?"

Ruination crashed upon Charlotte like an avalanche.

The duke moved to Lady Ablethorp's side, a frown wreathing his face.

"My lady," he said to the viperous Ablethorp. "I fear you make much out of nothing. Lady Charlotte and Lord Hawthorne are related."

"Vaguely," she said.

The duke, Patrick's good friend, eyed him with a pained expression. "My lord?"

It felt as if a thousand eyes peered at her. At least Mama and Claire knew what she was about, which mattered little, for all stared goggle-eyed at her and Patrick's misstep.

Charlotte could find no words, for she was compromised in the eyes of the *ton*.

Patrick appeared confounded, too. As a man who commanded a Royal Navy ship, he must feel as if he had stepped into another's life.

Patrick *was* confounded. True, he could reply to the duke, say nothing untoward had occurred. Charlotte's name would still be blackened.

Which was the coward's way.

As a man, he would escape unscathed—Lady Charlotte had no male relatives to defend her honor, unless he counted Rhys or himself. The irony did not escape him.

Charlotte would be brushed with scandal and called loose or wanton. Unconscionable epithets. The episode would be caricatured in cartoons, noted in *The Morning Post*, the gossip endless.

He imagined those faces multiplied by hundreds, rumors slithering through the *ton*, shaming Charlotte.

The clock on the mantle ticked.

Patrick did not wish to marry. Yet, as a gentleman, he could not abandon this woman to wolves like Ablethorp.

Charlotte peered at him, damming tears she obviously wished would vanish. Her back was straight, her chin high, but the fear and grief in her eyes touched him.

"An assignation, you say, Lady Ablethorp?" Patrick said. "That would paint our meeting in an unsavory light, given Lady Charlotte's and my betrothal."

Lady Ablethorp raised a haughty brow. "Is that so, my lord? And are you not to depart for your new command in the near future?"

"On the morrow." He nodded. "Hence, my farewells to my fiancée in private."

Ablethorp huffed. "And shall you leave Lady Charlotte dangling at the end of a string for years?"

Charlotte's eyes widened, and she went to speak, opening that pretty mouth of hers.

Patrick forestalled her words. "I shall not be absent for years but for a few months. Lady Charlotte and I intend to marry upon my return."

Charlotte closed her mouth, her face paling further, lips compressed tight.

Lady Ablethorp winked. "How fortuitous. And may I offer you both my heartfelt congratulations."

A hullabaloo of congratulations and back slaps ensued, along with their family's speculative stares as the guests filtered out.

Alone once again, Charlotte rounded on Patrick. "And what are we supposed to do now?"

"I assumed that was obvious."

"Become engaged? That is absurd."

"Extended engagements are not uncommon, and in truth, I have no idea how long I shall be gone on my next assignment. We shall have ample time to wiggle out of this challenging situation. In fact, the longer I am away, the more believable it will be that you tire of waiting and cry off."

"Ah." Charlotte grinned. "Not a bad thought, my lord."

Patrick winged out an arm. "Let us complete the sale after a dance, a waltz, to convince the Philistines that we are indeed a couple."

"I fervently hope," Charlotte said, taking his arm, "that our dance will not give you hives."

Patrick's soft laugh charmed her once again.

"I doubt that," he said, lips twitching. "But one never knows."

His cheeky grin appeared. "What say you to gifting me your father's painting? A token of our engagement."

Charlotte tapped a finger to her lips, then offered a saucy smile. "Not a chance, my lord. The price stands."

CHAPTER
TWO

Weeks after Patrick Lansdowne had sailed, Charlotte sat at her desk and dipped her pen into ink to hover over a fresh sheet of foolscap. Her daily correspondence to her friends and relatives complete, she had resolved to write Patrick in answer to his letter. But how to phrase her words?

A dollop of ink dripped to the paper.

Salutations, Lord Patrick!

How do you fare? Your letter sounds as if life at sea is treating you well. I am pleased you are bound for the Mediterranean, rather than Bermuda. Closer to home.

I hope you do not mind me calling you Lord Patrick. I find Lord Hawthorne or Captain Lansdowne too formal for an "engaged" couple.

Please continue with your vivid descriptions of the sea and sky, for I am painting a challenging seascape and hope to incorporate your details onto the canvas.

All is well at Halafair, though Claire has contracted a cold from her many treks to a nearby dig. I admire my sister's passion, but I confess her absorption with archaeology leaves me nonplussed. Gardening is the only dirt I wish to turn.

I recently read Percy Bysshe Shelley's "Ozymandias." What an exceptional work! I suspect you will find it so upon reading the poem. I shall enclose a copy.

Do you and your men play cards? I bet that you do so. Whist, piquet, vingt-et-un? I am curious. What else do you do aboard ship of a recreational nature?

Your descriptions of the native costumes and landscapes of the West Indies thrilled me. Though I may never see that exotic land, I feel I have been there due to your lively words.

I visited Woodbine to see Rose, and she and your brother are faring well. I have a surprise for their anniversary, a work-in-progress. Can you guess the subject matter? I suspect you shall.

Do stay safe.

Yours,

Lady Charlotte, Halafair Hall

While in port, Patrick's cabin boy handed him his correspondence, including a letter from Lady Charlotte. He opened it first, knifing through the seal, and upon reading her tepid thoughts on her sister's archeological fervor, he laughed aloud. He assembled his writing materials, for he must return an equally entertaining missive.

Dear Lady Charlotte,

How fare you? We are headed for the Black Sea, and I am in a sour mood as we have been becalmed for a solid three days. The men are restless, as are the officers and myself!

The painting I purchased from you now hangs in my cabin, a true pleasure and delight each time I view it.

You may find this as charming as I do—a cabin boy, not my own, mind you, has seen fit to attach himself to me. He is a fine little fellow named Henry, of about eight years. He has become my shadow, and his antics give me much amusement. He seldom speaks, other than to say, "yes, sir," yet he manages to convey a plethora of emotion in those two words and appears at the oddest of times. I fear a bad case of hero worship.

Did he know my many flaws, ones you are privy to, he would run in the other direction.

To answer your question, we indeed play poker, whist, and vingt-et-un, most often with my steward, Lieutenant Banby, who is somewhat of a card shark! Regarding other recreational activities...the lieutenant embroiders pictures, as do several of the other men, which are called woolies. A few tell entertaining stories, whilst others play musical instruments such as flutes or drums. Dice games are popular, as are woodcarving or model making. I admit to the latter pastime.

I began The Bride of Lammermoor *(Anonymous), but did not find it pleasurable, thus I have switched to* Frankenstein or the Modern Prometheus, *also published anonymously. A ripping read. Have you read it?*

No tales of adventure nor exotics in this letter, I am afraid, though I am wondering when you shall cry off our engagement. I fear it shall be an onerous task, and I do not envy you.

Whilst in the West Indies, I purchased a token for you from Barbados, a "painting" made of shells by a local woman. I suspect you will be amazed by its intricacy.

Do tell more about your gift to Rhys and Rose, for I suspect both Roddy and Dolce figure prominently! Those yearlings are full of mischief!

Yours truly,

Captain Patrick Lansdowne, the Royal Charles

How awful to be becalmed, Charlotte thought. How frustrating. She hoped the winds had picked up by now. Of course, they must have, given his letter arrived eons after posting.

Patrick had purchased a token for her from exotic Barbados! How kind...and intriguing. Shells, of all amazing things. Any art fascinated her, including Patrick's model building, and she was equally charmed by his lieutenant's embroidery, having seen other exquisite works by sailors at sea called woolies. She must tell him more of her current painting in her next letter.

Dear Lord Patrick,

I hope the winds have picked up by now! The rain here is unceasing and I am in the glums. I must light several braces of candles to paint, and that frustrates me excessively. Are you no longer becalmed? I fervently hope so, for it sounded rather tedious, as well as producing mischief amongst the crew. Do you still have your "shadow" cabin boy?

You make ship models! What a complex craft, and I can picture you, tweezers in hand, bent over your work. Upon your return, I do hope you will share some of your models with me.

I have begun a large piece for the Royal Academy of Arts' Summer Exhibition. I am pleased...so far, yet I have much work still to come before its completion. Perhaps this is the year the committee will approve my work for entry! I think you will approve, for it is a seascape.

Currently, I am reading Northanger Abby *by Jane Austen. It is exceptionally written and quite Gothic in tone. Also quite amusing. Have you read any of Austen's work? For years before her passing, her works were labelled by "A Lady." It is only with her sad death that her works bear her true name. I find that rather tragic.*

My ten-year-old pup, Titian, is ailing and I am rather distraught. He is a fine fellow and I would hate for him to leave us. When I visited Woodbine, I made sure Diablo was faring well. Your horse is in fine fettle, though I suspect he longs for his master.

Regarding our engagement, I am hoping to make our announcement ending it at the height of another's scandal, thus saving myself and you from an excess of chatter. Soon, I am sure.

Yours,

Lady Charlotte, Halafair Hall

Dear Lady Charlotte,

How is Titian? I do hope he is faring better.

At the moment, I am reading nothing, for I am on fire! A man I dislike intently—an admiral, no less—has ordered the Royal Charles join his Mediterranean flotilla. We were bound for home, and when the order came through, all aboard were greatly disappointed, myself included. He and I shall not interact a great deal, yet I loathe the sight of him even surrounded by the sea. He has an untrustworthy soul and is a man who derided our great Lord Nelson.

On a more uplifting subject or perhaps a laughable one, the boy's hero worship has only increased. I now call Henry my barnacle, for he is seldom far from my side. A more insidious case of hero worship I have not seen. My personal cabin boy's nose is quite out of joint! Yet I cannot find it in my heart to dismiss Henry, for he means well and his antics greatly amuse me.

Yours truly,

Captain Patrick Lansdowne, the Royal Charles

CHAPTER

THREE

After months at sea, Patrick stood feet braced on the afterdeck, hands behind his back, as the *Royal Charles* dove and rose through the churning waves of the Mediterranean, angry waters that presaged the storm to come. A dangerous one. Their flotilla was a beast, a commanding one, yet he sensed the storm would be vicious.

He signaled Banby to join him, and his steward strode to the afterdeck.

"I do not like the looks of this, Captain."

"Nor do I, my friend." Patrick leaned against the taffrail. He grinned. "We shall meet the challenge."

Banby raised his field glass. "We are far enough from shore."

"Would that we could heave to and batten down the hatches. I wish you to have the sails reefed and the bloody cannons checked yourself, for I have little confidence in Midshipman—"

"I am aware," Banby said. "It shall be done, as well as Cook's galley fire."

Sea spray lashed them as they peered into the heightening waves. A peel of nearby thunder shook his bones, the surrounding flotilla disappearing and reappearing in the mist, like specters from a ghost story.

Hours later, the crew weary, Patrick cursed as they swooped downward on yet another immense wave, and the *Royal Charles* surged upward, attempting to scale it.

The fallen night, the driving rain made it impossible to see the flotilla other than the few lights winking in and out as the ships strove against towering waves. The *Royal Charles* crested yet another, but an immense gust of wind sheered across the bow, followed by thunder, then a loud gunshot.

Except that was no gunshot. Patrick raised his lantern, rain lashing him. Across the bridge...Disaster. A crack in the main mast.

Shouts, stomping feet, men running to different positions. Patrick boomed commands, changed one sailor's trajectory, then a midshipmen's, to see Banby race toward him.

Another gust. A louder crack.

A boy ran past him to preserve a loosening stay.

Lightning struck again. The mast!

Splinters flying! The main mast bending...toppling!

A boy directly in the falling mast's trajectory.

Men screamed, ran, leapt as Patrick streaked across the deck toward the boy, fighting through bodies, rain, and wind, running... running.

He peered through the torrent. A crack boomed, the mast teetering.

The boy... Henry!

Patrick sprang, shoving away the child as the mast thundered downward.

Patrick regained consciousness with pain so brutal he wished to scream. He clamped his teeth tight. Royal Naval captains did *not* scream. Beyond the agony, waves rolled beneath him. He cracked his eyes to see watery light filtering in from cabin portholes.

The pain spiked, his back arched, and he collapsed, a bloody sweating mess. How...

He remembered. The mast falling, his leap to save the boy...

Had the boy been saved?

His uniform smelled of dried blood, and his breath hitched, trying to comprehend his situation. He was onboard a ship. But it was not the *Royal Charles*, though Patrick couldn't explain how he knew that.

He was alive, at least, though that shocked him, for he had been certain the falling mast would end his life.

When he widened his eyes, light momentarily blinded him, and he rubbed them. Even that simple movement caused pain.

His eyes adjusted to see two owlish ones, the color of blue frost, peering down at him. Patrick blinked, yet he could not recognize the face.

"Would you like some water, Captain?"

The voice was young, very young. He nodded.

Cool glass touched his parched lips, and when the glass tilted, blessed water coated his tongue. He swallowed.

More came into focus, the cabin belonging to an unknown offi-cer. But the boy...

"You...boy... Are you well?"

"I be good, Captain," the boy said.

"Your name?" His words sounded slurred. He *should* recall the boy's name.

"I'm Henry, sir," the lad said, his freckled face and dark blue eyes filled with worry. "I'm all right, Captain. You saved me."

The boy stretched to give him another sip of water, a hand resting on Patrick's thigh. Patrick saw it with his own eyes.

Except, where Henry's hand rested, he felt *nothing at all*.

Sleep took him once again.

Charlotte was penning letters, a stack of them, for she had been consumed by her work, dreading a maid delivering that day's post, which would only make the pile higher.

Her eyes drifted through the windows to the day outside, with a searing blue sky and early summer flowers abloom. She'd planned a walk with Claire and...

A knock and their butler entered with yet more letters. After thanking him, she rifled through the stack.

One from Patrick! His were her favorites, so entertaining.

Dear Lady Charlotte,

I hope you and your family are well and thriving. I have had little time to write, and as we prepare to leave port in Menorca, a Spanish port once in British hands, I finally have a moment to post my letter.

Impressive towers protect the harbor and the sea is near blue as the Caribbean. You would be charmed by the town, with its pristine white homes and public buildings, the sky a searing blue. Most days. This week, the weather has turned foul.

My stable visit to see the Menorquín horses was a highlight. Some say they have Arab blood, others claim them to be of Berber stock, and still others, mid-European. Whatever their source, these beasts are agile and stand a solid fifteen hands. All are black, with gleaming coats, and appear friendly and eager to work. I found myself enthralled.

The Menorcans claim their horses' fiery temperament is coupled with steady nerves, and I have observed their riders practicing Doma menorquina, a Menorcan riding style based on dressage. Their athleticism is unparalleled. Upon my return, I shall investigate purchasing a dam and a stud.

I do not know when I shall be able to write again, for as we set sail, the seas seem unhappy with our flotilla, the skies gunmetal gray, the waves churning.

What is your latest novel? One you might recommend? I have found no time to read while I assured our ship repairs complete, the Royal Charles *now shipshape and sound.*

I found a few moments to work on a new model ship, managing to build the frame and lay down the planks. A British frigate.

How goes your painting for the Royal Academy's exhibition? Five feet wide sounds immense, and I hope you are making good progress.

I have assigned Henry to post this letter. I am rather confounded by the barnacle's adulation, yet his cheeky words amuse me. The boy has a good heart.

Once our business in the Mediterranean is complete, we sail for home. I am eager for it.

Have you had the opportunity to dissolve our engagement?

Yours truly,

Captain Patrick Lansdowne

Charlotte lifted her pen to write Patrick, to tell him of Titian's passing, of her newest novel, *The Maid of Killarney*, and of her progress on her exhibition entry. Charlotte bit her lip, Patrick's question nagging. He had again asked about their engagement. Well, no, she had not cried off yet. Soon, she told herself, aware her hand was stayed by her increasing fondness for Patrick and her dislike of the commotion reneging would produce. Which was absurd. She *must* send the announcement to the papers. Soon. Charlotte would do it soon.

Opening his eyes, Patrick was near blinded by white. Walls, bed, sheets, floors—all white. Where in God's...?

Pain reminded him that all was not well, yet it was less severe than his previous awakening.

Lieutenant Banby sat to his right, and on his left, the boy, Henry.

As the bed did not move from the rocking waves, the soothing motion absent, they must be ashore.

"Greetings, Captain," Banby said. "Good to have you back, as you have been insensate for days. We are in the port city of Barcelona at the Hospital de la Santa Creu i Sant Pau. You are recovering from your accident aboard ship."

"How fares my ship?"

Banby shook his head. "I am grieved to report that the *Royal Charles* is lost."

"Our men?" he said with a rasp.

"All but three survived the sinking, and were taken aboard the *Lady Mary*."

Even three were too many to lose. "Who?"

"Lieutenant Proudfoot, Seaman James Tarlow, and..." The man sighed. "And Cook."

Cook had been with Patrick since before Trafalgar. An honorable and brave man. All of the three pained his heart, but Cook had been Banby's and his good friend. For no reason whatsoever, he remembered Cookie's incident and smiled. "Remember Cook's affair with the escaped chickens?"

Banby grinned. "How could I not?"

Patrick turned his face away. "*Christ.*"

"He shall be greatly missed," Banby said. "I believed you done for, too, Captain."

"I thought the same," Patrick said, turning to the boy in the room. "Why are you here, Henry?"

Rather than answer, the boy looked to Banby.

"He will not leave your side," Banby said.

Patrick processed Banby's words, but the emotion felt too complex to untangle. "My prognosis?"

Banby's stoic demeanor never changed but his eyes darkened.

"Banby, report!" he demanded, his voice as stern as he could make it. Which wasn't much.

"The doctors believe you are paralyzed from...your thighs down, Captain."

Patrick's world trembled. "And shall I walk again?"

"They have not speculated."

"I see," he said. "I would prefer to be alone."

Banby and the boy saluted him, the pair wearing pained expressions, and Banby quit the room.

Useless legs. Useless bloody legs. How would he possibly go on?

He sighed.

Henry, that pesky boy, remained and now stood tight against a corner of the room staring down at his boots.

"Why are you still here, Henry?" He hadn't meant to sound so agitated. Bollocks.

Henry's face whitened.

"*Well?*"

"I figure you might need somethin', Captain. I dunno, a drink of water, a bit ta eat."

Patrick didn't laugh. Christ, he had nothing to laugh about. Yet he found his barnacle amusing.

"So you plan to simply stand there until I need something, young man?"

"Yes, sir!" Henry saluted, touching his clenched fist to his brow.

"Then prove yourself useful. I wish to sit up."

Henry scurried to the bed. "You sure?"

"Henry!"

The boy saluted again but didn't move.

Christ! He spoke in a quiet but stern voice. "Am I your captain or not?"

The boy's expression turned pensive. "Well...As we's on land, I don't rightly know."

A barnacle with a mind.

Heaven help him.

Charlotte stood at her easel in Halafair Hall, her favorite place to be. Her current painting was of Roddy and Dolce, Rhys and Rose's two beloved foals, the work to celebrate the couple's first wedding anniversary. When the Marquess and Marchioness celebrated in a month, the portrait would be ready.

The delicious light from the window caught her engagement ring, a beautiful bouquet of emeralds and diamonds that sparkled in the sun. Patrick had posted the ring from the West Indies, a surprise.

Charlotte cursed, for she had once again forgotten to remove it whilst working. She shook her head, returning to work.

Charlotte cleaned her brushes and moved on to a second painting, a stormy seascape thirty inches by four feet. She had much yet to do on the work, but was pleased how it was coming along.

She left that easel and crossed the room to focus on her Royal Academy of Arts' Summer Exhibition painting. Entrants to the prestigious show did not have to be members, and though they accepted very few women into the exhibition, she hoped her seascape at dawn would do the trick.

This seascape challenged her—the most difficult painting she had yet to execute—a large piece more than six feet wide.

As she raised her brush to the restless sea, thoughts of Patrick intruded. Her fiancé. The time was long past for her to declare an end to their engagement.

She had hesitated again and again, pushing off the announcement of their engagement's dissolution. She was not sure why. Perhaps due to the ensuing stares and gossip? Charlotte cared little other than needing the *ton* for the sale of her father's paintings.

A more powerful reason lurked in her mind's recesses. Or was it her heart?

Perhaps because Patrick's offer of marriage had been noble? She must call herself a liar to claim that the reason.

She should be honest at least to herself—she found his correspondence lively and intriguing, his perceptions intelligent. In truth, Charlotte had begun liking the man far more than she could have imagined.

How surprising.

Patrick's carriage was loaded, the trunks with new clothes stowed atop, while Lieutenant Banby checked the horses. Within the carriage, Captain Patrick Lansdowne, Viscount Hawthorne since the Battle of Trafalgar, lay on a specially constructed bed for the journey to Germany.

He was anxious for their leave-taking, yet he could do nothing to speed the process along. Out the window, the barnacle trotted to the front of the carriage.

Why was the child still here?

Had Henry's parents been contacted? Did Henry even have parents?

Many cabin boys came from naval families, but others were orphans from The Marine Society or the Foundling Hospital, while others with a criminal bent were conscripted. He fervently hoped this boy was amongst the former and would be collected soon.

"Banby!" Patrick hollered.

In seconds, the side door was flung open. "How can I help you, Captain?"

God's blood! Patrick wanted to scream. How many times had he heard those words over the past month? He was sick to death of them. Sick of the pain. Sick of his useless legs. He should have died beneath that mast aboard the *Royal Charles*, rather than lived as a useless hulk of a man.

The barnacle materialized beside Banby.

"Why are you not on your way home, Henry?" he asked.

"The *Royal Charles* were my home, Captain," Henry said.

Fury, frustration, exasperation filled every pore. Yet he must not release it onto the boy. "Do you have another home back to England, one with your father and mother?"

The boy stood straight, hands tight to his sides, though his lower lip quivered.

"Henry?" Patrick said.

"I ain't got no home, Captain, leastways not one as you described."

"You are an orphan?"

The boy's cheeks pinked. "I am. I were const...conscrp..."

"Conscripted?" Banby said.

Henry nodded. "I were in the orphanage and someone took me. That's how I landed on the *Despoina*."

Why hadn't the boy told them thus when he had come aboard? The blistering curses circling Patrick's head were not suitable for a child. Barnacle, indeed. "Then you shall come home with us."

CHAPTER
FOUR

The celebration for the Marquess and Marchioness of Ravenscroft's first wedded year was small, consisting of family and close friends. Charlotte's painting of the colt and filly was a success, but a moment of joy in an otherwise concerning celebration. The festivities weren't somber, not exactly, but worry slithered through the group like an asp seeking prey.

Two months earlier, Patrick's letters had gone from chatty to infrequent, the family and Charlotte receiving terse notes that explicated nothing. Patrick was alive, they knew that much. Yet he had not returned home nor indicated what he was doing nor why he remained away.

Rose insisted Patrick would return soon. She "felt it in her bones."

Charlotte suspected Rose's words were intended to soothe her husband, who near daily contacted the Admiralty with few results, other than knowing the *Royal Charles* had sunk and three aboard had died, though not Patrick. The family, Charlotte, too, worried as well.

Rose, Charlotte's sister-of-the-heart, pulled her aside at the first opportunity. "Have you received any explanation from Patrick?"

"None," Charlotte said. "Only brief notes. A line or two that told nothing of his condition or whereabouts." She missed his chatty letters with his thoughts and feelings about life at sea or in exotic lands.

"Rhys is not doing well," Rose said.

Charlotte glanced at the marquess. His eyes were tired, his demeanor weary. "He looks rather wan."

"He is not eating properly and he even went off on one of his retreats. He has not done so for ages."

Rhys' retreats, Charlotte knew, were the result of his participation in the war against Napoleon. Months earlier, after the family had settled at Woodbine, Rhys had ceased them. Their renewal was a bad sign which must stress both himself and Rose.

"I am so sorry," Charlotte said. "Thankfully, Patrick has not perished, and yet..."

"My pain-in-the-ass brother has failed to explain *where* he is or *why* he has not returned."

Patrick *was* a pain in the ass. But he was also kind and funny and possessed other fine qualities. He positively vibrated with life.

Charlotte knew not what to say and remained silent.

Patrick's pain merely hummed now, ever-present but tolerable, as they traveled away from *Schloss Salder*, a stately home where an agent said the Farffler chair resided. The chair was unique, as it was *self-propelled*, which would give Patrick a modicum of independence. He must find the damned chair. Nothing less would do.

Once Patrick had been strong enough for travel, he, Banby, and the barnacle had traversed numerous uncomfortable miles in search of a self-propelled wheeled chair, each stop ending in disappointment.

Patrick had tried a Bath chair, but that wheeled contraption was anathema, for he must be either pushed by a man or pulled by a horse, the indignity too much to bear. During his research, he discovered most chairs were the same until he'd found a sketch of Farffler's. Early on, Patrick had written letters and engaged agents to suss out the chair, and one reply from Italy claimed a chair that might suit.

Six weeks had passed as they'd made their way to Italy, but the recumbent chair their agent had discovered was again too heavy for Patrick to push himself, even with his increased upper body strength. That egregious disappointment was lightened somewhat by the agent pointing them to an ephemera dealer. There, they discovered the schematics for the Farffler chair, originally constructed in 1655 for the man's own use.

At the very least, they now had the plans. Yet they had ventured to *Schloss Salder* in hopes of finding the actual chair...with no luck.

Patrick's strength had grown daily through his demanding calisthenics, his arms, torso, shoulders, chest, and neck all gaining strength. But though Banby exercised his legs each day, they remained useless sticks.

As *Schloss Salder* grew small in the rear window, Patrick wanted to throw something, hit something, anything to rid himself of his overwhelming loss of agency.

He reached for his flask and emptied it. Only water, when he longed for a sip of scotch or bourbon. But he had sworn not to indulge, at least until they found a proper chair.

When the pain had been intolerable, when he hated what he had become, he imagined killing himself. That would surely end his suffering.

He sighed, lifting a two-week-old English newspaper, *The Times*. Of course he would not kill himself. A tossing cowardly thing to do.

Dear God, but he was bored. The pain was bad. Disability was bad. But the boredom...That might be what killed him.

Patrick reached for the leather portfolio and pulled out the plans for the Farffler chair. The person sat on a low-sided wooden seat, with two tall wheels alongside. Across the recumbent legs sat a box covering gears, with two crank handles projecting from either side. A third smaller wheel was situated in front. Farffler had used the cranks to propel himself.

Though his hopes had been repeatedly dashed, he refused to quit. He thumped one of his two canes on the carriage roof, the sticks near as useless as his legs, but they gave him the leverage to stand without aid.

The carriage soon drew to a halt, and Banby appeared, along with Henry.

"You called, Captain?" Banby said with a raised brow.

The man thought he was funny. "I have been reviewing the sketches of Farffler's chair."

"I see," Banby said.

"Let us have done with this mad dashing about. We shall build our own cursed chair, then return home."

Days after the anniversary party, May in full bloom, Charlotte had returned to Halafair to focus once again on her smaller seascapes. The painting nearly done, the light perfect, and her factor now possessed preliminary sketches for clients. A wealthy farmer *and* Sir Alex Morrison had expressed interest, which might presage a bidding war—a good thing.

Time for the signature, the most challenging part of the process. For the name she would place on the work was Reginald Pheland, her father, famed for his paintings of landscapes and seascapes. Though he had passed away years earlier, he allegedly left a cache of his work in the attic, work their family continued to sell.

Only her mother Beatrice, and her sister Claire knew her forgeries paid Halafair's taxes, funded their staff, and many other estate-related expenses.

Her papa, whom she dearly loved, had been a fine, albeit traditional, artist. As a child, Charlotte had been fascinated by his work, enough so that she had picked up a paintbrush at the age of three. Years later, her mother and sister claimed she had surpassed her father's artistry. In her most self-reflective moments, she was forced to agree, due to her studies with the great J.M.W. Turner.

Women who worked in oils were few, discouraged from the pastime by ignorant men, the proceeds from those sales minuscule. On the commercial market, paintings with *her* signature would receive far fewer pounds than those bearing her father's name. Or any male name, in fact.

Her family needed money to survive, hence Charlotte had become a forger to ensure their survival.

As she attributed the painting before her to her father, she fervently hoped Papa was looking down upon her with approval.

Charlotte returned to her work. Hours later, she cleaned her paints with turpentine and washed her hands with Castile soap, discarding her painter's apron on a hook set for that purpose. She retired to the yellow salon to pen replies to letters she owed. A stack of them.

Once she had answered her friends' letters, adding questions on fashion and *on dits* around town, she wrote Mr. Turner. She regaled him on her proposed entry into the Summer Exhibition and asked after his current project.

A knock broke her focus, a maid appearing at the door. "Excuse me for disturbing you, Lady Charlotte, but Lady Ravenscroft has arrived and wishes to speak with you."

A surprise, and she began folding her completed letters. "Lovely. Please have refreshments brought."

Halafair was but an hour's ride from Woodbine, the Lansdowne stud farm in Devonshire. That Rose would travel without prior notice said something was up.

"Lottie!" Rose said, arms wide for a hug.

Charlotte clasped Rose to her, this sister of the heart. Standing back, she noted Rose's appearance, a bit sallow, and couldn't help but see the bruising beneath Rose's eyes.

"Are you well, dear sister?" Charlotte said.

Rose grinned. "Yes! Though I spend much time bent over the chamber pot."

Charlotte gasped. "Are you...?"

"Indeed!" Rose said, grinning. "The little sprog performs the scotch reel within my belly. I am told it will pass. I hope it is soon!"

"As do I!" She hugged Rose again. "When shall I meet the wee Lansdowne?"

"December, or thereabouts." Her sister frowned. "Though I wish my babe were the only cause of my fatigue."

"Rhys?" Charlotte said.

"He is well enough."

Charlotte leaned forward. "Then what?"

Rose pressed her fingers to her closed eyes. "As you know, Patrick's ship sank during a terrible storm. We have learned that in saving the life of a cabin boy, Patrick was gravely injured."

"How badly?" A pit yawned in Charlotte's belly for that brave, irritating man. He'd escaped unscathed from the Napoleonic wars, only to suffer this. "Will he live?"

"Yes. But it is terrible, Lottie." Tears filled Rose's eyes. "He is paralyzed. His legs, I mean. They no longer work."

For such an active man, the loss would be a devastation. She had first met Patrick at Fielding Manor, Rose's former home. An intense man, one quite different from his brother the marquess, his sarcasm and quips could be funny...or lethal. Yet she would never forget his honorable display saving her reputation at the Devonshire ball. Not all men would act thus, and she owed him much. But it was his letters, missives that illuminated the inner man, that intrigued her. He had revealed a reader, a model shipbuilder, and a captain who cared for his crew. A man who found humor and delight in a small cabin boy. Patrick Lansdowne was more than she had first perceived.

"Will he walk again?" Charlotte asked.

Rose opened her knitting bag, removed her current project, and began weaving stitches. "The doctors refuse to give a definitive answer, only hints that Patrick's debilitation is permanent."

"God in heaven, I grieve for him." Charlotte rubbed her forefinger and thumb together again and again as if aching for a paintbrush.

"I wanted you to be apprised," Rose said, her fingers swiftly weaving stitches onto her needles. "He is, thankfully, on his way home. Three sailors died in the storm, and they were blessed not to lose more men."

"I suspect," Charlotte said, "Patrick does not feel particularly blessed."

"I am sure he does not," Rose said. "You understand, yes? To decide?"

"Decide?" Then Charlotte realized Rose's implication. "You mean our engagement?"

"His injury puts you in an awkward position if you renege."

Charlotte enjoyed life at Halafair with her mother and sister and would be content to remain there. The only stick in the spoke was that without access to the *beau monde*, Charlotte would have trouble selling her forged paintings. And without the paintings' sales, her little family would suffer.

Rose knew they were not flush in the pocket, for they often spoke of personal matters, but Charlotte would never reveal the dire state of their finances.

"Given the loss of his legs," Charlotte said, "I cannot imagine how Patrick will deal with his injury upon his return. It frightens me a bit, if I am honest. I would also prefer the *ton* not vilify me."

"I doubt they will," Rose said. "They disdain anyone with disabilities."

"*Fools!* Because of Locke's and others' words." Charlotte sighed. "But that is for another discussion. No, they will turn on me because Patrick is a viscount and the brother of a marquess. The *ton* will find my rejection offensive. But in truth, Rose, I like the Patrick I came to know during our letter exchanges, and I shall not cry off, at least not until Patrick returns."

"In a week, Rhys and I go to meet the ship carrying Patrick," Rose said. "Of course, Patrick did not tell us when his ship was docking. Rhys discovered it on his own. Just like him to be that inconsiderate.

"Sister," Charlotte said. "You are being harsh. Patrick has been through much."

"You are right, Lottie." She wove another stitch. "I sometimes cling to the memory of the boy who was such a pain in my arse."

Charlotte smiled. She could picture that boy, all full of himself. A second son's life was often a challenge. She suspected much of his bravado had come from that.

"I thought you might join us," Rose continued. "We plan to bring him to Woodbine."

She very much wished to see Patrick and to help in any way possible. "I shall eagerly accompany you." Her thumb rubbed back and forth, back and forth. "Though what I shall do afterward is a conundrum."

"Nor can I advise you," Rose said, shaking her head.

Charlotte peered out the tall windows, where early summer blooms rioted.

"His accident will change him," Rose examined her knit stitches. "He may want nothing to do with us."

"He will get us no matter his mercurial mood."

"Are you *sure* you will not break your engagement, Lottie?" Rose peered at Charlotte. "Before his return?"

"I will not. For I wish to think and to spend time with Patrick."

Rose squeezed her hands. "I suspect you already know that answer, dear sister."

"I suspect I do."

Charlotte sat in the Ravenscroft carriage, though this one bore no crest, Rhys disinclined to announce their arrival at the pier.

Her heart was too warm for Patrick to cast him off. Ending their engagement upon his arrival home would send the worst sort of message—that Patrick was no longer a whole man. She simply could not. Perhaps, together, they would find a workable solution.

Their carriage was positioned in the long line awaiting the ship's passengers, the ship having docked, though it seemed to take forever for the passengers to disembark.

"How do you think he will be?" Rose said to her husband.

Rhys' face was tight, his hands fisted. "Angry?"

"Do you not think he will be sad?" Rose said.

"I suspect his lordship has the right of it," Charlotte said. "Patrick will be furious."

"Perhaps," Rose said. "I confess, I am wary of his reaction."

Charlotte was as well. She peered out the window. Sailors lowered the dock ramp, a line of passengers queuing up behind them, disembarking once the ramp was secured. Would Patrick be carried or on a stretcher? So hard to imagine for such a formerly vigorous man.

Charlotte failed to imagine him unable to ride, to run, to dance. How would that spirited man cope?

A bit of a hullabaloo on deck as the passengers parted, their carriage too distant to see the rumpus' cause until...

"Look!" Rose said, pointing. "Do you see that tall naval officer beside a man in a chair, the blackamoor?"

"Yes," Charlotte said, peering out the window.

The chair seemed to move on its own, rolling down the gangway with its passenger and traveling up the pier.

"Patrick!" Rose said.

Her fiancé drove the chair, pushing its large wheels, whilst the tall dusky officer walked alongside, with a boy trotting after them.

"God's breath!" Rhys said.

Standing at the front of the crowd was Lady Ablethorp, a dreadful gossipmonger, her mouth flapping.

"What shall we do?" Rose said to Rhys.

"That woman is the worst gossip," Rhys said. "If we all leave the carriage, it will cause a hullabaloo, an event my brother would hate in the extreme."

"Lottie," Rose said. "Rhys can go meet Patrick. We will wait here."

Nerves aflame, Charlotte shook her head. "As his fiancée, I should be the one to meet him, and *damn* Lady Ablethorp."

Rhys knocked on the carriage ceiling, and a footman opened the door and let down the steps. Charlotte took his helping hand, lifted her skirts, and proceeded, her eyes never leaving the man in the rolling chair who grew closer by the minute. She prayed she was up to this particular challenge.

The nearer Patrick came, the stranger she found his chair. Unlike Bath chairs, his was crafted of large wooden wheels, the third at the front quite small. The chair Patrick used was spare, made of wood and cane. A marvel.

Charlotte clasped her hands tight as if they could compress her nerves into a ball. Patrick's face was clearer now, clear enough she saw fresh lines scoring his tanned cheeks. But other than those, he looked much the same, a raven-haired handsome man, though his torso looked more broad, his arms thick enough to strain against his uniform's fabric.

The moment he spotted her was indelible, his blue eyes aglow, though she couldn't tell if they were filled with fury, fear, or joy.

She approached the dock as he neared land.

"Lady Charlotte!" cried Lady Ablethorp. "How delightful to see you."

They exchanged curtsies. "Lovely to see you as well."

"Are you waiting for your betrothed?" Lady Ablethorp said, her tone arch.

"I am, my lady." Charlotte nodded and walked on.

The moment neared when Patrick would reach her, and he neither sped up nor slowed down. Now, all she saw was Patrick, the crowd receding to form a sort of bubble between herself and her fiancé, its circumference ever-shrinking. Charlotte prepared for it to burst.

CHAPTER

FIVE

Patrick ascended the last bit of the dock, its slight hill giving him little trouble, for all he saw was Charlotte, tendrils of raven hair escaping her bonnet in the breeze.

Why in God's blazes had she come? However the woman had gotten here, she could damned well return the same way.

"Get the carriage, Lieutenant," he said, yet again thankful the Admiralty had agreed to assign Banby as his adjunct during his recovery.

The lieutenant nodded, bounding the rest of the way to land, as Patrick once would have done, heading for the carriage Patrick had specially constructed, with modifications for his condition. Thank Christ he needn't be lifted into its seat, as a child would, for all to see.

His barnacle remained glued to his side, and Patrick pushed his wheels a bit slower loathing the inevitable.

"Your lordship!" hollered that cursed Lady Ablethorp. "Welcome home! I see your fiancée is here to greet you."

He nodded to the woman and pushed his chair onto level ground, turning right to bring it before Charlotte.

"My lady," he said, nodding his head. "Do forgive me, but a bow is out of the question."

Ablethorp reared back, aghast, the repressed giggle coming from Charlotte. Over the past months, Patrick had imagined this scene—a friend or family member's first sight of him and his wrecked body. He'd vowed not to care and simply get on with it.

Charlotte curtsied to him and stretched out her hand. Dammit, he must take it. Not an easy thing, for since his accident, he disliked touch.

He took her hand and bent over it, though he did not kiss it, quelling the urge to do just that. A surprising burst of joy shot through him for no reason whatsoever.

"Rose and Rhys are here to bring you home," she said. "They await you in their carriage."

"I have arranged my own conveyance," he said.

"Have you?" Charlotte smiled. "I should not be surprised for you are such an efficient man."

Patrick choked on a snort as the lieutenant returned to stand by his side.

"Do introduce me to this handsome fellow, Patrick." She held out her hand to the lieutenant, who took it and bowed.

Patrick snarled. "Lady Charlotte, meet Lieutenant Banby, a Royal Marine, my steward, and a pain in my arse."

"The captain's a pain in my arse, too," Banby said in resonant tones, followed by a grin. "A pleasure to meet you, Lady Charlotte."

Charlotte smiled, enjoying their banter. "Good to see, Patrick, that your scathing tongue has received no damage. And that your steward has a sense of humor." She peered up at Banby and winked.

Patrick's lips twitched, for this saucy woman often surprised him.

"Might this be Henry?" Charlotte leaned down to be eye-to-eye with the boy.

Patrick actually growled. "My barnacle. He shall be joining us. Permanently."

The boy grinned.

"How nice to meet you, Henry."

The boy's face flamed. Henry looked to Patrick, who nodded, then he gave her an adorable bow. "Ma'am."

Charlotte liked that Patrick had taken on this boy whom she suspected had no family. "You will be living with the captain and Lieutenant Banby." She rose, turning to her alleged fiancé. "That sounds like an excellent plan, Patrick."

"Indeed," Patrick said, though his face gave no hint of his feelings. "I thank you for coming to greet me, my lady." Patrick nodded, then wheeled toward his carriage.

The infernal woman walked alongside him, his dismissal apparently sailing over her head.

"You need not attend me, my lady," he said.

Charlotte smiled, though it failed to reach her eyes. "Of course I must, my lord, for I have every intention of accompanying you to Woodbine."

"I plan to go to Ravenscroft."

A glance showed Lady Ablethorp's eyes fastened on them, a dragon smile pasted on her face.

"Do come to Woodbine, my lord," Charlotte said, her voice brittle. "Your sisters await you there and are most eager to see you, as are Rose and his lordship."

The inevitable drew near. The questions. The looks. The sympathy. The *pity*.

He would have none of it!

Except...His dear Susannah and Thomasina would be crushed if he failed to visit them. Susannah might understand, but Thomasina would not, for her less complex mind would find his apparent lack of interest confusing.

For all that he loathed the idea of the impending meetings, he could not deny them. "I will come." He had not meant to sound so churlish.

"That will make them very happy," Charlotte said.

"And you?" he said in equally harsh tones.

"Of course." She beamed him a smile, one he suspected was crafted for Lady Ablethorp's observation.

"As I am your fiancée," Charlotte said. "Rose has invited me to Woodbine as a houseguest. Is that not delightful?"

Good Christ, why hadn't the damned woman cried off? She should have done months ago. Curse her. She could very well renege now and make them both happy.

As astonished as Charlotte had been by Patrick's wheeled chair, she was equally amazed by his carriage. Outwardly, the vehicle looked similar to the many vehicles lining the quay until Lieutenant Banby proceeded to the carriage's rear. He and the driver unwound lengths of rope secured by cleats on each side of the carriage and lowered the back of the carriage as if it were a gate that when resting on the ground formed a ramp comprised of interlocking boards.

When the two stepped away, Patrick wheeled up the ramp and into the carriage. Charlotte peered inside to see him pull a strap through each chair wheel and buckle them to rings on the floor, locking the chair in place. How very clever.

Charlotte climbed the ramp, ducking her head to enter. Patrick's arms must be mighty, indeed, to wheel that chair upward. She took the cushioned bench facing Patrick's chair while the driver and the lieutenant lifted and locked the ramp to the carriage.

The opposite side door opened, and the lieutenant peeked in. "Are you settled?"

"I am."

"Then I shall join Henry and the coachman up top."

"Tell him we travel to Woodbine," Patrick said. "He knows the way."

The lieutenant gave them a final nod and closed the door.

Patrick raised a brow. "No maid, Lady Charlotte?"

"As my fiancé, I saw no purpose in bringing along another. We have much to discuss."

"Why the hell have you not ended our engagement?" he said with a snarl.

"I never got around to it." Charlotte shrugged.

"You can damn well do it now!"

Charlotte sighed, a fake one she exaggerated. "I think not, my lord. Were I to cry off now, the *ton* would denigrate me."

"I doubt that. You know what they think of cripples."

"I cannot be cut off from the *ton*. My family needs the income from my late father's paintings to sustain us and Halafair."

He chuffed. "Use Christie's or Sotheby's."

"I have a factor, as you know, but an auction house is out of the question."

"Why is that?" Patrick said, his face inscrutable.

Charlotte had prepared for his question, for the scrutiny of reputable auction houses could prove disastrous. "Mother objects. She forbids it for she and Papa had two execrable experiences and loathes them. There is also my sister."

"Lady Claire?"

"Were I scorned by the *ton*, which I care little about, it would harm my sister's chances for a good marriage. You must see that. I cannot subject my mother or sister to increased gossip. Not at this time."

"That is ridiculous. As a marquess, my brother can smooth the way for Claire to make a suitable match and assure your mother is welcomed by all."

Charlotte nodded. "Perhaps. But while your brother is a powerful man with great status, the risk remains. The Phelands cannot become pariahs, especially with Claire lacking a dowry."

"Then *what*?" he said.

"We marry, of course."

Patrick filled the cab with his wild laughter, sobering only to bore those dark blue eyes into her. "In other words, you wish to tie yourself to a wreck of a man, one who cannot even put one leg before the other?"

Now it was Charlotte's turn to chuckle. "Really, pouring it on too thick, my lord. You are no wreck, and certainly your sour humor and vicious barbs remain fully intact."

He huffed, looking away from her out the window. "And if *I* renege?"

Charlotte's breath hitched. He would not do that, would he? Consign her to perdition and bequeath her mother and sister to the same fate?

Though she did not know Patrick terribly well, he was a man of honor. "I do not believe you would do that, good sir."

His lips thinned, but he remained silent, peering out the window as the carriage rocked forward, the pace glacial due to the line of carriages and milling people. The marquess and Rose's carriage followed, making their way up narrow streets headed for Devon.

Part of Charlotte dreaded the challenges to come, yet a frisson of excitement wound through her at Patrick's return.

Rose had instructed the staff not to make a fuss over Patrick. A good thing, as he was in a foul mood upon his arrival at Woodbine. The staff were cordial, and though Susannah had tears in her eyes, she held her excitement in check. Patrick roughly accepted her kiss and hug.

Thomasina was another story. Though the elder sister, Sina appeared younger, as she was petite, her unique eyes slanted upward, her speech somewhat muddied. But her memory was capacious. Sina could recall exact moments from her childhood to the present day, and her small form held a powerful heart and a preternatural way with animals, especially horses. Rose had a gift with them, as well, and the pair now ran the Woodbine stables alongside the stable master to near-magical results.

Thomasina could not stop hugging Patrick until Susannah finally said, "Enough, Sina! You will suffocate him."

Thomasina pulled away, laughing. Patrick was smiling, too, the first smile Charlotte had seen from the man. With reluctance, she admitted the sight breathtaking, for he was devilishly handsome.

"I have worked with Diablo on a special project," Thomasina said.

"And what might that be, my little troublemaker?" Patrick said.

Sina's smile held secrets. "You will soon see, Patrick."

"It will be good to visit Diablo," Patrick said. "Though I shall never ride my old friend again." The last was tossed away on a whisper, but Charlotte caught them.

Patrick introduced Lieutenant Banby, a man with a military air and a ready smile whose dark curly hair complemented his dusky good looks. Charlotte wondered at his story.

"Come," Rhys said. "Let me show you your rooms."

"I wish to see Lieutenant Banby and young Henry settled." He peered up at Rhys with sharp eyes. "They shall stay in the manor house, of course."

"We have prepared rooms for them, too," Rose said. "An outrider rode ahead to inform the staff."

"My thanks, Rose," Patrick said.

Rhys began to push Patrick's chair down the hall accompanied by the family, herself, Banby, and the boy.

"Stop," Patrick said, raising a hand. "I prefer to wheel myself."

Rhys released the chair. "Your wheeled chair is a marvel. Tell us about it, brother."

Patrick's jaw bunched. "Perhaps another time."

Their procession arrived at a former morning salon transformed into a bedroom suite. A large low bed, a desk with stationary and accoutrements, and a good-sized sitting area at the opposite end.

"Look how the light pours through the windows," Charlotte said.

Rose beamed. "Which is why we gave you rooms on the same side down the hall. Come see."

Charlotte followed, and Rose swung open a door two rooms

down the hall. Charlotte gasped. Before her stood a medium-sized room with an easel, light pouring onto the wooden frame.

"Your studio. As with Lord Hawthorne's room, we thought the light ideal for your work." Rose waved her back to the hall. "Through here…" She swung open a door to reveal a sitting room with a sofa, chairs, and a large hearth, and pointed to a side door within the room. "That leads to your studio. And this…"

Beyond the sitting room lay a bedroom with a high poster bed, a large armoire, and a corner screen meant for her daily ablutions. "Your trunks have been unpacked."

"These rooms are perfect," Charlotte said.

"We did not unpack your paints or canvases," Rose said.

"Thank you. I prefer to do that myself." Charlotte must paint while she was at Woodbine, and this arrangement was splendid.

Down the hall, a bellow. "Get out of my sight!"

Rose sighed. "We have a challenging situation."

"We do," Charlotte said.

"Out NOW!" Another boomed command.

"You are truly going to go through with it then?" Rose said. "Marrying that irascible man?"

Charlotte was surprised Rose had asked, for Rhys had obtained a special license for them to wed. "I am inclined to do so."

"I fear you will be in for a rough time of it." Rose straightened a pillow on the bed.

"I do not doubt it." Charlotte shrugged. "But I have an odd fondness for that contrary man. And I am also curious."

"About what?"

Charlotte smiled. "I enjoyed hints of that inner man—kindness, curiosity, humor—through our letters. I wish to discover what is beneath that crusty exterior."

"Patrick does possess fine qualities." Rose closed the door behind them as they left Charlotte's rooms. "But all your digging may reveal is more crust."

They disbanded to rest after the day's doings, and as evening drew near, Charlotte changed for dinner. Passing Patrick's room, she found his door ajar. She couldn't resist peeking inside.

He lay in bed, reading, his chest bare.

Oh, my. She swallowed. A dusting of black hair covered a torso that bulged with muscle, his arms equally firm and large. Her eyes drifted to his lower extremities, suspecting he was naked beneath the sheets. Charlotte blinked repeatedly in an effort to regain her composure.

When she stepped inside, Patrick looked up, a frown instantly wreathing his face. "Why are you here, my lady?"

He leaned forward, slipping a blue silk banyan over his shoulders and chest.

"I assume you will be joining us for dinner," she said.

"I have no reason to do so. I have ordered my dinner delivered here."

What a crosspatch. "Your family expects you, Patrick. They are looking forward to sharing a meal with you."

"This evening, I choose not to do so."

Charlotte sat in the chair by the window. "That is a shame." Charlotte notched her chin. "As I do not wish you to eat alone, I shall join you."

Patrick's face tightened into severe lines. "That is unnecessary."

Charlotte smiled. "But of course it isn't. I *choose* to do so."

Patrick lay down his book. "I do not wish you to. In fact, I wish you to leave."

Her laughter peeled, and she speared him with a knowing glance. "I am sure you do, but since you cannot make me, I shall stay."

Patrick threw the book. Charlotte easily ducked, the tome sailing nowhere near her head to slam against the wall.

"Close," she said. "A shame your aim was off."

"My aim was perfect."

"Then why did the book not hit me?"

"Because…Goddammit. You are a nuisance. Annoying in the extreme."

"La," she said, pressing her hands beneath her chin. "Such compliments make me blush."

A knock, then a maid entered carrying Patrick's meal. "Your dinner, your lordship."

He had the girl place the tray across his lap.

"Excuse me," Charlotte said. "What is your name, miss?"

"Elowen, my lady."

"I will be joining my fiancé for dinner. Please bring me a tray as well."

"She will *not* be joining me," Patrick said to the girl.

Elowen's eyes bounced between Charlotte and Patrick.

"Indeed, I shall," Charlotte said.

The poor woman's jaw dropped, panic writ large. She fled.

Charlotte smiled at the stubborn man and rose. "I shall go fetch my meal."

Patrick tossed back the covers, sending dishes and food flying.

Thank heavens he'd put on the banyan. Charlotte waited.

Scraping fingers through his short hair, Patrick heaved a sigh. "Apologies."

She called up her courage and clasped her hands before her, squeezing tight. "I refuse to pretend that your injury does not exist, good sir. That it does not affect us. I am sorry, so very sorry for the loss of your legs. But do not mistake my sympathies as seeing you for a lesser man, for I do not. You are simply a different one." Patrick's cold face told her nothing as she said her piece. Now, she stiffened her spine and waited for the explosion.

"Please fetch Lieutenant Banby, Lady Charlotte," Patrick said in a measured voice. "I will attend the family dinner."

CHAPTER

SIX

The following day, Patrick awoke disoriented and in pain, the latter a frequent companion since his blasted accident. He plowed through it as best he could, sat up, and swung his legs over the bed to sit sideways. He reached for his wheeled chair's arm, always placed near his bedside by Banby, and pulled it close. He slid onto the chair in a most unceremonious manner, panting.

Paralysis did not allow a man much dignity.

Naked, he wheeled to the chamber pot, took care of business, and then scrubbed his face and hands in the wash bowl, drying them afterward.

Did he have the energy to dress himself this morning or should he call for Banby?

A knock at his door.

"Go away," he said. "I am not yet dressed."

He slid back onto the bed, covering himself as best he could, in case Lady Charlotte or anyone else chose to barge in on him. Were he at Hawthorne Hall, his viscountcy's seat, he could get angry, throw things without people cutting up his peace. Even in need of repair, Hawthorne would give him the isolation he craved.

The door opened and Charlotte breezed in wreathed in a wide smile.

"I said go away."

She halted, eyes wide. Given that he was naked, albeit his lower half was covered, he was unsurprised at her startle. But she recovered well and actually curtsied, this ridiculous woman who was fast becoming a pest.

"What is it now, my lady?" he said with annoyance.

"Thomasina has a surprise for you, so make haste to get dressed."

He grumbled. "I can no longer 'make haste,' my dear fiancée. I have yet more letters to write, and, devil take it, I wish to break my fast first."

"My lord, if you are going to growl every time I say a word, we shall have a fractious marriage."

He snorted. "You are ridiculous, woman, imagining a wedding."

Ignoring his words, she retrieved an errant stocking and placed it on a chair. What nerve. Patrick had been obeyed by everyone from cabin boys to captains and this woman dared disregard his orders.

She again pasted on that fake smile, and he far preferred her genuine one, for then her blue eyes glowed like beacons.

"Oh!" Charlotte said as the door opened. "Here is your breakfast which I ordered for you, thus you cannot use that as an excuse. Eat up, and I will send Banby to come get you."

He needed no one to "come get" him. He studied her beneath lowered lids. A complicated woman. Understanding her was like reading the seas. For all one could assess them, they never failed to surprise. How many more bombshells did she have awaiting him?

A pain shot up his back, and Patrick clamped his teeth so as not to groan.

Charlotte's canny eyes widened, and she took the tray from the maid and laid it across his lap.

"I shall return in a half hour." She smiled, and this time her eyes did warm with that beautiful blue light. "We shall journey to the stables."

The very last place he wished to be, for he had loved riding with a passion, particularly on Diablo. Nothing for it, he supposed. He would never hurt Thomasina's feelings.

"As you wish." He scooped up a honey cake and shoved it into his mouth.

Henry, Charlotte, and Banby accompanied Patrick to the stables, the boy skipping with excitement for he loved horses near as much as Patrick. Thomasina met them at the entrance to barn one and hugged him, then kissing each cheek. Rhys and Rose were there as well, along with the stable master, Lucy, and Arjuna. His "surprise" had turned into a circus.

"Come." Sina took his hand.

An awkward situation, as he could not wheel his chair one handed, yet were he to drop Thomasina's, he would dampen her spirits.

"Banby," he said over his shoulder. "If you would."

The lieutenant moved behind his chair, and they rolled into the barn, Thomasina's body vibrating with excitement. Down the long aisle, his old friend, Diablo, stood in the crossties. He nickered as they neared.

The barn aromas and sounds tore him back to his childhood at Ravenscroft, a blissful time when he learned to ride Snowflake, his first pony.

When they reached Diablo, his head bobbed down for a scratch and Patrick obliged, breathing in his stallion's familiar scent. The horse did the same to him, which evoked Patrick's smile.

"Well, won't you look at that," the lieutenant said. "A smile and your face didn't fall off."

"You are such an ass," Patrick said.

"Asses are fine animals." Banby grinned, eyes lit with humor. "If I do say so myself."

Thomasina unhooked the crossties and led Diablo to a ramped platform.

"We built this for you," Thomasina said.

Susannah flew around a corner, red-faced and brushing at her skirts. "Roddy is misbehaving. Again."

Grinning, Thomasina shook her head. "You must be more firm with him, Susannah. I told you that."

"Yes, yes I know," Susannah said. "But he is so terribly adorable! How fare you, Patrick?"

"Undecided," he said.

"We are just beginning." Thomasina clapped her hands in glee.

Their stable master, Grimes, neared carrying the oddest saddle Patrick had ever seen with its myriad of buckles, dangling straps, and an unusually high cantle. Grimes swung it and its accompanying pad onto Diablo's back, positioned it properly on his withers, and then fastened the girth.

Patrick eyed the saddle with skepticism.

"Our plan is for you to *ride* again." Thomasina clasped her hands before her, eyes bright.

Patrick bit back *"impossible"* and attempted a smile. "A fine thought, Sina, but I do not see how I am supposed to accomplish that without working legs."

"When the family learned of your injury," Susannah said, "we researched how to get you in the saddle again. We have come up with a solution."

"We considered putting you on a less fiery horse than Diablo," Sina said, scratching behind the huge horse's ears. "But you and he are friends, and I suspect he will soon learn what needs to be done."

This would end with him eating dirt, Patrick was sure of it, but he would survive. If it pleased his sisters, riding was worth the attempt.

He rolled up the ramp and locked his chair, a clever bit of mechanics he and Banby had thought up. Thomasina checked Diablo's girth, then slipped on his bridle, handing the reins to Rhys.

Though Charlotte smiled, he caught worry and fear there, too. His intended had always been skittish around horses, though she valiantly overcame that fear the day of the fire at Fielding Manor.

At Sina's signal, Banby hefted Patrick from the chair, Patrick gritting his teeth, for he loathed being carried like a child. Susannah stood beside Diablo, and she eased Patrick's right leg over the saddle, and then Banby planted him on the seat.

Hell. Diablo beneath him once again felt bloody good. Perhaps he would ride off into the sunset never to return.

Rhys walked Diablo from the ramp and halted him in the aisle, while Thomasina moved to his left side with Susannah on his right. They lifted his boot-clad feet into the stirrups, and for the millionth time, he cursed the lack of feeling in his legs. How would he direct Diablo without his legs?

Next, they buckled thigh straps around his legs.

"These are to secure you," Thomasina said. "Or your legs will flop around."

Her graceless speech didn't offend, for Sina's speaking manner was always straightforward. Banby reached for a leather strap sewn to the cantle and buckled it around his waist.

"The waist strap is a dangerous option," Susannah said. "But the only way for you to not slide from the saddle. Diablo is sure-footed and the chances of him falling are slim."

Perhaps his giant horse would be the death of him yet. Not such a bad way to go.

"The key, as always," Thomasina said, "is balance. You are changed, Patrick, but you can regain that balance in your new form. I have seen it."

Rhys began to lead Diablo down the barn aisle, and Patrick took up the reins. Being atop his horse felt good—right and strong—though his balance was off without his legs.

"Look who's coming!" Sina said.

Over his shoulder, Lightning Rod pranced down the aisle toward them. Nicknamed Roddy, the colt was a four-legged devil. A handful, true, but one with a sweet nature. His paint coloring and fine conformation made him the most gorgeous colt Patrick had ever seen.

Several things happened at once—Rose made a grab for Roddy's loose lead line, while Sina widened her arms to corral the playful colt, and...

Roddy leapt, outmaneuvering them both, to nip Diablo's rump.

His horse screamed, and off they went.

Shouts and cries followed him as they galloped from the barn, Patrick's body momentarily freezing, as if his flesh disremembered the countless years he'd spent in the saddle.

The cacophony dimmed as Patrick focused on staying upright.

Terror squeezed Charlotte, pumping her legs as she dashed outside along with everyone else.

Diablo was galloping off with Patrick atop him.

No, no, no. This could not be.

"God's blood!" shouted Rhys. He ran back into the stable shouting for a horse.

Charlotte gasped. Patrick had careened to the left in the saddle.

Please, please, please.

He tilted further.

As if Patrick were remade, he caught Diablo's rhythm and a sense of rightness clicked within. By leaning forward, he found a steadier seat, and his hands relaxed, his upper body swaying with the horse's great strides.

Patrick tilted to the left and felt the change in Diablo's gait from his crotch up his hips to his shoulders. He straightened, then leaned right, feeling out the boundaries of this new legless riding.

Straightening, he brought Diablo down to a canter and breathed in scents of the meadow's wildflowers, a field's fresh-mown hay, and the home wood's rich pine. Patrick laughed aloud as they cantered across a pasture.

His seat did not feel as it once had, but rather like a new thing he could practice until it became rote. The promise of a new adventure energized him.

They flew past Woodbine's majestic oaks, and he caught a whiff of sea air, Diablo's thundering hooves eating up the ground.

Joy fountained through him. He was mobile, in command of where he went and how he went.

They approached a stone wall that bordered another pasture.

He should not.

Hell yes!

Over they soared, and Patrick laughed, giddy as a boy with his newfound freedom.

As he gradually slowed Diablo, the horse was panting and sweaty and so was he when he turned the great horse back toward the barn, toward his family, toward the woman who both intrigued and enticed him, though he suspected Charlotte hadn't any idea of the latter.

He brought Diablo to a walk, and as they neared the barn, he waved, their alarmed faces transforming to smiles.

Charlotte had seldom felt such fear turn to joy as she watched Patrick on Diablo, who walked toward them at a mellow pace. Leaping over that wall, as if the pair had wings, had taken years off Charlotte's life. Two? Perhaps three?

Thomasina clapped, bouncing on her toes as the pair drew close, man and horse puffing with exertion.

"Brother!" Rhys said. "The last ten minutes I have lived several lives."

Patrick patted Diablo's neck.

"As you practice, Patrick," Thomasina said. "Riding will again become second nature."

Patrick stared at them all, unable to stop grinning.

"I thought you was bound to die," Henry said with a grin.

"For a moment there, young Henry," Patrick responded. "I thought so as well."

"I'm mighty glad you did *not*," Henry said.

"On that, I must agree." Patrick cast a glance at Charlotte and frowned. "My Lady Charlotte, are you well?"

Charlotte scrubbed tear-stained cheeks sure she was now tomato red. "They are tears of joy, Captain. You looked splendid riding Diablo. Absolutely splendid!" She laid a hand on his thigh, realized he could not feel her touch, but left it there anyway.

Touching Patrick felt good, for he was alive and well rather than crumpled in a pasture with a broken neck.

"Banby, let us get me out of this rig. I am famished."

Rose and Rhys sat in his study after dinner, Rhys reading the papers from town, Rose on the sofa perusing her newest tome on horse breeding. Racing about the room were their two Cairn Terriers, Bram and Isla, as they play-fought.

"In God's creation, why?"

"What is it, my love?" Rose said, massaging her flat stomach, eager for their babe to show.

He stalked toward her slapping the paper against his thigh and dropped it on her lap. "This."

Rose searched for but a moment.

What handsome Captain recently returned from ports unknown to be greeted by his lady fiancée? Though he may be broken in body, their reunion looked to be a happy one observed by many. Will the lady now accept his changed status? If so, when shall wedding bells ring?

Rose sighed. "It is nothing more than we expected, Rhys."

"That old biddy spreads her gossip willy-nilly."

"It could have been worse," Rose said.

A bellow of fury sounded from the library.

She looked at Rhys. "Oh, dear."

Patrick had spent long hours since that first ride practicing on Diablo, and several days later, he wheeled down the hall to Charlotte's room and knocked. He had a plan.

From his visits to Fielding Manor, he well knew Charlotte's apprehension about riding, yet her love of animals was fierce. Rose had worked with her, and according to his sister, Lottie had improved her seat. He had an idea, one he imagined would ultimately please her, and hoped she would join him on a jaunt.

"Hello, Patrick," she said with a smile upon opening the door.

She was lovely, tall, and curved, wearing a blue day dress. "Would you consider riding out with me?"

Her lips tightened. "I am not terribly accomplished."

He took her hand and squeezed. "I have taken that into account. I chose Beauty for you, a gentle mare not easily startled and Rose suggested you ride astride."

"I would prefer that." Another smile, though her eyes shined with apprehension. "It will take me but a minute to change."

Charlotte reappeared wearing a navy split-skirt habit, and though her unease was obvious, off they went.

Once atop the petite mare, Charlotte's hands tightened and released, her back rigid, and Patrick was thankful for Beauty's placid disposition and calm demeanor.

Charlotte had not noticed much about her horse, praying she would not slide off Beauty, for each moment astride was a balancing act she never quite accomplished. Even with Patrick's infirmity, he now rode as if he were bred to the saddle.

A log they must step over looked immense, a rise in the earth, mountainous. Sweat beaded her upper lip. Her tension increased.

Beauty bunched her muscle and Charlotte stiffened further, the log drawing close, the mare beginning to prance at Charlotte's tense seat. She had done this before, felt the same horrid sensations, yet she could not relax.

She began to slide.

The ground reared up, her fingers tightening on the reins, her right foot slipping from the stirrup.

Just as she teetered, a hand caught her upper arm. Patrick's. He straightened her in the saddle.

"Dear Charlotte," Patrick said. "I cannot fathom how you did that slide towards the ground, though I did see you stiffen. We must discover a way for you to relax in the saddle."

"I have tried, Patrick," she said, mortified. "Rose has practiced with me again and again, but I never seem to find that seat you and she endlessly talk about."

"I have an idea."

That terrified her even more. "I should stop striving to be that which I am not."

"You like horses, yes?" he said, his eyes gentle.

"Exceedingly, and once or twice I have felt that balance and the freedom it brings. I enjoyed those sensations. Very much. But..."

Charlotte was nearly in tears, her fear of a fall quelling her attempts to relax until she *did* sit properly.

Patrick drew alongside Beauty, Diablo much taller, and he leaned down, took mare's reins from Lottie, and lifted her onto Diablo's back in front of him. She sat straight as a poker.

"Why did you do that?" she said.

"Because I shall not have our ride lead to disaster."

He threaded Beauty's reins through a saddle ring, then tightened his left arm around her waist. "Relax against me, Lottie. I want you to feel Diablo's rhythm as we fly over the earth."

"I do not wish to fly—eep!"

They'd broken into a slow lope that ate up the earth with Diablo's huge strides. The world breezed by and gradually Charlotte relaxed enough in Patrick's arms to note the beauty in the canter, the freshness of the air, and the magnificence of the beast beneath her.

Patrick urged Diablo faster, then into a gallop. They flew, and Charlotte felt she sat atop Pegasus, hooves barely touching the earth. Glorious.

When the barn reappeared, Patrick slowed their mad speed to a canter, then a walk. Charlotte laughed.

"Do you see?" he said.

"Oh, yes! I could ride with you forever."

CHAPTER

SEVEN

Forever. Patrick saw their future rolling out across the years. Much to his surprise, that vision brought him an unexpected burn of pleasure.

Once their horses were unsaddled, they watered and fed them, then brushed them down, Charlotte diving into the task with gusto. At a young age, Patrick had learned to take care of his mount, and while his infirmity often made help necessary, he continued to do as much as possible after a ride. A matter of pride, which his brother claimed he had in abundance. A ridiculous assertion were it not so true.

While Charlotte washed her hands, Patrick wheeled away in search of a barrel. He found Arjuna, who led him to one behind the barn. Per Patrick's instructions, the man rolled the barrel inside and down the aisle toward Charlotte. Arjuna was about to lift it when Patrick said to leave it as it was.

The Indian man's eyes lit with understanding, and he nodded and smiled before he left.

"You have brought me a barrel, my lord." Charlotte said with a saucy smile. "A rather odd gift, I must say."

He grinned. "I want you to mount the barrel as you would a horse. I will hold it steady."

After giving Patrick a skeptical look, Charlotte swung a leg across the barrel and sat.

"Now position your legs as if you are riding, so your feet do not touch the ground. Good." He held the barrel steady.

"But what about sidesaddle?" she said.

"The barrel will increase your overall balance, and you shall practice astride. Once comfortable astride Beauty, you shall work on your sidesaddle balance, which I suspect will come naturally. Now I will remove my hands. See if you can steady it."

Charlotte did as asked, and the thing teetered, almost spilling her off, but each time Patrick anchored the barrel.

"Any minute, you will see me upended," she said, voice thin with nerves.

"No, I will not, my lady. With practice, you will soon balance atop Beauty with ease."

Her face lit with a smile, one so lovely it seized his breath.

The following day, all at Woodbine had read the *on-dits* about Patrick and Charlotte in the *Morning Post, The Morning Chronicle,* and even *The Times.* Patrick's silence on the subject thundered, but Charlotte could not stop cursing Lady Ablethorp. How *dare* that awful woman refer to Patrick as "broken" and "damaged." He was changed, yes, but most certainly *not* broken.

Those were her thoughts as she stood before her easel, making haste as she put some finishing touches on a painting when the door burst open.

She whirled, screeching. "Get out!"

Heavens, it was Patrick. And she'd just screamed at him.

She didn't cover the work, as it was a painting in *her* style, not her father's. "Apologies, my lord. Truly."

He wheeled inside, a curious expression on his face.

She dropped her brush into the turpentine and approached, a

hand reaching for him until she noted the smears of paint covering it.

"Please do forgive me," she said, trying to explain away her shout. "At home, I lock my door when working. People always knock, you see, and I was startled by your entrance...Do you forgive me?"

"Charlotte, the error is mine, you see, for I imagined you at work and wished to observe." His gaze traveled to the easel, his face an unrevealing mask of sangfroid, utterly handsome in its stillness. "An interesting subject."

Oh, dear. He disliked the painting. "Indeed."

Patrick was astonished at the fluidity and grace of the small piece—fishing boats plying the waves. Light, dramatic, yet not overly so, streamed from between churning clouds, the waves so fraught and evocative he could almost feel the sea spray. How exceptionally fine.

Patrick's absorption was so complete Charlotte wondered if he was preparing critical salvos. Her confidence, wobbly at best regarding her own work, vanished as a will-o'-the-wisp. "Whilst here, I paint on a smaller scale."

"That makes sense, given the space." He wheeled toward her second easel, a covered one that hid a forgery, and she scurried toward him.

"Indeed," she said, irritated by her breathless voice. She must regain her composure, for if he discovered his fiancée was a forger...

"I do much larger works at home," she blurted out.

Patrick gestured to the small painting. "This is the first one of yours I have seen. Do uncover this one."

Oh, heavens. "La, the work is not complete, and I hate showing anything when it is in such an early stage." Her voice, high-pitched, evoked a girl just out of the schoolroom.

"Is that so?" Patrick inched closer and she paralleled him in some strange dance.

Charlotte reached for the turpentine rag and began to clean her brushes and hands. "I am starving and must go change for dinner."

"As am I. Two hours is too long to wait, I am afraid." His eyes tracked her as a hawk's would prey. "Shall we ring for tea? With biscuits, of course."

Charlotte did *not* want to ring for tea, for if she walked to the bell pull, Patrick could lift the muslin covering the forgery.

"Tea will spoil our dinner," she said.

"Nonsense. I am ravenous, and tea and biscuits will hold me over."

Were Charlotte to deny him, it would look odd. "Of course." She walked to the bell pull and tugged, but as she feared, Patrick unveiled the painting.

A forged work already signed with her father's name.

She stared at him, hands clasped so tight her fingers might break.

"Are you touching up one of your father's works?" he said.

His tone was even, but she caught the inference beneath the question.

Patrick struggled to believe his eyes. It was obvious Lottie was not "touching up" her father's painting, but *creating* one, signature and all. An astonishing feat, for Charlotte had wholly replicated Pheland's style.

Why on God's green earth would his intended *forge* paintings by her father?

Charlotte read Patrick's distaste, along with his curiosity, which made her frantic. She and Patrick seemed to be reaching an accord, for in truth, she liked him a great deal. Now this.

She removed her smock and hung it on its hook, buying time. She could lie. But his eyes said he knew of her forgery. She pulled over a low stool to sit across from him. Time for the play to end. "I painted this seascape in my father's style."

"His *style*?" he said, his tone cutting. "Is that not Reginald Pheland's signature?"

"Well, yes, a facsimile of it." His frown made her want to flee.

"Those many months ago, did I purchase a painting by your father or by you?"

Charlotte rubbed her forefinger and thumb together again and again. "The painting was my work."

The man's face went blank, giving nothing away, but the energy around him was charged, a combustive thing that might ignite.

Her deceit. Her humiliation. Those were bad, but worst of all was Patrick's disappointment in her.

Lottie's eyes were lowered, thus Patrick could not read her thoughts. His were ones of utter astonishment. Her skill was unparalleled, yet her actions unconscionable. He could not reconcile the woman he knew with the deeds she had done. She must have a sound reason for doing so. Mustn't she?

He pondered this. He would consider her possible motivations before his anger and accusations flew. He wheeled toward the door as a maid opened it, a tea tray in her arms.

Over his shoulder, he said, "I fear I have lost my appetite, Lady Charlotte. I will see you at dinner."

Patrick flew down the hall at a furious pace, ancestors' portraits streaming by, so distracted he nearly crashed into Rose.

"I have been looking for you, Patrick," Rose said. "What has got you in such a bother?"

He was not about to tell Rose of the forgeries. "I am out of sorts with my fiancée, a trifling thing." He peered up at Rose, her willowy form still slim, though she had told him of her pregnancy. He daren't look her in the eye.

Rose stared down at him, her clever mind always busy as a bee, and she moved to a bench down the hall beneath one of the portraits, his great-great-grandmother.

Rhys' Rosie had been a pest and a bane to his childhood, but she had grown into an intelligent and perceptive woman. He moved to her. "What is up in that lively brain of yours, sister?"

"I wish to talk about a particular matter," she said.

"Which is...?"

"Henry. The boy needs more." She slapped her lap. "He is a cocky child, which is not a bad thing. More importantly, he is a sweet one as well. I also suspect he has a sharp mind."

"I agree he needs more," Patrick said. "Which is why I plan to hire a tutor or governess for him. I have written to friends noting my need for a governess or tutor." He wondered at Charlotte's thoughts on the matter, and was certain she had some. Then he recalled the forgeries.

Rose's eyes brightened. "Excellent. If you do not object, I shall query our vicar. He may know of someone suitable. I am amazed at how well Henry rubs along with the family and staff."

"For which I am most thankful."

"He is deeply fond of you, Patrick," Rose said.

His lips quirked. "I have noticed."

"Whilst he and Lieutenant Banby sleep in the manor as one of the family, I believe Henry needs more than a tutor."

That took him aback. "What more?"

"I am talking of..." She bit her lip. "I fear he still sees himself as your and Banby's cabin boy, rather than viewing Woodbine as his home and us as his family."

"He and Lottie get on well. I have told the boy he will remain with us when we decamp to Hawthorne Hall."

Rose nodded, rubbing circles on her belly. "Excellent. You know, he often plays with Isla and Bram."

"Does he?" Patrick chided himself for not noticing.

"He follows them around the house," she said, grinning. "Then pounces on them to play, most often when he believes no one is watching. The pups adore him."

Patrick was not focusing on Henry as he should, too caught up in his concerns for himself, for Lottie, and had been remiss with the child. Henry should have his own pup, though the results would be chaos. Yet the idea appealed. "A pup for Henry, a creature of his own to love and care for. A fine idea, Rose."

She reached out a hand and squeezed his. "Exactly where I was headed. Grimes has found a stray pup lurking in the stables." Her lids dropped. "A mongrel, but sweet as pie."

Patrick recalled the day he had met Rose, when the eight-year-old child had marched onto Ravenscroft land in hopes the family would take her pregnant dog, Tessa, a purebred setter. Her pups were *not* purebred and Rose's despicable father intended to kill the lot, including the dam. They had taken in Tessa and that first litter was one of many, her pups outstanding hunters.

"Shall we take a gander at this pup?" he said. "What does he look like?"

Rose's eyes danced. "A rather odd, unusually tall, black cocker spaniel."

"Good God!" He grinned. "Let us go see him."

Dinner was awkward. An understatement. It had been painfully obvious that Patrick had no intention of talking to her or even looking at her. Even Rhys and Susannah noticed. At least Rose had the good grace not to stare.

A day later, Charlotte avoided Patrick with ease, as he'd once again gone to the workshop where he must do mysterious things. Perhaps the model building he'd noted in his letters.

Charlotte had painted, studio door locked, the pressure intense on completing the three works she had committed to buyers. She then slunk to the library, fearing any moment Patrick would shout the truth to one and all.

She was being a coward. That wasn't her. Was it? She tended to confront situations head-on. Not this one, her behavior that of a mouse. But all she wanted to do was hide, her budding accord with her husband-to-be in shambles. That she was diminished in Patrick's esteem disturbed her greatly. A courageous man, both frustrating and delightful. *His* courage given his infirmity plucked a deep chord within her.

Charlotte lifted a book from the side table. What if she lost the use of her hands? Could no longer paint? She doubted her response would come close to the pluck Patrick exhibited.

The book dropped to the floor when the man in her thoughts rolled into the library. "I have been waiting for you, Lottie. Had we not planned a riding jaunt?"

She retrieved the book, which hid her shock. They *had* arranged an outing. Before. "I confess, since your anger on discovering my... activities, I assumed you would not wish for our ride. I thought..." She paused, then blurted out words she wished to contain. "I thought, mayhap, you wished to end our engagement."

Patrick wheeled close wearing a frown. "Tell me, fair Lady Charlotte, are you marrying me for my money, so you no longer must create fake paintings?"

Charlotte started. What a horrid thought. "No!"

His lips quirked. "I was making a joke, a poor one. Breaking our engagement never occurred to me."

"I had planned to keep painting after we wed. To fund my family. You know they and Halafair need the money. *Do* you have money, Patrick?"

He threw his head back and laughed. "Money? My dear, I have gobs of it. More than I know what to do with."

"But...I had no idea as we have not drawn up marriage contracts."

"I have substantial prize money from the war and additional wealth courtesy of an uncle on my mother's side. He left me a well-financed estate, a charming place in Westmorland."

"Your earlier anger—you felt I was immoral? Greedy? A trickster?"

"None of that." He shook his head, a lock of hair falling to his forehead. "After much thought, I was most angry with myself. I was also embarrassed."

"Embarrassed?"

"For being duped with my purchase, like everyone else. Yet as I thought on it, I found whoever painted a work I admired should not matter. When you sent the sketch of the seascape you wished to sell, I was moved by its beauty. The painting itself? I found it exquisite, and well worth the pounds spent. It brought me to the sea I eternally long for."

"But the forgeries, Patrick."

"Being not a total dunce, I am aware working in oils is a long and painstaking process, thus a powerful motive must push you to forge paintings. As you have noted, your family needs money. Hence, that is your motive."

His compliment about the seascape and comprehension of why she did the unthinkable stilled Charlotte's tongue. She was both embarrassed and touched by his perception.

"Am I correct?" he said.

Charlotte nodded, scraping at the paint beneath her nails she had failed to scrub away. "Papa was never wise when it came to funds, nor was he a man who prepared for eventualities. When he died, we were bereft. For all he loved us and we him, that emotion failed to put food on our table or pay Halafair's taxes. We sold many of his few remaining paintings, but when those funds disappeared, I saw only one path out of our predicament."

"I see," Patrick said. "Necessity is, after all, the mother of invention. What of the late Earl Fielding? Did he not leave your family well provided for?"

The earl had been a rat bastard, though it would be most indelicate to voice those words. "Our lot improved when Mama married Fielding, but his death left us nearly as destitute as our father's passing—he, too, had failed to prepare. His will left no mention of us."

"Lady Bea's dower contracts?" Patrick said.

"When they were written up, our second cousin assisted, our single male relative." Charlotte threw up her hands. "Both Fielding and my perfidious cousin wished to get their hands on Halafair and, yes, I suspect a possible collusion. The dower contracts? Mama receives one hundred paltry pounds a year from Fielding's estate."

"What of the new earl...?"

Charlotte snorted. "That prancing fop? No, he most certainly did not offer assistance. The odious man came for a visit and refused to aid us, whether unable or unwilling I do not know. Thank God Halafair is unentailed, for at least we have a home. After Fielding's death, I again took up my father's brush."

"Have I ever seen a painting of *yours*?" he said.

Charlotte nodded. "The one with the fishing boats. But mine are for mere pleasure, any sale producing but a few pounds sterling."

"How can you say such? You are a gifted artist."

"I am also a *woman*, my lord!" Her voice was heated, this old saw endlessly repeated by myriad women frustrated by men's perceptions. "My gender severely diminishes my worth as an artist and selling my paintings for mere pence holds little appeal."

"I want to see more of your work," he said, his eyes filled with sincerity, which ruffled her composure.

"But the forgeries...You truly do not revile them?"

He wheeled closer and took her hands. "Forging artwork is wrong, you and I both know this. Yet I see in you a courage to do what must be done to survive."

Charlotte shook her head. "I am not courageous, Patrick. Far from it."

"I am well familiar with simply getting on with it, Lottie. But you acted when necessity called, though the task unpleasant, one that, I suspect, rips at your soul."

Patrick squeezed her hands, his warm and calloused, his grip firm.

"And has *your* soul been ripped in two, Patrick?"

A flicker of grief joined the fire lighting his eyes, and she reached for him, though she shouldn't. Too dangerous, too open to rejection. And yet she cupped his cheek.

He leaned into her hand, eyes hooded. "During battle, when you must choose between victory and the lives of your men...It tears you apart, for victory is your only choice. Yet the maneuver you execute will end comrades, as well as enemies. The decision takes but a split second. A wisp of thought. When it is done, you are left endless time to cradle your grief at lives lost, made worse by the ensuing triumphal celebrations, for all you can hear are the cries of the dead."

Charlotte cupped his cheek, searching for adequate words not cradled in cliche. "I am profoundly grieved, Patrick."

"As am I."

CHAPTER
EIGHT

R hys strolled into Rose's dressing room, hands in pockets, amid the excited yips and leaps of Bram and Isla.

Rose's heart thumped, it always did when her husband entered a room. Lucy, her friend and former governess, had insisted on arranging Rose's hair for that evening's small get-together. Rose dared not gainsay her, the woman acting as a mother for years.

Rhys dropped a kiss to Rose's temple, making her shiver, before ruffling each pup's fur and taking a seat in the Sheraton chair near her vanity.

"Greetings, Miss Lucy," Rhys said. "How fare you this fine evening?"

Lucy paused before placing a final pin in Rose's hair. "I am well, my lord. And yourself?"

"Well, indeed," he said. "Have you and Arjuna set a date for the wedding?"

Rose swiveled to see Lucy's mahogany complexion turn a dark pink.

"That Arjuna," Lucy said. "He pesters me about a date. What is the rush, I say?"

Rhys chuckled at Lucy's wry tone. "I see."

"Are you driving your fiancé to drink, Lucy?" Rose said.

"Drink can harm the body," Lucy said, eyes glinting with humor. "I do not partake."

Rose threw up her hands. "It is an expression, Lucy."

"If you say so, *Minnu*."

Rose stood, lips twitching. "*I* am ready for your wedding, dear one."

Lucy winked. "You and Arjuna both." She bowed and swanned from the room.

"She is a treasure...and a character."

"She has done so much for me, Rhys."

"I know." He walked to Rose and pressed his lips to hers, and she sank into the bliss of her husband's affection. When they parted, admittedly with much reluctance, Rhys frowned.

"What disturbs you?"

"I have stumbled upon a bit of troubling information." He led Rose into their sitting room, and once on the settee, took her hands in his. "Earlier today, I found the door to Lady Charlotte's studio ajar. When I entered, two maids, Elowen and Hermione, were inside chattering away."

"They should not have entered," Rose said. "Not even to clean it."

"Agreed," Rhys continued. "Both maids are new and claimed not to know of the prohibition."

"That sounds not like a *grave* discovery, Rhys."

He squeezed her hands and leaned back against the cushions. "No. But after I shooed them off, I moved to the paintings, all uncovered. Two were unsigned, and one had Pheland's signature. One of those unsigned was of a fox hunt. The piece gave me an uncomfortable feeling, though I would swear it was Pheland's work."

Rose shrugged. "Perhaps the baron was painting it when he died or never put it up for sale, thus leaving it unsigned."

"Possibly. I overheard Lady Charlotte comment on how she was selling several works of her father's to collectors. She noted a fox hunt and remarked how distasteful she found the painting's subject."

"I am discomforted by what you are implying, Rhys." Rose lifted Bram and cuddled him.

"No more uncomfortable than I am, my love. I examined the four works in the room. Charlotte had signed one with her name, one I found quite beautiful, in fact. But the other three..." Rhys cleared his throat.

Bram leapt from Rose's lap as she stood, her mind awhirl. She disliked this discussion in the extreme. "And?"

"I touched a small corner of the fox hunt painting." He held up a finger dabbed with green. "The work is fresh, Rosie. Recent. I would suggest Charlotte has been forging her father's work and selling it as such."

Rose walked to the balcony's French doors, both pups following. The once-sunny day now brooded with inky clouds accompanied by a chill drizzle. She turned back to her husband.

"I fancy you are correct," Rose said. "S'truth, I have suspected this for some time."

"You said nothing."

"What was there to say?"

"This trickery troubles me, deeply."

"It does me, as well. I have not addressed the subject with Charlotte. There must be a reasonable explanation."

His eyes narrowed. "What the deuce could that be?"

"I do not know." If someone from outside the family discovered Lottie's chicanery... Too upsetting to contemplate.

"The woman is to marry my brother!"

"I know that!" She went to Rhys, sliding her arms around his waist. "I did not mean to sound so—"

His forehead met hers. "I know, Rosie. The question is, do I inform Patrick or remain silent? Devil it, I cannot see myself doing the latter. I wish Angus were here as a sounding board and not off in America."

"Give me a few days, Rhys," Rose said. "I will speak with Charlotte and learn her thoughts."

"How can I, Rosie? Were Patrick to enter this marriage without knowledge of his wife's forgeries… That would do him a grave injustice."

"I see." Rose bit her lip. "All right then, yes, tell him. I will speak with Charlotte. I am sure she has a reasonable explanation." Though Rose found the situation worrying.

Rhys found Patrick in the stables with Henry, who was playing fetch with a pup who looked much like a black cocker on stilts, all floppy ears and wide grin.

"What ho!" Rhys said. "What have we here?"

Henry tossed the stick, and the mongrel raced down the aisle. "My new dog! *Mine!*"

Rhys chuckled. "What are you calling him?"

"*Her* name is Stella!" Henry said with a roar. "The Captain told me 'stella' means star. She is *my* star. The Captain and Lady Charlotte said he was to be my very own!"

Such a small thing, really—a pup for a boy—yet Henry was in transports, his chest puffed with pride. Rhys doubted the child had ever owned much, certainly not a dog. What a grand gift.

Patrick's eyes shined at Henry's enthusiasm, the emotion warming Rhys' heart. His brother's accident and his resulting paralysis troubled Rhys, particularly Patrick's loss of joy. Yet lately, he saw sparks of the old Patrick, a man who once found delight in much. "Well done, I say. Stella is a fine girl."

The pup, perhaps nine months, reappeared, prancing with the stick in her teeth. She dropped it at the boy's feet, eyes focused on Henry, bright for another go. He tossed the stick, and Stella raced for it.

"Henry, might I steal Lord Hawthorne for a few moments?" Rhys said.

"A course, my lord."

"I doubt we shall be missed," Patrick said, as he wheeled down the aisle.

"Indeed," Rhys said. "What a fine gift."

"Stella has taken to sleeping at the foot of Henry's bed," Patrick said with a smile. "I suspect those two shall make mischief. Come to the workshop." Patrick reached for a lantern hanging from a support post and handed it to Rhys. "Night is coming, and it appears you are chewing on something. I shall work whilst you emote."

The workshop was a largish building beyond the barns where repairs or builds necessary for Woodbine's function were created. Entering the small room Patrick had taken as his own, Rhys hung the lamp on a hook as Patrick rolled to his bench, newly constructed to suit his wheeled-chair's height.

"What is your current project?" Rhys strolled over to inspect.

Patrick took care laying out his tools and materials before a miniature, a Royal Navy frigate, with thirty-six guns.

"An Apollo-class," Patrick said.

An odd choice, for his brother most often crafted hundred-gun first-rate ships of the line similar to those he captained.

Patrick slipped on his enlarging goggles, ones Patrick had cobbled together for his miniature work years earlier. He lifted a pair of tweezers and inched a miniature board into place on the ship's hull, utterly absorbed.

"Why a frigate, of all things? In my memory, you have never served on one."

Patrick swiped glue across the plank and hull, then fixed the board. "This ship is a...well, a unique memory."

"In what way?" Rhys laid a hand on Patrick's shoulder.

"I need a drink." Patrick laid down his tweezers and stretched his arms over his head.

"I could use one, as well," Rhys said. "I suspect the ladies have retired for naps before tonight's small gathering."

"Gathering?" Patrick froze.

"Devonshire and some of his friends will be joining us."

Patrick backed up his chair and wheeled to a counter which held a bottle of Scotch whisky, pouring them each a glass.

Rhys pulled over a stool, took the scotch, and sat.

"Cheers, brother." Patrick raised his glass.

They clinked glasses. "Tell me about the frigate"

"It represents my resolve to discover and bring to account those behind commandeering a Royal Naval ship as a slaver."

"A slaver," Rhys whispered.

Patrick swirled his drink, downed it, and poured another. "Near the war's end, during a pause in engaging the enemy, we came upon a Royal Navy war frigate offloading chained slaves onto a cargo ship. We were in British waters, which made the exchange highly illegal, thus we hastened toward the pair." Patrick took a sip. "When they spotted us, both the cargo ship and the frigate set sail." He clenched his jaw.

"I am aghast," Rhys said.

"There is worse to come." Patrick downed his second scotch, his face tight with strain, to slam the glass on the table. "While underway, the frigate forced the remaining slaves aboard into the sea, chains and all. I watched men, women, and children sink to their deaths. We were too distant to reach them in time."

"Bloody hell!" Rhys held out his glass for a refill.

"We were all horrified, but Banby, the son of a former slave and a white Jamaican, was deeply affected. They sank like stones, of course, yelling for help that would never come. We tried, but it was impossible for all but one who began to swim toward our ship."

Rhys' was wide-eyed. "What did you do? Go after the swimmer? Pursue the frigate?"

"We saved the boy."

"A good choice."

Patrick nodded. "The swimmer was Henry."

"Good Christ!"

"A logical decision, as well. Given the frigate's speed, we could not have caught them. Through my glass, I watched as those maggot pies sailed into the distance. Who in Christ's name has the cruelty to drown chained people?"

The horror of it seeped into Rhys' bones.

"Why toss Henry overboard with the slaves?" Rhys said.

A smile whispered across Patrick's lips. "It seems our intrepid Henry had made friends with two of the slaver boys and he strenuously objected to their being tossed into the sea. Hence his own dunking."

Patrick swiped a hand across his face. "Upon our arrival in port, I reported the incident and the *HMS Despoina,* a name I did not recognize, to the Admiralty. Unfortunately, war's end and my subsequent injury affected my pursuit. To date, I have heard nothing, but I am far from done."

"A loathsome tale," Rhys said. "Slavers are contemptible. How can I help?"

Patrick stiffened. "I do not wish to involve you at this time."

"But—"

He wagged his glass. "For now, Rhys. I suspect someone at the Admiralty is involved. I must feel things out a bit more to have a better sense of the situation before I bring you aboard." Patrick grinned. "You are my heavy guns."

"If you say so." Rhys rolled the smoky scotch over his tongue. "Were you able to glean any information about the slavers or ship from Henry?"

Patrick returned to his model. "Someone at his orphanage gave him over, conscripting him onto the frigate as a cabin boy. The boy saw many comings and goings before they set sail, but has no idea the men's identities. Enough of this, dear brother. You did not beard me earlier to discuss slavers. What do you need to thrash out?"

"Will you marry Charlotte?" Rhys said in clipped tones.

Patrick cut him a sharp look, knowing Rhys expected his famed temper to reveal itself.

"If you choose not to do so," Rhys said. "We will devise a strategy which does not hurt the lady's good name."

"I fail to see how that is possible."

Rhys had noted the changes between Charlotte and Patrick since his brother's return. Though subtle, when the two occupied the same room, an undeniable frisson flew between them.

Unlike many younger brothers who followed the elder like a puppy, Patrick always acted the opposite of Rhys, such as when Rhys joined the cavalry, Patrick chose the navy. Surprising them both, his brother had fallen in love with the sea.

Yet he and Patrick were bonded tight, and as enigmatic as Patrick often appeared, one thing always remained—their love of family and one another.

"What shall you do?" Rhys repeated.

"I will marry the girl of course."

"A harsh solution, given the long-term commitment that may wear on you as the years pass."

Patrick shrugged. "I like her. Quite a bit, to my surprise. Enough to wed, surely. We shall muddle through."

Rhys could not picture "muddling through" a marriage. He loved Rose with depths he could never elucidate. Without that...

"I know my viewpoint is unusual," Rhys said. "But Rosie and I have such affection—"

"Ah, brother, we all know you and Rose are besotted, and I applaud that. Perhaps love shall grow between Charlotte and myself."

Rhys was frustrated, but he also allowed Patrick's life was not his. "You are certain..."

Patrick chuckled. "Nowadays, I am certain of little."

Rhys walked to the ship model and examined Patrick's work. Impeccable as always. Patrick watched him with keen eyes.

Rhys was stalling and fiddled with his pocket watch.

"What is it, Rhys?" Patrick said. "You are positively bursting."

"Yes, well..." Rhys again sat on the stool, eye-to-eye with his brother. "I have a disturbing suspicion about Lady Charlotte."

"Which is?"

Patrick watched with eyes keen as a raptor's. Rhys cleared his throat.

"Get on with it, man!" Patrick said.

"Her ladyship appears to be forging her father's paintings. She puts his name on works she has created."

A lopsided smile was Patrick's response, which Rhys found quite odd.

"Are you not shocked?" Rhys said.

"I am not, for I knew of my lady's deception."

"I see." Rhys failed to comprehend Patrick's *laissez-faire* attitude. "What shall we do about it? Your wife cannot be a forger."

"No, she cannot," Patrick said. "But I know her purpose. Fielding left his countess virtually penniless, as did the baron before him, neither giving a thought to their own demise."

"How improvident," Rhys said.

"Lottie and her family own Halafair outright, but they had few funds to support themselves or the manor. The three devised a scheme, claiming a host of Baron Halafair's paintings remained. In reality, Charlotte was painting them."

Rhys leaned forward, resting an elbow on his knee. "To sustain themselves. I can understand that and their untenable position. But nonetheless..."

Patrick nodded. "Charlotte will not continue with the fraud. Three paintings remain to be completed and delivered. Once handed over, she is done with it, finding the ruse as repellent as we do."

"An acceptable plan," Rhys straightened. "As long as no one else learns of her secret."

Patrick's frown acknowledged the truth of it, for if the forgeries were made public, disaster would follow. Charlotte would be ostracized, perhaps even prosecuted and jailed, their family tarred with the same brush.

Rhys imagined his brother's marriage of convenience to a forger disturbing in the extreme.

To Charlotte's delight, she and Patrick had come to an accord and they rode out daily. Having practiced her barrel riding, she felt increasingly secure atop Beauty and much to her joy, her mother and sister had arrived from Halafair Hall.

The day was sunny, and Charlotte flung open the bedroom window. The soft breeze played with her unbound hair and she drew in the scents of garden and wood that mingled with the sea, a heady concoction.

Had Patrick risen? She padded down the hall and knocked on his door. Silence. Easing the door open, she stepped inside. His bed was rumpled, but he was not in it.

She dressed quickly in her split-skirt habit, hastening downstairs to find Susannah at the desk in the family drawing room, writing away, reminding Charlotte she owed many letters. She must set aside time later.

Susannah was penning a novel, an open secret that went unmentioned by all the household, as Patrick's sister was shy about her work.

Susannah turned, spotted her, and covered the page. "Lottie!"

"Good morning!" Charlotte said, bussing Susannah's cheek. "It is a lovely day. Would you care for a ride?"

"I am afraid not." She folded her notebook closed. "I have an appointment to practice my shooting."

Charlotte was incredulous, for Susannah was the gentlest and most retiring of the siblings. "Your *shooting*?"

Susannah grinned. "Sharpshooting is a passion since I was little. Have you met Billy Broad?"

"Indeed, I have." The one-armed former soldier always had a good word. "He seems a stalwart fellow."

"That he is," Susannah said with a nod. "He was a sharpshooter during the war and has immensely improved my aim. Even with one arm he remains a lethal shot."

"I confess your passion surprises me."

The pretty blonde quirked a smile. "Ah, women should not be good shots, eh?"

Charlotte chuffed a laugh. "I simply cannot picture you out in the woods hunting a buck!"

"I do not hunt." Susannah shrugged. "I simply enjoy shooting. Hitting a bullseye gives me great satisfaction."

"I will leave you to your practice, then," Charlotte said. "I must find my fiancé."

"I believe he went to the stables. Barn one, I think."

Outside, Charlotte hastened toward barn one only to be halted by epithets and shrieks. Following the sounds, she found Henry and a stableboy a good stone heavier engaged in fisticuffs, Henry's Stella bouncing around them.

"I can too!" Henry barked, throwing a punch.

The stableboy dodged. "You lie!"

"I doesn't!" Henry threw another.

"Stop!" Charlotte yelled, to no effect whatsoever. She bustled over to the pair, both bloodied, but neither unbowed.

"Henry!"

The boy turned to stare at her, eyes wide. Which was when the stableboy planted Henry a facer, knocking him to the ground.

"I should'na done that," the stableboy said. "You was lookin' the other way."

Henry shrugged, a cockeyed grin wreathing his swollen, bloodied face. "All's fair. I fight dirty, too."

The stableboy jammed his fisted hands to his hips. "I never fight dirty."

Henry leapt to his feet, eyes narrowed. "You just did!"

The stableboy raised his fists. "Take it back!"

"You are both behaving like mad hatters," Charlotte said. "Stop it *immediately*."

The boys surfaced from their pugilistic fugue, staring at her and bowing.

"Come," she said, taking each boy's hand and walked to a nearby bench, Stella trotting along. She sat, a boy on each side. "What were you two fighting about?"

"This one 'ere says he can ride a horse." The stableboy jabbed a thumb toward Henry.

"I can!" Henry said, leaning across her, chin thrust forward.

"Cannot!" The stableboy crossed his arms.

"Can so—"

"What is your name, young man?" Charlotte asked the stableboy.

The boy reddened, mumbling something.

"Pardon?" Charlotte leaned in.

"Augustus," he said with disdain.

"A fine name. Augustus—"

"Please don't, m'lady," he said. "I hate it. Call me Spider."

"Can you ride, Spider?"

"A course! Mr. Grimes himself taught me." He looked at Henry, chest puffed. "So there."

At eight, Henry was smaller than Spider, who appeared older and larger boned. "And you claim Henry cannot ride?"

"He can't," Spider said.

"Perhaps he can. Or perhaps not." She glanced at Henry whose lie made him drop his eyes. "I have a suggestion."

"What's that, Lady Charlotte?" Henry said.

"Spider, why do you not teach Henry to ride rather than fighting with him?"

"Cause he be a liar!"

"I ain't no liar!"

"I shall find Mr. Grimes and he will settle this." Charlotte rose and straightened her skirts.

"Wait!" Spider said.

Both boys jumped up to stand before her stick straight, Spider giving Henry a dour look.

"And what should I wait for?" Charlotte said.

"Don't tell Mr. Grimes," Spider said. "Please."

She clasped her hands. "Then how shall we proceed?"

"I ain't a very good rider," Henry said.

Charlotte doubted Henry had ever been on a horse.

Spider's hooded eyes slid to Henry. "I weren't either when I started."

"I can help Henry, too." She gave the boy a smile.

"Captain said horses scare you," Henry said.

"Once," she said. "But not so much anymore. You shall ride my barrel. You shall see how it helps."

Spider bit his lip. "The first thing Mr. Grimes taught me was how to take care of the beasts. I can show you, Henry. Um, if you wants."

Henry's face stiffened to mulish, looking ready to sass Spider.

"Knowing how to care for a horse is essential to riding, Henry," Charlotte said. "I learned, too."

Henry shoved his hands deep into his pockets. "I guess I should."

"Good!" she said. "Now shake, boys."

Henry thrust out a hand, Spider's moving more slowly, but when they shook, Stella nosed her way in seeking pets. The boys laughed.

"C'mon!" Spider said. "Let's go!"

Off they went, and Charlotte hoped the rest of her day proved less frenetic.

Patrick wheeled around a corner and gifted Charlotte with a smile, Claire following. She waved to her sister.

"Are we riding, Lottie?" Claire said.

"Indeed, we are!"

CHAPTER

NINE

Their trio trotted across the Woodbine meadows and pastures toward the east.

"Your seat is greatly improved, Lottie!" Claire said. "I am amazed."

"You, Lady Charlotte," Patrick said. "Are acquiring all the hallmarks of a fine rider."

"Thank you both." Her demure words masked her bubbles of joy at their compliments.

Charlotte rode on Patrick's left, noticing his preoccupation. She wondered what troubled him, but hadn't the courage to ask.

Perhaps he no longer wished to marry her.

Perhaps he was leaving Woodbine.

Perhaps...

Her fears were childish, yet Patrick had come to mean more than a mere acquaintance or, if she were honest, even more than a friend. She delighted in their rides, their conversation always interesting, and relished his watching her paint. His concern for her, his smiles, his humor, which was increasingly in evidence. Yet she refused to consider what those feelings meant, for they unsettled her.

Their trio ascended a small hill and before them spread meadows of clover, vetch, and wildflowers waving in the breeze. A splendid sight. "The prospect is beautiful, is it not?"

"Oh, yes," Claire said.

The day was warm, and Patrick doffed his coat, strapping it to his saddle beside the basket with their luncheon. Charlotte was about to do the same when the Duke of Devonshire appeared atop a knoll, accompanied by three companions.

Patrick waved, and the quartet rode toward them. The duke's estate marched alongside Woodbine, and he welcomed them on his land as eagerly as they welcomed him.

"What, ho!" His Grace shouted.

After exchanging greetings, the duke introduced Lord Cardingcom, Lord Ashworth, and Lady Eloise Farnam.

Devonshire was very blond, very tall, and very handsome, as well as quite robust. His countenance and bearing would have intimidated Charlotte were he not good friends with the Lansdownes. In truth, he was the most amiable of men.

Unlike the duke, Cardingcom appeared a smallish man, with a fine build and brown hair styled a la Brummell. Yet his dandyisms failed to appeal, his clothes and bearing somewhat ostentatious. Lady Eloise's eyes gleamed when presented to Patrick, her blonde good looks enhanced by her red riding habit. Charlotte disliked her predatory examination of her fiancé.

Claire had stiffened at Lord Ashworth's introduction, her sister's eyes hungry. The earl, dressed all in black, with auburn hair and a bronze complexion, was a striking man, yet Claire seldom noticed such things. Something brewed in her sister's busy brain.

"Ashworth, you old dog," Patrick said, and the men clasped forearms.

"Good to see you atop a horse, Lansdowne!" Ashworth said.

Lady Eloise stared at Patrick's legs and sniffed. "I was just commenting on the straps binding your legs."

How utterly offensive.

Lady Eloise raised a brow. "I assumed his lordship would no longer ride due to his enfeeblement."

Enfeeblement! Charlotte gritted her teeth, then tossed Patrick a grin. "Not only has Lord Hawthorne regained his exceptional seat, but he flies over jumps others would not dare."

"You are bound for a picnic, is that not so?" Devonshire said, ending the unpleasant exchange.

"We are, your grace." Charlotte smiled. "Do join us." Cook always packed enough for an army. Or rather, a navy.

"Jolly good," Cardingcom said.

"I fear we cannot," Devonshire said. "Even as we speak, our chef is preparing luncheon."

Lady Eloise brushed a stray curl from her face. "I am truly fascinated by that rig you use, captain."

"Are you, indeed?" Patrick's tone was pleasant, but his eyes had chilled.

Curse the woman. Patrick's quiet inflection and those frigid eyes signaled the emergence of his rapier tongue.

Charlotte hoped he did not immolate the woman. More than Patrick's own injury, others' wounds and deaths often absorbed his thoughts. He would speak of injured seamen, ones with no loving families, ones who were poor and could ill afford proper treatment or aid. Some became beggars, while others were consigned to a parish workhouse, a deadly place. Their ruined lives troubled him greatly.

Lady Eloise pressed a hand to his arm. "Should your horse fall..."

"Fall?" Patrick chuffed. "Diablo does not fall, my lady, and if he did, I would happily go with him to the end."

"Forgive me, my lord," she said with a frown. "My brother's horse fell at Waterloo, his legs crushed, his death a consequence."

The ire in Patrick's eyes cooled. "I am deeply sorry."

"As am I," Charlotte and Claire said in unison.

Lady Eloise's beautiful gray eyes radiated superiority. "He survived the battle, you see, a medaled cavalry officer. For him to live, his legs would have to be amputated. Naturally, he refused. A noble death."

"Noble?" Charlotte blurted out, shocked to her toes. "Your brother could have been with you and his other loved ones."

The lady puffed up. "A cripple? Half a man. We Farnams pride ourselves on our perfection of style and address, though I confess I always wondered how it would feel."

"How *what* would feel?" Patrick said in a clipped voice.

"Having useless legs."

Devonshire and the two men stared, the duke exclaiming, "My lady!"

Patrick would explode, perhaps injuring his friendship with Devonshire. Charlotte reached across to squeeze his hand.

Patrick gave her a wink and boomed a laugh, surprising all. "But you see, Lady Eloise, I cannot feel them, so I have no answer to satisfy your curiosity!"

During their exchange, Cardingcom had stared at Charlotte through his monocle. Patrick must have noticed, for he said, "Are you previously acquainted with Lady Charlotte, Lord Cardingcom?"

The man flushed and Devonshire chuckled.

"Cardingcom here," the duke said, waving a hand. "He is rather taken with your father's work, Lady Charlotte."

The man looked abashed. "Indeed, forgive my scrutiny, m'lady. As a collector, I find Reginald Pheland's work head and shoulders above all others."

"How kind," Charlotte said while Beauty stretched her neck to nibble the grass.

"I noted several Pheland paintings at Devonshire's," Ashworth said. "Quite striking. I was particularly charmed by your father's portrait of Chatsworth House."

"I am a Pheland devotee as well," Patrick said with a jaunty smile.

Oh, dear. Charlotte would *not* look at him for she suspected his pesky sense of humor was about to appear.

Cardingcom opened his mouth to speak, but Patrick continued. "I find the works sold since his passing, the ones he left to his family, to be his most exceptional."

Heaven forfend. "Do you, my lord?" Charlotte said in a clipped voice.

"Why, yes," Patrick breezed on. "For they show a confidence that appeared to grow in his later years."

Charlotte's cheeks heated.

"I have seen several, Hawthorne," Cardingcom said. "I must agree."

"Lord Ashworth." Claire leaned forward, eyes alight. "I am an admirer of *your* late father's work."

"He assisted in the acquisition of the Parthenon friezes," Cardingcom said. "Did he not?"

Ashworth scowled. "Yes."

Interesting. Had Ashworth not been associated with archeology, Claire would have remained silent.

Her sister smiled, and the men took notice, for Claire's comeliness stunned one and all, her sweet nature charming whomever she met.

"The friezes are exquisite," Cardingcom said.

"Naturally, I have seen them, as well," Lady Eloise chimed in.

Ashworth speared them with a hostile glance.

"Lord Ashworth," Claire said. "Many talk of your father's sculpture room with awe."

Ashworth spoke through gritted teeth. "That would be one way to describe it."

Claire started at his hostile tone. "I apologize if I have offended."

"Not at all!" Devonshire chimed in. "Theseus here is a grumbler."

"God's blood!" Ashworth mumbled under his breath.

A stag pranced from the wood, saw them, and sped away.

"Fine hunting now for bucks!" Devonshire enthused.

Saved by a deer, much to Charlotte's relief. Lord Ashworth's demeanor was most unappealing.

Their talk turned to hunting, and she addressed Patrick and Claire. "Shall we not find our picnic spot before it grows too late?"

They said their farewells and rode off, Charlotte happy to be quit of the appalling Lady Eloise.

"An odd group," Claire said as they trotted toward a hill with a towering maple.

"Ashworth is a good friend to Devonshire," Patrick said. "Where the duke dug up the other two, I cannot imagine, for Ashworth does not suffer fools."

"Fools or not, the man was quite discourteous," Claire said. "A disappointment."

"In what sense?" Charlotte said.

"In truth, I was hoping to discuss my research with him." Claire patted her horse's neck as they climbed a grassy hill. "He is a renowned antiquarian, near as much as his father. I ache to see his father's marbles for my research. They say the room, stuffed with Greek statuary, is incredible. Given Ashworth's demeanor, I doubt he would allow me entry."

"Perhaps you are hasty, Lady Claire," Patrick said, for he was used to Ashworth's taciturn nature.

"Perhaps," Claire said, then grinned. "Or perhaps not."

They reached the knoll's crest with views of the surrounding countryside, a glimpse of the sea in the distance.

"I am off," Claire said.

"But our picnic?" Charlotte said.

Mischief gleamed from Claire's eyes. "Lucy and I are to practice with my knives, for she has great interest in my technique. We meet at the small copse near the house and thus I must leave you two lovebirds."

"But…" Charlotte said.

Claire cantered off across the pastoral fields.

"What a mercurial sister I have," Charlotte said.

"Nay. She is playing matchmaker, Lottie." Patrick untethered his legs and waist strap, then pulled his right leg over the front of the saddle, so his legs rested together. "I have a bit of a surprise, my lady."

"I love surprises." Charlotte beamed.

Patrick drew his newly crafted crutches from his saddle, resting them beside him on the saddle.

Charlotte dismounted. "What are you about, Patrick?"

He took a crutch in each hand, gripping the handles, leaned forward, and slid off Diablo, catching himself with the sticks.

"My word!" Charlotte said.

Patrick took a couple of breaths, then moved the right stick forward. True, his legs dragged, yet he had the strength to *move*.

"What a feat you have accomplished!"

A bead of sweat tracked down his temple. "All this while—the accident, dashing about for a proper chair—I held the hope that sensation in my legs would return. That hope has dimmed, thus, along with work on Diablo, I have used these to build my strength. I cannot go far, of course."

Charlotte clapped. "But that is no matter! You can dismount on your own."

"I intend to stretch my abilities as far as my injury will allow."

Charlotte spread out the blanket beneath the maple, near enough Patrick could seat himself, and he lowered his hands on the crutches, muscles straining, sweat running down his spine. Then he released the sticks and sat with a thump, arranging the crutches beside him. Awkward, true, but damned doable.

"I shall show the Admiralty," he said, "I may be confined to a desk job, but I am not chair-bound."

She kissed him, a mere brush of the lips.

Lottie's eyes were closed, her lips warm and plush, and he slid a hand to her neck, then dipped his head and kissed its nape. She sighed, her hands coming to his shoulders, his lips returning to hers. She sighed again. He wanted more, much more of his sweet woman, and he deepened the kiss.

She finally drew away on a gasp, her eyes large, her breathing rapid, her cheeks a-blush.

"Well done!" she said, her hand flying to her mouth.

He found their kiss mighty fine, as well, which pleased him enormously.

Charlotte's laugh, light and strained, burst forth. "I meant your use of the walking sticks. You are a man to whom obstacles are but a trifle."

He shook his head. "Not a trifle. But some mountains are scalable."

"Shall I tie Diablo?" Charlotte said.

"No need," Patrick said. "I have trained him to stand when the reins lie on the ground."

Charlotte laid out their meal of sandwiches, lemonade, and other sundries. "How clever."

"A necessity, given the awkward nature of me trying to tie him." He reached for a sandwich and bit down.

"When do you move to Hawthorne Hall?"

"Soon. Though needing much repair, workmen are seeing to it, and we will reside in the former priest's cottage until the house is livable. I think you shall like it."

"I am sure the estate is lovely, disrepair or no."

"It overlooks the sea and has much charm, and lies but an hour or so from Woodbine."

"Perfect for visits," she said, wearing a faux frown. "Your comments on my father's later works were outside of enough, my lord, as you well know they were mine."

His lips twitched. "I only spoke the truth, my lady."

She wagged a finger. "You are a devil who aimed to get a rise out of me, sir."

"I am." He spread his arms wide. "For I adore when your cheeks flush that delicious shade of peach."

"You are bamming me, sir."

He badly wanted to kiss her again, and from the glint in those sapphire eyes, she might feel the same.

That, or cosh him on the head. "Bamming you? I think not, Lottie."

Charlotte tilted her head. "How came you by your interest in art?"

Patrick leaned back on his elbows. "I never thought much about it."

"Never?" she said.

"We have much art at Ravenscroft, including a Gainsborough, a van Dyck, and a Hogarth. Bird paintings abound, as well, due to my father's obsession. My greatest influence was my mother. She died when I was fairly young, but I recall her at her easel where I would sit beside her and watch. Rhys would tease me, saying I was cuckoo, but I was captivated by how her strokes, mere dabs of paint, magically transformed into people and trees, pastures and mountains." He chuckled. "Though at the time I could not elucidate that. Thomasina paints, as well."

"I have seen," she said. "Have you ever tried?"

He shook his head wearing a smile. "Once. But I had not the patience for mixing the powders, for cutting the canvas, or laying on the primer. The preparations failed to hold my attention."

"And yet your miniature ships are filled with preparation, detailed and precise in every aspect."

On a shrug, he said, "I took up crafting them during lulls at sea and a passion was born. I shall leave the painting to you, love, and enjoy the products of your labor."

He'd called her "love," and though a trifle, she became all tingly. "Tis no labor, for painting is my obsession, and I am always eager to face a blank canvas."

The pear he bit was green and shiny, his sensual lips stealing her attention as he chewed. He licked away a drop of juice with his tongue, his eyes capturing hers, smoldering blue gems, that made her fuss with a loose thread on the skirt of her gown.

"How do you feel today atop Beauty?" he said, his voice a low rumble. "Your seat looks rather fine."

Her cheeks bloomed with that peach color Patrick now considered a favorite. "Much better. Surprisingly so."

"Why surprisingly? You have been practicing, have you not?"

"Yes," she said, in a hushed voice, as if someone nearby might hear them. "I pulled the barrel into an empty stall and I usually close the door so no one can see me."

"Usually?"

She took a bite of the sandwich and chewed. "Sometimes I forget. Grimes came upon me yesterday and I nearly died of embarrassment."

"I am most pleased you did not." He, too, had spied her practicing, and she had been both adorable and determined, her face scrunched in concentration. Patrick found it charming.

Charlotte was lovelier than she had any right to be, and he would swear each day she grew more beautiful. He'd heard Rhys say that regarding Rose, at the time finding it ridiculous. How wrong he had been.

No denying he was drawn to her, her artistic pursuit no small part of that attraction. Her figure was lovely, as well, though he had always imagined himself with a petite blonde. One soft and malleable who would admire his mastery of the sea.

Malleable? Not his Lottie.

The breeze quickened and he scented the ocean brine, saw the gulls wheeling nearby, their cries audible. He longed for a deck beneath his feet, for the sway and roll as his ship challenged the waves.

No one triumphed against the sea, but one could be in accord with its rhythms and appreciate its inconstancy, where in seconds a terrible storm could rise, only to be followed by an exquisite sunset.

"You look far away, Patrick. I suspect you are back aboard your ship. Do tell me of your time at sea?"

"With pleasure." He raised a brow. "Do you know why I joined up?"

"So as not to be outdone by your 'perfect' brother?"

"Exactly." He chuckled. "Whilst I knew little about sailing and less about the sea, I discovered a gift for both."

"Tell me," she said.

He peered through the leafy tree to the endless blue sky above, picturing the vast ocean. "I love all of it, for I fell unexpectedly in love with the vastness, the freedom."

"Freedom. Yes." She smiled, eyes sparkling, and offered him an apple.

Bloody blazes, she was Eve, her face sun-kissed, her eyes blue stars...

He was waxing poetic. God's teeth, he'd gone daft. He took her offering and bit down.

"What are you thinking now?"

"How my purchase of your seascape now lies at the bottom of the sea, along with the numerous trinkets I'd planned to gift you."

"I am touched," she said. "I shall paint you another."

She'd surprised him. "Would you?"

Charlotte fussed with a jar's recalcitrant seal, her eyes not meeting his. "It would not be an exact copy, but—"

He pressed a hand over hers. "Nor could it be, each of your works is unique."

She nodded. "We should start back, my lord."

"Not quite yet, Lottie, for I wish to renew my proposal of marriage."

CHAPTER
TEN

Charlotte gulped her lemonade, thankful for the glass in hand to hide her surprise. She had pondered their marriage a great deal, imagining the years rolling out before them. Patrick would make an admirable husband—intelligent, interesting, thoughtful. And who would not be attracted to such a handsome, commanding man? He was catnip for the ladies.

"As I told you earlier," he said, "my wealth is ample enough to support Halafair, your mother, and a dowry for Claire. That is my intention."

She went mute, and no wonder. That Patrick would erase her family's financial woes left her imagining her freedom from debt, from worry, from fear. No more forgeries, nor leaky roofs, nor concerns for Claire's future. To be safe. Charlotte could not recall when she had last felt thus.

"I am deeply honored, Patrick," she said. "But I have come to realize I cannot."

His face remained unchanged at her rejection. "Why is that, Lottie?"

Heat scoured her cheeks—damn her pale complexion—but she

held his gaze. "As I have come to know you…I hold you in great esteem, so much that I would not shackle you to someone to whom you do not deeply care. What if in a month or a year you found a woman you *did* feel great affection for?"

He frowned. "I do not think that way in the least."

"We can find a way out of this conundrum, do you not think?"

"Knowing what may or may not come is impossible. I like you well enough, Lottie. Very much, in fact, and I enjoy our time together. You provoke my mind, insist I see the world in different ways. You even make me smile, sometimes when you did not intend to."

Charlotte feigned shock. "How dare you find humor when I do not mean a joke!"

There it was, his soft laugh that so charmed her.

"I believe you are doing so right now," he said. "But with intention. We have many shared pastimes, such as your painting and my enjoyment of it."

"What about riding?" she said, her voice quiet. "And gadding about the ocean? I am not terribly good at the former and I do not know if I would like the latter."

Patrick shook his head. "You shall never have to lock-step with me, Lottie. Think. Marriage will give you a freedom that must appeal, your family comfortable at Halafair. We shall have Hawthorne Hall and Edgecombe, the estate my uncle left me. Both will be your homes."

"Of course I see the advantages, Patrick."

"While you do not love me, nor I you, we rub along well, do we not?"

"We do," Charlotte echoed, though when Patrick said he did not love her, Charlotte's heart had pinched. A feeling to be examined later. "You said you plan to return to duty."

"Soon. Though I will dearly miss being at sea, I can accomplish much."

"I doubt that not." She bit her lip.

"You must see the advantages to our union."

"Yes, but…"

Patrick took her hand, kissing her palm, then looked up. "Love can grow, Lottie."

She struggled with her words, embarrassing ones. "I…I wish for children, Patrick."

His eyes danced with humor. "This is plain speaking, indeed, my lady."

Charlotte wanted to die.

He leaned forward and cupped her cheek. "*Our* children would be a possibility."

"In truth?"

His grin was wide. "Dear Lottie, I function as any other man in that regard."

A startling admission, one that made her down her lemonade in one gulp. "Well good!" she said in a high-pitched voice. She reached again for the lemonade jar, but he took it from her, set it aside, and enfolded her hands in his.

"Marry me, Charlotte. If you say no, that will be the end of it. I wish to give you an opportunity to decline as everyone assumes a *fait accompli*. You deserve a voice in this. A choice."

What a thoughtful gesture, a meaningful one. But it was his look of hunger that stole her breath. Hunger and want and warmth.

"On my behalf," he continued, "I suspect we will enjoy each other and find our way."

She stared at their held hands, then at the desire she saw in his eyes and the warmth she felt in her heart. "All right. *Yes*, I will marry you, Patrick, and I am honored to do so."

He took her in his arms, running a hand up and down her back, then he kissed her, taking his time, exploring her lips to dizzying effect.

Woozy when Patrick released her, he continued. "Rhys has procured a special license. Shall we wed day after tomorrow?"

Two days. A swift nuptial, which appealed, for she was never patient with the inevitable. "Yes. You are sure about your finances? My paltry dowry will not help."

He shook his head on a low chuckle. "Dear Lottie, I have ample funds. Your family shall not know want again."

Growing bold, she kissed him, oddly pleasing sensations prickling through her.

"God, you are sweet," he said when they parted. "I adore much about you, Lottie. We shall do well."

Charlotte warmed, and they stared at each other in something like surprise.

"Let us return," Patrick said. "I am eager to tell all the news."

The air thickened with promise as they gathered their luncheon detritus.

"How shall you regain the saddle, Patrick?" The thought just occurred, and she was abashed.

"All prepared. Would you fetch Diablo?"

Charlotte did as asked, and the big horse nickered, eager for the ride. Patrick lifted his crutches, pressed on the sticks, and rose, vaulting belly-down onto the saddle. He hefted his right leg across the stallion's rump and rose to a seated position. What strength and determination to accomplish such a feat.

"Brilliant, Patrick!" she said.

"I aim to please," he said with a jaunty grin.

Charlotte admired him more than she could say.

As they neared Woodbine, Patrick leaned across Diablo for a kiss, then peeled off to tell Rhys their news, while Charlotte rode to a small copse behind the barn. There, she found her sister and Lucy throwing knives like circus performers.

Claire's penchant for the pastime was born when a traveling carnival decamped near Halafair to perform for the nearby town. She was seven, her curiosity vast, and she had observed their doings in secret. Somehow, she inveigled their knife thrower to teach her, with

Mama's surprising support. Charlotte was fascinated, but she didn't want to touch the things.

Dismounting, she tied Beauty and approached, staying well behind the two women. Lucy, an expert in the martial art *kalari*, watched Claire with a raptor's attention as her sister threw her knife. Once complete, Charlotte cleared her throat.

Claire set her knives on a stump and ran over.

Lucy gathered her knives. "I shall return to the house." She raised a brow at Charlotte. "I suspect I will have many projects in the days to come."

"You must be a seer, Lucy!" Charlotte said, laughing.

Lucy's face pleated on a laugh. "So Arjuna says."

After Lucy strode off, Claire bounced on her toes. "News?"

She flushed at Claire's grinning face. "Patrick and I shall marry in two days."

Claire whooped, then took Charlotte in a fierce hug. "You are pleased, yes?"

"I am," she said with a smile. "My heart has warmed to Patrick." He spoke to her as if her thoughts mattered, rather than as a "mere" woman reciting nonsense, while his small jokes or humorous comments charmed her. And when their eyes met over a shared event or amusement, a pleasurable frisson arced between them. "Though we have not a love like Rose and Rhys, who knows? I hope his feelings deepen, as mine have. I must go tell Mama."

"I am happy for you, Lottie!" Claire gripped Charlotte's hands. "Lord Hawthorne will make a splendid husband, for I sense he holds you in great affection. Have you discussed children?"

More mortification. Ridiculous. Claire was her sister, a woman more plainspoken than most. "Patrick says all is…" She cleared her throat. "All is well in that regard."

"Excellent!" Claire said. "I will spoil any nieces or nephews you bring into this world as marriage for me is on permanent hold."

"Wait…You do not plan to wed?" This was new, a surprise, for men flocked to Claire like drones to a queen.

Claire tucked an arm through Charlotte's. "My research has led me to a pivotal place, a conundrum that, if solved, will change our perceptions of the ancient Greeks and Romans."

"Will it, really?" Charlotte said. "Your Greek trip in the new year with Fauvel's group will aid this?"

"I believe so. Fauvel is both esteemed and renowned for his antiquarian research. He continues his diplomatic service in Greece, though his primary focus remains on antiquities. I cannot even think of a husband until I have uncovered the truth of my studies."

"To marry or not is your choice and no other's."

"We shall see."

Picturing her own children with black hair and blue eyes near overset her. "Either way, I am certain you will make a most marvelous aunt."

"Of that, you can be sure!" Claire laughed. "We had best fly, Lottie, for we have much to do!"

Their wedding was a small affair attended by their family and a few friends, including the Duke of Devonshire. Charlotte insisted upon one thing—to be *seated* across from Patrick as they took their vows. When she walked down the aisle and took her seat, his eyes glowed. She suspected hers did, as well.

All went beautifully until the toasts at the nuptial breakfast, which went on forever. Everyone spoke, from Mama to Rhys to Thomasina and on, all except for Charlotte, overwhelmed by the reality of having a *husband*. Not that it felt real.

That would happen this evening.

Oh dear.

The toasts wound up with the duke's speech, a delightful one, loving and grand, just as the man himself, until...

"In honor of the newly wedded couple," the duke said. "I shall host a musicale at Devonshire Manor in their honor."

At least it wasn't a full ball.

Rhys, about to open his mouth, shut it, while Rose's eyes grew as wide. Susannah fussed with her napkin, Mama and Claire smiling.

Patrick simply nodded, his face tight and pale.

"How very lovely, your grace," Charlotte said.

"Not at all!" the duke responded. "A pleasure."

For all his kindness and amiability, he occasionally misread others' sensibilities.

"It shall be an intimate affair," the duke continued. "No more than one hundred or so guests."

Could it get worse?

The duke winked at Patrick. "I expect Admiral Saumarez will attend as well."

Patrick had mentioned the admiral to her in passing, his obvious dislike for the man due to his crass words about Lord Nelson, whom Patrick had greatly admired.

Ah, my. The situation had worsened.

Late that morning, after the wedding hullaballoo, Patrick rode off on Diablo, explaining he needed to clear his head. Not the most husbandly thing to do, but Charlotte understood. He was tense as a strung bow. She felt the same, perhaps for a different reason as she was unable to pry her mind from that night's *event*.

While Patrick rode, Charlotte painted, for it had the same calming effect as Patrick's gallop. Distracting her was her search for India yellow, only to find the bladder near spent.

Dear heavens, she was a married woman. Yet nothing felt changed.

Tonight...*all* would change.

Shoving her fear into its box, she jotted India yellow in her notebook beside the list of paints to order, all part of the pallet she used for her forgeries, which differed from her own more lively one. She returned to the largest easel and began to work, pausing to thin the lead white with turpentine.

A storm had come up and rain pounded the windows, the trees

whipping like dancers, the sounds lulling her. She hoped Patrick had returned before the downpour.

Charlotte became lost in the idyllic world of the Somerset pastoral, and she entered that elusive space where she painted full tilt, where the world receded and all that existed were the strokes of color she laid on the canvas.

A pounding at the door and Charlotte jerked.

"Who is it?" she said.

"Your husband!" Patrick said.

"Come!"

Charlotte grinned as Patrick's chair whooshed across the carpet, then onto the canvas she had laid beneath her easel.

"Hello, husband," she said, a smile in her voice.

"Hello, *wife*."

She turned to him, finding his hair damp. "You and Diablo survived the storm, I see."

"That we did. It was exhilarating."

Charlotte could understand that. "You love storms." She did as well.

"A great deal." Flying across the fields, Patrick had found himself missing Charlotte. A trifle odd, that.

Charlotte had come to a particularly challenging portion of the Somerset sky, and she slipped her brush into the jar of turpentine, massaged her hands with the turpentine cloth, and moved to the settee, a better venue for her new husband. *Husband*—how strange.

"I shall order tea and biscuits," she said, struck by the beauty of his face. Tanned and lined, his blue eyes a beacon, she raised her hand to touch his cheek. "We can share."

"How do you fare this afternoon, Lottie?"

She wrapped her shawl close. "I am at sixes and sevens, which is why I hastened to my studio when you left for your ride. I always find work comforting." She shivered.

"Are you chilly?" he said. "Shall I have a footman bring more wood for the fire?"

"No, but thank you. I do not feel the chill when I paint, I become so absorbed." Charlotte fumbled for a suitable topic, something unexceptional. "I suspect the promise of the duke's musicale discomforts you."

He rolled to her paints, examining each color with interest, then on to her brushes. "I shall do my duty." He tossed her a jaunty grin, patting an arm of his chair. "As much as I am able."

"We shall do fine," she said. "Together. I would like to learn more about your chair."

"Would you indeed?"

In for a penny and all that. "About how you created it, for it is quite different from most wheeled conveyances." She nibbled her lower lip.

Tea interrupted their conversation, and Charlotte poured and made a plate for Patrick.

"Your chair is very much a part of you."

Patrick cleared his throat. How could Charlotte possibly be curious about his infernal chariot? "Why did you never ask before this?"

"I guess, mostly..." She stared at her hands, coward that she was. "I did not wish to offend, Patrick. You do not talk about your chair, yet it is a vital part of who you now are. Frankly, I am fascinated by it."

His hand slid over hers and squeezed. "Did you know the Bath Chair was named for the town where the inventor lived?"

"I saw them when we visited!" Charlotte said. "Clever contrivances."

He nodded. "That they are. But the damned thing was too heavy for me to push. Self-propulsion was my singular necessity." He leaned forward and fingered her shawl. "What a pretty thing, and so soft."

"Cashmere. A gift from Rose who knitted it for me. Its deep blue reminds me of your eyes." Had she said that aloud? Her cheeks flamed.

Patrick leaned forward and bestowed a sweet brush of the lips. "A German watchmaker in the sixteen hundreds invented a self-propelled chair for himself."

"Did he? I have seen none until yours."

"That is because no other exists. We failed to find his original chair, which frustrated me beyond measure."

Charlotte laughed. "I can imagine. I would have been frustrated, too."

"May I?" He gestured toward one of her notebooks scattered about the small table between them. She nodded, and he drew a pencil from his pocket and sketched Farffler's chair.

"That looks heavy. Yours looks much lighter as you replaced much of the wood with cane. Farffler's third wheel was in front, while you have placed yours in the rear. And you do not crank it, as you have drawn, but push the wheels for propulsion."

"We tinkered." He cleared his throat. "Banby has an aptitude for mechanics, as do I. Henry is quite interested, as well. We found Farffler's plans in Italy, and after finding issues with Farffler's design, we experimented beyond it."

"Coming up with this masterpiece!" Charlotte said.

"Banby and Henry were a great part of it."

Charlotte took a sip of tea. "I am very fond of both. Banby amazes me with his understanding and acumen."

"He has those qualities. He also can be annoying beyond words."

They laughed, their eyes catching in wonder at the connection between them.

Charlotte cleared her throat. "I do enjoy the lieutenant's sense of humor. And Henry...he is special. I am glad you took him with you."

Patrick snorted. "Not by choice. Well, not at first, for he clung to me like the barnacle I call him."

"Confess. You care for the boy."

He grumbled. "Well, yes. It appears the miscreant has burrowed beneath my skin." He lifted a figurine, crudely done of a painter at work, and turned it in his hands. "We shall modify my chair further. I have designed some new wheels for the outdoors, wood and steel. Banby is executing them."

"How so?" Charlotte said.

He moved closer. "We first turn the wood on a lathe to achieve a cylindrical profile. We use the roughing gouge, and next, the spindle gouge as a shaper, followed by the skew—"

"Oh, my!" Charlotte leaned back, laughing. "As I am not of mechanical inclination, I fear that is too much detail for my poor brain to conjure. I hope I have not offended."

He grinned, all white teeth and warm eyes. "Not at all. I am used to Banby and Henry, equal enthusiasts of mechanicals."

A tap at the door, and Patrick rolled to open it to find a maid he did not know.

""I do not believe we have met," Patrick said.

"I am Hermione, my lord. I been here near on three months. I'm here to pick up the tea tray."

"I am afraid we are not quite finished."

"Oh!" She bobbed a curtsy and fled, and Patrick returned to the table before the settee.

Charlotte's head quirked. "That was odd."

"How so?"

"I did not ring for her."

"She said she was new."

Charlotte shrugged, and offered him a biscuit. "Tell me about your childhood. Something you would change."

He laughed. "My name."

"What is wrong with Patrick?"

"*That* is not the name to which I refer. My full name is Falcon Patrick Percy Lansdowne."

Charlotte started. "I see nothing offensive."

He shook his head, a smile wreathing his face. "For as long as I remember, Father was obsessed with birds and insisted on birds in all of our names, though Rhys' first name is Griffin, a nonexistent creature."

"But an epic one with wings and the head of an eagle!" Charlotte said.

He shook his head. "Falcon. Who wants to be called Falcon, I ask you?"

"I think it is quite dashing," she said.

"I think it is quite ridiculous. And to be named after a parrot? Appalling."

"Our Percy, of course. He could not be—"

"Oh, he is, the same one from my childhood, for the damned bird will live for fifty or more years. Thankfully, our mother called me Patrick."

"I do see why your feathers were ruffled."

"Bloody hell, Lottie!" he said, fighting his smile. "Thomasina is dammed fond of that bird, and she insisted we bring him when we decamped to Woodbine. Were it up to me, I would rid ourselves of the pest."

Charlotte waved a hand. "All bluster, m'lord. You would not. Sina does love strutting about with him on her arm. Was she as attached when you all lived at Ravenscroft?"

His eyes grew distant. "You know Sina is different from the rest of us. Better in many ways due to her sweet nature and prodigious memory, not to mention her preternatural harmony with horses. To all our sorrow, Father saw only her surface differences and sent her from the family to live here with the stable masters. When Rhys became marquess, he reunited us all, her meeting with Percy, love at first sight."

"I did not know," Charlotte's tone was serious. "How very sad."

"It was, but no longer so," he said. "What about your childhood? Would you change anything?"

CHAPTER
ELEVEN

Her eyes burned, for an image of Papa came to mind. She reached for a pencil and a notebook and began to sketch a parrot. "I wish Father had lived longer. My papa was an eccentric who too often spent too much on gifts. He was a collector, too, of snuff boxes, ladies' fans, and a copious amount of feathers, as well as taking on assorted wounded wild animals." She smiled at the memory. "He was a jolly man, seeing humor in much, particularly the human condition. He brightened our world with laughter and warmth."

"I see." Patrick was not terribly jolly, and he wondered if Charlotte wished she'd wed a more high-spirited man.

How very serious her new husband looked. On impulse, Charlotte kissed him, his lips warm and fervent, as if he would gobble her up. Oh, she liked his kisses.

"You are not jolly, Patrick. But rather, witty, which I appreciate far more." Charlotte grinned. *And* he was a delicious kisser.

Later that day, Patrick rolled into the family dining room, where a cold collation graced the sideboard. He had hoped Lottie would be here, but she was not. Only Rhys sat at the table near sideways, leg crossed, reading *The Morning Post*.

"Good day, brother," Patrick said as he wheeled to the lower sideboard Woodbine's crafters had constructed for him. A surprise. The estate's housekeeper said it was the least they could do for a boy she'd known since he was in skeleton suits.

Plate made, he rolled to the table while mulling over his recent conversation with Charlotte.

"How fare you this afternoon, brother?" Rhys laid down his paper.

He did not miss the humor in Rhys' words. "Charlotte surprised me today."

"Wives do that, surprise us. How?"

He told Rhys about Charlotte's question regarding his chair. "At first, I was displeased, which sadly, I conveyed to my wife."

"Your typical reaction to anything regarding your infirmity," Rhys said. "I hope you did not—"

"No, I did not. When I understood she was truly interested in the mechanics and creation of the thing, I explained the process to her. It still surprises me, her question."

"Why?" Rhys said. "Charlotte is your wife. Wife or no, I have observed her interested in all you do."

"You think so?"

"I do. It is rather obvious she holds you in affection."

He took a bite of beef, then downed it with a sip of wine, buying time. Charlotte liked him, that he understood, and she seemed to welcome his kisses. But affection? "Does she?"

"I thought your accident affected your legs, not your brain."

Patrick's self-deprecating smile was followed by a chuckle. "No, but I would say we both agree I can be rather thickheaded, particularly when it comes to Lottie."

"Fear not, younger brother, for that affliction besets me as well. Rose tells me as much."

They laughed, then Patrick sobered. "I hold Lady Charlotte in great esteem as well."

"Do you?" Rhys said in a dry voice. "I never would have guessed."

Charlotte was performing her nightly ablutions in preparation for bed. Her hand was on stroke eighty-nine when she paused. Bed. With Patrick.

A knock at the door. "Hello?"

Mama. "Come in!"

Her hands shook so hard she ceased brushing and laid her silver-backed hairbrush on the dressing table.

"I gave you that," Mama said coming to stand beside her. She ran a finger over the silver back. "Papa chose the style, you know."

"I did not."

She plucked at the low-cut neck of her nightrail, a garment gifted to her by Rose for her wedding night. The silk was soft and warm and clung to her curves like a lover.

Oh, my. A *lover*.

Mama pressed her hands to Charlotte's shoulders and squeezed. "All will be well. Trust your mama. Love you, my darling girl." She bussed Charlotte's cheek and left.

Would all be well?

Given Patrick's legs, Charlotte anticipated *his* unease. Their intimacy would not be easy for him, for his limbs must be terribly thin. She must not react poorly, did not wish to hurt her new husband's feelings, for she admired him and found him...desirable? She did, indeed, yet how that desire translated to sexual congress muddled her brain.

Another knock.

Charlotte massaged her temples. "Enter!"

"Lottie!" Rose said.

Charlotte swiveled on the seat. "Rose?"

Rose entered the bedroom, hopped onto the bed, and patted the place beside her. "I thought to have a chat."

Panic clutched Charlotte's heart. "A chat?"

Her sister-in-law's face glowed with a smile. "I thought...well, I wondered how much Lady Bea has told you about this evening's events."

What to say? "I know, um, Patrick will come to me and we will..."

"Yes?" Rose leaned forward.

"Um..." Charlotte leapt, nearly twisting her ankle, to straighten her things on her dressing table.

"Lottie. My dear sister."

She did not look up. "Yes?"

"Come sit beside me," Rose said, entering the sitting room and taking the divan.

Charlotte whooshed a sigh and seated herself beside Rose.

"Do you trust me?" Rose said.

"You know I do."

"Then trust me when I say tonight's events will go more smoothly if you hear what I have to say." Rose again took Charlotte's hand in hers. "He will touch you."

Charlotte nodded and straightened. "As I understand it, he and I will look at each other naked, and that will possibly produce a pregnancy."

The rapid blinks of Rose's eyes testified to her sister's shock.

"You see?" Charlotte said in a chipper tone. "I know just what is required of me. Though Mama said to think of other things—like painting or archery—while it is happening. Are we done?"

Squeezing her eyes tight, Rose sighed. "I am afraid, dear sister, that what you have described will produce nothing other than a chill."

Charlotte's mouth made an "oh."

"Let us talk about horses!" Rose said, eyes bright. "Now, you have seen horses mating, yes?"

She peered at Rose from the corner of her eye. "Perhaps. I am not sure I actually have."

"All right, then," Rose said, her tone serious. "First thing, the mare is teased."

"Teased?" Charlotte's voice was high, closer to a squeal.

"You will be teased, too, when Patrick touches you and—"

"*Where?* Exactly where will he touch me, Rose?"

"Your face, your breasts, your..." She pointed.

"There?" Oh, my!

"If he is as skilled as Rhys, and I suspect he is, you will like it."

"I do not see how that is possible. Mama said not to touch down there and..."

"Have you never?"

Charlotte chewed her lip. "Perhaps we should continue this later."

"Soon, dear sister, there will be no later."

"No later!"

Rose enfolded Charlotte in a fierce hug. "You will be *pleasured,* Lottie."

"No. No, I will not."

"I suspect you shall, Lottie." Rose continued. "Once the mare is teased."

"There is *more?*" Oh, this sounded very involved, not to mention worrisome.

"The stallion then mounts the mare from behind and—"

"Patrick will mount me from the rear?" Charlotte said, or rather, screamed the words.

"No, dear sister. I doubt that." Rose giggled. "Though the position is quite pleasurable, too! I am making a muck of this. Try to calm yourself."

"I do not see how, since this whole...performance sounds like something out of a bad theatrical!"

"But once you are teased, you—"

"Do stop with the horse analogies, dear Rose, for my imaginings are too awful."

Rose grinned. "I cannot help myself!" Rose shook her head. "Our stable master, a dear man, explained the act of making love in horse terms. I find it easier to clarify the process that way, you see?"

"Since childhood, Patrick approaches all he adopts with forethought, deliberation, and care. I am certain he will do the same with your lovemaking. Do you enjoy touching him?"

"I...yes." Charlotte loved caressing his face, his cheek, and she relished his kisses and his hot breath on her neck. Why, even his smile could make her prickle in that delicious way. But this talk of them doffing their clothes and being naked and touching untouched parts...She wished to take up her paints and never stop.

"Making love, Lottie," Rose said. "It is the most natural thing. Once you are, um, desirous, he will face you. Then, he will insert his penis into your private place."

Charlotte froze. "That cannot be," she said, her voice a whisper.

"There will be a pinch, and yes, it hurts only the first time. The pain passes near instantly, and Patrick's movements will begin to feel lovely."

Movements?

After Rose completed her tutorial, Charlotte returned to brushing her hair. She took a deep breath.

Mama had congress. Rose, too, who said it was pleasurable. All married women must have experienced marital relations. And survived. She would, as well.

Earlier that evening, the women of Woodbine had prepared her bower—rose petals on the bed, flowers adorning the room, a full pitcher of chilled water, and other niceties.

After tonight, she would be changed.

That change would hurt, as Rose said, though she had assured Charlotte the pain was brief.

In the days since Patrick's renewed proposal and the arrangements for their wedding, Charlotte had painted in a frenzy. She had succeeded, for the new seascape, Patrick's wedding gift, was in *her* own style. If he wished, she would replicate his original purchase, but she thought he might like a painting of her own work.

Her eyes drifted to the wrapped package resting against the wing chair. She hoped it pleased him.

Frazzled nerves squeezed her heart—a combination of fear, excitement, and worry that she would be inept. Earlier, Rose had said nothing about what *she* was supposed to do while Patrick was "teasing" her. What if Patrick found her unappealing?

Along with her discussion, Rose had sneaked in a tumbler of scotch from Rhys' study and Charlotte lifted the glass and sipped. Though it seared, soon a welcome heat suffused her just as Rose had assured.

Patrick cared for her. He had said as much.

Now, minutes before his arrival, Charlotte did not see how a man atop her, thrusting his member inside her, could be anything but discomforting. She downed the rest of the glass as the creak of wheels sounded in the hall.

Patrick neared their rooms, and wasn't that an oddity—*their* rooms. He hadn't shared a room since he'd been at the Royal Naval Academy. He desired Charlotte, desired her rather voraciously, if truth be told, but it had been eons since he had been intimate with a woman. Never since his accident.

A cat crossing a puddle of water was less nervous than he.

Charlotte shivered. She could hear Patrick outside the door. Her hands shook as she smoothed her nightrail, and she dashed to her full-length mirror.

A knock.

"One moment!"

She smoothed a wrinkle, then held the gown wide so it flowed properly. She laid a lock of hair over her shoulder, shiny from brushing. Her nightrail was such a pretty, diaphanous thing, trimmed with exquisite Belgian lace. She twirled.

And froze.

Oh, no. It could not be.

A red splotch marred the back of her nightrail.

The Scarlet Lady had arrived. Now. Of all times!

How had she not read the signs? Felt the ache that accompanied her courses? Been prepared?

Foolish woman! She had ignored the signs because her thoughts had obsessed over her engagement and marriage.

"One minute, Patrick!" she called out again. Charlotte washed, and then retrieved her belt from the dresser, wrapping it about her hips and looping the muslin over the front and back to make a sort of loincloth. Within, she placed the stitched pad she used for such occasions, washed her hands again, and donned another nightrail, this one not nearly as pretty and made from a thick lawn.

Heaven help her, how would she ever tell Patrick?

Patrick wheeled into the room to find Charlotte seated at her dressing table, her gown a cloud about her, her raven hair a cascade down her back as she brushed the long strands.

Breath failed him at the sight of her. Charlotte was blindingly beautiful.

His nightshirt felt too small across his chest...and too large, the thing tangling in his legs. He had slept naked since he had left skeleton suits behind, and he wished to divest himself of the rig. A mad urge wished Lottie to see him, *all* of him, including his withered legs.

However, the idea of revealing them to Charlotte was more harrowing than facing an enemy ship of the line.

Did she pity him? Perhaps look at him with disgust?

"Patrick, if you're tired..."

He reached out and ran a hand down her hair. So soft. Had she any idea how he longed to be inside her? "I am not tired."

She smiled, a warm open one that rose to those midnight-blue eyes of hers, yet he caught a hint of fear before she returned to brushing her hair.

Lottie confounded him. She had never troubled over his infirmity, never made an issue of it, though she would speak plainly about his accident in the most mundane of words. He liked that. Charlotte appeared to accept him as he was, even if broken, and he could not but wonder if those feelings would remain after she viewed the scars and wreckage that were his limbs. She seemed willing enough for sex. He wished he could say the same.

Patrick caught the moment she again glimpsed him in the mirror. She lowered her hairbrush and swiveled to face him.

"You look like you are in pain, Patrick," she said, rising from her seat.

His self-deprecating grin was genuine. "All of this is new to me, my dear."

"Is that so?" She clearly remembered the gossip, and her words flew without her volition. "From the *on-dits*, you are quite adept with the ladies."

"Before," was all he said, for he tried never to think about the before times when he could walk and run, vault onto a horse, or climb a mast with ease.

The bed covers had been drawn back, and Charlotte plumped the pillows. Over her shoulder, she said, "Did you not say all was in working order?"

His smile was conciliatory. "Of that, I can assure you."

Devil it, how sensible she seemed. All a ruse, he suspected, for her hands shook smoothing a pillowcase.

He wheeled to the bed and took her hand. "Relax, my pragmatic wife, and does not the word "wife" sound strange?"

"It does. Shall I help you onto the bed, husband?"

Bollocks. The bed was a challenge, for Lottie's was a great deal higher than his own. Mounting this Everest would be awkward as hell, but manage he would. "Thank you, but no."

"As I anticipated." Charlotte clasped her hands in front of her so her knuckles shined white. "For I expected you to say as much."

"Canny woman. You are coming to know me too well."

"I am glad." She peered down with the sweetest smile.

In days past, she would have had to look *up* at him, as he had been a tall man. Once.

"Let us wait a moment," she said. "I have a gift for you." Charlotte hurried to retrieve the package and handed it to him with a shy smile. "To celebrate our marriage."

He lifted his own gift from his lap and held it in the palm of his hand, a far smaller package, but one he thought she would enjoy.

"Shall we open them together?" Her eyes sparkled as she took the velvet box.

They dove in, and once again, his breath was stolen. Lottie had painted him a seascape, one much like the one he'd hung in his cabin, and yet different. The rendering struck him as more vivid, more...alive. He smelled the brine, felt the roll of the waves, heard the snap of the sails.

"Oh, Patrick," Charlotte said, interrupting his thoughts. Her eyes were wide as she stared at the ring in its simple setting.

"I purchased this diamond in India and recently had it set for you. When I presented your engagement ring, you noted your love of emeralds, but said diamonds intrigued you."

"They do." She held up the ring so the gem sparkled in the lamplight. "For they hold all the colors of the spectrum."

"Shall I slide it onto your finger?"

"Please do."

Charlotte slipped off her wedding ring and held out her trembling hand, and he slid the diamond onto her finger. He replaced her wedding band, leaned forward, and took her lips with his.

Patrick made the kiss different. More. Not only did Patrick put his feelings into it, but also his promise to care for her all of his days, to watch over her, to be her friend and refuge. When he released her, she stared at him, tears pooling her eyes.

"Too much?" he said.

Her lips compressed, but a smile peeked out and she shook her head. "No, it was more. Much more."

He ran a hand down her shoulder. Gods, how he wanted her.

Thank Christ the numerous folds of his nightshirt hid his erection. "You are quite lovely, you know."

"I do not know, but I am glad you see me as such. I...I must speak to you of something."

Her words boded poorly, and though he ached to touch her further, to move inside her as one, to express his feelings for her in the most primal way, he hesitated. "Indeed?"

"The Scarlet Lady has put in an appearance."

"Scarlet Lady?" Patrick had not a clue what she was about.

Charlotte paled. "A term I invented. Claire calls hers the Red Dragon, given her quiet flare for the dramatic."

"Lottie, what the hell are—"

"My courses." She fiddled with her ring. "They arrived in a rather untimely manner."

His hands trembled and he squeezed the arms of his chair. A ruse to avoid their wedding night? Or truth? He searched her face, but found no answer.

"I see," was all he said.

"I am sorry! I had no idea. I usually do, you see, but I was so overset by, well, the wedding and this evening, that I—"

"You need not continue, Lottie." He took her hands and kissed both, then spun his back wheels toward the door.

"Stay," Charlotte said. "Please. Sleep beside me?"

Patrick paused to peer over his shoulder. "I awaken in the night, Lottie. Nightmares. You do not wish to sleep with someone so troubled."

She appeared beside him and kneeled. "I care not about your nighttime ramblings, Patrick. I have ramblings of my own. Do stay."

"In truth?"

She reached out a tentative hand to cup his face. "Please."

He turned his head to kiss her palm. "Then it shall be so."

Patrick faced the bed, a four-step climb, with trepidation. His upper body strength was impressive, but he was unsure if he could make this ascent without aid. Christ! The thing looked tall as St. Paul's.

He must try, for he would not tolerate his new wife assisting him on his climb into the thing.

Patrick reached up with his arms, bracing them on the mattress, and lifted, straining mightily, holding himself aloft, perpendicular to the mattress, arms straight.

Lottie moved toward him, but he shook his head, and she backed off.

His arms shook, but it would take but one more push to see him atop the bed.

With a massive heave, his torso flopped onto the mattress, and he paused, breathing like a bellows. *Christ*, he loathed his paralysis with such fervor he saw red.

Charlotte had not moved again but had taken up a book and was reading by candlelight. Canny woman.

Patrick pulled forward further and further toward the headboard until his legs followed. Thank all that was holy he'd made it. He took several more calming breaths, then rolled face up to stare at the ceiling. Lottie put aside her book and rested her head in the nook of his shoulder, slipping one leg across his unfeeling ones. She sighed.

"You are warm and cozy, Patrick."

He wrapped his arms around her, her curves giving him a stunning cock-stand, a hand running across her glorious hair. She sighed. He did the same and was soon in a dreamless slumber.

CHAPTER

TWELVE

Charlotte had fallen asleep embraced by Patrick's warm, strong arms, the feelings of safety and care, heavenly. She hoped he was equally pleased with the arrangement. Except now she was awake, Patrick tossing like a storm-driven ship. Charlotte considered waking him, but...

"Murderers!" he screamed.

"Patrick," she whispered.

He awakened in an instant, eyes wide, sitting up, chest puffing like a bellows.

"You were having a bad dream," she said, cupping his cheek.

"I was. A recurring one."

"Something troubles you deeply." She ran a hand across his chest. Though he wore night attire, but she felt the steel-hard tension that had seized his body. "What is it?"

He flopped back onto the pillows. "Not a pretty tale."

"I would still like to hear."

Patrick ached for a drink to settle his nerves. Dare he tell his new wife what he had seen?

He imagined her lovely face, scrunched in concern, her eyes deep blue pools of worry. Rhys knew. But Lottie...? "The tale is grim."

"The better to free yourself from it haunting you. For a bit, at least."

Moonlight filtered in from the bedroom windows, casting its pale glow across the wood floor and flowered carpet.

He was stalling.

On a huff, Patrick began his tale of the slaver and the frigate, her expression transforming to shock.

"The plot worsens, sweetheart." He reached over and clutched her hand. Charlotte lay across his chest, wrapping her arms about him, and he held her tight. Which was when he told her of the slaves' despicable deaths. And of Henry.

Tears welled in her eyes. "Those poor men and women. Children, too, and we could have lost Henry, as well."

Patrick noted his reporting the incident to the Admiralty. "I planned to follow up, but after my accident...Things somewhat fell apart."

"Evil," Lottie said with fervor. "The idea of *owning* human beings...I see why that event haunts you."

"I shall follow through now to discover who captained the *Despoina* and to bring the owner to account. *He* is the one responsible and those drowned deserve justice."

"I could not agree more," she said. "I can write letters, help out in some way?"

He shook his head. "These are deadly men who would not think twice about harming you."

He kissed her for her understanding and simply because he must. She answered in kind, and his heart was content. For now.

At six the next morning, Patrick found Rose in the kitchens eating bone marrow pudding, of all things.

"A rather odd snack, sister."

"The babe ached for some." Rose shrugged, taking a chair, and rested the pudding jar on her lap. "'Tis the morn after your bridal night. It is a wonder you are up, Patrick. What troubles you?

He scraped a hand through his hair. "Do you think Charlotte is content with our marriage?"

Rose startled. "Why, I believe so. It is obvious you have a fondness for each other."

"I imagined that to be the case." He nodded. But Lottie's Scarlet Lady...Was that a ruse to avoid intimacy? Or genuine? He had categorically refused to plunder her soiled clothes seeking proof.

A smile quirked Rose's lips. "From what I saw, you spent the night with Charlotte, did you not?"

"What you saw?"

"I happened to be up for a late-night glass of milk." She rubbed her belly. "The babe has many demands. I saw your bedroom door open, you absent from your room. So I assumed..."

"All we did was sleep, Rose." He whooshed out a breath. Heat rose to his cheeks, a most alien sensation.

"Ah." Rose's color was high, as well.

"Never mind." He turned his chair toward the door, but Rose laid a hand on his shoulder.

"Patrick?"

"While we failed to have relations," he said, keeping his back to her, "it is not what you think."

Rose squeezed his shoulder. "I see."

"You do not." *God's blood*, this was more torturous than engaging Napoleon's flagship. He turned his chair to face her. "Charlotte claimed...She asserted her Scarlet Lady had arrived."

"How awful. On your wedding night, of all things."

"So, you believe her? She was not avoiding my attentions?"

Rose tipped her head. "I doubt she was feigning excuses. That has never been Lottie's way. She dislikes deceits."

Except for her forgeries. "Thank you, Rose. I appreciate your insight." Her words had produced a profound relief, even though he could not entirely accept them.

Charlotte awakened, her stomach churning with feelings that tore her to and fro. Patrick had held her through the night, where she felt warm and safe and wonderful. But when she had roused, he was gone.

Perhaps she had angered him. Or maybe he regretted telling her of the slavers. Or he may have seen her Scarlet Lady as her excuse to forgo congress.

Oh, he could not believe the latter.

And yet, any newlywed husband might find the launch of her courses a way to avoid intimacy.

But how could he? Patrick was handsome, imposing, a man she desired, for she wished to touch him, hold him, and have him do the same for her. Yet those urges still confused her, and she did not know how to deal with them.

Dressing, she discovered a note from Patrick on a side table.

Off to practice on Diablo, Lottie. Enjoy your morning slumber. I shall see you later today! Your husband, Patrick

She'd slipped it into a dresser drawer alongside his other letters, warmed by his consideration.

On her way to the morning room, Henry and Stella erupted from a side hall and raced to her. "Good morning, *Lady Hawthorne!*" he shouted. Stella barked. "We're off to see Spider!"

She laughed, hugging him so tight, he squeaked. Staring down into his dear face, she nearly came to tears picturing him struggling in that frigid ocean, death minutes away. After she kissed Henry's cheek and gave Stella a pat, they tore off, and Charlotte proceeded to the morning room, though she'd rather trail Henry, assuring herself he was safe. Silly, of course.

At breakfast, none treated her differently, but as she chewed a dried cherry, she caught covert glances around the table, as well as smiles exchanged between Claire and Thomasina.

If they only knew she was not yet a wife, not in the strictest sense, nor in her estimation.

She could do nothing about their joining, not until the Scarlet Lady had fled. Rose might give her some insight, but both she and Susannah were off to visit two of Woodbine's tenants, the couple about to give birth.

Knowing the one activity that would soothe her fears, she repaired to her studio. The three works nearing completion were all sold—one to a viscount, one to a banker, and one to a gentlewoman farmer.

Her clients had received sketches allegedly done by her father, and all had requested to purchase their respective paintings and sent a sizable deposit.

The idea that she would no longer have to forge paintings made relief fountain within her. The forgeries weighed heavily, and with that burden lifted, Charlotte felt a freedom she hadn't in years. Free to paint what she desired. Free to explore new colors, new brush-strokes, new compositions.

Hours passed, and when she checked the mantle clock, after-noon was advanced. Charlotte stepped back to view the landscape for the lady farmer, a bucolic scene of sheep and streams and fields, with a manor house anchoring the work. She had made great progress.

Silly, really, but she missed Patrick and would go hunt him up.

A knock at the door and Charlotte quickly covered the landscape. "Come in."

Patrick wheeled inside.

Her cheeks heated, a mighty blush, at the sight her new husband. Last night, he had seen her nearly *naked*. In truth, she wished *he* had been naked, the muscles of his torso and chest making her mouth water. She wanted to see all of him.

To imagine why that was so, would make her flee the room in mortification.

"What are you working on, wife?" Patrick said wheeling closer.

A thrill echoed within at the word "wife."

Last night, his tale of the slaver had been horrific. Even more vivid was the memory of his arms holding her. And his kisses.

Patrick closed the door, wheeled to the canvas, and flipped its muslin covering up.

She rubbed her forefinger and thumb together. "It will be done in but a few days. I am pleased with it."

"This is a fine facsimile of your father's work," Patrick said.

He hadn't frowned, and yet she caught his hint of disdain. Charlotte nodded. "I must complete my final three sold works, Patrick."

Patrick shook his head. "My dear Lottie, this needs be stopped. I comprehend your need to support your family and the estate. That need no longer exists, thus, you must put forgery in your past."

She drew a chair over beside Patrick. "I could not agree more, but for these three. They have placed deposits on them."

He squeezed her hand and released it. "Return the money. Easy enough."

"I cannot." She walked to the easel and re-covered the painting. "I *will* not. The buyers will fuss, as they are most desirous to own my father's work."

"But these are *not* your father's work."

"I know that! Do you not see how canceling will invite scrutiny? I also gave my word, Patrick. That matters to me."

His face hardened. "I understand and appreciate your reasons, but we can weather whatever occurs."

"I will not go back on my word, Patrick."

"I feel you must," Patrick said.

Charlotte cleaned her brushes, for she needed to busy herself while she thought. Patrick had no right to tell her such. Except he did. As her husband, he literally could lord over her as she was, essentially, a possession. Chattel. She wiped her hands with linseed, except she used the wrong cloth, she was *that* disturbed.

"Talk to me, Lottie," Patrick said.

Charlotte tossed the rag away and cleaned her hands with a proper one. She scrubbed and scrubbed, her fingers becoming raw, as she wished away the conversation along with the embedded paint. "I shall not renege, Patrick. You must understand that."

"I *must?*" Patrick said in a quiet voice. "You will *not* sell those paintings, Lottie. What if your forgeries were discovered? You could be imprisoned."

"That has *always* been the case." Anger and hurt consumed her. "But my word matters greatly to me, Patrick, as much as any man's sacred bond. Have you ever broken a promise or an agreement?"

His fingers tapped the arms of his chair. "That is neither here nor there."

"Well, have you?"

"In truth, I cannot recall."

"I doubt so." One day of marriage. One single day, and already Patrick was dictating to her, as if his thoughts and opinions outweighed hers, as if her wishes mattered less than his, as if her bond signified little.

Was this how they would go on? Him commanding and she obeying?

For years—first, before Mama's marriage to Earl Fielding, and then after his death—Charlotte's hard work had enabled her little family to thrive.

Now, with one brushstroke, Patrick was stifling her sense of value and worth, for he was not taking her decisions and promises into consideration, plowing through them with a scythe.

How dare he treat her thus?

"If you will excuse me, my lord." Charlotte bobbed a curtsy and fled.

The stable had become a sanctuary of sorts where Charlotte practiced on her barrel to improve her seat, often imagining future paintings while she teetered back and forth.

Today, she had no patience for it but wished to fly across the fields and hills as she had done with Patrick. To erase their earlier conversation, to feel free and in control.

Too impatient to run down a stableboy, she groomed and saddled Beauty. As she rode off, Arjuna called after her, but she ignored him, ignored all of them to get away, to find a calm place within where she could untangle their conversation to further reason with him.

Patrick dictating to her as he would to his sailors on one of his warships would not serve. True, she had promised to obey during the ceremony, but those words were scripted long before women had any agency whatsoever.

Now, it occurred to Charlotte that she had none, either, when it came to Patrick. Her husband was her lord and master, a concept she found rather awful. And yet Mama had bowed to both Papa and the earl's will.

Rose did not simply bow to her marquess' will. Truth be told, she sometimes acquiesced, yet she often did not. Rose and Rhys seemed in accord about that sort of thing, their disagreements settled, and they continued on.

Beauty hopped over a log.

Charlotte wobbled. She wasn't paying attention, and she must, for Beauty was rather frisky today, wanting to break into a trot. She rode astride, in the split skirt borrowed from Rose, and except for that one wobble, she felt secure, her barrel practice paying off.

After settling Beauty with words of praise, they left the home wood for a meadow that unfurled before them. Of a sudden, Beauty broke into a canter, and Charlotte let her have her head. They flew across the meadow, faster and faster. Too fast.

Charlotte clung to the mare, nerves running riot, muscles stiffening. Her seat began to feel jelly-like at such blinding speed.

She pulled the reins, then sawed them. All without effect. Beauty had the bit between her teeth.

Hell and damnation!

She tried to relax, tried to find her seat, but at this speed, terror choked all reason. A wall approached, its height immense, though she knew it to be but a few feet.

Charlotte pulled hard on Beauty's right rein, trying to turn her, but her normally biddable horse refused, determined to leap the wall. One of Charlotte's gloved hands clung to her mane for dear life.

All would have a good laugh about her jaunt when she told the tale. If she survived.

A shout to her right, but she daren't look, instead focusing on Patrick's lessons on how to fall, taking care with her seat, legs, and hands.

Closer, closer, the moss-dappled rocks neared.

Beauty's hooves pounding. A lock of hair flying across her face. The world a blur.

Oh, heavens!

Beauty raising her front quarters...Charlotte flung backward... gripping the mane...holding on, holding on...

They soared.

Charlotte clamped her jaw, refusing to scream.

Then they were over, and just as she thought they had made it, Beauty landed and stopped, all four hooves planted hard.

Charlotte flew over the saddle to thud onto the unrelenting ground.

For long moments, she lay stunned, assessing her body, clearing her mind.

Beauty.

She pushed to a seated position, head ringing, pain blooming through her. The mare was grazing on tufts of grass looking sweet as pie. Charlotte was no Thomasina and unable to assess whether Beauty was injured or not.

A warmth coated her face. Touching her cheek, her fingertips came away red. Oh, dear. The pain had eased to tolerable, and she took a deep breath. A scrape, nothing more.

Charlotte went to stand but found that wish more challenging than expected. She finally got her legs under her and rose. "Ouch!"

She thumped back on the ground, ankle throbbing.

"Hold up there!" came a male voice.

A man dressed in black cantered an equally black horse toward her. Lord Ashworth, one of the men with Devonshire she'd met days earlier.

A chill breeze stung her cheek. Heavens, she felt poorly.

The horse thundered to a halt, and the man leapt from the saddle to kneel before her.

"I saw you sail over that wall, Lady Charlotte. I can help you stand, but I am unsure if you are too severely injured to do so."

"I am shaken, Lord Ashworth." Charlotte nodded, clearing her throat to regain her composure. "But I doubt my injuries are grievous, though my ankle throbs like a beast."

"Stay put while I check your horse's condition."

Stay put? Really. "Her name is Beauty, a lovely girl with a bee in her bonnet this morning. She is usually sweet and amiable."

Lord Ashworth smiled, and his looks went from brooding to compelling. He was tall and muscled, perhaps in his early thirties, with an air of competence about him.

Upon returning to her, he said, "Your Beauty does not seem seriously injured, though she is favoring her right leg. We can walk her back to Woodbine. Now let us get you up, shall we?"

He wrapped an arm around her waist and lifted her to a stand.

Charlotte's laughter was of the nervous kind. "It seems both Beauty and I have hurt our legs. Will she be all right?"

"Hard to tell, I do not believe she has broken it. Now, I shall set you on that wall, mount my horse, and lift you up beside me. How does that sound?"

His deep-set green eyes were kind and filled with concern. Charlotte brushed off her habit as best as she could and straightened her bonnet.

"How do you know His Grace?" she said as Ashworth collected Beauty's reins.

"We are old friends from Harrow. We attended Trinity College together, as well." He grinned. "He has an interest in antiquities, and though I am an earl by birth, I am an antiquarian by choice."

"How very bold." She suspected Claire knew of Ashworth's pastime, which explained her original interest in him, though he had offended her that day.

"Ready?" he said.

She nodded, and he hefted her atop the stone, then retrieved his horse and Beauty. If she was not mistaken, his huge black horse was a Friesian.

In moments, Ashworth was mounted and soon swung her up into the saddle before him. Charlotte took a minute to settle and arrange her skirts.

"How do you feel?" he said.

"Sore." She smiled over her shoulder. "But I believe I will live."

"You will most definitely live, my lady."

He signaled his horse and they began the walk home at a glacial pace.

"Devonshire talks endlessly about the inhabitants of Woodbine," Lord Ashworth said. "And in a most favorable light. I have yet to meet Lady Susannah or her sister Thomasina, both favorites of the duke's. Am I correct that only yesterday you married Lord Hawthorne?"

"Indeed, sir, you are well informed." She had been sitting straight, her back inches from his chest, but that was exhausting, and she leaned her weight against him, easing her aches.

He took out a kerchief and dabbed at her face.

"Ow!"

"Apologies! It is just...well, you look rather terrifying with all that blood on your face."

"It is but a scrape."

"I suspect so, but I fear you will terrify Woodbine's inhabitants."

Charlotte shrugged, thinking that after their argument, Patrick deserved to be terrified. "Thank you for the warning. They will soon see I am well, only sore."

"And your ankle."
"Yes, there is that. I believe it is simply sprained. A trifle."
Charlotte hoped Patrick did not make too much of her escapade.

THIRTEEN

Once the family caught sight of her, clucking and shocked expressions surrounded Charlotte. Thomasina took her hand as Susannah and Rose drew her inside, Lord Ashworth seeing to the horses.

"I wish to go with Ashworth," she said. "To make sure Beauty is well."

"Heavens, forfend!" Rose said, taking her hand. "Come along, Lottie. We must get you patched up."

"A sprained ankle," Charlotte said in chipper tones. "Nothing worse."

"Lean on me," Rose said.

Mama appeared. "Charlotte! You look terrifying!"

Claire, following, tittered. "Like a ghoul."

In the kitchens, a hullabaloo ensued, with Susannah hauling out the medicine chest, Mama washing her face, and Claire dunking her foot into a bucket of ice water. After Thomasina retrieved the horse liniment, Rose applied it to her bumps and bruises.

"What the bloody hell!" Patrick said, wheeling into the room beside Rhys.

Fustian!

"Patrick!" Susannah said in shocked tones.

"I have heard you swear like a sailor, sister." Patrick wheeled close, his eyes shooting from Charlotte's bloody face down to her foot in the tub. She lifted her skirts over the bowl to hide her swollen limb.

"What happened, Lottie?" Patrick said.

Charlotte explained about Beauty taking off. "Are you going to rail at me, Patrick? I've a beastly headache, everything hurts, and I remain furious with you and your dictatorial manner."

He reared back. "That is plain speaking, my lady."

Ashworth entered, shrinking the room yet again.

It was all too much, her eyes welling. She beat them back and composed herself, then cleared her throat. "How is Beauty, Lord Ashworth?"

He nodded. "With some rest, she will be perfectly well, Lady Hawthorne. A strained fetlock, nothing more."

Thomasina peered at Charlotte wearing a frown. "How did that happen?"

"I am afraid when we jumped the wall, Beauty did not land properly."

"Jumped the wall," Patrick hissed, hands raking his hair. He appeared to wrestle with a powerful emotion, then he took her hands, his eyes welded to hers. "Our next lesson shall focus on runaway horses and how to control them."

She tried a smile. "A good plan."

"Arjuna said they gave Beauty oats this morning," Lord Ashworth said. "She was running hot."

"Hot?" Charlotte said.

"Full of vim and vigor," Rose said. "Too much so."

Patrick reached to cup her cheek. "You did not know, and thus cannot be faulted."

Rhys notched his head at Ashworth and his brother. "Let us

repair to my study, shall we? A fine scotch has recently arrived for you to sample."

Patrick kissed her on the lips, in front of them all, and when the kiss deepened, the world dissolved.

Breathless, they withdrew, to stare at each other with a sort of wonder.

"Until later," Patrick said on a wisp of breath. "When we shall discuss my dictatorial manner and can pursue more kisses."

In truth, Charlotte was quite eager for later.

The scotch having sanded away much of Patrick's fear, he went in search of Banby, finding the man in the family drawing room at work on a large embroidery hoop. Beside him, Henry wielded a smaller one, the dog Stella at his feet, a lesson in progress.

Henry leapt up and saluted.

"Forgive me for disturbing you," he said. "I must speak to the lieutenant. Henry, how would you like to curry Roddy and Dolce?"

Henry bounced on his toes, hoop dangling from one hand. "Really?"

"It will be good practice," he said. "Tell Arjuna I sent you, and he will fix you up with all you need."

"I know what to get, Captain," Henry said. "I've been learnin'."

"Excellent. Now off with you."

Banby placed his hoop on the table. "Captain?"

Patrick always appreciated the man's calm, and he took several moments to find the right words, ones hard to voice. Given Banby's dark skin from his mother, the slaves' deaths had been a cruel reminder that he could have been one of them. "I must apologize for my stumble these many months in not pursuing the slavers."

Banby tilted his head. "Given your injury, I cannot blame you for that."

"Nonetheless..." Patrick nodded. "I sent off several letters to the Admiralty in pursuit of the frigate *Despoina* and her captain. A starting point."

Banby ran a hand across his mouth, nodding. "I am glad, sir."

"Another letter to a friend at the Admiralty asked him to unearth the *Despoina's* original name and ports of call during the war."

Shadows danced across Banby's eyes. "A good thought."

"I shall not let the episode pass, Banby," Patrick said.

"Nor did I think you would, sir."

"Your formality is wearing on me, Euan Banby. Call me Hawthorne or Patrick."

Banby's horrified look near made him laugh. "I cannot, Captain. I have served you far too long to adopt that informality."

Patrick quirked a brow. "Is that so? Alongside our roles of steward and captain, we have been friends these many years, have we not? Work on it?"

Banby grinned. "Is that an order, Captain?"

"Of course!" Patrick said with a wink.

They both laughed.

His next stop was Rose, whom he found in her sitting room.

"Might I disturb you, sister?" he said.

Rose's needles clicked as she knit a bonnet for the babe. "Believe it or not, Patrick, I can talk and knit at the same time."

"I never doubted it." He rolled close, brushing his fingers across the soft yarn, trying to imagine his own child and failing. "A beautiful bonnet for the beautiful child to come."

A flush tinged Rose's cheeks. "We hope you will stand godfather to the babe, with Lottie as godmother."

He was taken aback. "That will be my privilege, Rose."

A saucy smile lit her face. "After this morning's excitement, you remain out of sorts? I can see you are simply dying to ask me something."

He swiped a hand across his face, masking his grin. "An exaggeration, my lady, something you do with great alacrity."

"Ha! Trying to wind me up as usual!"

"Just a bit." How to broach the subject of Charlotte's forgeries? What words to use to soften the revelation? "In truth, I have a serious matter to discuss. Charlotte has been forging Reginald Pheland's paintings to support her family."

Rose wove another stitch, nodding. "Rhys and I concluded as much. Rather confounding, is it not?"

"Very much so." He detailed his earlier discussion with Lottie where he forbade her to sell her final three paintings.

"You *forbade* her." Rose paused completing a stitch.

"Of course," he said, whooshing a puff of air. "Charlotte refuses to obey me and says it is due to giving her word to the buyers."

"I see." She resumed knitting the pretty confection, face creased in thought. Patrick waited...and waited.

Rose sighed. "You are not at sea to command those around you."

"As the deck is stationary, I have noticed."

"Hrumph. I say this because *forbidding* your new wife to complete a task she has promised can only lead to disaster."

"Disaster?" He ground his teeth. "Revelation is disaster. Being incarcerated for forgeries is disaster."

"For your marriage, I mean. It is new, your relationship has only begun to bloom. Pronouncements are a surefire way to make a hash of it."

Patrick knew that. He also knew he could not go blithely along with Charlotte selling forgeries.

"Mend your rift, brother," she continued. "Know this, a woman can value her given word as much as any man does. I suspect Lottie knows the wrongness of the forgeries."

"Indeed, that is true."

"Perhaps Charlotte will promise and cease painting them."

"She already has done so," he said. "With great enthusiasm, in fact. You must not think that Lottie takes pleasure in this farce."

"I never would," Rose said. "I am glad you do not misunderstand, either."

"So where does that leave me?"

"The question I ask—is the damage to your marriage worth forbidding your wife something she feels compelled to do? Charlotte's intention is risky, but the danger is minimal. I fear were you to succeed in halting the current sales, your relationship, your future, will be greatly damaged."

Charlotte was showing Claire the Covington painting, a bucolic meadow scene.

"Why did you add that dab of yellow?" Claire said.

"Step back and look."

Her sister did just that. "Oh, my! The light on those wildflowers."

"Yes." Charlotte grinned.

Charlotte sat in a small slipper chair, a cushioned stool propping up her injured ankle. It throbbed but was more than tolerable. Now, if she could only get her paint strokes to do what she wished, she would be content.

Claire kissed her farewell, but Charlotte barely noticed, intent on rendering the oak trees. Minutes, or perhaps hours later, she sighed and sat back, working the cramps out of her fingers. When she looked up, she found Patrick observing her.

"Oh, my! When did you arrive?"

"A good ten minutes ago." Patrick wheeled across the room. He had again altered his conveyance. The wheels were smaller, perhaps lighter, easier to push, with metal strips banding each wheel. Nor did his feet dangle, but rested on a wood support at the chair's base. He rolled closer, grinning.

Though out of sorts with him, Charlotte could not resist that smile and grinned back. "I did not hear you enter, your wheeled chair is so quiet now."

His grin turned jaunty. "The better to sneak up on you, Lottie."

"You have made alterations."

He chuckled. "Improvements. Yes. Henry, of all people, was the spark, asking why the wheels were so large. The cooper crafted this new chair, the metal wheel strips making it hardier and more maneuverable outside. They surprised me with it."

"But do not the metal strips make it a further chore to push?"

"I do not even notice them." His eyes fell to his legs, his face sobering.

"Your infirmity is troubling you," she said.

"*Yes.*" His eyes turned to her painting. "I once stood more than six foot, if you recall. Now..."

This was the first time he had voiced feelings about the loss of his legs. That he would trust her meant a great deal. She took up her brush and returned to work.

"In truth, your injury is terrible, yet you have not merely made the best of it. You have triumphed."

"And how, wife, have I triumphed?" he said, his tone sharp.

Charlotte smiled. "Do you not see, silly man? You have created this chair when you could have sat back and bemoaned your fate. You have exercised, you have ridden Diablo, even dismounted with the sticks. You are a man of action, and you have taken it."

"Is that so, *wife?*"

"I am amazed. And impressed." Still smiling, she said, "Sometimes I think you use the word 'wife' as an epithet."

"Nay. For I say the word with much affection." He turned his attention to her easel. "I see you are working on the meadow painting."

Any minute he would explain—*again*—how she should not continue with the paintings. Charlotte strengthened her resolve, but it was a challenge, for he was happy with his new chair and his increased mobility. "Just a few touches and it will be complete and ready for the signature."

"Which will be your father's, correct?" he said, his face unreadable.

Charlotte laid down her brush. "Yes." The word bounded out, as if aching to be free, a line in the sand of sorts. She turned a stern face toward her husband, making to rise.

"Wait, my lady." Patrick grasped her hand. "I wish to offer..." He paused, kissing her palm. "I wish to offer an apology for my dictatorial comments this morning."

Charlotte startled. Did ship captains ever apologize? His words meant much, though he had not retracted his earlier pronouncement. She swiveled on the stool to face him, resting her injured foot on the floor.

"Once Earl Fielding died," she said. "You see, I imagined marrying in the far distant future, if at all. Until we were discovered at the ball, that is. My life has been somewhat unconventional and…" She gestured toward the painting. "These consume me. Without them…"

"Your family would not have thrived. Darling girl, you have been steadfast and resolute. I admire that greatly."

Words fled, for Patrick's admiration moved her, her feelings for her spouse far deeper than she had admitted. She thanked the heavens that he understood her motivation.

Charlotte straightened, her smile sheepish. "I am making a hash of this, am I not?"

He wheeled closer. "You are not."

"I know our situation is as challenging for you, as it is for me. You never intended marriage, not at least one to me. You acted the gentleman, though it was a detriment to yourself. I suspect you always do the right thing."

"Perhaps, well, as much as possible, for doing what is right and good matters."

She brushed his cheek with her fingertips. "I know you are used to command, and these changes in your life have been profound. I wish for us to rub along in harmony and will try to be more explicable in my actions. My aim in our marriage is to compromise, Patrick, though I shan't always. I will not give up these final three sales. Do you not see why?"

They sat eye-to-eye, a lovely sensation, for he must loathe people peering down at him.

"I see a woman," he said, "whose word is her bond, which is

worthy of commendation. Though I disagree with your plans for these paintings, I shall not interfere with their sale."

She sucked in a swift breath, startled in the extreme. "Thank you, Patrick. I must deliver two of the paintings myself, as my factor has retired."

"Can you not hire another?" he said.

"Would that I could," she said. "The process is too time consuming, as it involves trust. I wish these works gone. What if you accompanied me?"

"I could." His face gave nothing away, but she saw that mischievous glint in his eyes.

"Would you?" she said. "Truly?"

He grasped her hand. "A fine solution. You must never feel unworthy, Lottie. I wish you to have a voice in our marriage, one equal to mine." He offered a lopsided smile. "Mostly equal."

Charlotte giggled. "Shall we see how the 'mostly' works, my lord?"

"I would hope we shall."

"As would I. What brought about your change of thought?"

"Who else but that pesky, infuriating..."

"Rose!" Charlotte pealed a laugh. "Bless her contrary soul, for my will is far less sturdy than hers."

"The woman is a termagant and read me the riot act."

"Rose has a knack for dealing with Lansdownes."

"She is a true terror! Has been since she was a child. But my brother adores her, thus I tolerate her prickly nature."

"Prickly? Is that not the pot calling the kettle black? Ha! I fail to believe you, my lord. Oh, the prickly part, yes, but I have seen your affection for Rose many times."

"With the exception of the chrysanthemum debacle." He regaled her with the tale of Rose's and Rhys' wedding and her chrysanthemum allergy, which he had known none of, for he had filled the room with them for their wedding. A disaster.

The air around them softened, and Patrick took her lips in a long, satisfying kiss. "I am lucky to have found you, Lottie, for you do not seem the least bothered by my controlling tendencies."

For a moment, Charlotte lost herself in his eyes, warm pools of affection. "I am not unaffected, sir, but rather those tendencies make me wish to challenge you. I suspect no one onboard ship ever did so."

"There, my dear viscountess, you would be wrong. Banby, for one, never missed an opportunity to offer a contrary point of view. That is one of the reasons I requested him as my adjunct after my injury."

"Banby can be as cutting as you, sir, which is saying something!"

"More importantly, he is a trusted friend. Though my tendencies toward autocracy are fierce, I have learned the advantage of collaboration."

"Are we one of those collaborations?"

He leaned forward, so very close his breath brushed her lips. "Indeed." He took her lips with hers.

No perfunctory kiss, this, but a deeper expression, one which held the promise of sweet tomorrows.

The following morning, she returned to her studio, delighting in the fact that Patrick had slept beside her yet again, and they had cuddled and warmed each other, no nightmares troubling their slumber.

An hour into her studio work, Patrick appeared. "I have a surprise, Lottie."

Surprises always delighted her, but at the moment she was too preoccupied to pay it much mind, bone tired from her race to complete the three paintings.

But this was Patrick. She gave him a smile. "And what might that be?"

"We are going on a jaunt if you are willing."

Charlotte wished for no jaunt, for finishing these three cursed works was her singular goal.

Patrick wheeled over. "You are weary. I see it in your eyes. Is the Scarlet Lady troubling you?"

"No more than usual." Once again, she went red as an apple, embarrassed enough to waggle her paintbrush at him.

He stole the brush and plopped it into the turpentine. "You are worn out, sweetheart. All we need is half a day for our adventure."

The light in his eyes, his hopeful demeanor swayed her. "Shall we ride or take the carriage?"

He grinned, and there went her heart again, thumping madly.

"The carriage for Banby and Henry join us as well. I wish to be ambulatory and they shall assist."

"When do we leave?" Charlotte began cleaning her brushes, then worked the turp cloth over her hands, scrubbing at her nails, Prussian blue clinging like the devil.

"Within the hour. Time enough?"

"Yes." Curious about their outing, at the very least, she could doze in the carriage.

CHAPTER

FOURTEEN

Patrick was pleased the day was sunny as their well-sprung coach thumped and bumped along the road, Banby and Henry up beside the coachman, their usual preference.

His wife had fallen asleep near instantly, and as they approached their destination, Patrick hesitated to wake her.

Worry made him frown. What if Charlotte hated Hawthorne Hall? He had visited the place several times overseeing the ongoing work to make it livable.

Empty for years, the manor now played host to vermin, spiders, and much damp that added to its deterioration. Workmen had been setting the manor to rights for months, but he could wait no longer to show Lottie, for he hoped to incorporate her ideas into their new home.

Though spending hours each day at her easel, she remained sweet-natured and seldom lost her patience with the staff or with his curmudgeonly self. He disliked pulling her away, but he worried about her health, hence today's small adventure.

They neared Brixham, the nearest village to Hawthorne, and he wanted her to view the seaside town of about three thousand souls.

He nudged her. She did not stir. Lord, she must be weary. Then his hand brushed her cheek. A fluttering of lashes. A kiss made Lottie come alive in his arms, a delightful reaction, and he was hungry for more as their tongues tangled. A harsh bump in the road jarred him to his senses.

"Look, Lottie," he said as he drew away. "Look outside."

Her eyes fluttered momentarily, as if coming back to herself, then looked out the window. "How picturesque!"

"Brixham, named for an early resident, Brioc, followed by the Old English suffix, ham meaning home. Its other moniker is 'Mother of Deep-Sea Fisheries.'"

"I see why. Look at the endless fishing boats bobbing on the waves! The sea." She sighed. "Is it not glorious?"

"It is, Lottie. We are almost home."

"Home?" Her widened eyes made him grin.

"Hawthorne Hall is but a short distance, located in Higher Brixham, near Sharkham Point."

She slid forward, hands pressed to the glass, peering out the window.

Leaving the town behind, the road grew bumpier as it climbed a hill, chuckholes abounding.

"Where is it?" Charlotte said, hands tapping her skirts.

"Patience, love. We are almost there."

They turned onto a drive lined with ancient gnarled oaks, then around a corner.

A tumbledown wall appeared and beyond that, a two-and-a-half storied manor about the size of Woodbine, with several outbuildings marching nearby. All looking rather sad. Perhaps this was a poor idea, showing Lottie the manor before it was put to rights.

"See there." Patrick pointed to a small cottage to the manor's left. "That is the former priest's house, Hawthorne once a medieval monastery. They built the existing manor during the Tudor reign."

"But the front is Georgian," she said.

"The manor has experienced many iterations over the years."

Their carriage rolled around a circular drive, stopping before the entrance, the courtyard's center an overgrown riot of wild-flowers.

Charlotte was both shocked and entranced by the estate, for the charming main house had much potential, yet appeared in a poor state and she suspected the interior needed as much attention as the exterior. The thought delighted her, for she and Patrick could put their own stamp on the place. A rather exciting project.

Patrick had grown quiet, his thoughts locked down tight, as they often were. Did he love the place? Or find the idea of making it livable distasteful?

She held her tongue, for Patrick would share his opinions in his own time.

After he rolled out of their carriage, Charlotte followed him down the ramp and up the long slate path to the front door, painted a cheerful yellow. True, the paint was peeling, a project she added it to her mental list of "must-dos."

Banby and Henry assisted Patrick's chair up the two steps, with Banby unlocking the door. He eased it open, the door creaking like an old man's bones.

Charlotte entered to be met by a dank, musty front hall, the door's side windows covered in grime. Before her, the central stair wound upward, splitting in two at the second floor, many of its boards missing or warped.

Patrick wheeled inside flanked by Banby and Henry, the boy barely able to contain his excitement.

"Is this our new home?" Henry said, bouncing on his toes.

"It is, Henry." Charlotte grinned. "Or will be, once the repairs and improvements have corrected the disarray."

Henry cupped his chin. "Seems to me, it'll be years afore we can—"

"It will be habitable sooner rather than later, Henry," Patrick said.

"And where'll I sleep?"

Patrick frowned, but his eyes danced with good humor. "In the stables?"

"Cor!" Henry said with a grin. "That would be spot on!"

Her husband chuckled. "You shall have a room within the manor house, of course."

Hard to keep a straight face, for Henry looked crestfallen.

Off the main entryway to their left stood a pleasant receiving room decorated in dust and cobwebs coating the few pieces of rickety furniture, moth-eaten curtains and greasy windows blocking the light. Yet the room's exquisite oak panels featured intricate designs—quatrefoils, rosettes, and linenfold patterns—enough to make her swoon. They lined the walls interrupted by large windows that would offer views of the gardens and outbuildings once cleaned. Beyond, the abandoned gardens were riotous with wildflowers as they meandered toward the sea cliffs.

In one corner, Charlotte found an industrious spider had crafted an intricate web, one she wished to paint. She withdrew her pad and pencil from the pocket of her pelisse and drew a quick sketch.

Patrick cleared his throat. "It needs work."

Charlotte whirled. "Yes! How thrilling! We shall have great fun, shan't we?"

Her husband threw back his head, booming a laugh. "You shock me, Lottie. I feared you would be horrified at the manor's current state."

"Not I," Charlotte said. "The opposite, in fact." She crossed the entryway to the grand hall. And grand it was, with a cavernous fireplace, floor-to-ceiling windows, more oak paneling, and a stone floor. "We shall make it our own, Patrick, yours and mine. Look at that view!" Beyond lay a courtyard garden enclosed on two sides by the manor's wings. "Oh, it is splendid!"

Patrick tugged her onto his lap, kissing her with unbridled passion until Banby's cleared throat. They continued their inspection of the first floor, the second too dangerous to ascend, to find a sunny room with French doors, a perfect for a morning room, with gardens and outbuildings outside.

But first, the sea.

Charlotte opened the French doors with a tug, then raced to the gardens' far end where a low wall marched along the cliff's edge. Beyond that, the sea. Winds buffeted her as she walked beside the wall, discovering a break where a path led downward to a small sandy beach.

The prospect lured her, but she would not take the path today. "We can swim here!"

"We will, along with our many projects." Patrick rolled up behind her.

"Ones I look forward to." She turned to face him, and found this view of their new home equally enchanting, almost as much as her devilishly handsome husband.

They rambled the grounds, peeking inside outbuildings—cottages, a brewhouse, a garden shed, and a dovecote, then returned to stand before the manor house itself.

Patrick tossed Charlotte a sinful grin. "They say ghosts walk these halls."

His Lottie giggled. "Do you believe in ghosts, Patrick?"

He didn't. Not really. Yet as a man of the sea, he allowed for the possibility of spirits. How could he not, having spent so many hours facing nature's whimsy and wrath?

"Perhaps," he said.

"And who are these alleged ghosts, husband?"

"One specter is that of a pre-Reformation monk who lived here when the house was a monastery."

"I hope the fellow welcomes us warmly!"

"Ha! I agree. The second ghost is a woman. She may prove less amenable, for in 1604 she was forced to marry and haunts an upstairs room."

"An unhappy soul. Mayhap we can cheer her, then."

Leave it to Lottie to not be put off in the least. He waggled his brow. "Mayhap we can."

A day later, after Henry had returned from their new home with the Captain and his lady, he had completed his duties with Lieutenant Banby. With Stella romping beside him, he strolled to the barn, all casual-like. For he had a plan.

Henry liked a horse. Well, it might be a pony, but he didn't care. The white fuzzy creature would whinny whenever he entered the stables, and when Henry went to pet him, it was even better. The white horse would lay his head on Henry's shoulder and sigh.

His name was Dante, and Henry had wanted to ride him forever... but he didn't know how.

Which was why he ended up standing in Dante's stall in a dither, Stella chewing the bone he'd brought along. Spider had done good on his promise, showing Henry how to curry Dante. He said horses sweat beneath a saddle, so if you don't brush 'em, the horse'll shake to remove the loose hair. He'll remove you, too!

He also learnt to clean a stall. Nothin' to it but a little labor and he'd done worse aboard ship emptying the slop buckets. Next, Spider showed him how to put on a halter so he could lead a horse around, and then the tack—a saddle pad, a saddle, a bridle, and reins to steer.

But Spider had not taught him to *ride*. Henry kept waiting and waiting, but the day never seemed to come.

He was about fed up.

Dante was so friendly. A pal. He wouldn't hurt him.

Nobody'd taught him how to sail when he'd gone to sea. Same thing.

Preparing Dante was hard. He brought all the equipment into the stall, so nobody'd see him. Dante moved a lot, but Henry had carrots to get him to stay still.

Finally, it was done, and he cracked open Dante's stall door and peered up and down the aisle. A couple stable boys were far down the aisle, but they were too busy to notice him.

"Come," he whispered to Stella.

Henry led Dante from the stall and climbed the mounting block holding Dante's reins, like he'd seen others do.

Stella peered up at him as if asking to join in.

"A course you can come, pup!" he said.

Her tail wagged. She knew what he was about 'cause he'd told her.

He got on Dante, and the horse's rear bumped up, but he'd been at sea and Dante the waves. Easy as pie.

"Go," he said.

Dante didn't move.

He thrust the reins forward, jiggling them. "Go! Go!"

Oh, he'd forgotten to kick. He knew about kicking.

"Go!" His legs flared then he kicked Dante's sides.

His horse took off at a trot!

Henry rolled and a foot lost its stirrup, the metal bouncing against Dante's side. His horse went faster!

Fenced fields sprawled outward like the endless sea as Dante picked up speed.

Henry whooped!

In the distance, a horse and rider cut across the fields, jumping fences as they galloped his way. A black horse. Diablo! *Uh, oh.*

The pair swooped in and the Captain leaned down and grabbed Dante's reins, pulling him to a halt.

"Henry!" the Captain said in his command voice.

Henry saluted, fist to brow.

The Captain handed the reins back to Henry, who stared bug-eyed. Stella stared, too. "Thank you, Captain!"

"You were out of control."

"We was having' a ride, is all."

The Captain's face got all tight. "How in all God's creation you think you were riding, I do not know! One foot from the stirrups, your mount out of control. You could have been killed."

The Captain was mighty angry.

Henry slipped his foot in the stirrup and kept his head down. He was ashamed Captain Lansdowne had seen his adventure.

"What do you have to say for yourself?"

He peered up. And up. Diablo was a big 'un. At least the Captain's face weren't an icicle no more. Henry shrugged. "I wanted ta ride."

"And whom, might I ask, has been teaching you."

He stared at his mud-covered boots. "Well, um, Captain I—"

"Do look at the person you are addressing, Henry."

He did, and fear shook him. Though he wasn't sure why for the Captain had never hit him, not once, nor had the Lieutenant. But he was still powerful scared.

"Answer me, Henry," Patrick said.

Henry weren't a snitch. Period. No point in mentioning Spider 'cause it weren't Spider's fault. But he wouldn't lie.

"Well?" the Captain said.

"I just wanted ta ride, Captain." He shrugged, then leaned forward to pat Dante's neck. He was a fine fellow.

"He is a friend," the Captain said.

"My pal, along with Stella, a course." She sat beside Dante peering up at Henry and yipped.

His girl needed a hug, so he slipped off Dante to give her one, getting a face bath in return.

"Can you remount on your own?" the Captain said, raising one of those black brows.

Henry looked at the stirrup, then at the Captain. He shook his head.

"Lead Dante to the fence."

He did, seeing the Captain's plan, and scrambled atop it still holding the reins.

But Dante stepped away. The Captain brought Diablo alongside and pushed Dante closer.

"How'd you do that, Captain?" *Oops*. He'd annoyed the Captain. Again. Henry knew 'cause he made that whooshing sound.

"Get on the pony, Henry," the Captain said.

"Dante is a horse!" Henry slapped a hand over his mouth.

That made the Captain laugh. Thank his lucky stars, 'cause he could'a got mad. Henry slid onto Dante's back and settled his boots into the stirrups.

"Do you know how to direct a horse, Henry?"

Henry's lips went tight and he shook his head.

Another of those whooshes. "I will teach you."

"You will?" Henry's heart swelled.

"Yes."

First, the Captain described how Henry should hold the reins, then how to use his legs. The Captain pulled one rein out to the left, and Diablo moved in that direction. "Do as I did with the rein putting pressure on your right leg."

Henry complied and Dante did as asked.

"Good," the Captain said. They ambled around the field at a walk practicing left and right.

"Time for home," the Captain said. "Remember to squeeze, not kick, to get him moving."

They aimed for the stables. A good thing, 'cause Henry was all atremble.

"You enjoyed the lesson?" the Captain said.

"I did, Captain. A *powerful* lot!"

"From what I have seen today, you have some aptitude. All right then. We will practice each day."

Henry was so shocked he twisted in the saddle. Dante disliked that, 'cause Henry jounced a bit with his fussing. "Really truly?"

"Really truly. It will be a learning experience for the both of us, I suspect."

He couldn't wait to tell Spider! And Banby!

They returned home, Stella galumphing beside them, to see Spider waiting outside the barn. Henry waved with much enthusiasm, telling Spider all the details of his lesson as he brushed down Dante. Replacing his tack, he raced to find Banby, whom he discovered embroidering in the family drawing room.

"I rode Dante, Lieutenant! I rode him all over! I turned him left and right. The Captain showed me!"

Banby looked up from his work. "And did you fall?"

Henry grinned. "Nope! The captain's gonna teach me to ride like him!"

One of Banby's rare smiles appeared. "Excellent."

"You making another thread painting, Lieutenant?" Henry sat beside Banby and examined the work. "That's beautiful, sir!"

Banby frowned. "Aye, it is. Beauty, with horror beneath." His eyes found Patrick.

"The slaver and the frigate?" Patrick leaned in to examine Banby's threadwork.

"Aye." Banby set another stitch. "I shall work until the miscreants who drowned those slaves are brought to justice. Then I shall burn the thing."

"Oh, no!" Henry said. "It's so beautiful."

"Aye, 'tis coming out well," Banby said. "And I look forward to the conflagration."

CHAPTER

FIFTEEN

That afternoon, Patrick mused over Lottie's reaction to Hawthorne Hall, for he had anticipated her displeasure at the state of their new home. Instead, she saw Hawthorne as a challenge, an exciting one, continuing to surprise him in the most pleasing ways.

His heart, desiccated from his unrelenting anger at his injury, had begun to fill with...was it joy? Delight? Hope?

Over the following days, Patrick was gratified with the way he and Charlotte rubbed along. True, they still guarded their words. Nor had they made love due to the cursed Scarlet Lady. He had begun counting the days, with perhaps three remaining.

If Lottie was not dissembling, his twisted legs revolting her...Had she lied about her courses?

He refused to believe so. And yet...he failed to abandon the worry.

The sun blazed in a cerulean sky, not a hint of breeze, as Charlotte entered barn one the following day to practice on her barrel, having given Beauty her morning treats. It surprised and pleased her how the exercise improved her balance. Then again, given Patrick had suggested it, she should not be amazed.

Her husband was so worldly, had done so much, had so many adventures. He was also well-versed in the classics, in languages, and in a myriad of subjects disregarded by a lady's governess.

Charlotte knew little more than the womanly arts and painting, the latter a worthless accomplishment in the eyes of the world. She sighed. She wished to be more for Patrick, know more, have greater understanding, for she feared she would ultimately bore him.

As she took in the barn's sounds and scents, calm suffused her. Once, barns had ruffled her nerves, all due to a fall from her pony where she'd broken her arm. It had taken Beauty and Patrick's quiet care to assuage those fears.

Thomasina exited a stall, and Charlotte hastened to her, noting not a single twinge from her ankle. "How are you this fine day, Lady Thomasina?"

"Excellent!" Thomasina replied.

Though Sina's physical contrast to her siblings was pronounced, her personality was her greatest deviation, for she bubbled with an emotional effervescence, a joyful one. Those who mistook her for "simple" were fools. Sina was canny in her own way, her memory prodigious, and her emotional awareness of humans and animals, exceptional.

Thomasina took her hand and led her to the barrel stall. "I have watched you."

"Have you?" Charlotte replied with a smile.

"You are much improved in the saddle," Sina said.

"Coming from you, that is a high compliment."

"You were afraid for a long time. Now...you are not."

Charlotte leaned down and hugged her sister. Sina reminded Charlotte of a girl not yet come out, though she was older by two years than Susannah, her enthusiasm disdained by the *ton*. How inane, for it lent great joy to life.

Thomasina slipped a hand into the pocket of her barn coat. "This is for you."

Charlotte's name was written in imprecise letter blocks across the wax-sealed missive Sina handed her. Odd.

"From you?" Charlotte said.

She shook her head.

"Who delivered it?"

Thomasina shrugged. "It feels wrong." She pointed to the letter.

"How?"

Thomasina shrugged, blonde curls bobbing. "Just...bad."

Only a fool would fail to heed Thomasina's instincts. "I will remember your words, Sina."

Charlotte would read the letter after she practiced, yet not two minutes atop the barrel, she slipped her feet to the floor and opened it.

I KNOW WHAT YOU DO!

Charlotte stilled atop the barrel. *No.* Could this mean...?

In a daze, she dismounted and slipped the letter into her pocket, thankful she had added one to her habit.

Who would write such a thing? What should she do?

Mind awhirl, Charlotte returned to the manor. Once inside her studio, she locked the door. All was as it should be—her paints, her brushes, the empty canvases, and her work mounted on their easels.

She straightened her brushes, made sure the turpentine was properly sealed, checked that her chrome yellow was where she had left it.

Her heart galloped.

What to do about the missive? *I KNOW WHAT YOU DO!* A threat if ever she'd seen one.

Hours later, Charlotte worked on a corner of the stormy seascape nearing completion, all troubles and fears, hopes and wishes dissolved to mist.

A knock, and she unlocked the door to find Patrick waiting, a roguish grin on his face.

"Might I watch you paint?"

She smiled in return. "Please do, though I should be answering my ever-increasing stack of correspondence piled on our secretary, guilt my constant companion."

Charlotte moved her easel a tad to catch better light and again lifted her brush. The cloudy day suited both the piece she painted and her mood.

"When you are preparing to execute a fresh work," Patrick said. "Do you have an image in your mind? A subject? A color?"

Charlotte laughed as she dabbed burnt umber onto the ship's hull. "Sometimes all of those things. Sometimes one. Sometimes none. When I have an overwhelming urge to paint, I simply must. So I begin. Of course, life often intrudes."

They talked of seascapes, art, and artists.

"I admire Thomas Lawrence," Patrick said.

"I do somewhat, yet he tends to flatter his subjects, rather than paint truth."

"Does truth matter in art?" Patrick said.

Charlotte's brow arched at the question's irony, though she knew he was referring to a greater truth. "I believe so, though it is often hard to achieve. Do you care for etchings? Caricature? I enjoy Thomas Rowlandson's political satire and social observation."

"As do I, though my favorite artists, excepting your father and yourself, m'lady, are John Constable and J.M.W. Turner."

"I studied with Mr. Turner," she said. "Did you know?"

"I did not."

She nodded. "His guidance showed me things I was blind to earlier. He taught me how less could be more, how abstraction can create emotion. It was he who taught me how to burrow deep, to reach the heart of my subjects. He has greatly influenced my work."

"And thus, your style differs from your father's."

"It does." Something was wrong with her seascape, and Charlotte held up a finger trying to identify it, pausing their discussion. She backed away from the canvas, and a sharp breath later, she rushed to the easel, picked up her brush, and performed a mad flurry of brushstrokes.

When the madness passed, she stepped away once again, sighed, and smiled.

"You have such confidence when you paint," Patrick said.

"Not really." Charlotte shook her head. "Or at least not often. I will have bouts of inspiration such as this one, and that is heavenly. But most often it is my craft that sees me through, particularly when I work on my father's paintings."

She pulled over a chair to sit beside him, finally gaining the courage to show him the letter. "Something disturbing happened today."

His face grew serious. "What troubles you, love?"

She withdrew the note with its screaming *I KNOW WHAT YOU DO*, and handed it to him, explaining where it was left.

Patrick brought it to his nose. "If I am not mistaken, this is vellum."

"Yes. A terribly expensive medium for a mere note, not to mention an odd one."

Patrick held it up to the light. "No watermark."

"I looked as well," she said.

"The letters appear written by an uneducated person," Patrick said. "Which tells us little, as I suspect whoever wrote this intended such."

Charlotte's hands clenched. "It is nasty."

"Yet no request for money," Patrick said. "No threats. This was meant to frighten you."

Charlotte went to clean her brushes, fussing with them. "I fear it has succeeded."

Patrick wheeled closer. "Put those down, Lottie."

She did so, and he lifted her onto his lap and wound his arms around her. She rested her head in the crook of his shoulder.

"While the note is worrisome," he continued, "I suggest you put it in its proper place."

"Proper place? I find it alarming, for I cannot help but picture how our lives would unravel were my forgeries to become known."

"Do recall the accuser's aim is to provoke fear," Patrick said. "If he indeed knows the truth, who would believe him? You've noted the Royal Academy displays works by your father, one of which you painted. Even they cannot tell the difference. Who would accept someone bringing allegations? What proof could they possibly have? We can deflect any charge and you are surrounded by loved ones, Lottie, people who would protect you. Fear not. Complete the three paintings, and you are done with it. Let this scurvy note go where it belongs—into the fire."

"You make good sense, Patrick. I shall try."

"Do not try. Accept it."

Patrick was in a grump the next morning when Charlotte breezed into his dressing room. Understandable, for Devonshire's musicale was that evening.

"Shall I wear this tonight?"

Lottie held up a sapphire-blue confection sparkling with beads, silver stars, and diaphanous chiffon, but to his pleasure, no ruffles. He had little concept of women's clothing, a situation that had gotten him into trouble with his sisters more than once. "It is exquisite."

Charlotte laughed. "You are saying that to get rid of me!"

"Now why would I want to get rid of you, wife?"

She bussed his cheek. "So you can brood in silence about tonight. Shall I try it on for you?"

He gave her a roguish grin. "Please do, that way I shall have the opportunity to take it off you."

Lottie rolled her eyes. "Patrick, this is serious. Tonight is a big event designed for *us*."

Once, he had been a fine dancer, women eager to partner with him. Now? He would resemble one of Devonshire's statues, a fixture on the sidelines.

Lottie perched on the bench. "I have hurt your feelings. I did not mean to do so."

He raised an eyebrow. "You have not, my dear." Dammit, his voice was chillier than the Arctic. He hadn't intended thus.

The dress spilled across her lap, highlighting how it matched her eyes. Eyes now darkened to indigo with concern. Such lovely eyes. "The dress is perfect, for it makes your eyes shine like stars."

Her face slackened. "Really?"

He took one of her hands and kissed each finger. "I speak the truth, fair lady."

Lottie laughed. "You may have the sullens, my lord, but your tongue is quite clever this morning."

"I confess, I dread this musicale."

"Your first time in society after your accident..." she said. "It will be a challenge."

"Indeed."

"I am proud of you and will be by your side."

She'd taken him aback. No small thing having Lottie by his side. But proud? "Why in God's name would you be proud of me?"

"Your bravery, of course."

"What? Wheeling myself around like a trained pet?" He could not contain the bitterness in his voice.

"Doing it up a bit brown, are you not, husband? You were brave to save Henry, brave to take on Henry, brave for that first ride on Diablo, brave to pursue the slavers. Brave to accept this evening's musicale when I imagine you would rather do anything but attend." She winked. "Unfortunately, it is in our honor."

"Lottie!" Rose shouted from somewhere distant. "I need you!"

She kissed Patrick's cheek and flew out the door.

A surprising woman, his wife, and a now-familiar warmth bloomed in his chest. *Most* surprising.

The musicale was in full swing. A thousand torches and candles lit the night at Devonshire's estate, an immense manor house, though not the duke's primary seat. She suspected Chatsworth House in the Derbyshire Dales was even larger. The food was lavish, the orchestra fine, the beeswax candles luxurious. Opulent flowers adorned the many areas set aside for the guests' amusement—for billiards and cards and other pastimes. A mime troupe performed, and on the front lawn, a fire eater held sway.

Devonshire's "small" affair resembled nothing Charlotte had ever experienced, except perhaps a night at Covent Garden. The duke had even provided one of his smaller rooms for dancing, "smaller" being relative given the size of rooms in this pile. Woodbine would neatly fit into one of the wings.

Charlotte sat beside Patrick where he had stationed himself beside a large tree dotted with perched doves, having insisted they peek in at the dancing. She failed to care, for none of the men who might ask her to dance were near as interesting as her Patrick.

Charlotte leaned toward him. "Can we leave...damn." Devonshire approached, another man in tow. Both men bowed, and the duke presented Sir Alex Morrison, an intensely handsome man with a pleasant smile. Devonshire took a seat and began chatting with Patrick. Morrison glanced at Patrick and shuddered.

That did it. Sir Alex was one of many discomfited by Patrick's infirmity and chair, seeing her husband as defective. She suspected they pictured themselves as Patrick was and could not bear the thought. Fools all, with their delicate sensibilities and small minds.

Morrison turned his gaze on her, finally asking, "Would you do me the honor of a dance, Lady Hawthorne?"

Charlotte opened her mouth to decline, but Patrick leaned close. "Do dance, Lottie. I would enjoy watching you twirl around the room."

They took to the floor, thankfully a quadrille. Morrison appeared a pleasant man, but as the dance progressed, he had little conversation to recommend him as he prosed on about her father's artistry, then babbled on about goats, of all things. Patrick's eyes followed their movements, even as others approached to converse with him. His lips held a faint smile, his eyes sharp, and if she were to confess, she enjoyed his scrutiny.

When Morrison returned her to Patrick, she leaned in. "An abysmal partner." She told him about the goats, making his lips twitch.

"When we repair to Hawthorne Hall," he said in a faux sonorous tone, "we shall acquire goats. What think you?"

"I like goats a great deal." She grinned. "Perhaps some hedgehogs, as well?"

"Those, too."

"What of squirrels?"

"You go too far!" His mock serious tone made her laugh.

"Shall we adjourn, my lord?"

"Not yet, Lottie." Patrick scanned the room yet again.

"Who are you seeking, Patrick?"

Lord Cardingcom and Lady Eloise approached.

Dear Heavens. They had met the pair out riding, the day of their picnic, when Patrick again asked her to marry him. A sweet memory soured by their arrival.

The next thing she knew, she was performing a reel with Cardingcom, his lordship struggling with the steps. When they came together, his conversation showered compliments on her father's work before moving on to Patrick's infirmity. The daft man actually made allusions to the bedchamber. Beyond offensive.

Glimpses of her husband showed him again watching her, much as one would salivate over a bonbon to be devoured, pleasure coursing through her. All the while, Lady Eloise chattered away to Patrick.

They rejoined the group when the dance ended, and Cardingcom and Lady Eloise swanned off.

"Was her ladyship awful?"

"I do not recall," Patrick said. "All I need do was nod as she droned on."

"Shall we see the jugglers?" Charlotte said.

Captain Lord Uffington approached. Heavens, not another dance. When she again sat next to Patrick after the scotch reel, sweat trickled down her spine from the energetic dance. Her husband flourished a handkerchief, and she dabbed her forehead.

"All Uffington talked about was war," Charlotte said.

"Have some punch." Patrick handed her a glass, for which she thanked him.

"Can we not please leave?" she said. "The musicale will begin soon. Shall we not...Oh, no."

Baron St. Michaels bore down on them, a swagger in every step. A tall, blond, good-looking man in his late thirties known as a bruising rider to the hounds and for his interest in the arts. After bowing, he stared straight at Patrick rather than avoiding his gaze.

Uncaring of the crowd or St. Michaels, Charlotte whispered in Patrick's ear. "One final dance, for I wish to be with *you*." She kissed his cheek and gathered her remaining energy as the baron led her onto the floor.

A waltz and St. Michaels swept her with grace amidst the revolving dancers.

Charlotte stole a glance at Patrick. He, Rhys, and Rose were conversing. Would that she were with them.

"I met Pheland several times," St. Michaels said, forcing Charlotte's attention back to her partner.

"Did you?"

"The first was when you were a child of perhaps ten at Halafair Hall, the second at the academy. His demeanor was most agreeable, his work, exceptional. An outstanding man and artist. My father's enthusiasm for his work birthed my own passion for Pheland's art."

"How lovely." Charlotte sifted around in her brain for something to say. Anything to say.

Would this dance never end?

As Lottie danced, Patrick delighted in her graceful movements, imagining himself as her partner. He had been a fine dancer. Once. He had once been many things, most of which were lost to him. All of which infuriated him.

And yet, he found pleasure in observing his wife, who presented an elegant figure, blue eyes snapping, black hair agleam, her gown floating about like a cloud. Watching her gave him joy, a reminder that though his accident had stolen much, he had gained much in its aftermath, as well.

He must accept he was forever changed. Yet he yearned to walk, to run, and, yes, to dance. God's blood, acceptance was hard.

His glance around the room halted as the sight of the dashing Admiral Saumarez, a middle-aged lothario fawning over a blonde girl less than half his age. A child, really, whose blushes were obvious even from this distance.

Saumarez spotted him, and to Patrick's surprise, dismissed the girl and headed his way.

Interesting. The man disliked him, a mutual feeling, but he feigned a smile as Saumarez neared.

Patrick's letters to the Admiralty regarding the *Despoina* had produced little but for one cogent fact—during the war, decommissioned frigates, their repairs too costly, were sold to private individuals. His friend's research was ongoing as to the purchasers, particularly of Apollo-class frigates. Though not on any Royal Navy roster, the *Despoina* had flown the RN flag. A ruse, it appeared. Bad luck the *Royal Charles* had stumbled upon the slave exchange.

Apollo-class ships were built but for two years, greatly narrowing the field. Three of the Apollos had been sold, one of which Saumarez had purchased, his personal wealth from shipping.

Shipping *what*, Patrick wondered.

Saumarez's current notice was odd, for Patrick had been beneath the man's regard—honors at Trafalgar or no. Only *after* the *Royal Charles* encountered the slave ship had the man begun a whisper campaign disparaging Patrick. The curious timing might mean nothing. Yet he could not discount it.

The admiral reached him and bowed. "What ho, Lansdowne! I see you are still legless. No more sailing for you, my good man."

"True," he said. "Yet soon I take on a position at the Admiralty."

"How intriguing," Saumarez said. "A desk job."

"The Admiralty shall suit me well."

"Is that so?" Saumarez stared down at him.

An empty chair sat beside Patrick, yet the admiral continued to stand, a tactic. Saumarez had a purpose, his fatuous. But the enmity in his eyes revealed intention. A purpose.

Patrick was eager to discover exactly what.

Saumarez shook his head, running a hand over his full head of hair, a source of pride. "I question your return as a possibility, for you have ruffled feathers at the Admiralty."

"Have I?" One time ashore, Patrick had discovered an insect in his bed in Trinidad, a thick-tailed scorpion. Fatal if mishandled. Much like Saumarez.

The air thickened, Saumarez's powerful personality containing a simmering fury. But the admiral smiled, waving his monocle. "What has you worked up about those frigates, Lansdowne?"

Ah. His casual question said Patrick's path to the slaver was on track. Patrick smiled, all teeth, and in an analytical voice detailed the events regarding the slavers, which would alert Saumarez to his mission. But it would put him on edge, too, were he the villain Patrick suspected.

As he recounted his tale, Saumarez's eyes flickered with interest and momentary shock, though his bearing remained merely curious.

"A terrible tale," Saumarez said on Patrick's conclusion. "I doubt you will find the miscreants."

Patrick grinned. "A long shot, indeed, but worth the effort. Do you not agree?"

Saumarez slid onto the seat beside Patrick and leaned in, his smile missing an upper canine, transforming him from handsome to demonic. "I hold sway with the Admiralty."

"Do you?"

"Of course. Great sway." Saumarez nodded, leaning close, noise from the dancers and orchestra receding. "The purpose of my conversation is to *help* you, Lansdowne."

Any "help" Saumarez gave would be poisonous. "How is that, sir?"

"Why, many see your useless legs as a hindrance, even on land, while others find your malady repulsive. I can smooth the way to your reassignment on land, if..."

He could picture Saumarez's manipulations, offered only if he dropped his investigation into the slave ship and the frigate. Patrick had thought the man subtle, yet he now used an anvil to persuade. He hoped he hid his disgust well.

"Think on it, Captain," Saumarez continued, rising to his full height to again peer down at Patrick. "Though you are a captain no more, are you?"

"Rest assured, Admiral. I shall certainly contemplate your thoughtful offer."

CHAPTER

SIXTEEN

The musicale in the main ballroom had begun, except it was opera, much to Charlotte's chagrin. She was not an enthusiast, and now the soprano was on her *third* aria, one from *The Devil to Pay*. Charlotte wished to run from the caterwauling.

She should like opera. Mama did, Claire did, everyone did, or so it seemed. Yet, sadly, she loathed it, which made for a long evening, made even longer by the fact she and Patrick had been seated in the very first row with little chance of escape.

Patrick leaned toward her. "I desperately need some air."

That had been said through gritted teeth. He must be uncomfortable, perhaps in pain.

The aria concluded with applause, thumping canes, and shouts of "Huzzah!"

Charlotte leaned down. "Shall we repair to the terrace?"

"An excellent idea." Patrick wheeled toward a set of French doors, Charlotte beside him, as attendees chatted during the brief break. When they started up the aisle—Patrick's muscled arms pushing his chair, Charlotte walking beside him—all eyes swiveled their way.

On the terrace that embraced the back of the manor, Patrick wheeled to a bench where Charlotte could sit. The wind increased, the trees waving like mad dancers. No star shined, the moon hidden by clouds, the night black as Hades but for the torches Devonshire had set out.

"Thank you, love," Patrick said.

"Are you in pain?" Charlotte said.

"Only from that woman's screeching."

"I feel rather guilty for disliking opera."

He snorted. "You should not, for I loathe it, as well."

"Tonight is all a bit much, is it not?"

"An understatement, dear Lottie."

The air thickened with the scents of impending rain, the wind tossing her curls to and fro.

"We shall have a storm soon," Charlotte said.

Patrick inhaled deeply. "Ah, but the breeze is delicious, is it not?"

"Most invigorating," she said, her gown whipping about her.

"I noted you encountered the admiral, as you had hoped."

"I did," Patrick said, his sarcasm sharp as Toledo steel.

Charlotte had watched their exchange from a distance. Much of the time, the admiral could have been eye to eye with Patrick by taking a seat. Yet he had chosen to hover, Patrick forced to look up to converse. Rather than inconsideration, Charlotte suspected it was a stratagem to make Patrick feel small. A pathetic tactic.

"Did you mention returning to duty?" she said.

"I did," Patrick said with a smirk. "But Saumarez was more interested in my quest to find the *Despoina*. Interesting, no?"

"Very much so."

"His pressure that I drop my frigate search was not terribly subtle." Patrick leaned back in his chair. "He implied, if I left off, he would grease the Admiralty's wheels for my return to duty."

Charlotte tapped a finger to her lips. "As if he has stakes in the outcome."

"Yes. The man's inducement was blatant, yet the obvious question remains as to why he cares about a lone frigate."

"This confirms your suspicion Saumarez is behind the slaving incident?"

"Him, or a friend, perhaps. Somehow, Saumarez is involved."

Patrick turned his chair to face the impending storm, nostrils flaring, eyes a-glimmer.

"You enjoy storms," Charlotte said.

"I do."

"I think they bring out the wild in us all."

Though Patrick was making the best of the evening, though the musicale sadly highlighted Patrick's infirmities. At Woodbine, they could have played chess or discussed the Royal Academy's newest exhibition. Ah, well.

Charlotte had an urge, an odd and daring one. Patrick might dislike it, but she could not resist. She slid onto his lap, wrapping arms around his neck. "I remember dancing with you here, in the large ballroom."

He slid his arms around her, and it felt delicious, his warmth seeping into her, his arms holding her tight.

"*Do* you recall?" she said.

"Of course," he said. "The night you sold me the painting."

"Yes, before all the ensuing chaos."

"As I recall, you found me rather acerbic." He kissed her neck.

Charlotte sighed. "I confess I did, for you seemed a proud and arrogant man."

He chuckled softly. "I was. Probably still am, though I have been brought down a peg or ten."

"You were a fine dancer. And yet I prefer the current Patrick, a more thoughtful and considerate man, one who still could best any one of those gentlemen."

He cleared his throat. "I fear you are rather prejudiced in my favor, Lottie."

"I speak only truth, for you were one of the most lauded and accomplished men I had ever met. You still are."

"Fustian." He chuckled. "Though I admit your point of view charms me."

She leaned close and stole a kiss, his lips warm and soft and eager. His tongue brushed hers and she sighed. When the kiss ended, Charlotte rested her head on his shoulder.

The thick air dampened sounds from the ballroom, while lanterns flickered and danced in the wind. The air smelled rich, lush with promise and the scents of the sea. Charlotte lifted her face to catch a smattering of rain droplets, though the storm itself held off.

A clinking sound, nearby, then a slapping of wood against wood.

"Did you hear that?" Patrick said.

"Like glass breaking and a door hitting the jamb."

He nodded. "Stay beside me and silent, if you would."

Charlotte rose, and they proceeded around the meandering terrace until a flicker of white flapped in the glow of a torch.

A crunch beneath the wheels of Patrick's chair as they moved closer. He reached beside his chair to lift a glass shard, then pointed to the fluttering drapes. The door was ajar.

Charlotte leaned down. "I shall peek in. If you do, the crunching from your chair wheels may alert someone within. Do you know which room this is?"

"No, but whoever is in that room is doing mischief."

Charlotte eased a drape aside, keeping her body hidden, and peered within. She could see little in the torchlight but silhouettes of furniture.

"Anything?" he said.

"The room looks empty," Charlotte whispered.

"I enter first."

Patrick proceeded, and when she stepped inside, the torchlight illuminated a pool of satin on the floor.

Charlotte gasped, pointing. "Look!"

From an inside pocket, Patrick withdrew a striker and matches, lit one, then rolled to an end table holding a brace of candles and lit them.

The room was indeed empty with the exception of a supine body, the woman's face turned away from them, a fireplace poker piercing the woman's chest. Great strength was needed to plunge a poker through flesh and bone. Blood draped the woman's torso to pool on the Persian carpet.

Charlotte pressed her hand to a table, steadying herself, then took tentative steps toward the woman. She tiptoed around the blood and crouched down.

"Do not touch," Patrick whispered in a commanding voice.

"I shall not." She shuddered, fireworks of fear bursting inside. She inched closer, then peered across the body to view the woman's face.

"Oh!" Charlotte trembled, bounding to her feet. "It is Lady Eloise!" She swallowed hard, bile filling her mouth, then sidled around the woman, holding her skirts tight to avoid the blood oozing across the floor.

Charlotte had not cared for Lady Eloise. In fact, she disliked her in the extreme. But the woman did not deserve this ending. "Lady Eloise had a viperous tongue. But this...A rather extreme reaction, would you not agree?"

"The poker changes things," he said.

Charlotte nodded, teeth jammed together tight so as not cast up her accounts. "Suggesting her death was one of opportunity, rather than premeditation."

"An astute observation, Lottie." Patrick's eyes glittered with humor. "I have seen many a violent death, but you have not, wife. Have you been studying with Bow Street?"

A nervous giggle leaked out. "I am rather overset, I confess. No runner, but I have long been an observer of human nature. For my art."

"Do sit before you collapse."

She wobbled to a wing chair. "We should get the Duke and Rhys. Send for the magistrate."

"In time. Speed will not aid Lady Eloise. Are you well?"

"I think so, I... Yes. Yes, I am."

"Good. As a keen observer, what else do you see?"

Charlotte gasped a few calming breaths and peered around the room, the miscreant long gone. Patrick wheeled the room's circumference holding aloft a candelabra, his gaze moving from object to object.

"Look there, Patrick." Charlotte pointed to the empty wall. "A painting hung above the desk. Do you see? Or perhaps a coat of arms or some such."

"I do."

She pushed up from the chair, lifted a lit candle, and moved to the gallery of oil paintings on the far wall. "Look here. This is a van Dyck worth many pounds." She held up the candle to the painting beside it. "And this Rembrandt is worth many more pounds. Whatever the thief took, it must have an ever-greater value."

"Whatever it was," Patrick said, "I would suggest the missing object as the motive behind the break-in and murder."

"It could be." She crouched down beside her husband and rested her head on the arm of his chair.

He stroked her hair. "It will be all right, Lottie."

"I had never seen a dead person before. Not like this. Not one who was murdered."

"I shall remain with Lady Eloise while you retrieve the duke and Rhys." He kissed the top of her head. "You have been very brave, my love."

On wobbly legs, Charlotte left the room.

Minutes later, Patrick's lady wife reappeared beside his brother and Devonshire, both of whom goggled at the corpse on the floor. He held out his hand to Charlotte, and she tucked her ice-cold hand in his, coming to stand beside him.

In clipped words, Patrick explained why they entered the room and what they had discovered.

"We found only one missing item," he said. "Charlotte, do sit before you fall down."

She blinked rapidly, then traipsed to a wing chair, hands trembling.

Devonshire circled the room, while Rhys crouched to inspect Lady Eloise.

"An opportunistic crime," Rhys said.

"Yes," Patrick said. "Well, your grace?"

Devonshire crossed his arms over to his chest before his desk, staring at the empty space above it. "Dammit."

"What hung above the desk?" Charlotte said.

"An old painting. A landscape depicting Chatsworth House, my primary seat."

"By whom?" Patrick said. "The perpetrator left valuable paintings behind."

Devonshire cleared his throat, then darted a discomforted glance at Rhys.

"Why are you prevaricating, Devonshire?" Patrick said in a harsh voice.

The duke spared Charlotte a glance. "Reginald Pheland painted the work."

"My father?" Charlotte said. "How odd."

"My father commissioned the painting perhaps twenty years ago. It was a favorite of his."

"That does not explain things," Charlotte said. "Why would a thief steal the Chatsworth painting, not to mention murder Lady Eloise, when a Rembrandt and a van Dyke hold far greater monetary value?"

"That is the question, indeed," Patrick said.

Their party returned home in the wee hours, all exhausted. Once arrived at the rooms they now shared, Charlotte flung open the door and began to pace the sitting room.

"You are overset, Lottie," Patrick said wheeling inside.

Charlotte paused, eyes wide, hands clasped tight enough to break. "I am somewhat shattered that I am not more...well, shattered at seeing a body, a *murdered* one. I should be horrified by Lady Eloise's demise. Yet my mind persists in focusing on the missing painting."

Patrick took her fisted hand, uncurled it, and clasped it tight. "I admit the theft of your father's painting is rather curious, given Rembrandt and the van Dyke."

Charlotte slid onto his lap, arms winding around his shoulders, and sighed.

"Why not the sterling candlesticks?" she said. "The costly paper-weight? The other valuables scattered about the room? Why would they steal only my father's painting?"

"I believe you startled him," he said. "When you peered inside, he had only just killed Lady Eloise and lifted your father's painting from the wall. I suspect he intended to take other items, but hearing you, he affected a quick escape, the remaining valuables left untouched."

He felt the tension in Charlotte's body dissipate.

"Of course," she said. "That makes perfect sense. The theft was merely circumstantial. He had to leave or be seen."

"Exactly." Patrick nodded.

She brushed a wing of hair from his forehead. "I like your longer hair."

He wanted to be in bed, holding his wife.

Charlotte rose. "I am all at sixes and sevens and am making too much of this, I suspect. I shall retire."

"As will I," Patrick turned his chair toward the bedroom. For the thousandth time, he wished her Scarlet Lady would depart.

Entering their bedroom, Patrick startled. The bed was far lower to the ground—the previous one requiring Charlotte to use steps and him calisthenics to ascend the thing.

"Oh. I can explain," Charlotte said. "I saw no reason for you to jump hoops to ascend, so I asked Rose to replace the bed with a lower one."

Patrick wheeled closer and raised the bed skirt. He began to laugh.

"What is it?" she tried to peer around him.

"This is no new bed," he said. "Rose had the legs cut down."

They were both amused, though Charlotte felt guilt for the maiming of a perfectly fine bed.

"Is your Scarlet Lady still with you?" he said.

She ducked her chin, looking adorable. "Indeed."

Patrick was coiled tight with desire. True, there were other ways to accomplish his and Lottie's release, yet refused to initiate her into the love arts using them, not for their first time, *her* first time.

"Then you shall rest in my arms, lovely Lottie, as I find great joy in holding you."

Her lids lowered and she smiled. "As do I in being held, Patrick."

The musicale continued for another day, as did the hullabaloo, for the magistrate came to call, along with a Bow Street Runner hired by Devonshire, each insisting Charlotte and Patrick repeat the previous evening's events. Worse, Lady Eloise's mother added to the chaos, poor woman, while Lady Ablethorp gathered on-dits like flowers for her tainted bouquet.

When they arrived home late that afternoon, Charlotte returned to her canvases and work.

Two days later, a knock on the door preceded a whirlwind flying inside. Charlotte was thankful she'd donned her dressing gown, as Henry stared back at her with anticipatory glee.

She understood why, for he was dressed in his new riding habit of black top boots, black pantaloons, a white shirt, a blue jacket, and a proper hat, all due to the lessons Patrick was giving him on Dante. According to Patrick, Henry showed great aptitude.

"Yesterday was grand fun," he said. "Shall we ride out again today?"

"It certainly was enjoyable!" she said. "You look quite dashing, Henry."

Charlotte wished she could ride, and she scooched down to speak eye-to-eye with the boy. "I cannot, I am afraid, for I have much to prepare for a small trip in two days. How does the day after that sound?"

Though Henry tried to don a smile, he was only half successful. He nodded and turned to leave.

"A moment, Henry."

"Mistress?"

"I have news. First, the captain and I have sent out inquiries regarding a tutor or governess for you. How do you feel about that?"

His hands delved into his pockets and he shrugged.

"He or she will teach you maths, literature, and science, as well as comportment and other useful things."

The boy peered up at her, and she led him to the settee.

"What about mechanicals, mistress?" he said once seated.

"As I am not your mistress, but your..." What was she? Perhaps motherly, but she was not his mother. Why wasn't there a word, dammit! "Perhaps call me Lady Charlotte?"

"But you are Lady Hawthorne."

"True, but Lady Charlotte is more friendly, do you not think?"

He punched the air. "Lady Charlotte it is, mistress!"

Charlotte shook her head, laughing, and wagged a finger. "No more mistress, Henry! Patrick and I are more like guardians and you are our ward."

"I dunno what that means."

"We shall care for you. Feed you. House you. Take responsibility for you, which is quite a serious matter."

Henry had been nodding, his eyes filled with thoughts.

"Most of all, we shall give you affection, as both the captain and I are very fond of you."

"You are?" he said, eyes wide, hope gleaming.

"Very much so."

"I is very..." He stood. "I *am* very, very fond of you and the captain. Very."

She peeled a laugh, then kissed his cheek. "Then we are all very, very fond of each other!"

"As you say, Lady Charlotte!" Henry sketched a bow and raced from the room.

Charlotte found Patrick in his workshop building a miniature ship. He had progressed far and was now at the painting stage, working on the hull with the tiniest brushes imaginable. She waited until he paused.

"Patrick?"

"Much as I am delighted you are here, I must finish this hull stripe."

"Of course. I shall wait with pleasure."

He proceeded to drag the brush back-and-forth, periodically re-dipping it in the paint jar. Long minutes passed where he fussed with a section of the bow until he sighed a long breath and sat back in his chair.

Charlotte walked behind him and began to knead his shoulders

"God's good grace that feels fine."

"You have been hunched over for hours. I suspect you are all knotted up."

"I find it hard to cease my labors when I create my ships."

Charlotte smiled. "That is not so different from what I do. In fact, I find all creativity springs from the same place within."

"An interesting point of view, Lottie," he said. "Focusing on my models helps me think, and I have been mulling over the murder and theft as Devonshire's."

"Have you come to any conclusions?"

"An attendee at the musicale must be the perpetrator." He laughed. "Though I confess I find that hard to believe."

"Perhaps a server?"

"Possibly." He tapped her hands and she ceased her ministrations, then turned his chair to face her. "And what, my fair lady, has brought you to my den? Do you wish for tea? A biscuit?"

"No, thank you," she said. "I have much to ready for my trip."

"Ah," he said, "the delivery of your final work..."

She frowned. "You mean my final forgery."

"Yes, well, I will be glad when it is gone."

"No more than I, husband, particularly given its subject. I abhor fox hunts. No, I have come about Henry."

"Our barnacle?"

"Yes, our very own...I wish to bring Henry more into our family."

He tilted his head. "In what way?"

"We spoke of hiring a governess and the vicar has pointed me to a friend, a parishioner. He says she is able to teach him proper speech, maths, history, and geography. The boy has such an inquiring mind."

"Too inquiring if you ask me," he said, eyes a-twinkle. "What else does this vicar have to say about his governess?"

"She is oriental," she said. "I believe of Japanese extraction, but with a fine command of English and highly educated. What do you think?"

"I care not where she is from, but whether she can handle such an obstreperous boy."

"Obstreperous? Henry is lively, no more."

"Lively?" He rolled his eyes.

"Oh, come now," she said. "You put on a great show, Patrick, but you care deeply for him. Play the crusty captain all you want, but you could have abandoned Henry on your travels."

"I could *not*." He chuffed. "Why do you think I nicknamed him barnacle?"

Charlotte clasped Patrick's face and brushed her lips with his. He startled, and she deepened the kiss, finding that magical pleasure in touching her husband and knowing he wished to touch her as well.

A workman's shout disturbed the moment, and Charlotte eased back. "You are as much Henry's barnacle as he is yours."

She leaned in to kiss his cheek, and, oh my, he smelled good, like fresh lemons and pressed linen. "Shall we engage in another duel of chess again this evening, sir? I am quite eager for it."

"You shall not win again, Lottie!"

His chuckle followed her out the door.

CHAPTER

SEVENTEEN

T he sun shined bright the following day when Charlotte said farewell to Mama and Claire, who were returning to Halafair. She would miss them, but they were little over an hour's drive from Woodbine, which would allow visits aplenty.

She went to work with a vengeance, knowing in little more than a day, her deception would done and dusted. *Never again!*

Patrick wheeled inside, a tray piled with food and drink across his lap. "I thought we might share luncheon, my dear, as I have scarcely seen you for this past day."

Her brush hovered above the final signature on the final forged painting. She completed it with a flourish and sighed, noting an area needing touch up. Why had she not noticed it before? She was simply too tired to care and would take but a few minutes to correct.

"Luncheon?" she said, her voice soft with exhaustion. "That would be lovely, husband. I must clean my hands and brushes first."

"This is tomorrow's delivery," he said. "Will it be dry enough?"

"These last few touchups will six or eight hours to dry, for I shall not use Megilp or varnish, which would only cause problems."

Patrick moved to the small table and slid the tray atop it, then began setting out plates, cutlery, and linens. "You appear to have drained yourself, Lottie. Your face is white as chalk."

"I wanted to finish, get this last one gone, and…"

"And what?" he said.

She took the sofa across from Patrick, days ago having moved the original wing chair that sat opposite, so he would have a welcoming space for his wheeled chair. "I am eager to paint my own work. At last. Have you any word on the theft or Lady Eloise's murder?"

"None."

The display of cheeses, warm bread, and cold meats made Charlotte's stomach rumble, and they dug in.

Patrick buttered a slice of warm bread. "Once your final commission is fulfilled, we shall move to Hawthorne Hall and at that time, we shall bring this governess you have found aboard." He held up a hand. "The priest's house repairs are complete, as are several other outbuildings and cottages. We shall take the first while Henry and Banby can take one of the others. The foreman assures me that the manor shall be ready in a month, as the remaining work is largely superficial. What are your thoughts, Lottie?"

The fact that Patrick had asked for her input warmed her. Charlotte handed him the plate she had made, then filled her own. "I think supervisors are notoriously fickle with time. Nonetheless, I am eager to live at Hawthorne."

"As am I. I am also keen to see more of your own work, for I dearly love the seascape you gifted me on our wedding day."

Her breath hitched. "Why…why thank you, Patrick." Truth be told, Lottie was nervous about his reaction to her work as he was such a devotee of her father's.

"I leave for Dartmouth tomorrow," she continued, nibbling a bit of cheddar. "Where I shall deliver the awful fox hunt to Lord Elias Archer."

"I shall accompany you." He waggled his brows.

Charlotte grinned. "Then it shall be a pleasurable journey, indeed!"

Henry was a curious boy. Aboard ship, he had gotten into trouble more than once for going where he should not and doing what was forbidden. Since coming to Woodbine with the Captain, he had curbed his terrible desire to see Lady Hawthorne's...Lady Charlotte's father's paintings. He must remember to get her name right.

Henry had entered Captain Lansdowne's cabin many times and seen the painting that hung above the captain's desk, the one of the sea and a ship during a mad storm. Henry believed it had bewitched him, for he could not stop looking at it whenever he was in the room.

In his short life, he had viewed few paintings. He wanted to see more, for the Captain's now rested at the bottom of the sea.

Lady Charlotte had some paintings by her father here, ones she was selling to toffs with plenty of blunt. Henry wanted to see them very much.

And as the itch had grown, Henry had fought mightily against it until today, when Banby was occupied, and the Captain and his lady had gone for a ride. His picks burned his pocket, ones he had cobbled together after being taken from the orphanage.

He should not, he thought as he sauntered near Lady Charlotte's studio door.

And then luck! A favorite lady of his. One of the new maids, the pretty black-haired one he liked, breezed from Lady Charlotte's studio. She failed to lock the door!

The maid should not have been inside. The room was forbidden to all without her ladyship's permission. The rule broken, Henry felt no compunction entering, and so he did.

He hoped to see a painting like the one that was no more, one so beautiful it made him imagine someday captaining his own ship.

He flew inside the studio, eased the door closed, and froze.

Four easels sat around the room, all covered with cloth. Henry approached the first easel. It held something small, a size similar to the one in the Captain's cabin. He took great care lifting the muslin.

His breath hitched. Another painting of the sea, a frigate battling the waves, was everything he hoped for.

Except...He turned away, thinking of Bala and Lamin—though the slavers onboard the *Despoina* called the boys Oscar and Abraham. Henry liked their real names. They were good friends, especially Bala who was full of mischief, just like him.

They were the same age as him, too. And dead. Long dead now. His hands curled into fists. He'd tried so hard...tried to save them... and he'd failed. His eyes got all watery, which was really dumb, and he swiped the back of his hand across his face.

He returned to the pretty seascape, and once again, he stood on deck, riding the waves, streaks of sun parting the cloudy sky. Memory said the Captain's painting was less beautiful than this one. But he was not sure.

Footsteps in the hall. Henry stilled. When they moved on past, he relaxed, walking to the second, larger easel. A view of a manor house. Nice, but not wondrous like the sea painting. The next one was a fox hunt. He'd never seen a real fox hunt and they did not interest him. Where was the fun in hunting a small creature with men, horses, and dogs? Henry shrugged and moved to the last painting, another large one.

Surprise filled him when he raised the cloth. The craggy countryside with a castle overlooking the raging sea was finished, the sea so real it...He touched the canvas with great care, but his finger came away blue. That confused him. How could Lord Halafair's painting not be dry? The man was dead.

"What the hell, Henry!"

He whirled. A furious Banby stared daggers at him.

Henry colored up. "I...Um..."

"Fiend seize it," Banby said as he approached. "Why are you in this room?"

Henry's eyes fell to the floor. "I wanted to see the paintings, sir."

"Look at me!" Banby said.

Henry raised his eyes. "I know I shouldn'a, but..."

"The door was locked for a reason, Henry."

"No, it *weren't*," Henry said with emphasis, shaking his head and shoving his hands deep into his pockets. "One a them new maids left the door open."

Banby's face tightened. "Pardon?"

"I saw her leave and she did not lock the door. I ain't cutting a sham."

Banby would not hit him. Probably. But he might. Early in life, Henry had taken so many blows, he could not help but anticipate pain.

"And?" Banby said.

"The Captain's painting, sir, the one in his cabin onboard ship. I saw it, and it was so beautiful. I wanted to see the others Lady Charlotte's father painted."

The lieutenant's eyes softened. "His paintings are exceptional, I will admit. Now that you have seen them, let us depart, shall we?"

"Of course, Lieutenant, but I got a question."

"And what might that be?"

Henry pointed to the seascape, showed Banby the spot he had touched, and held up his finger with blue paint. "If these paintings be by Lady Charlotte's papa, how come this one is wet?"

Banby stared for long moments, then raised the cloths to examine the other three paintings.

Henry walked to the fox hunt and stuck out a finger.

"Never touch a painting!" Banby said.

"This one's dry! Can't I—"

"No!"

In a stride, the lieutenant stood beside him. "You will say nothing of this, do you hear? Not to anyone, including Lord or Lady Hawthorne. Are we clear, Henry?"

"Mum's the word."

At breakfast the following morning, Charlotte dressed in her favorite travel outfit, both excitement and relief made her near dizzy. Plus, that morning, the Scarlet Lady had departed. Hurrah!

Of the forged paintings, only Viscount Lord Elias's fox hunt remained. She would meet the viscount in Dartmouth, but a few hours by coach, and in a few days, their household would move to Hawthorne Hall, where she would set up her permanent studio. Never again would she have to replicate her father's work.

With Patrick accompanying her today, they would have a fine jaunt discussing all sorts of things or, as Charlotte suspected, Patrick would get frisky, an even more desirable pastime.

Surprised her husband had not joined her at breakfast, she poked her head into their bedroom to find him sitting up in bed, Banby hovering over him like a worried grandmama.

"My lord?" she said.

Banby excused himself as she walked to her husband.

Lines of pain bracketed Patrick's mouth, and he spoke through gritted teeth. "I would suggest you postpone the delivery, my dear. I am afraid this back of mine has decided to let itself be known."

She took the chair beside the bed. "I am so very sorry, Patrick."

"These attacks have become increasingly infrequent, and for that I am grateful."

"As am I. But Patrick, I cannot postpone the delivery."

"Why not?" He took her hand, raising it to his lips for a kiss.

"The buyer's estate is in Coventry, and he is traveling from St. Ives home, Dartmouth on the way. Do you not see?"

He grumped. "I suppose I do. What say you to taking Banby and the barnacle with you?"

"All right." She smoothed the covers. "I hate leaving you in pain."

"Nothing to be done for it. The pain will pass. It always does."

But how he suffered during these spells, battles he must fight over and over. Her heart squeezed.

"Do not look so solemn, Lottie," Patrick said. "I have endured worse, and I believe the exercise, particularly riding Diablo, is improving my condition and strength. Are you looking forward to setting up our household?"

"Very much, indeed."

"Once this mission of yours is complete, we shall only look forward."

"Yes." Lottie leaned close and kissed him, one filled with all the passion she felt for this man. It shocked her how swiftly they had come to an accord, and how well they rubbed along together. Thought fled as Patrick wound an arm around her and pulled her close.

The day had turned broiling, the sky cloudless, the humidity cloying for his poor Charlotte, who must be uncomfortable in the confines of the coach. Patrick was eager for her swift return.

Rhys barged into the bedroom, much to Patrick's annoyance, for battling pain shortened his temper in the extreme.

"How do you get on, brother?" Rhys said.

"What business is it of yours?" Patrick snarled, his eyes dropping to the book he had been reading.

"Oh, ho, I see you are in discomfort."

Patrick did not look up. "Astute of you brother. Now go away."

"I shall not. Your sheets are damp from sweat, which is unhealthy. I propose—"

"Nothing." Marking his place, Patrick prepared to deal with Rhys, who was in one of his get-up-and-go whirlwinds. "I wish to do nothing."

"That is unfortunate," Rhys said. "As I need a swimming companion."

Patrick's eyes flashed and he paused, setting the book aside. "I confess, a swim holds some appeal in this heat."

"Excellent, I suspected you might think such."

Rhys, his ever-prepared brother, called to a pair of footmen hovering in the hall to assist Patrick into his chair, something he could routinely do on his own when this blasted pain wasn't driving him to madness. Though he mumbled and grumbled, they were soon off.

"You are a genius, damn you." Patrick lapped across the placid water, its buoyancy and chill easing his pain. This particular pond was shaded by tall trees, giving them some surcease from the unrelenting heat, the cool water completing the job. "I believed I was unable to swim until on a scorching day in Italy we found a pond. Happily, I was proven wrong."

Rhys paced him in the pool, and they swam back and forth till near exhaustion.

Naked, they now floated atop the water, the slight breeze cooling them further.

"I do not know why I did not think of this myself," Patrick said.

"Because you were in agony."

"It does that to a fellow, scrambles the brain and emotions."

"I am quite familiar," Rhys said. "Your pain has eased?"

"Very much so," Patrick said, fluttering his hands to move in circles. "Had I felt this well, I would have gone with Lottie."

Rhys chuffed. "Jouncing in a coach? I think not. Do you look forward to taking possession of Hawthorne Hall?"

"Indeed, I do. The estate has a lovely prospect overlooking the sea, and Charlotte will be most pleased to have a large studio, one where she can sprawl to her heart's content. She left off working on her submission for the Royal Academy's summer exhibit while here, as the piece is too large. I have had it transported to Hawthorne and she can resume work it whenever she chooses. I have set up her studio which I think she will like."

"You are not giving her a choice of rooms?" Rhys chuckled. "Dangerous ground, brother."

"Of course I will give her a choice. I am not that much of a fool. But the space I have chosen possess exquisite northern light which I believe will be ideal for her work."

"This folderol with her father's paintings will be ended?" Rhys said.

"Finally," Patrick said.

"I cannot help but be glad," Rhys said.

"As am I," Patrick said.

A rabbit paused by the pond's edge, sitting on its hind legs, observing, while it nibbled grass.

"We are being watched," Patrick said.

"Cheeky fellow!" Rhys laughed. "You and Charlotte seem to be rubbing along well."

A grin spread across Patrick's face. "In truth, I would never have anticipated that outcome, yet it is so. Lottie is a delight in myriad ways. I am a fortunate man."

"Indeed, we are both fortunate in our wives. Are you still determined to work at the Admiralty?"

"I have a little use on this earth without it."

"That, brother, is a gross underestimation. Have you considered taking your seat in the Lords?"

Patrick was silent for long moments as he drifted closer to the bank. "I would be dreadful at it."

"I disagree," Rhys said, stroking to shore and lifting himself from the water. "Your mind is sharp, your energy high, and your address exceptional."

A laugh burst from Patrick as he followed Rhys, pulling himself from the pond to sit on the bank. He grabbed one of the towels, then dipped into the near-empty picnic basket for one of the remaining peaches. "I shall think on it."

Charlotte arrived at the Floating Duck, a public house in Dartmouth feeling rumpled and out of sorts. The road had been incredibly rough, the humidity suffocating, and she had spent her time making sure the precious painting's crate did not fall to the floor. Foolish, for it was bound to the opposing coach seat, but her nerves were on high alert. A faint air of unease wound through her, an elusive discomfiting breeze, perhaps due to the painting's subject.

When Lord Archer had asked whether her father had painted a fox hunt, one with the hounds cornering the small red creature, she had dithered in her answer. Though her dislike of the subject was extreme, she forced herself to assure him that, indeed, her father had painted such a scene. Which he had not.

Charlotte had ensured the pinks worn by the men were of the era, rather than their current iteration. The same held true for the ladies' riding habits and saddles—subtle differences that mattered. Fortunately, she recalled two of her papa's works with foxes gamboling in a wood. With luck, all would be well. Charlotte sighed. Never again.

Her maid, an anxious sort, moaned the entire trip. She wished Patrick had been hale enough to accompany her, a solid and comforting presence. When he was by her side, she worried little.

They stopped with a lurch in a cloud of dust, and Charlotte donned her mask, the same one she'd worn meeting Patrick at the ball. She wished for none to see her face, not even the grooms holding the horses.

Banby assisted her down, and she brushed out skirts dusty from the hours-long trip. Both Henry and the lieutenant had ridden beside the coachman, though the boy wished to ride on the roof, Charlotte putting a period to that idea.

The public house was dark and loud as she entered, and it took a moment for her eyes to adjust. Given the hour, not yet three, the taproom was full to bursting with revelers, men's talk and laughter near deafening. An odd choice for the exchange—one Archer had insisted upon due to his tight schedule. She was somewhat reassured by the buyer's letters, which implied he was a measured and serious man.

Henry and her maid remained with the coach to guard the painting, while Banby strode before her, an imposing presence.

The lieutenant parted the throng enough for them to reach the bar.

"Good sir," she said to the barkeep. "I have an appointment here with a gentleman, Lord Elias Archer."

The man's caterpillar brows rose. "Lord Archer, you say?"

"Indeed," Charlotte said.

He hollered over his shoulder, and a young man appeared. "Take the bar, Felix. I'll escort the lady."

They proceeded down a dark corridor alongside the bar toward the back of the inn, the barkeep casting furtive looks at Banby. The cacophony dimmed as they reached a door at the end of the passage. The bartender knocked three times, and the door cracked open.

"Thank you, sir," Charlotte said.

"Happy to accommodate," replied the bartender, who entered the room.

Banby strode inside next, with Charlotte following.

The scene made her freeze. Two burly men held Banby in their grip, while a third covered his mouth with a cloth. In the shadows sat a fourth man wearing a hideous mask, a nightmare-inducing one. The seventeenth-century physician's mask bore a curved beak above his exposed lips and chin, the latter bearing a stitched wound, while thick glass covered the mask's eyes. The man smiled.

A tremble coursed from her head to her toes. Even so, the artist in Charlotte noticed the mask's poor construction and sloppy red swirls surrounding the eyes. No antique, then, but a cobbled-together replica. What game was afoot?

Given his long legs and torso, the masked man was tall, and a whiff of recognition tickled her brain only to dissipate.

"Sir!" Charlotte barked. "Release Lieutenant Banby immediately!"

He smiled again, but remained silent.

Banby's eyes widened, then he slumped unconscious and the men dropped him to the floor.

Charlotte was in danger, that was obvious. Banby would want her to run, yet she could not leave him in the hands of these villains.

Her mind scrambled. *Be assertive.* "Do explain you purpose, sir! Your behavior is unconscionable!"

The masked man's smile widened, an unpleasant curling of his thin lips, for even through the thick glass, his eyes gleamed with hunger. He rose and bowed low. "I have a bargain for you, my lady."

Charlotte gasped at his faintly familiar voice. She must be smart and clever. These assailants were brutish in the extreme, the masked man in charge playing some horrid game. "And what bargain might that be, sir, since you are obviously not Lord Archer?"

"Ah. You may call me simply 'my lord.' Lady Charlotte—"

"Lady Hawthorne to you, *sir!*" Even wearing her own mask, he recognized her, though she had written that a woman factor would deliver the work. No point dissembling.

"I wish..." he said, with an accent she could almost place. "You are to accompany me to Penrhyn Creigiog, my estate in Padstow. I wish you to paint for me."

Ridiculous. "*Paint* for you? I am uncertain the reason for your odd request, but my husband awaits me at home. I cannot accompany you anywhere."

The masked man flicked a finger at the barkeep, and the man departed, closing the door behind him. A blackguard for leading them into this trap.

The leader rose, moving close, near enough to feel his warm breath across her cheek. She refused to lower her eyes.

"If you choose *not* to accompany me," he said. "I am afraid I must end the lieutenant's life. A tragedy. Do you not agree?"

That rat bastard, threatening her, blackmailing her with the possibility of Banby's death. Good heavens, of course she would not allow him to kill Banby. Nor would she go with him, this lordling who thought he could order her about.

"I do not believe you, good sir."

He grinned. "Oh, there is little good about me." He walked to

Banby's prone form and fisted a clump of his short hair, raising his head to expose his neck. He drew out a wicked-looking knife and rested it against Banby's throat.

"I do not enjoy this sort of thing, but rest assured," he pressed the blade tighter to Banby's neck, "it is but a trifling to end his life. Do you wish to watch?"

She flew to where he stood gripping Banby like an animal to be slaughtered.

"My lord, this is all rather extreme." What *else* would he do to her if she relented? "Why do you want me to paint for you?"

"Why?" he said with a chuckle. "Because I want your art and you, of course."

CHAPTER

EIGHTEEN

Her kidnapper's coach was plush and well sprung, but not enough to soften the pitted road that only worsened with each mile. All of which made little difference to Charlotte. Her captor hadn't even bound her hands, assessing that she would not leap from the carriage to escape, as Lottie would break her neck. No leaping. Not yet, at least.

As the miles thumped by, the topography changed from the plush green of Devonshire to a landscape of rock and sparse trees, the wind bending the beeches in a fierce gale. Which perfectly suited her mood.

Her captor did not remove his mask within the carriage, and when Charlotte tried to converse, for information was power, he failed to answer. For the remainder of the interminable journey Charlotte dozed.

She awakened to briny sea scents filling the cabin, noting their many leagues from home. From Patrick.

Would he think she had abandoned him?

No, of course not. Banby, her maid, and Henry would explain at least part of what had happened. But Lord Elias Archer was obviously a fake name with an equally fake estate sitting in the Midlands. Far from the direction they were headed.

Exhausted, Charlotte became lost to a deep sleep until she was jarred awake by the coach's halt.

Outside loomed a gloomy manor of gray granite and high turrets now washed by the rain that beat against its forbidding stones. A brooding presence. Her throat dried, her brain muzzy. Above the downpour, Charlotte heard the crashing waves. They were near the ocean, a marker of sorts.

A black liveried footman opened the carriage door, and her captor descended, turning to offer Charlotte his hand. "Welcome to Cornwall, my dear."

Calmer now than at the inn, she took note of her captor's ungloved hand, hoping to identify the man. Sadly, he wore no rings or other identifiers. Given his speech and the way he moved, he seemed of the upper classes, perhaps even the *ton*. He had claimed to be a lord. If true, given the calluses on those hands, he was likely a sportsman.

The steps were slick with rain, yet she sidestepped his hand to manage the descent on her own, unwilling to touch him.

As fled the rain to the front portico, the urge to weep roiled through Charlotte. Oh, she must not show weakness, which would give the villain more power over her.

But how she wanted to cry for Patrick and the family, who would worry terribly for her. For on the day she would have ended her years-long masquerade, her captor had ripped her away in a most cowardly fashion.

Lottie sniffed and sharpened her voice. "Now what?"

He led Charlotte up the steps to the landing where a woman awaited, all in black but for white cuffs, she looked much like a sour nun.

"This is Mrs. Hastings," he said as they approached. "Our house-keeper. She will show you to your room where you can change out of those wet clothes and warm yourself."

"Change into what?" she snapped.

"I procured several dresses for you, as well as paints, smocks, and other accoutrements."

Dresses, smocks, accoutrements! Dear God, he must have planned her abduction for months. How would Patrick ever find her?

The hour had grown late, nigh on seven when Patrick heard the crunch of gravel, Charlotte's coach returning to Woodbine. He was eager as a schoolboy to see his lady, finding he had missed her presence excessively.

He had accompanied her to deliver her painting to a gentlewoman farmer, the Scottish buyer reneging on the work. Before her marriage, Lottie would have been devastated by the loss of pounds, but Patrick had reassured her the matter was a trifle.

Would that she had shipped Lord Archer's fox hunt, but the peer had insisted upon hand delivery, as many of her buyers did, the venue set by Archer for the exchange.

That mattered little now. No more trickery, no more forged paintings. His Charlotte was free of those burdens.

He wheeled into the entry hall with much anticipation. The swim had eased his back, and he was in fine fettle. Once Lottie's Scarlet Lady was gone, he anticipated much joy between the sheets with his lady wife.

Sounds of feet racing up the steps, the door flung open, only to see Frieda and their coachman supporting Lieutenant Banby.

Patrick wanted to bellow. Instead, he bottled his wrath. "What in God's name is this?" He wheeled backward for Banby and his helpers to enter the house. "Where is Lady Hawthorne?"

Henry peered at him with haunted eyes. "She be gone, Captain."

In the drawing room, Patrick listened in silence to the tale, joined by Rhys and Rose, and his sisters. By the end of Henry's recitation, Patrick's gut tight was enough to hurt.

"What of the barkeep?" Patrick said. "Did he not sound the alarm?"

Banby scrubbed his face. "He claimed innocence, that he was constrained as well. I was unconscious, so I do not know the truth of the matter. I questioned him, not well, I admit. He stuck to his story. Nonetheless, I believe he colluded with the kidnappers."

Rose had rung for a tea tray, pouring Banby a cup which he downed, then she served the others.

"Sounds like kidnapping for ransom," Rhys said.

Silent tears had begun rolling down Claire's cheeks.

"They din't get the picture!" Henry chimed in.

"That cursed fox-hunt," Patrick said with a growl.

A cloak of calm descended on Patrick, much as in battle, for he sensed the fight to come would challenge his mettle, ideas bursting like lightning strikes on how to proceed.

"I do not understand," Thomasina said. "There are lots of people to ransom. Why pick our Charlotte?"

"Because she painted that!" Henry slapped a hand across his mouth.

"How came you by that knowledge, Henry?" He had kept his voice gentle, but the boy began to shiver.

"I seen the paintings, Captain."

Did everyone know about Charlotte's forgeries? Christ. For all his travails at war and the accident, Charlotte's kidnapping anguished him like none other. He thought he understood pain. Until this very moment, he had not.

Charlotte awakened the next morning aching from her long ride in the poorly sprung coach.

That would not do.

She slipped from the bed and stretched her arms up to the ceiling, then down to the floor ten times. Then, hands on waist, she tilted left then right, again ten times. She also ran in place, something Patrick said got the blood flowing. Exercise complete, she dressed.

A knock before a housemaid entered.

"I'm to help you dress, miss," the girl said, a plump young woman with envious curves, brunette hair, and a wide smile. She breezed into the room, took a dress from the wardrobe, and helped Charlotte into it. "Me name's Mercy."

Charlotte did up the front buttons while Mercy plaited her hair, chattering away about the weather.

The door flew open, her captor entering. He wore that foul mask, and though his dress was gentlemanly, it hid a diabolical mind, one she must outwit.

He bowed, and Charlotte almost laughed. *Really*. Her kidnapper bowing to her? The absurdity tickled her. She did not reply with a curtsy but folded her hands in front of her.

"Have you broken your fast?" he asked.

"I have not."

"Do you wish to breakfast or see your studio?"

"The studio, if you would."

He nodded. "As expected. Follow me."

Blast the man to *Hell*.

Two doors down the damp hall, he paused, Charlotte noting a bucket catching water that dripped from the ceiling. Perhaps all was not idyllic at Penrhyn Creigiog.

He pressed the latch handle and swung open the door. "We shall address any imperfections or missing items, as I want your studio to contain all you need to paint."

The large room was done up in mahogany and gilt, with dark green velvet drapes, a table and two chairs, and a gold tapestried fainting couch. She drifted to the folded easels resting against a wall, of the finest quality, as were the powders for paints from T&R Rowney. She peered more closely to read the colors. Modern ones, unlike her father's palette, the ones she used for her forgeries. A mistake on his part. "Which direction does this room face?"

"North, my lady. To capture the best light."

She planted herself in the center of the room. "You sent me that note, left on Lady Thomasina's dresser."

He grinned. "A bit of folderol."

What an *ass*. "And what am I to paint?"

"Since your people stole away the fox hunt—"

"Painted by my father."

"You shall paint that in your father's style, as you have done these many years."

How had he known?

He most certainly was no intimate of hers and the few trusted staff at Halafair would never reveal her secrets. Someone at Woodbine, perhaps. A spy?

Implausible, as the servants were loyal and steadfast to Rhys and his family. Many had served for decades, and numerous staff positions were held by former soldiers. None would betray them.

Yet Charlotte recalled coming upon two new parlor maids dusting the library. Perhaps one of them?

At present, she could do nothing about that. Nor would she dissemble about forging her father's works. Her captor was canny, and she wished to avoid igniting his temper.

And yet... "So let me understand this, sir. You adore my father's paintings, yet you are having me churn out a copy. For money?"

"I need the money, but I am also a serious collector of your father's art. And now yours, as I know Reginald Pheland never painted a fox hunt!"

She flushed. "Is that so?"

"Over time, I suspected you were forging your father's work, for filthy lucre, I assumed."

His words rang with sincerity, his toothy grin making Charlotte's stomach churn. When she remained silent, he asked, "How do you like your studio?"

"It will serve. I presume you have kidnapped me, not merely to paint, but to ransom me for a fat sum."

His lips curled into a smile. "In that, my lady, you would be wrong."

Charlotte loathed being confined, her first few days at the manor miserable with chills, skin crawling, all due to Claire shutting Charlotte in the ice house. A silly, childish trick that left her in utter blackness for what felt like hours.

Though allowed to roam the manor at will, she still felt confined —the outdoors off limits unless accompanied, eyes watching wherever she walked, the guards' stares, lascivious and predatory. She must learn to deal with it, Charlotte admonished herself, for she could be locked in a cell. Or a cellar. Or an attic.

Her captor was pushing her hard, so hard her fingers had become chafed and sore from the work, her anger surpassing her fear. "I cannot paint with such speed. I *will* not. Look." She held out her hands.

Her captor reared back, effusively apologizing, then eased the pressure to a less injurious pace. Would that he did the same for her confinement. Would that he release her.

Charlotte's hands ached, her body weary, but most debilitating was her mind—a panicked herd of horses galloping this way and that.

Those first days, she had investigated the manor's doings in search of a possible escape route. Her third-floor bedroom had several windows, which overlooked an endless drop to the ground. Sheets came to mind, as Rose had detailed their use to escape her home. But each day they were replaced by the maid Mercy. One set would not nearly be long enough. Tearing the diaphanous drapes was a thought, but the manor's denizens would notice.

When her kidnapper was gone on his various hunting excursions, several men cradling rifles prowled the grounds. At home, he roamed the manor halls in silence wearing black garb and that awful physician's mask. She'd come upon him several times and it had scared the wits out of her. No healer he, but a specter haunting his own castle, the personification of death.

She wondered if his staff had ever seen him without it.

Many of the manor's rooms, the public ones, contained original paintings by her father and forged ones by herself. Charlotte remembered watching her father work on many of those in the dining hall, study, and parlors and suspected more were displayed in less-public rooms. She had not ventured there yet, fearing he might discover her alone. Seascapes and landscapes, town scenes, and ones of Scotland hung in dark and dank rooms with little done to improve the manor's moldering ambiance, the air scented with decay.

In a salon tucked away from the house's daily bustle, she found a small painting hung above a divan, the day's watery light filtering in to shine on the work. She gasped, then pressed a hand to a chair back to steady herself. The painting was again by her father, one she had never seen before. Yet she knew it. For its subject was Chatsworth House, her father's signature, an early iteration, in the bottom right corner.

This was the painting stolen during the musicale, the one resulting in Lady Eloise's murder.

Her captor had attended the musicale or been part of the staff. Not staff, no, for he was too high in the instep for that possibility.

Why, the man might have danced with her. That she knew him, perhaps had held her in his arms, chilled her to the marrow.

Each day before her easel, Charlotte dashed a blue stroke on the back of an empty canvas, keeping track of the days. She took note of comings and goings to at the manor, including deliveries. Few came or went, though the previous Monday a wagon of fruits, vegetables, and meats had appeared.

Each night, she collapsed into bed, weary from her work and imprisonment. Her captor's presence sapped the joy from her work, an ever-present gladness that existed while she painted. She questioned whether she would find it again.

And Patrick...Her thoughts never strayed far from her husband, particularly in the wee hours. They had just begun as a couple, finding their way in an awkward marriage that held the promise of possibility.

What if Patrick were further injured while looking for her? What if her captor intended him harm? What if Patrick was killed?

What if, what if, what if...

Her fractious sleep contained nightmares of plague physicians or dreams of Patrick, ones where dried tears crusted her face when she awoke.

She had taken to calling her captor "the monster," for monstrous he was. The irony of him attending church services that first Sunday did not pass her by and she was glad whenever a hunt or other sporting pursuit tore him from Penrhyn Creigiog.

During those early days, he perched like a fat spider observing her as she worked. But he grew bored with the pastime, and much to her pleasure, his visits became more infrequent.

Eavesdropping, conversing with Mercy or Jane or Cook or simple observation gleaned a wealth of information. She prayed for the opportunity to use it.

The monster appeared moneyed. Hiring guards cost a pretty penny and his clothes were impeccable. Having visited the stables attended by a guard, his horseflesh appeared in fine fettle, too. Yet the stables leaked, too.

Given the manor's condition, the monster must funnel his money into sporting events or more art.

The manor's air was suffocating, the few servants cowed by their master near as much as she. Fear was the currency of Penrhyn Creigiog, and she would lock her door each night, even knowing he had a key. Charlotte would cry and beat her fists against her pillow, whispering, "Why me?" After the tumult, she would gather the shreds of her composure, knitting them back together. How foolish to rail against fate, rather than devise a way out of this hideous mess.

Charlotte managed her fear well enough to further explore the first floor. Most of the less public rooms sagged with neglect, the thin house staff inadequate for the manor's size. More buckets graced the floor, the curtains dust-covered and moth-eaten, while filthy windows barely let in light when the sun shone, an infrequent occurrence. The manor's air spoke of penury and abandonment.

It was all rather Gothic, and she wondered if the townspeople gossiped about her captor. Perhaps, though she had no idea if there was a nearby town or not.

Could she know the monster? If he were, indeed, a member of the *ton*, no one with such an unbalanced nature came to mind.

A week into her incarceration, Charlotte fired up her courage to explore the upper stories in search of more paintings by her father.

Past midnight, Charlotte's hands still ached from long hours at her easel. Mrs. Hastings, housekeeper *terribilis*, had tended them, reeking of disdain at Charlotte's discomfort.

Charlotte peeked to see if a guard stood outside her door. None did. Unsurprising. Where would she go with gunmen peppering the estate? She lit a lantern's candle and proceeded down the hall.

She passed her studio, moved down the hall lit with torches, then up the staircase to the fourth floor, the boards creaking with her passage, the air redolent with musty age.

No torches greeted her arrival, the space cold enough she shivered. She clutched her shawl tighter, lantern high in the Stygian darkness, with small plumes of dust bursting as she walked. Half a dozen paintings by her father lined the walls, and at the hall's end, moonlight pooled from a window, drawing her to the open door and beckoning her inside.

An immense ballroom lay before her smelling of damp. Tall windows marched across the room's far side, allowing the moon's light to filter in. Water streaks darkened the flocked damask walls, while cobwebs adorned the moth-eaten draperies. A single wing chair and table with something atop it sat at the room's center, a tiny island in a sea of darkness.

Holding her lantern high, she approached the first artwork hung a few steps beyond the door. Another of her father's seascapes.

Moving close, Charlotte gasped. The painting had assumed a frosty look from water seeping into the varnish layer, blanching it.

Equally bad, mold darkened the painting's edges and crept toward its center.

The next painting and the next were damaged the same way. If not restored soon, they would be unsalvageable.

More than a dozen of Reginald Pheland's valuable works hung in this frigid, dank room, en route to destruction.

Why?

She paused. It seemed nonsensical that the monster, an obsessive collector, was allowing his precious paintings to deteriorate. An absurdity Charlotte failed to understand. None of the works on the lower floors showed this deterioration. All the baron need do was move these to a warmer, drier location.

Yet he had not.

She'd known from the first she was dealing with a man whose faculties were disturbed. But this desecration of paintings he allegedly loved…She could not fathom it.

Raising her lamp high as she moved closer to the table with an object resting atop it. A doll house.

Closer still, and Charlotte reeled back upon seeing the building in full.

Halafair Hall.

A replica of her home, a miniature, complete with Palladian windows, columns and…Taking great care, Charlotte opened the front door. The maker had replicated Halafair's black-and-white marble entry, the hall's chandelier a near match, as was the double staircase rising to the second floor.

Peering through a tiny window into the main salon, she gasped. Above the fireplace, hung a miniature replica of *Halafair*, painted years earlier by her father.

Chills raced down her spine, and she flew from the room, her nightrail swishing dust, glad to have left the room behind. She sneezed.

"God bless, my dear."

Charlotte froze.

"Are you in need of a handkerchief?" the monster said as he approached.

"No, thank you," she said, her words thick. She would not back away, even if her flesh kept screaming, "Run!"

"Might I ask, why you are up here?" He came to stand before her, wearing his ubiquitous mask—a tall lean man all in black and white, his waistcoat zigzag patterned. His eyes gleamed like an adder about to strike. "This floor is a dangerous place."

"I wished to see if any of my father's paintings were hung here."

"Ah!" he said, pitching his voice low, so low Charlotte had to strain to hear. "All this belonged to *my father*." The words "my father" were spat as an epithet as he took her elbow and guided her back into the ballroom. He waved his lantern toward the dollhouse. "He built this himself. Did you know he dealt in art?"

"I did not." How could she, considering the monster had not revealed either his or his father's name?

"Oh, indeed, he was famed throughout England. Art was his *raison d'etre,* taking little notice of his family, his estates..." He took her elbow, returning them to the ballroom. "The evidence of his care. Nonetheless, he birthed my love of art, particularly your father's. Has your curiosity been satisfied?" He hovered over her, his black garb one with the hall's darkness.

She daren't speak of the paintings' disastrous state, of which he seemed uncaring or oblivious. "It has, sir."

The monster leaned close, his breath reeking of spirits. "I am a lord, and you will refer to me as thus."

A thousand fears fluttered her mind, her terror threatening to eat her whole. She wanted to scream, to flee.

Instead, Charlotte raised her lantern high, her face a mask of curious inquiry. "When may I leave here, my lord?"

"Leave?"

His laugh sent panic buzzing through her. She must deflect. "Shall we repair to the drawing room, my lord?"

His hand darted out to brush a curl behind her ear.

Bile surged. And fury. How *dare* this madman intimidate her! She must *do* something. She must escape.

He began to pace a circle around her. "Do you know, my dear, *you* are your father's finest creation. Standing in this hallowed room," he said with much irony, "I believe now is the time to speak of our marriage."

Marriage? "I am wed to Lord Hawthorne."

He waved a hand. "Easily set aside, as I suspect you have not consummated your marriage."

That was neither here nor there. Truth be told, she knew little about the intricacies of vows, but of a certainty, he must have her consent to set them aside.

"You speak of personal matters between a husband and wife, which I find inappropriate," Charlotte said. "But let me assure you, my husband and I have indeed consummated our marriage. Many times." His only refutation would be to examine her. Dear heavens, would he dare?

A gust of wind rattled the windows. "To be discussed later for it is early days, is it not?" he said. "I am sure as time passes, you will see the advantages to our union." He took her hand, raising it to his lips for a kiss, then tucked it into his winged arm.

"Come. You appear chilled, my lady. Shall we proceed to warmer environs?"

Charlotte nodded and they walked at a stately pace when all she wished to do was run.

NINETEEN

Once a day, Charlotte was allowed outdoors for a constitutional, always accompanied by her captor or one of his minions. The manor's oppressive atmosphere increased her distress and the paintings she created suffered for it. By week two, the gowns he had purchased for her began to hang loose and Charlotte felt her soul fading away with her flesh.

She discovered a peephole beside one of the framed paintings hung in her bedroom, a chilling find. Given the angle, the observer could see her in bed, even changing her clothes. She stuffed it with a handkerchief. And while the kerchief was removed daily, each night she stuffed the hole again. She suspected the game amused the monster.

Charlotte worked on a second fox hunt, this piece more vile than the previous one. The first was nearly complete, yet he had demanded she begin another portraying a group of riders surrounding a pack of hunting dogs ripping apart the fox.

"No, no, my dear." The monster loomed above her, his hand on her shoulder gripping vise tight.

"My lord?" she said.

"You have obviously not attended a fox hunt."

"I have not."

"We need more blood! Our fox may be small, but there is always copious blood." He squeezed her shoulder hard, making her cry out.

"Of course," she said, forcing down an angry retort.

As she worked, her loathing for the subject only increased, and she found his implicit threats of pain infuriating.

This creature wished to marry her? Ludicrous.

When she had begun the work, she decided to fill this new painting with clues. The work depicted men on horseback hovering over the poor bloody fox, with hills and trees in the background.

Three men appeared in the painting, all with differing expressions. The monster's cut on his chin had been stitched when she'd met him, the stitching now gone to form a bright pink, raised scar. So she painted a rider with that very same scar, along with his blond hair.

Were the family to catch a glimpse of the painting, they might recognize the man or realize Charlotte had painted the work while in captivity.

She added a second identifier—the Darley Oak—a gnarled, ancient tree said to be the oldest in Cornwall, one Charlotte had seen. Though Charlotte had no idea whether the manor was situated near Bodmin Moor or not, someone might recognize the tree and note it stood in Cornwall.

Perhaps a hopeless folly, yet she must *do* something to effect a change in her situation. Since devising her clues, Charlotte worked with greater purpose and energy, all the while planning her escape.

Tomorrow was the day. If she failed...

Best to think positive.

The monster insisted she leave the studio door open, for he enjoyed sneaking up on her whilst she worked and did so with frequency. At least she had come to sense his approach. Now, nary a muscle twitched.

Her thoughts scattered as the air changed. Charlotte girded her loins.

"This is coming along nicely." His voice held a smile as he strolled near, a pleasant voice, deceptively so.

"Thank you." She did not cease working and prayed he failed to notice his scarred chin in the painting.

He strolled over to the first fox hunt, still incomplete.

"This will set a pretty price," he said.

He did not exist. Nothing existed except Woodbine while Patrick looked on as she worked.

"I think you shall paint another hunting scene next," he said. "One where they blood a young hunter."

Charlotte nodded.

"Add my Irish hunter, Clementine, and perhaps Harold, my favorite foxhound."

She could not resist. "I am sure Harold and Clementine will make the work exceptional."

When he let her quip pass, she asked, "What size?"

"Large. Yes, I think sizable." He leaned down to sniff her, the mask's beak poking her neck.

Her stomach wobbled, though she remained outwardly serene. *Please do not look closely at the painting.*

The monster had provided canvases in varying sizes, paints, brushes, turpentine, cloths—all for her ease of work. Though peace of mind was sadly lacking, that treasure out of reach.

"Come," he said. "Put down your brushes and we shall share tea and biscuits."

Since they had breakfasted earlier, an odd time for tea. Charlotte cleaned her brushes and hands, and he pulled out a chair at the table set before the windows. She sat as Jane placed a tray loaded with sweets, savories, and a pot of steaming tea on the table.

Charlotte was quiet as they ate. He was not.

"Dear Lottie, you must be careful roaming the manor, for there are many hidden nooks and crannies that are unsafe."

How dare he use her nickname. Few but Patrick called her that, and it sounded foul on his tongue. "My name is Lady Hawthorne, my lord. Thank you for your advice."

"I have considered sharing my rooms with you to keep you safe."

"As you know, I am a married woman," she said with heat. "I would decline."

He reared back. "Decline?"

She backtracked, softening her tone and offering a smile. "That would be a betrayal of my vows, which I take seriously."

"Do you?" He grinned. "Yet you are here, without any comfort at night to allay your fears."

"My fears are perfectly manageable, my lord."

He withdrew a large knife from his boot and poised it above her left hand. Charlotte froze, schooling her features to curiosity, rather than the horror she felt. Were he to stab her hand with that knife, she doubted it would heal well enough to paint. He knew that as well as she.

The monster lowered the knife until the point made a dimple on her skin, then a bit more pressure, a sharp sting, and blood oozed from the shallow wound.

Charlotte contained her tremble, staring into the mask's glass eyes. "What is the purpose of this, my lord?"

"Ha! Do not move your hand!" He flung the knife into the air where it twirled and whirled.

Would he truly allow her hand to be damaged?

No. This was yet another game to break her will and sense of self. Her hand remained firm on the table.

When his hand darted out and he swiped the handle just before the point reached her flesh, she near fainted in relief.

"Danger is everywhere, my lady. Would you not agree?"

Charlotte wanted to grip that distended nose and rip the mask from his face. But tomorrow was the day for her escape. "As you say, everywhere."

He slid his knife back into his boot, then resumed eating as if he had not just played cat-and-mouse with her.

"I must change for church." He took a sip of tea, then rose.

"I could accompany you, my lord."

He snorted and sauntered toward the door. "I think not. Have you any thoughts on our marriage?"

"I fear I have been too busy to do so."

"*Do* think on it. What a powerful team we shall make!"

Once gone, her contained trembles burst. Long minutes passed, Charlotte walking through tomorrow's escape plan time and again until she composed herself enough to return to work.

Her escape, via vegetable cart, cheered her. Penrhyn Creigiog was but one of the many houses the delivery man attended, his wares covered with a canvas tarpaulin beneath which she could hide.

Hours passed until her back itched when her captor stormed in once more, bending over her and licking her neck.

"Pray do not distract me," she said. "I am at a difficult point in the work."

He laughed, so soft. "It is rather hard to resist, for you taste delicious, my dear."

Yes, escape was risky. But better than staying in this fetid place. If he caught her? She would suffer, but she doubted he would end her life, his greed for her art gluttonous.

Charlotte's brush dabbed at the sky.

"No farewell?" He boomed a laugh as he left, the sound fingernails across slate.

A week gone, easily the longest week of Patrick's life. The misery had trumped his battles at sea, the sinking of his ship, and even his accident. He finally understood why Rhys went on his "retreats." War had changed them both, yet they still lived a life, unlike to many others. Sometimes, that life became too much.

Upon Lottie's disappearance, they had hired twenty of Bow Street Runners sixty-eight constables, most the Red Robins, Bow

Street's horse patrol. All were highly trained and disciplined and would scour England for his wife. They had also disseminated gossip that he and Lottie were on their honeymoon.

Patrick rode daily to Dartmouth to question the innkeeper and others at the hostelry where Charlotte had been taken. Most claimed to know nothing, while two men described Charlotte entering the Floating Duck with Banby. Neither had seen her leave.

Yet someone at that infernal inn knew something about Lottie's kidnapping. They might be clams but he would pry them open.

Patrick became a man obsessed, though he tried to hide his compulsion from the family. He would venture to their rooms, pressing Lottie's pillow to his face to draw in her scent. Lottie's glorious scent.

They'd never had a courtship, and he gathered small tokens of his affection. A box of chocolates, a miniature dingy, "Lottie" on its stern, *Rosalind and Helen*, a recently released poetry collection by Shelley he'd ordered for her...but never given, and other emblems of his attachment. The gifts he'd purchased during his last voyage—the shell painting from Barbados, a colorful ceramic perfume bottle from Marrakesh, a sandalwood carving from India—all rested at the bottom of the sea.

He had not a single image of Charlotte, could not even look upon her face. When she returned, he would request a self-portrait. Entering her studio, he would peruse her paintings again and again, trying to feel her presence, trying to suss out who had taken her and where she was, for he did not believe her dead.

Her kidnapper would not have orchestrated her abduction in such precise detail only to end her. Yet no ransom note had arrived.

Charlotte was a beautiful woman, and perhaps her looks had obsessed her kidnapper. Yet Patrick trusted his instincts which had held him in good stead during the war years. He sensed her captor wanted Lottie for her art.

He questioned Banby and Henry, even Lottie's maid before her resignation, hunting for any obscure detail that might give him a clue to her whereabouts.

He wrote daily to Lottie's mama and Claire, for they must be as frantic as he, informing them of any progress and, most especially, reassuring them he was doing all possible to bring Charlotte home.

Letters also flew from his pen to auction houses and art dealers, requesting information on any Reginald Pheland painting coming up for sale, as well as directing three runners to attend auctions with Pheland paintings for sale.

Even so, this disaster made no sense.

On the eighth day of Lottie's kidnapping, Patrick wheeled from his coach onto the grounds of the Floating Duck, Banby assisting.

"Stay here, Lieutenant."

"But sir…"

"I will call if need be."

Banby reeked of annoyance as he saluted.

Entering the inn, hazy with smoke and smelling of spirits, silence reigned. He spotted a suitable table and wheeled over, the Duck's denizens resuming their chatter.

Patrick noted the innkeeper's absence as he glanced toward the bar. On his previous excursions, the barkeep nowhere in sight, the innkeeper claimed he was visiting his sister. Having the man's description from Banby, Patrick was pleased to find him drying glasses behind the bar.

He would get answers today.

Patrick moved a chair aside, wheeled close to the table, waving the barmaid over, a comely girl with expansive breasts beneath her white blouse.

She approached with a swish of her hips. "How can I help ye, handsome?"

He smiled, putting all of his charm into the effort. "Your best ale, miss."

With a smile and a hip swish, she departed, returning in minutes with his frothing tankard.

"Many thanks," he said. "By the by, might you tell me the barkeep's name?"

"Brimley," she said, her brow furrowed.

"Would you ask Mr. Brimley to join me? I have an offer for him."

"Do ya, now?" She eyed his chair. "What's a toff like you want with old Brimley?"

Another smile. "I am afraid that must remain between the man and myself." He slipped two shillings onto the table.

She swiped them up and nodded. "A moment, sir."

Minutes later, a stocky older man wreathed in graying curls approached his table.

"Mr. Brimley, I presume?" Patrick said.

"I be Brimley. Whatcha want?"

Patrick waved him to a seat, and Brimley looked at it askance.

"If you do not sit, I fear our conversation will give me a stiff neck."

Brimley pulled out the chair and thumped into it.

Patrick removed a sovereign from his pocket, setting it on the table, then took a sip of ale. He waited.

"Well?" the man said eyeing the sovereign, his eyes darting from the money back to Patrick.

"I have a few questions, my good man, about some events last week."

Brimley's eyes narrowed. "Last week, eh?"

Patrick gave him his captain's stare, cold as ice and commanding. "The day my wife was kidnapped."

Brimley jerked and started to rise. Patrick's hand shot out to clutch the man's arm just above the elbow. "I would not be so hasty as I have several more sovereigns in my pocket, which you will receive if you cooperate."

The wheels obviously turned in Brimley's head. "Alright. Aye, I'll stay. But yer playing a dangerous game." He stared at Patrick's chair. "One you might not be man enough for."

Patrick's smile was pleasant, but his eyes remained cold. "Shall we see?" He shoved the sovereign in Brimley's direction. "Can you identify any of the men from that day?"

Brimley shook his head, his shaggy hair wagging.

"What about their leader? What can you tell me of him?"

The man shrugged. "He wore this funny black mask with a long curving nose." He gestured to show Patrick.

A medieval doctor's mask. Charlotte's kidnapper had disguised himself. Interesting. Perhaps Lottie would recognize the man. Perhaps he would, as well.

"Did you hear him speak?" Patrick said.

"Aye. He sounded like a toff. Like you."

Curiouser and curiouser.

"Was there any part of his face you *could* see?"

"Aye."

A short, round man entered the inn and Brimley's eyes darted toward him, his spark of fear dissipating.

Extracting the man's information resembled hauling up a thousand-pound anchor. By hand. "Anything unusual about what you saw of his face? Perhaps a beard? His lips? A chin divot?"

Brimley rubbed his hands across his pants. "A stitched cut on his chin. Looked to be deep, too."

Patrick eyed the man, knowing he concealed more. Much more. He extracted another sovereign, flipping it with his fingers. "How did they originally contact you?"

"What makes ye think they spoke ta me?" he said, eyes following the coin.

"Because someone at this inn aided them. I suspect it was you, Mr. Brimley."

"Me! Why I—"

Patrick leaned close. "I do not intend to harm you, sir, but rather glean information."

The barkeep laughed. "How could you do me harm, you with..."

The knife Patrick thrust beneath the man's chin froze him.

"Let us not play games, Mr. Brimley."

The barkeep went to nod and stopped. "No games."

"Good." The knife vanished. "Continue."

The man eyed the sovereign, then Patrick. "One a his thugs got in touch and told me what to do when the lady arrived."

"Did you know him?"

Brimley shook his head. "He were blond with long hair. Don't know where he be from, either."

"His accent?" Patrick said.

Brimley shook his head, curls bobbing. "I dunno. He weren't from around these parts."

"Clothes?"

"All except the toff wore regular ones. He was all decked out in fine clothes, like you."

"How much did they pay you to aid them?"

He flushed, the man's nose turning beet red. "A pound."

"Anything else?"

He scraped his nails across his unshaven chin and peered at the sovereign on the table. "You gonna give me that?"

"Possibly."

The man glanced around the room, then dipped his head. "I were out of the room, so I didn't *see* what was going on, but two of the thugs raced from the room out the door, then ran back inside minutes later. I mighta followed them back down the hall and heard something through the door."

"Good Christ, man, *what*?"

"That sovereign?"

Patrick slid it across the table, showed it to Brimley, then fisted it.

"There was shouting somethin' awful. Screeching."

Patrick unfurled his fist. "And?"

"'I must have the painting!' the leader screamed in that plummy voice a his. Then another said 'the coach left.' And another, 'Why in hell's name did you not follow it?' That were the toff. More words I couldn't hear cause a the shouting. Then, and this were the toff again, 'I have killed for less! My prize will paint me another! Get out!' Then smashing came and I backed away 'cause it sounded bad. I weren't going in that room again for nothing!"

Banby sat across from Patrick on the return trip to Woodbine, keeping silent while Patrick mulled over his conversation with Brimley.

"The barkeep enabled the kidnapping at the inn," Patrick said.

"What will you do about him?"

Patrick shook his head. "Nothing. He is simply a greedy man uninvolved with the heart of the situation."

"Was he acquainted with any of Lady Charlotte's abductors or where they were from?"

"Sadly, no, but not a waste of time. Her kidnapper knows my lady paints."

Only a flicker in Banby's eyes showed his concern. "Interesting."

"The barkeep heard him say, 'My prize will paint me another!' His prize! Christ! Proof enough."

"The use of that word." Banby shook his head. "Most disturbing."

"That it is," Patrick said. "Charlotte's abductor appears to be of the *beau monde*. 'A toff' in the barkeep's words. Though how elevated I cannot be certain. He wore a gentleman's clothes, as well."

"Someone of the *ton*," Banby said with surprise.

"Certainly possible. He bore a slash on his chin, one that would likely scar."

Banby rested an elbow on his knee. "That will help."

The carriage hit a vicious hole and Banby jounced, his head thumping the roof, while Patrick's secured chair never moved.

"Paralysis has certain advantages," Patrick said, humor in his voice.

"So it appears," Banby said, eyes alight.

"It is worth noting the kidnapper's men chased after the painting, the one you and Henry spirited away in the carriage. How did you end up in the carriage?"

In a dry voice, Banby replied, "I was unconscious at the time. Henry said they found me in a back room and had to get help carrying me to the carriage."

"The leader was in a great fury at its escape." Patrick raked a hand through his hair. "He said he had 'killed for less,' to quote the barkeep."

"Killed," Banby said. "Lady Eloise's death...?"

"Perhaps. Wise to pursue that, but let us take care hypotheses do not lead us astray."

"A man obsessed is never safe."

Patrick peered out the window, his thoughts scrambling. They had learned much, yet he felt no closer to finding his lady.

TWENTY

Charlotte's rare artistry was known by few. Yet her abductor seemed aware of her talents, the barkeep's quote, "My prize will paint me another," giving Patrick hope that a man obsessed with her art would not end her life.

Once Patrick's information had been disseminated to the family, all continued their search in one way or another. Claire and her mama pitched in, as did Devonshire, Lucy, and Lord Ashworth.

They spread no word that Charlotte was missing, the honeymoon faradiddle holding sway. Patrick and Rhys agreed that were her disappearance known, chaos and possible harm to Charlotte could be the result.

"After yesterday's visit to Dartmouth," Patrick told the gathering. "We must again review the guest and server list from the musicale. If Charlotte's kidnapper is indeed the painting's thief and Lady Eloise's killer, the perpetrator will be on those lists."

"Shall we give the staff list to Billy?" Rose said. "I shall ring for him."

"Billy Broad?" Patrick said turning to Rhys.

"The man has become invaluable as head of my..." Rhys turned to Rose. "What exactly *do* we call his position?"

Rose shot him an amused glance. "The head of your guards, perhaps?"

Rhys huffed. "We do not have guards."

"Then what would you call all those former soldiers who roam the estate with firearms?" A smile trembled on Rose's lips.

Rhys opened his mouth, then clamped it shut. "Billy is an excellent choice, Rosie."

Billy arrived, and Rhys produced Devonshire's two lists, giving the staff's to Billy. Their group sat around the dining table, each person taking a page. Given the one-hundred-plus guests, there were many pages, with each writing their candidates on the paper in the center of table.

"What about Admiral Saumarez," Susannah said. "The man has little love for you."

Patrick shook his head. "No interest in art whatsoever. His predilections run more to fleshy pursuits."

"Patrick!" Rose said.

He grinned. "It is the truth, Rose."

"Cardingcom should be added," Devonshire said. "He is an admirer of Pheland's work."

"St. Michaels is too," Thomasina said.

"How do you know this, my lady?" Devonshire said.

She tapped a finger to her lips. "He asked me to dance the gavotte."

"Did he?" Patrick said, surprised. Few ever requested a dance with Sina, and he was impressed St. Michaels had done so.

Thomasina nodded. "We talked mostly of horses, but he also talked of Lord Halafair's paintings."

"Added to our list," Rhys said.

"What about Lady Compton?" Devonshire said. "I have seen several of Pheland's paintings at her townhouse."

"We might as well add her ladyship," Susannah said. "Once we have gathered all the possibles, we can winnow the list down."

"A woman kidnapper?" Devonshire raised a brow.

"Why not?" Rose notched her chin.

Devonshire snorted. "Duly noted, my lady. Why not, indeed."

"Add Archway and Morrison," Patrick said.

"We must include the Countess of Oxford," Rose said.

"Byron's former lover?" Devonshire said.

"Yes," Susannah chimed in. "She is passionate about Lord Halafair's work."

"Lady Harley, as well," Rhys said. "At the musicale she begged me for an introduction to Charlotte, for, and I quote, 'I adore the girl's father's work!'"

"We now have as many women as men, or thereabouts," the duke said. "I simply cannot see a woman doing this, not to mention the doctor's mask was worn by a man who appeared to lead the kidnapping."

"I like the Earl of Home, a known art aficionado." Rose peered around the table.

Rhys shook his head. "Too fusty."

"You have a point," Devonshire said. "But let us add him in any case."

They worked through until a maid entered, asking when they wished to take dinner.

Rose glanced at the darkened sky.

"Is it night already?" Thomasina said. "We have been busy!"

"That we have, Sina," Rhys said.

Over dinner, conversation flowed around him, but Patrick could think of nothing but the names they'd gathered. Connecting Charlotte's kidnapping to Lady Eloise's murder was a key that might unravel the entire conundrum. Or mislead them entirely.

The following day, they narrowed their prospects down to five, four men and a woman—Cardingcom, Home, St. Michaels, Morrison, and Lady Harley. All lived far and wide, and their Bow Street runners would investigate each prospective kidnapper.

Two days later, the five runners returned empty-handed.

Ten more runners scoured the London shops, galleries, and purveyors of oil paints and artists' supplies. One runner learned the Earl of Home had purchased a Pheland three months earlier, while another discovered Cardingcom had ordered paints and an easel, the proprietor noting the man had recently taken up the study of oil painting. That same proprietor noted two recent shipments of art supplies, high-end ones, one to Scotland and another to Cornwall. Neither name matched those on their list, but they added them nonetheless.

Patrick tried to picture Charlotte, and though he saw her face or a gown she wore or a ride she took, he could not imagine his wife in full, as if his lady wife were but an illusion or a disembodied soul.

No word, nor even a hint reached them of Charlotte or her art.

Patrick was losing his mind one interminable day at a time.

Charlotte prepared for her escape. She donned her darkest gown, a rusty brown, pinned her hair tight, and wrapped her shawl around her, making her way to her studio as she did each day. When the clock noted five minutes to ten, she left for the kitchens, nodding to Mercy and a footman as she passed them.

The kitchen was abustle, with pots clanging, people shouting, and dogs barking, for vegetables, fruits, and other sundries were in the process of being unloaded from the purveyor's wagon. Charlotte entered the large pantry and scooped up a pear resting in a basket. She took a bite.

Nerves aflutter, her escape a long shot, but enduring one more day of imprisonment had become an impossibility.

Backed into a dark corner, she lifted her shawl over her head, covered her mouth, and bent her back, imagining an old crone, one who could not walk with ease.

Charlotte tottered from the pantry across the vast chaotic

kitchens. A tradesman bumped her, excused himself. She nodded in return and shambled outside, pressing herself against the manor's stone wall.

A few yards away sat the vendor's wagon, a man standing at the horses' heads, with the two other tradesmen hauling the goods to the kitchens. With purpose, Charlotte headed for the huge black poplar just beyond the wagon and hid behind its trunk.

Her biggest challenge would be sneaking beneath the tarpaulin as the vendor prepared to leave. She waited, nerves fraying, hands shaking so badly she had to clasp them in an iron grip.

After what felt like hours—in truth mere minutes—the two tradesmen returned to the wagon. Barrels, crates, and baskets remained in the wagon's bed, the canvas bunched to rest against the driver's seat. One of the men drew the canvas across the remaining deliveries, while the other hoisted himself into the driver's seat and took up the reins. After spreading the canvas, the second man leapt into the seat beside the driver.

The driver nodded to the man holding the horses to release them.

Charlotte's moment had come.

But Cook flew from the door, raising her fist, demanding the plums she had ordered specially for the master.

The driver yelled back, but the man beside him leapt from his seat, scrabbled around in back, and handed Cook a small basket of the missing plums. He hiked the canvas across the wagon bed once again.

Charlotte thought her heart would burst, terrified that Cook or one of the men would look toward the tree. She pressed tighter to the trunk, her eyes on the wagon.

None glanced in her direction, and Cook reentered the manor, while the tradesman hoisted himself onto the wagon seat.

Charlotte ran across shifting leaves, near tripping over a fallen branch, certain someone would stop her.

No one did, and she lifted the canvas and dove beneath, hitting her head on a barrel. She pulled in her legs but had to leave them bent, for the fit was tight. Then she straightened the tarpaulin where she'd displaced it.

She eased herself down, trying to conform to the barrels and crates, shaking with tremors. As she slid on her side, a bag of what felt like potatoes poked her belly.

With a whistle and a snap of the reins, the wagon jerked forward.

She was on her way to freedom.

Charlotte wondered if people ever died from this sort of thing, the whole process intensely terrifying. The wagon bed rocked faster, the pace picking up. No shouts or cries for a missing artist came from the manor.

She wasn't away, not truly, not yet.

Charlotte forced her muscles to relax, demanded her mind find a calm place, and she imagined Patrick, saw him smiling, his eyes warm and welcoming. She thought of Woodbine and of riding Beauty again.

Time became fluid as the miles bumped by. She was sure she would have bruises from the crate poking her shoulder. It mattered little. Her weary body muddled her mind, and she grew drowsy after days of tension.

Minutes or hours later, a shout startled her awake. Fear clamped her heart.

More shouts and the thunder of hooves. The wagon slowed and then stilled.

Tears welled, for she had failed.

Voices outside, one rising above the others, one she feared and loathed most of all.

Someone flipped back the canvas, exposing her.

"Do sit up, my lady," the monster said. "That is not a fit pose for a gentlewoman."

Charlotte did as asked, her joints stiff. At this juncture, there was no point in fighting. A guard offered her a hand down from the cart, which she took only because it would amuse her captor were she to ignore it. She tried not to imagine her punishment, but thoughts of beatings or worse peppered her mind.

Standing before the monster, hands folded before her, he peered down atop his huge bay horse.

"I tried," she said, notching her chin. "This time I failed. Perhaps the next, I shall succeed."

At her words, his hands fisted, unsettling his horse. He nodded to one of his men, and the bruiser grabbed her around her waist and flung her across his horse's saddle. She oomphed as she landed, her breath stolen, which mattered little as they pounded back to the manor at a swift canter, her head bobbing like an apple, the rider pressing down on her back. Her new objective was to catch a breath so she did not suffocate.

Once returned to the cursed manor, the bruiser dismounted and pulled her to the ground so swiftly she barely caught her balance. Charlotte leaned against the horse, clinging to its saddle until she regained her breath.

She stared at the men, six of them, who were complicit in her treatment and lack of freedom. Rough-looking creatures all, sporting guns, knives, and cruel faces. And the monster? As he neared, dressed to the nines in fine hunting regalia, she understood the poor fox's terror.

St. Michaels' hand clamped to her upper arm and she was tugged through the house to her bedroom. He shoved her inside.

She expected him to rail at her, or worse, raise a fist. He did neither but called for a man to fetch Jane.

In minutes, the little maid stood before her captor executing a curtsy.

"Hello, Jane," he said.

"Good day, your lordship."

His head whipped around to glare at Charlotte. "This is what happens when you try to leave Penrhyn Creigiog." He ripped open the bodice of Jane's dress, slithered a hand beneath the cloth, and fondled the maid's breast.

Jane gasped, her hands flying to her mouth.

"Stop it!" Charlotte said.

"Stop? Why, I have only begun. Jane, get on the floor."

If at all possible, the maid looked even more terrified, though she did as asked and lay supine on the cold floorboards. Her captor removed his coat, folding it in half, and placed it with care on the bed. He then began to unbutton the falls of his pantaloons.

"No!" Charlotte stepped toward him in hopes of preventing Jane's rape. "Do not!"

A ruffian clamped harsh hands around her upper arms and pulled her back.

"Will you try to escape again?" her captor said.

Charlotte stared at the stark choice before her. She must escape, must leave this place. Yet how could she allow the girl Jane to be raped?

"I will not, my lord."

"Do you swear?"

"I *do* swear." No vows given under duress would chain her, for he was a villain of the first order.

He paused in undoing his buttons and offered her one of his fatuous smiles. "Sadly, I do not believe you, and I am of a mind to taste this bit of muslin spread before us." He freed another button. "Would you care to watch?"

His falls' placket fell away, and he dropped to his knees, straddling Jane, the girl lying as if a frozen statue. "What do you think, Jane, shall Lady Hawthorne watch our sport?"

Jane's eyes were pools of hot fear, and she neither moved nor answered.

Her captor turned his head to peer up at Charlotte. "Unlike your husband, with his limp legs and even limper prick, I shall illustrate how a real man performs."

Charlotte fled the room.

Mid-morning, Patrick wheeled into the family drawing room somewhat muzzy, but they had received word a Bow Street Runner was on his way with news. He was the first to arrive, surprising, given his dearest desire was to sleep. Leave it to Banby to rouse him from beautiful dreams of his Lottie.

Two *damned* weeks since Charlotte had gone missing, her loss consuming him, and he poured himself a scotch.

To date, the runners had turned up nothing, not a word, nor a hint of Charlotte's location other than Home's purchase of a Pheland, and Scotland and Cornwall as possible locales. Flimsy, at best.

He pulled a deck of cards from a side table drawer and began to shuffle. Anything to halt his mind's whirlpool of thoughts, his feelings of helplessness unassuaged. He had written friends in Cornwall and Scotland inquiring about artists, painters, and collectors of Pheland's work, ridden again to Dartmouth, and even scoured the countryside and local villages for any hint of her whereabouts. All for naught.

All the while, Patrick forced himself to exercise daily on Diablo, while both Banby and Henry badgered him to eat. He had sat before his model ship, but unable to focus on the delicate project, had abandoned it.

Patrick would have remained in bed, stewing in his juices of failure and inadequacy. But he would *not* surrender to those feelings of hopelessness, reminiscent of when he was first injured.

Rhys breezed into the room, poured a glass of water from the tray, and offered him one, pointedly staring at the scotch glass in his hand.

Good thing his brother hadn't commented on the early hour. That surely would have set him off. "No, thank you."

Rhys thumped down on the sofa beside Patrick's chair with a glower. Thomasina arrived, all smiles, and gave them kisses on their cheeks.

"You should not, Patrick." Thomasina stared at his scotch whilst wagging a finger.

Christ, was everyone a parent these days? He scowled.

Unaffected, Sina poured herself a cup of tea, asking if either wished for one. They declined, and she added milk and honey, then waved Rhys to move aside and sat in his place.

"It is ten in the morning," she said to Patrick. "Are you drunk?"

He sat straighter. "Of course not."

Rhys snorted. "You are well on your way, brother."

Both Rhys and Thomasina stared at him with imploring eyes, like he had hurt her feelings.

Goddammit!

Rhys, always high-handed, he could ignore. Who was *he* to dictate? But Sina...Patrick's will crumbled.

He put the scotch aside and lifted the glass of water Rhys had poured. "No whisky before four p.m. How is that, my Lady Thomasina?" He smiled. She was petite and sweet, yet a powerful force within their family.

She snapped him a nod. "Would you not prefer some tea, Patrick?"

"In truth, I would," he said, setting the glass aside. He took her hand and cupped it to his cheek. "Thank you, love."

The rest of the family trickled in, all of them wan from sleepless nights and long, maddening days. Charlotte's kidnapping had taken a toll on all Woodbine's residents, including the staff, for she was a favorite of theirs.

Charlotte. *Charlotte,* where are you? His affection for her was boundless. Nay, not affection, but love. Why was it now simple to admit he loved his wife, for he had never shared those sentiments with her? He was a cad. A fool. What matter if he took an early drink...or three?

His tongue could near taste the smokey spirits, recalling how a sip eased his nerves and propelled him to oblivion. So very appealing.

He sampled his tea. Nay. He would hold to his word.

Devonshire arrived, and the chatter increased. Patrick leaned back, thoughts of Charlotte keeping him company. To sleep beside her again...

A songbird trilled on the maple just outside the French doors, sweet and merry.

Patrick would give all his wealth and all his remaining health to sleep beside his wife once again. To see her lips tip into a smile and her eyes warm. To hear that little gasp when she found something interesting, but slightly embarrassing too. God's blood, he could almost feel her gentle fingers brush his errant forelock back from his face. That morning, he had come across her toothbrush. It nearly made him weep.

Emotion roiled through him, a sorrow so deep, he turned away from the others.

The door opened, the butler announcing the runner, who strode into the room wearing the uniform of the Horse Patrol, black top boots, pantaloons, and jacket above their signature red waistcoat, hence their Red Robin nickname. The man's white-gloved hands held a package, perhaps a painting, for it had that same shape.

All went silent and they turned as one toward the runner.

TWENTY-ONE

"Greetings, Mr. Jennings," Rhys said. "Do have a seat and tell us your news."

The wiry man perched on the farthest chair, then tugged at his neckcloth. When he remained silent, Thomasina spoke, "Would you care for some tea, sir?"

"Why, I would, my lady." The runner nodded. "And I thank you."

Sina arranged a plate with treats, handing it to the man, then poured his tea.

"Sugar?" she said.

"Pardon?" Jennings said.

Thomasina's speech often challenged those unfamiliar with her, for her words tended to be muffled and imprecise.

"Would you like sugar?" Susannah repeated. "Or cream, perhaps?"

"I will take it plain, and I thank you," Jennings said.

Patrick leaned forward, caging his agitation so as not to bark at the man. "Have you news for us, Mr. Jennings?"

Jennings set aside his tea and lifted the package, unwrapping it with swift, precise movements. He held up a painting of a fox hunt with Reginald Pheland's signature in the lower right corner.

"I saw this advertised at an auction. You told me to be on the lookout, and so I was. I bought the painting. A mighty sum, I would add, but you gave me enough blunt, and I had a feeling. I listen to my gut, you see."

Patrick's nerves twitched as he perused the work, one he had never seen before. He looked swiftly away, for it hurt to imagine his wife being forced to paint. He prayed the coercion did not sour her for the art she so loved.

The painting was recent—a fox being ripped apart by hounds while eager riders observed the carnage. How Lottie must have loathed executing this work.

Jennings leaned forward, elbows on knees, to stare at Patrick. "Tell me, your lordship, was my gut correct?"

Patrick's body felt the flush of adrenaline, of battle readiness that focused his mind to pristine clarity.

This painting was proof Charlotte lived.

The family believed her kidnapper was forcing her to paint, for she would never execute a painting such as this of her own volition. This work confirmed that supposition. Her abductor must need money to sell the fox hunt. Could that be the singular reason for her kidnapping? Bizarre, for there were far less circuitous ways to acquire funds. Which left Charlotte, the woman, a beautiful one. Did he want her as his muse? As his...Patrick shied away from such thoughts.

"Would you excuse us for a moment, Mr. Jennings?" Rhys said.

The runner moved to the hall and closed the door.

"Charlotte obviously painted that," Rose said, pointing to the artwork.

"Not voluntarily," Patrick said, gut churning. "This fox hunt is bloodier than the previous one."

Susannah peered at the painting. "Lottie said her father had a fondness for canids of all kinds. I agree with Rose and Patrick."

They asked Jennings to rejoin them and handed him another cup of tea.

"You did well, Jennings," Patrick said. "Very well indeed. We need the details of the auction and, most importantly, knowledge of who sold the painting."

The grizzled man frowned, nodding. "I've got the former, but could not discover the painting's owner. I wheedled a list from the auction house of all the attendees—your coins again proved handy, Lord Ravenscroft. They claim the owner unknown as a factor handled the sale."

"The factor must know," Rhys said.

Jennings raised a finger. "I did check on that. A fake, my lord." He handed Patrick a slip of paper with thirty or so names from the auction.

"Some of these folks never bid on a thing." The runner pointed to the paper. "I expect one a them might be the seller, so I put a check-mark beside their names."

"Good," Rhys said. "Anything else to report?"

The runner raised a brow. "Afraid not." He bit down on a cucumber sandwich and chewed with deliberation.

Once the runner left, they repaired to the dining room, placing Jennings' list in the center of the table, while a footman brought pens, sand, and ink.

"Let us crosscheck this with our master list of suspects," Patrick said.

They passed the list from person to person, examining both bidders and observers. By the time it reached Patrick, several names were crossed out, with ten remaining, eight from the non-bidders list and two from the bidders.

"Why is Lord Home crossed out?" Patrick asked.

Thomasina shook her head. "He bought End Game from us to use as a carriage horse."

As if that explained everything. Sina's oft-circuitous route to a conclusion tested his patience. "Do continue, Sina."

She stared at him, wide-eyed. "Why?"

"Because I do not understand," Patrick said. "The purchase of a horse is not reason enough to discount Lord Home."

Sina slapped her forehead. "I know that, silly. When he bought the horse, he looked at Strider, too."

"And...?" Patrick said.

"I said Strider was especially good over the fences during a hunt," Thomasina said. "Then Lord Home said that he hated fox hunting in the funny accent of his. I do not think a man who hates fox hunting would ask our Charlotte to paint a picture like this one."

Patrick chuckled to himself for his sister's reasoning, which as usual, saw the truth of the matter.

"You make perfect sense, Sina," he said.

His remaining siblings explained their reasons for eliminating names as well, which left four from the auction—Cardingcom, St. Michaels, Morrison, and Lady Harley.

"Interesting to note," Patrick said. "These three—Morrison, St. Michaels, and Cardingcom—danced with Lottie at the musicale. Though that may mean nothing."

"Everything is worth noting, Patrick," Rose said.

Rhys' face stiffened, his lips harsh lines. "Let us highlight these three, as well as Lady Harley. We may come across another fact that points to one of them."

Rose nodded. "Though we must not discount the others completely."

Patrick's thoughts crackled, as when commanding a ship before battle, ideas clicking in quick spurts until he reached a conclusion.

He leaned forward. "We will send the runners to investigate each person's primary seat, as well as exploring other possible prospects."

"But as Rose remarked," Susannah said. "We cannot ignore other potentials."

"True." Patrick held up a hand. "Along with our search, we shall also take the initiative and hold an auction ourselves."

"Ah, Patrick." Rhys chuckled softly. "Clever. You think auctioning a Pheland painting will smoke out the perpetrator, correct?"

Patrick nodded. "Given the murder and theft at Devonshire's, along with the runner's painting, our kidnapper seems excessively enamored of Lord Halafair's work. As the fake Lord Elias Archer, the kidnapper tried to purchase a Pheland fox hunt. He failed. Now, Charlotte has painted another. Compelled? I assume so."

Patrick continued, "Pheland's work is the fulcrum on which all turns. I propose we auction a unique work of Pheland's, one perhaps never seen in public? Lady Fielding and Lady Claire can help and they must be prominent at the auction, as well. We can invite all the many potentials on our lists, keeping close watch on those we have particularly singled out."

"Yes," Susannah said. "Which painting we can use? One of Woodbine's Phelands would be too obvious."

Everyone talked at once. He was not alone in being driven batty by inaction. Patrick pulled out his brightest hope. "Years ago, I visited Halafair Hall and I recall a singular painting hanging over the estate's primary mantle—*Halafair*."

"I have seen it and noted Lady Bea's love of it," Rose said. "An exceptional lure."

"I agree, Rosie," Rhys said. "One of a kind."

"But will Lady Bea part with it?" Devonshire said.

Rose smoothed a hand across her expanding belly. "Her ladyship would relinquish the manor itself to rescue her child."

"I agree," Rhys said.

Patrick nodded. "But as you question, so might the bidders. We must craft a powerful reason for her selling it."

Thomasina chimed in. "Remember when we gave Far Flung to the Foundling Hospital?"

"A donation for a charitable auction," Patrick said, waving a hand. "Of course. The recipient must be one with that makes sense for Lady Bea to gift her precious painting. If our reasoning is correct, out lure will be irresistible to the kidnapper."

Rhys' fist slammed the table. "I think it is damned brilliant. Offering an unseen Pheland painting is a fine scheme."

"We should include a sketch of the painting on the invitation." Susannah turned to Thomasina. "Once you see the painting, do you think you can sketch it?"

Sina's eyes brightened. "I can."

"Excellent!" Patrick said, bussing Sina's cheek.

Rose squeezed her eyes tight. "My fear is filling me with doubts. What if the kidnapper fails to attend? Or sees the ruse? Or sends another to act for him, one we will not recognize."

"I doubt he will send another." Rhys clasped Rose's hand. "For he will wish to see this unique original himself."

"We shall rescue our Lottie!" Thomasina said.

"And catch the villain." Devonshire's grin was maniacal.

Patrick tapped the chair arms. "I shall go through Lottie's papers. She must have notes on her network of Pheland collectors."

"It shall be a glittering affair," Susannah said, jotting notes. "Extra staff will be needed, as we will host many attendees overnight."

"The staff must be carefully vetted," Rhys said. "Shall we set Banby to the task?"

All agreed.

"What of Billy Broad's staff list?" Patrick said.

"He is taking great care," Rose said. "So far, his search has found no servant from the musicale as a potential perpetrator."

"I have heard not a word of Lady Hawthorne's disappearance." Devonshire said.

"Word as yet has not gotten out," Patrick answered.

"Then would *she* not be at this prestigious auction?" Devonshire frowned.

"Oh, that is easy!" Thomasina said with a bright smile. "The auction would upset our Lottie. She would be too overcome to watch her father's favorite painting sold."

"As always, Thomasina," Patrick said. "You have the right of it."

A few days after Charlotte's aborted escape, she was working on yet a third fox hunt painting. Though she had been given the run of the manor house once again, now a ruffian cradling a gun trailed her everywhere. Maggot pies all. Each evening, the monster posted a guard outside her door, but he had yet to insist one sleep in her room. Thank all the stars in heaven.

Charlotte stilled, hands and brushes dabbed with paint. Everything she had done since arriving at this dreadful place was out of fear. Fear he would hit her. Fear he would hurt those she loved. Fear he would...She'd best not think about that.

Rose, for much of her life, had been in constant fear. Charlotte suspected the reason but had never asked. Her sister had overcome her fear and taken charge.

Charlotte must do the same. How?

The man's madness was subtle, unnerving. Perhaps she might begin to act crazy, too?

No. That would prove difficult to sustain. Charlotte was sure she would slip up.

Who could she emulate? Who did she know who was different, exceptional?

Ah. Charlotte didn't laugh aloud, but she wished to. Her Grace, the Duke of Devonshire's mother, came to mind. Devonshire was the most amiable of fellows, a good friend. The few times she had met his mother, the duchess was haughty, a high stickler, one who oft looked down her nose at others. Charlotte was never sure if it was because she disdained them or that was her perpetual expression. Either way, the duchess was perfect.

In future, when she was in the monster's company or walked the halls, she would assume the demeanor of Her Grace of Devonshire. Perhaps that would bolster her mental fortitude to devise a new plan of escape. In fact, her captor's reactions might be entertaining.

Charlotte cleaned her brushes and hands and left her studio for the kitchens, planning to hide food in her room for when she fled.

The place was bustling as it always was when her captor was in residence, and she maneuvered around bodies, eyeing a mound of sweet tarts perched on a shelf. As she walked past the pantry, Jane's laughing voice floated to her ears. Charlotte paused.

"It all were pretty funny," Jane said, giggling further.

"I do not see how." The second voice was Mercy's, the maid she very much liked for her gentle demeanor.

"Her ladyship," Jane said on a chortle. "She thought the master were doing the naughty against me will. She were horrified!"

"As well she should be," Mercy replied with indignation.

"Naw. It were all play acting. Hisself and me has an arrangement."

"An arrangement? You don't mean..."

"A course I do," Jane said. "The master's awful fine between the sheets."

"That was a mean trick to play on her ladyship," Mercy said.

A slap. "What do you know, Mercy? She got what she deserved, tryin' to escape like that."

Charlotte's hands shook, incensed with the deception. Her heart had broken for Jane. How cruel to play a trick of that nature. How unkind, though she was glad that Jane had not been forced. But why would the girl engage in such an awful ruse? Charlotte had *wept* over Jane's fate, and to learn it was all a diabolical prank made her ill.

She retrieved two tarts, wrapping them in a linen handkerchief.

"What have you there, my lady?"

Her body seized, so distracted by the girls' chatter, she had missed his approach. Charlotte turned to face the monster, donning a haughty demeanor. She sniffed. "Tarts, my lord."

He wore his physician's mask. He always wore it, and though she no longer reacted in fear, she loathed the creation near as much as she despised the man.

"I will have one if you please," the monster said.

An entire plate of them rested behind her on the shelf, yet he wished for hers. Did he never stop his awful games, his actions always intended to make her squirm? She sniffed again, peering at him through patronizing eyes. She drawled, "Of course, my lord."

Charlotte unwrapped her handkerchief and held out the tart.

He ran a finger down her cheek. "Hand one to me."

She batted her lashes, a small smirk tipping her lips. "You cannot choose? What a shame."

"What is *wrong* with you?" His spat words nearly made her smile.

"Why, nothing, good sir." She lifted a tart.

"No, the other one," he snapped.

He would touch again, and she loathed his touch. He knew it as well as she. Charlotte replaced the tart and handed him the other. As she did so, his fingers stroked hers, eyes eager for a negative reaction.

Charlotte shrugged, as if she were bored with the proceedings. "Do enjoy your tart, my lord."

She rewrapped the remaining one, pocketed it in her smock, and strode from the kitchens with her back rigid, her head held high.

Three days later, Penrhyn Creigiog was a hive of activity, like a colony of bees reacting to their queen's hissy fit. Charlotte had no sense of what was causing the hullabaloo, but something was up and she was determined to find out what.

Since overhearing Jane, she continued to work at befriending Mercy, though she couldn't say she was succeeding, the girl wary in the extreme.

Today, Charlotte cleaned up and proceeded from the studio at her "duchess" pace, measured, dignified, imperious, as if she were separate from the household, from *them*. She passed Jane in the hall, who smirked, and her perfidy still ached. Nonetheless, Charlotte's duchess decorum gave her a small sense of agency, something she needed as she was perpetually fighting her fear, anxious it would billow out and a guard or footman would view her as prey.

Passing the laundry, Mercy was pressing linens, while in the kitchens, Cook and a maid packed baskets. The monster was on the move, perhaps headed somewhere important, and she guessed for some duration.

She took a wedge of cheese and several biscuits to add to her food stash.

Once he had left, she could think of no better opportunity to flee.

On her return trip to her bedroom, Mercy passed her carrying a stack of freshly laundered shirts. The girl might not be a friend, but she had found Jane's feigned rape contemptible.

"Mercy, a moment?"

The girl's round face, red from exertion, reddened further, and she made an O of surprise, then bobbed a curtsy, the stack of shirts teetering. "How might I help you, m'lady?"

"When I went to the kitchens to get a biscuit, the place was in an uproar. You seem to be everywhere, and…I thought I might query you about what is going on?"

The girl smiled, as if pleased, then looked up and down the hall, which was empty but for paintings by Charlotte's father and forged ones by herself adorning the walls.

Mercy leaned in.

A footman rounded the end of the hall, and Charlotte jumped, Mercy startling as well.

"Mercy, what is for luncheon?" she said in a loud voice.

Mercy's eyes moved every which way, attempting to follow the footman's progress. "I 'spect it'll be cold." Mercy eyed the footman as he passed by them. "Cold meats and cheeses, m'lady."

Without a glance, the man hustled by them and disappeared down another hallway.

Mercy leaned in again. "Word has it, his lordship is going to an auction."

"Why, how exciting!"

"The master's powerful worked up about some paintin'!"

No doubt one of her father's. "Is that so? Is he traveling a great distance, I wonder."

Mercy shrugged. "Ain't no business of mine."

"No, perhaps not. But you are an important maid, are you not? One that is often asked for by those higher up. Is that not so?"

The girl flushed cherry red. "You think so?"

"I know so. I have seen you perform essential tasks." All of which was a big faradiddle, but if Mercy could discover the auction's location and how long the monster would be gone...

"You noticed?" Mercy said.

The girl was so hopeful, so innocent. Charlotte hated her manipulation, yet she must flee.

"I *did* notice." She beamed, putting as much warmth into her eyes as possible, then bent close. "Tell me, have you ever seen the master's face?"

Mercy shrugged.

"No?" Charlotte said.

"Well, once, when he got that cut on his chin and it had to be sewn."

"I see. What did he look like?"

Mercy's brow pleated. "Handsome, I suppose." She shrugged. "Like a toff, though I can't say I liked his eyes. My sweetheart has beautiful brown eyes with the longest lashes."

Her description hadn't helped much, but any information mattered. "You have a sweetheart?"

She grinned. "Jemmy's kind, too. And fit."

"How lovely. This is the most excitement the manor's seen in months! I am so curious. Do tell if you discover anything more." Charlotte pressed a finger to her lips. "It will be our secret, Mercy, yours and mine."

TWENTY-TWO

Woodbine's grand ballroom brimmed with auction attendees milling about, making it a challenge for Patrick to wheel through the throng in search of Lord Theseus Ashworth. Tomorrow's auction would be a circus.

He hoped to God their plan succeeded.

The previous day, Ladies Beatrice and Claire had arrived in a flurry accompanied by a wagon carrying the immense painting down from Halafair Hall. Lottie's mother, Lady Bea, looked wan, Charlotte's disappearance having taken its toll. Lady Claire wasn't much better, for dark circles bloomed beneath her eyes, which ironically served to enhance her exquisite beauty. Blonde-haired and amber-eyed, she stole the breath of whomever she encountered. Patrick smiled to himself. Claire was detached from the attention she received, a reserved woman who cared little for pastimes other than antique pillars, friezes, and busts, her archaeologic passions galloping unchecked. Yet he suspected a lively woman lurked beneath that retiring demeanor.

Woodbine was fit to bursting with participants come from near and far for the auction. They had set out a cold collation for the participants, one they would replicate on the morrow, as well as drinks, including fine spirits to weaken inhibitions and loosen purses.

The Duke of Devonshire was in the thick of things, helping in any way he could—the man was a saint—when he spotted Ashworth admiring the painting of Halafair Hall. The man—with expertise in antiquarian pursuits, ancient Greece, painted art and other related fields—was whom they had designated *Halafair's* winner. His purse was fat, thus all would find his win unexceptional.

Ashworth would lift the price to heady heights. After the auction's conclusion, when Lottie's kidnapper lost to Ashworth, they believed he would make his move to steal *Halafair*. They would be at the ready, prepared to catch the shit-sack who had taken Charlotte.

With *Halafair*, Reginald Pheland had outdone himself, performing magic on canvas with this, his finest work. Few had viewed it, never having been on public display, adding to the painting's allure. In truth, many of Pheland's followers were here simply to view the piece.

The kidnapper would be salivating for it, Patrick was sure, and he was eager to spring their trap.

Lady Bea designated the Devonshire Foundling Home for Boys and Girls as the intended recipient of the funds from *Halafair's* sale. Rhys' marquessate would donate the money to the foundling home, the painting returned to the family once they caught the kidnapper. Patrick hoped that soon thereafter they rescued Charlotte.

Hope was an elusive, slippery thing since his accident. Yet he had dredged up a morsel, for hope he did for his love's safe return.

Auction night, Patrick wheeled into the second ballroom to view the crowd, Woodbine's first ballroom set with many rows of chairs. Henry walked by his side like a young lordling, dressed to the nines. Patrick had requested the boy attend him on the chance Saumarez showed for the auction. He wished to know if Henry recognized the admiral and whether he had seen him on the *Despoina*.

"Are you well, barnacle?" he said.

"I am, Captain."

Henry's clenched hands spoke differently.

"We are surrounded by the men of Ravenscroft, Hawthorne, and Devonshire. No one will harm you."

The boy nodded.

The place was near to bursting, the drink flowing fast, abuzz with conversations about the auction. Patrick observed members of the *ton*, high-ranking military, and city toffs chattering away. Lady Ablethorp, in a glaring puce gown gabbed in a corner. Were she not invited, the Lansdownes would fare poorly in the press.

Many in the crowd intended to bid, while others were curiosity seekers, *Halafair's* fame far-reaching due to its rarity. Tonight was an opportunity for Pheland devotees to view and possibly acquire a unique piece of art.

Devonshire furthered the crowd's excitement with his presence and enthusiasm. Ashworth stood beside him wearing his usual somber black, which contrasted with the plumage worn by other attendees, blindingly so to Patrick's way of thinking. Purples and puces, scarlets and golds, and virulent blues and greens were the order of the day, much like Percy, their particolored parrot. Pray God he did not fly into the ballroom during the auction.

A shocking thought, and he wheeled to Thomasina who stood with Rose, Susannah, and Claire.

"Is Percy locked up?" he said, though he hadn't meant it to come out a growl.

Thomasina giggled. "Of course, silly. Though I do not see why he cannot attend!"

He was about to respond when Sina winked, his chuckle making her smile. Patrick checked his timepiece. Ten minutes. The proceedings would begin with much fanfare, and he searched for the men who had partnered with Charlotte at the ball, possible kidnappers all.

He spotted Sir Alex Morrison first, who had dandified himself up by wearing a purple waistcoat, but was outshone by Lord Carding-com, a true dandy who wore pink satin knee breeches, clocked stockings, and a bright green embroidered waistcoat. In a far corner, the third man, Lord St. Michaels wore understated black and white as he spoke to another attendee. Near each stood a Bow Street Runner wearing finery to blend with the crowd. Minutes later, Patrick caught sight of Captain Lord Archway, Charlotte's fourth dancing partner. He leaned against a pillar sporting his formal military dress, another runner hovering close.

All four had come, as had Lady Harley, their fifth possible suspect, dressed in an elegant black gown with silver piping. Patrick was pleased.

A tap on his shoulder to find Rose standing before him looking beautiful and worried.

"Are all five here?" Rose queried.

"They are," Patrick said. "As well as many others from our lists. Now, let us pray that our ruse succeeds and we discover the kidnapper."

The doors to the ballroom swung wide, and Rose and Henry accompanied him when he wheeled inside amongst the other attendees. He mounted a ramp and moved across the small stage to Lady Bea, who had forbidden the family to call her Lady Fielding. Understandable, considering her late and unlamented husband had tried to rape and kill her. Lady Bea would be principal in the opening ceremonies.

She, too, had dressed to the nines. Still a beautiful woman, Charlotte's disappearance had aged her. Now she seemed a composed ice princess about to address her subjects.

Patrick clasped Lady Bea's cold hands in his. "My lady, this will succeed. We shall win the night and bring Lottie home."

Her haunted eyes darted around the crowd, then back to him. "I dearly hope so, Patrick, as we have orchestrated a powerful lure." Her eyes hardened as she sucked in a breath, spine stiffening. "Nearly three weeks, and not a word. Tonight, we must succeed."

"We shall." Patrick kissed the backs of her hands, then wheeled down to the ballroom floor. As he moved, Henry beside him, he greeted friends and acquaintances until he narrowed his eyes, stiffening. Saumarez had come. Arsehole.

He turned to Henry and whispered, "Do you see that man wearing a naval uniform standing next to a young woman in a peach gown?"

"I see him, Captain," Henry said, his voice wavering.

"Do you recognize him?"

"He's too far away, sir."

Patrick wheeled closer, but still too distant for Saumarez to take note. Henry's eyes widened, and then he leaned close.

"I saw him, Captain!" the boy whispered. "He wasn't wearing his uniform, but regular nob's clothes. It was at night, but there were plenty a torches when he boarded the *Despoina*. He talked a long while to the captain and first mate. They were drinking rum and laughing, having a fine time as the slaves were loaded aboard."

Patrick's breath caught, his fury sparked.

Which was when Saumarez looked directly at them, his face transforming to one of disdain.

Blinded by fury, Patrick shoved the wheels of his chair toward the admiral.

Hands gripped his chair, halting him.

"Stop, Captain. *Please.*"

"Let go, Henry."

"No, sir. I will not. Look, you don't want to be makin' a fuss about this now. Not now. Tonight's for Lady Charlotte."

Charlotte. He inhaled a breath, whooshing it out, taking a few more. "You are right, Henry. I thank you."

Fury dampened, Henry beside him, Patrick moved to his designated spot, with its line-of-sight on the five possible kidnappers.

Let the party begin.

Having befriended Mercy with no small amount of guilt, Charlotte began to hide a sheet every other day or so in the bottom of her wardrobe, stuffed in a corner. Mercy, perhaps sensing her plan, now carried extra when she changed Charlotte's bed and bath linens.

Though her captor was not in residence, Charlotte continued to paint—it would do no good for the staff or guards to sense her plan to escape. Late at night, a pale candle her only light, she would remove the hidden linens and craft her knots the way Rose had shown her.

More than a year ago, Rose had escaped from her childhood home using just such an invention. Though her rope required much fabric, Charlotte placed her knots relatively close together, for Rose had explained how her feet should rest on each one to make her descent easier.

Rose also said to affect an escape by rope, she must also strengthen her upper body and arms, which would see her to the rope's end in one piece. To build her muscles and endurance, Charlotte's daily walks became more brisk. She also practiced the few *kalari* martial art forms taught to her by Lucy, which created a circulating flow of breath, movement, and energy.

Charlotte's moves were not very skilled, but she performed *kalari dand* well enough. She lay prone on the floor, legs stretched out, arms bent beside her, and pushed up on her hands and toes. She lowered herself again, then thrust her upper body up on her hands, like a snake rearing, until her elbows were nearly straight. At first, she could barely complete a single *kalari dand*. Now, after practicing daily, she could accomplish twenty in a row. Each day, she strived to do more.

Focusing on her goal to escape, time flew, and she must leave before her captor's return.

From his position, Henry alongside, Patrick studied the audience as Rhys and Lady Bea walked onstage, the crowd's volume rising with anticipatory excitement.

When Rhys stepped to the podium, the room quieted. "Greetings all and welcome to Woodbine!"

One fellow started to clap and soon the assemblage joined in. Patrick's eyes darted between the possible perpetrators.

The room quieted, and Rhys threw back the linen covering *Halafair* with a dramatic flourish. Oohs and ahhs ensued.

The unveiling was perfunctory, given guests could view the painting prior to the auction.

Rhys nodded, first to Lady Bea, then to the crowd. "Let the auction begin!"

They'd hired a Christie's auctioneer, and the middle-aged man dressed in evening attire stepped to the podium and opened the bidding.

Patrick expected the night to be a long one. Yet within fifteen minutes, the bidders had been culled to five—Sir Alex Morrison, St. Michaels, Jane Harley the Countess of Oxford, Lord Ashworth, and, Saumarez, the latter's enthusiasm surprising. Nor did he miss the covert glances the admiral gave Henry. Fury at the man's deceit roiled through him, but that was for another day.

Patrick doubted the countess was the kidnapper, but anything was possible. The more likely perpetrators were St. Michaels or Morrison, the bland Morrison surprising him. Both men's wealth was said to be substantial, yet Susannah had noted an *on dit* that alleged two of St. Michaels' ships had recently been downed in the Atlantic, a costly disaster. Interesting.

The bidding grew frenzied, hands spearing the air one after another, Ashworth having no trouble matching the rapid pace.

Morrison fell away with a shake of the head, the pounds sterling reaching astronomical heights, and Patrick was near enough to see the hunger in St. Michaels' eyes. Yet he was next to fall, surrendering with a shrug.

On and on the bidding went between Lady Harley and Ashworth until the countess stormed off in a huff, giving Ashworth the win. As planned.

When the hammer boomed, Morrison's face was one of crushing defeat, Lady Harley furious as she peeked back into the room, while St. Michaels laughed.

Now came the tricky part.

Lord Theseus Ashworth had a low tolerance for fools and a high tolerance for tension, his nerves frosty as ice. Patrick knew the man little, for Ashworth kept his own counsel until he wished to arrow a point home. Then, he most often hit the matter's bullseye.

As planned, Ashworth stayed the night, as did other guests, the distance home too far to travel. A good man for this mission to trap the thief who had taken Charlotte and, they hoped, would attempt to steal *Halafair*. At two a.m., his lordship was feigning sleep, the immense covered painting on the floor, leaning against the wall.

Patrick had insisted on joining the final coup, and he sat in Ashworth's darkened dressing room, just inside the open door. Rhys was stationed in the wardrobe, poor sod, a hole having been drilled in the door so he could see.

Ashworth had left the curtains surrounding the bed open, but the moon was on the wane, casting but a pallid light across the darkened room.

Patrick's adrenaline flowed, his anticipation monstrous. Yet his nerves were battle-ready, calm masking his desperation to find Lottie.

Once they found her, he would assure her she was safe and loved, and that she would never suffer captivity again.

A crack at the door interrupted his musings.

Soon, it widened to reveal Morrison. Strange. He'd believed the man a long shot. Morrison might be bland, but he was also reputed to be an honorable man.

He tread on stockinged feet toward the painting.

Patrick expected Morrison to lift the painting, an awkward prospect given its size, and leave. Instead, he raised its linen cover, squatted, and struck a match, expelling a soft susurration of breath.

Morrison ran a hand down the painting's gilt frame.

Patrick's gut said he wasn't their man just as Ashworth sprang from the bed and Rhys bolted from the wardrobe amidst a din of shouts.

"It is not him," Patrick said, sitting in Rhys' study with Ashworth, Devonshire, and Rhys. They'd locked Morrison in a windowless room, something he had submitted to without question or argument.

"What makes you so sure?" Rhys said.

"I agree with Hawthorne," Ashworth said. "Morrison has not the heart for thieving."

Devonshire lifted his snifter, sipping his brandy. "All well and good. But that gives us no certainty that he is not Lady Hawthorne's kidnapper."

"Has the runner been dispatched to Morrison's seat?" Patrick said

"On his way," Rhys said. "It is not terribly far and he should be back by mid-morning."

"She could be anywhere," Devonshire said. "For Morrison also has estates in Scotland and Wales. Where is the painting?"

"Locked in Charlotte's studio," Rhys said. "Two footmen accompanied the painting and stand by the door, a third within the room itself."

"What of Lady Harley and St. Michaels?" Patrick said.

"Each is resting in their room," Rhys said. "I have put a watchful eye on both, as well as the other overnight guests, posting footmen beside the doors and in the halls on the off chance that an attendee we failed to focus on, is Charlotte's actual kidnapper."

"A wise move." Patrick scrubbed his face, weary. Hours were ticking by, and he feared their scheme had failed. Perhaps *none* of the attendees had kidnapped Charlotte. If so, they must begin their search anew.

Now they must wait until the runner returned from Morrison's estate, inaction making him restless.

Morning came early, the sun blessing them with a cloudless day. Patrick had slept like the dead, but his restless mind insisted he rise to greet the day, for good or for ill.

He slid into his chair, relieved himself, and wheeled to the window overlooking the drive. One of the myriad carriages was leaving Woodbine at a rather smart clip.

His bedroom door was flung open by Rhys, wearing but pantaloons, Hessians, and a billowing shirt. He charged inside.

"The guards before Charlotte's studio were rendered unconscious," Rhys said. "The one within, coshed on the head. You heard nothing?"

Patrick shook his head. "I slept soundly. Obviously, too soundly. Who?"

Rhys grimaced. "No idea, but *Halafair* is gone."

Charlotte sat in the tattered wing chair and sucked in a large breath, hands fisted. The room was cleaned daily, but it remained musty from the incessant rain, the atmosphere cloying. It was three in the morning, the castle silent but for the howling wind, its moans only serving to increase her apprehension.

Soon, she told herself.

Her hands trembled from fear or exhaustion she was unsure. Her captor was still off gallivanting, her rope knotted and ready for her descent, Charlotte having tied and checked the final knots.

Two nights hence, there would be no moon. That would be her chance. When the time came, she prayed for little wind. Shimmying down the rope in a gale would batter her against the unforgiving stone walls.

She could make two more days. She must.

Charlotte pushed from the chair and stowed the rope in the wardrobe. Unable to help herself, she stole to the window and unlatched the casement, peering down into the abyss.

Impossible.

How would she find the courage to toss the rope out the window? How could she crawl downward into *nothingness* on a strip of linen?

She rushed to the wardrobe to check the split skirt she'd fashioned with scissors and thread Mercy had acquired for her. She found it, the fabric cool between her fingers. Back at the window, she planned to hitch herself onto the sill, and...

No.

There must be a better way. Of course there must be. She would find it.

Charlotte closed the window, padded across the room, and slipped beneath the covers. She lay on her back, attuned to the slightest sensation. The tick of the clock. The rattle of the windows. The scent of her snuffed candle.

If Patrick were here, she would find her courage, her longing to touch him once again near overwhelming.

She traced his face on the sheet beside her—his strong cheekbones, his mobile lips, that devilish grin. Especially the grin. The way his eyes warmed when he spotted her. How they drew her in until the world fell away and there was nothing but Patrick.

She smoothed her hand across the cool linen and tried to sleep.

Charlotte awakened not to a sound, but a sense, that of oppression. Opening her eyes, that hideous mask stared down at her, the monster's lips smiling.

"You are awake." His tone was everyday, as if he were asking the time.

She tried to clear her muzzy mind, a bit of moonlight casting patterns on the wood floor.

He had lit a candle, and his teeth gleamed bright as he leaned close, a forearm on either side of her head.

"I am biding my time, fair maiden."

"I am no maiden," she blurted out, though he wasn't wrong. "But a married woman."

He brushed a hand across her braid. "You are the culmination of Reginald Pheland's brilliant work."

His chest pressed against hers, a boulder seeking to suffocate. No *kalari* move could save her in this position. She turned her head away, thinking of biting his wrist. That would only spark his ire.

"I shall soon return with that which is most precious. Then, we shall marry."

He was back at it again. Ridiculous.

"My anticipation is delicious." He grinned and poked her cheek with the mask's nose, then leaned close, closer still, jamming his lips against hers in a wet, disgusting kiss.

Charlotte clamped her teeth tight to prevent invasion and just as bile surged up her throat, he lifted off her and stood.

"Until my return, fair lady."

CHAPTER
TWENTY-THREE

"Morrison is out," Patrick said. "As is Cardingcom, who returned to London once he dropped from the bidding, according to the runner assigned to him." He watched Rhys pace circles in the morning room, hands clasped behind him.

Though scotch appealed, Patrick took another sip of tea. His brother looked awful, complexion pasty, fresh lines scoring his brow, hair mussed. Patrick suspected he appeared the same, for the loss of Charlotte and their subsequent hunt had taken much out of them.

"Archway, too," Rhys said. "For he did the same as Cardingcom."

Rose trundled in, though it was but eight in the morning, looking daisy-fresh, hand resting on her pregnant belly.

"I wondered where you had gone, my lord." She walked to her husband and bussed his cheek.

He wrapped his arms around her and tugged her onto his lap. "The painting is gone, the guards knocked out, though thankfully none dead."

"No!"

"Shall we focus on St. Michaels?" Patrick said.

Rhys sighed. "We cannot discount Lady Harley."

"I agree." Patrick's back had begun a small tattoo of pain. Familiar and unwelcome.

"I cannot see it," Rose said. "We chatted before the auction and Lady Harley babbled on about 'the cursed married colonel,' her words, and his inappropriate attentions to her daughter. Her ladyship returned from the continent particularly for the auction and planned to hasten back to Italy once it concluded. With so much on her mind, I fail to see her perpetrating such a theft."

"A cogent point, Rosie," Rhys said.

"That could all be a smokescreen, sister," Patrick said. "I like St. Michaels for it. Either way, the thief had help, help within Woodbine."

Rose's eyes widened, then narrowed. "We have a spy."

"Or two!" Rhys said. "Though I am loathe to admit such, I see no other possibility. Given the guards, the thievery could not have been committed by a single person. Yet St. Michaels and Lady Harley remained in their rooms through the night. Who at Woodbine would betray us so? It is hard to imagine. Most of our retainers have been with us for a decade or more, many brought over from Ravenscroft by our father."

"I hate imagining our loyal staff was involved." Rose slipped from Rhys' lap, made herself a cup of tea, and eased into the burgundy leather chair. "Perhaps another bidder assisted?"

"None of the overnight guests left their rooms."

"A recent hire, then," Rose said.

"We cannot be sure of that," Patrick said, as a maid entered with a fresh tray of tea and coffee, that bitter brew Rhys so enjoyed. He recalled the maid's name as Elodie? No. "Thank you, Elowen."

They remained silent until her departure, Rose serving them tea and taking a slice of honey cake for herself.

"Much as I loathe saying this," Rose said, "our staff are the most likely prospects for the theft. Let us make note of the newest members."

Rhys barked a laugh. "That will be a short list, Rosie."

"Which makes it all the easier, do you not think?" She winked.

"Shall we gather the others?" Patrick said.

"Let them sleep," Rhys said. "Plenty of time to bring them into the discussion." He retrieved a pen, ink, sand, and paper and handed them to Rose. "You have the most experience with the household staff, Rosie."

"The conspirators may not be of the household," Patrick said. "But rather the stables, the coachmen, our woodworkers, any of them."

Patrick and Rhys gathered more writing materials and began their lists.

"Not the handymen nor the woodworkers," Rhys said. "All have been with us ten years or more."

"What of Jonesy?" Pain speared up Patrick's back, and he forced himself not to grimace. His discomfort had increased each day of Charlotte's absence, a fitting reward for losing his wife. "I should have gone with Lottie to deliver that cursed painting."

"Should you?" Rose said. "As I recall, you were unwell."

"If I had been there—"

"What fustian," she said. "Instead of Banby, you would have been rendered unconscious or worse."

He scraped his hands across his face. "Charlotte's absence is driving me to madness."

Rose approached and kneeled, cupping his cheek with a hand. "Remember that Lottie is resilient and strong, not one to give up. We *will* find her, Patrick."

He was mortified to have Rose kneeling before him. "Get up, Rose, do."

She stood, graceful as a swan even carrying a babe.

"You are a good woman, Rosie." He chuckled. "Though at times a pain in my arse!"

"As you are in mine, my lord!" She laughed as well, which eased the tension between the three of them. "Shall we get to work?"

An hour later, they reconvened, the others still abed. Rose took her same seat as Patrick entered with Rhys. Patrick had spoken to Grimes, Arjuna, and Spider, all three intensely loyal. Grimes had raised Thomasina after Patrick's father had removed her from Ravenscroft due to her "differences." Arjuna was engaged to the devoted Lucy and Spider best friends with Henry.

Woodbine's steward, housekeeper, cook, and butler had served the Lansdowne family for more than a decade, the same as the head gardener.

Rhys blew out a breath, then presented a paper. "I have but two names—Jonesy, a coachman, and Cadan, an assistant gamekeeper. Both hired within that past year."

"I came up with none," Patrick said. "Both Arjuna and Grimes vetted the stable hires and none have been brought on this past year."

They looked to Rosamund.

"We hired housemaids Elowen and Hermione within the year, Elowen from Cornwall and Hermione from East Riding."

"I believe St. Michaels has an estate in Yorkshire," Rhys said. "Does he own others?"

Neither Patrick nor Rose knew.

"We will bring in all four," Patrick said. "And bludgeon them until they speak."

Rhys raised a brow. "Brother?"

Patrick uttered a soft laugh. "If only...We should question them individually, with Rhys and I speaking to Jonesy and Cadan, while Rose talks to the maids."

"Do we know their origins?" Patrick said.

"Elowen is Cornish," Rose said.

"Jonesy served with me on the Peninsula," Rhys said. "I doubt he is our man."

"We shall see what we shall see and pray for a positive outcome." Patrick again wished for a drink. A stiff one.

Rose bathed and changed, then joined Patrick and Rhys in the morning room, her eyes feeling like papered sand, her mouth a desert. She poured another cup of tea, then buttered a slice of toast as the rest of their family and friends trickled in. Claire and Lady Bea, Susannah and Thomasina, Devonshire, Banby, and Ashworth took seats at the table until the room was fit to bursting. A subdued Henry finally appeared, though he said not a word. The poor boy missed Charlotte terribly.

Once all were settled and eating, Rhys detailed their thoughts on who had orchestrated the theft and rendered the three guards unconscious. They bandied about additional names but ended with those chosen earlier.

Rose would interview Hermione, and after her, Elowen in the morning room, while Thomasina and Devonshire moved to the library, researching the various estates owned by the St. Michaels and the Countess of Oxford. Rhys and Patrick peeled off for Rhys' study to question Jonesy and then Cadan, while Susannah and Ashworth would search the rooms of the potential accomplices whilst they were being interviewed.

Rose waited in the family salon for her interviews. She'd swear the sprog, sensing her high emotions, was dancing the gavotte in her belly.

A soft tap at the door.

"Come in," Rose said.

Hermione entered, a pretty girl with a tip-tilted nose and canny brown eyes. Rose recalled hiring her, for she'd replaced another maid who'd left precipitously. Earlier, Rose suggested Lucy query the staff on why the original maid had quit her post.

"Hello, Hermione." Rose gestured to a chair opposite hers.

The girl, who couldn't be more than eighteen, sat at the very edge of her seat, though she appeared composed for a servant talking with Woodbine's mistress.

"You have been with us for six months," Rose said. "Which is when I always like to have a chat." A Canterbury tale.

"I see, m'lady."

"Do you like it here at Woodbine?" Rose asked, knowing her response would be positive.

Hermione smiled, transforming her face from pretty to beautiful. "I do."

That smile...Perhaps the girl was older than eighteen. Twenty? "I am aware you and Elowen entered Lady Hawthorne's studio, did you not?"

The girl lowered her eyes, but not before Rose caught a flash of anger. "I wanted to see the paintin'. Elowen did, too. I am sorry."

"You shall not enter a room that is forbidden again."

Hermione nodded.

"You hail from East Riding, do you not?" Rose said.

"I do."

The girl sat perfectly still and composed, which tweaked Rose's gut. Where were the nerves? "How did you end up here, such a distance from your home?"

"Not so far, as I were serving in Cornwall before here."

"No, that is not terribly far. Where did you previously serve again?" She should have noted that when she had hired the girl. Yet she had not.

"Baron Arundell of Trerice."

"Ah. I see." Again, that twinge, though the why proved elusive. "Do you wish to ask me anything about Woodbine or your employment?"

"No, m'lady. I likes it here. I truly does."

"I am glad. Thank you for your time, Hermione."

After the girl left, Rose scribbled notes while awaiting Elowen.

Elowen's copper skin alluded to Moorish or Romany heritage, and she recalled the girl saying she had been denied many positions due to her lineage.

The girl arrived and, unlike Hermione, she was jittery as a mouse before a cat.

"You have been with us for more than seven months," Rose said.

"I always try to have a chat with new staff at six, but we have been behind, what with all the goings on, you see?"

Which Elowen clearly did not. "Oh."

"How has your time been here at Woodbine?" Rose asked.

The redhead screwed up her face.

"Elowen?"

"Well, the way I sees it, all these goings on, as you called 'em, upset the household. Me, too. And..."

Rose leaned back in her chair. "And...?"

"Ya see, I prize my position here. I does. But, well..." Her busy hands worked the skirts of her dress.

Pulling teeth was easier. "Do relax, Elowen."

"Relax, m'lady? How can I relax when such doings threaten me livelihood?" Elowen pressed her lips tight.

"If you have seen something or know something untoward, please tell me."

"It ain't nothin', m'lady. Nothin' a'tall."

The remainder of Elowen's answers were one-syllable mumbles, the girl was so overset.

Admitting defeat, Rose dismissed Elowen and awaited Rhys' and Patrick's results at questioning Jonesy and Cadan.

Later that day, Patrick rolled alongside Banby, who would help him in and out of the bath. He could do it himself, but he'd made a hideous mess, water splashing everywhere. Liking it or not, he now accepted Banby's assistance. Once settled in the soothing water, he contemplated that morning's interviews, including Rose's.

Both or either maid was suspect. He and Rhys had spoken to Jonesy, a woodworker with a solid alibi—he and two others had gone to Torquay to purchase oak and pine and had only just returned to Woodbine. The coachman, Cadan, proved to be more elusive, as he was alleged to have gone to the pub the previous evening. He had not returned. A solid suspect.

Cadan hailed from Cornwall, as did Elowen, though that fact might be but circumstantial. Yet coincidences disturbed Patrick, always had, and the connection buzzed his brain like a hungry bee, for at least two perpetrators from Woodbine were involved in disabling the guards.

The bath water had chilled during his ruminations. Rather than call Banby, Patrick heaved himself to the edge of the tub, scrubbed his hair with a towel, hair that had grown considerably longer in Charlotte's absence. He wondered what she would say, or if she would comment at all.

His mind turned to Lottie at the oddest of moments, as if she were his magnetic north. He supposed she was.

Balancing on the edge of the tub with one hand, he lifted his legs with the other, swinging them out of the bath. The useless things dangled and he dried them as best he could. The way of the world now, he supposed. He slid into his chair positioned just so by Banby and wheeled to the bed where the lieutenant had laid out his clothes.

He sighed—exhausted by his infirmity, their search for Charlotte —he barely had the vigor to don his smalls.

The crystal decanter of scotch in Rhys' study glittered in his mind. A drink would be fine. Very fine.

But he had promised Thomasina, a good vow for the surcease drink offered no true relief.

"Bloody hell!" Patrick reached for his smalls.

The door flew open. "What the devil, Patrick!"

Who else but his caring brother? The man had an excessive resolve to fix everyone's ills.

"All is well!" he hollered back.

"I think not." Rhys stormed to where he sat naked in his chair. "I shall help you dress."

"No."

"Must you be so stubborn?"

He peered at Rhys' face, tight with fury. He wore that same look as a boy, and Patrick chuckled, then burst into a laugh.

"What?" Rhys said.

"Ah, you are just what I needed this morning to lighten my heart."

A brow raised. Now Rhys wore his imperious marquess expression, which only made Patrick laugh harder, clearing the cobwebs from his tangled brain to set him on his determined path once again.

They would unearth the miscreants and then they would find his Lottie.

Atop Diablo the following day, Patrick mentally reviewed Rose's notes regarding interviews with the maids. Cadan remained missing, which left him as a prime suspect, yet a house servant must have been complicit, as well. Rose wished to wait to re-interview Elowen and Hermione until that afternoon. The waiting chafed, but they had set two men, trusted former soldiers of Rhys', to keep an eye on each woman.

His thoughts went round and round, circling that which failed to fit.

"That is it!" His shout was loud enough to spark two ravens into flight. "We have got you."

Banby and Henry assisted him in dismounting and settling into his chair. He would have done it himself, but the speed of their aid allowed him to fly down the ramp, the pair running to keep up. "Gather everyone to the salon."

They appeared one by one and a more tired and sorry group he'd seldom seen. Once seated, he began to speak, only to have Devonshire and Ashworth fly into the room. He waited until they were seated.

"Hermione, Rose."

"Yes?" She leaned forward, hands clasped.

"Did she not say that while in Cornwall, she worked for Baron Arundell of Trerice?"

"That is correct," Rose said.

"There is no Baron Arundell of Trerice. The barony died out in the last century."

Everyone seemed to move at once, with Rhys in pursuit of Billy Broad, the one-armed former soldier who had been shadowing Hermione.

Patrick sat beside Rhys, whose imposing desk separated them from the maidservant, Hermione. They said nothing, allowing the tension to build until...

"Why have you brought me here, your lordship?" Hermione said, hands clasped tight.

"Do you not know?" Rhys said, brow raised.

The girl shook her head.

"We have a few questions about your previous employment, Hermione."

The girl shrugged, though she was no longer a girl, but a woman grown.

"You told Lady Ravenscroft," Rhys said, "that your previous employment in Cornwall was at Baron Arundell's estate of Trerice."

"What of it?" she said.

"Who told you to say that?" Patrick asked.

She shrugged. "Nobody. It's where I worked."

"Interesting," Rhys said. "As the barony is extinct and has been for decades. So do tell us how you worked at an extinct barony."

Hermione's face blanched.

"We believe," Patrick said, "that you aided our coachman, Cadan, to steal the painting, *Halafair*."

"I did not!" she said.

"No?" Rhys said.

The girl's belligerent eyes stared back at them.

Too much shilly-shallying. Gods, they were close to finding Lottie. "Tell us *now*."

Hermione jumped, then began to cry.

"Enough!" Patrick bellowed.

Notching her chin, eyes watery, she clamped her mouth tight.

"Where is Lady Hawthorne?" Rhys said, his voice soft, yet filled with menace.

She shrugged.

"I shall repeat myself, where is—"

The door flew open, banging against the wall, and Theseus Ashworth hauled Cadan inside, a bruise resting beneath his cheek, his lip bloodied.

"Bring that blackguard here!" Patrick barked.

"Cadan!" Hermione screeched as she leapt from the chair toward the man.

"Sit down, Hermione," Rhys said.

His brother's commanding tone planted her back in her seat.

Ashworth waited until the hubbub quieted. "Cadan here was making for Cornwall on a broken-down nag. I found him near the Cornish border." He shook his head.

No painting, Patrick surmised. The man must have handed it off to someone.

The air thickened with antipathy. Patrick wanted to pummel the man, while Rhys appeared to wish the same, rising from his seat to stalk to Cadan. The man paled.

"We gave you a home." Rhys clasped his hands behind his back. "Gave you a safe place to recover after the chaos of war."

Cadan sneered. "So what, I say."

Rhys returned to his seat. "Ashworth, take the man to the dungeons."

They had no dungeons.

"I ain't done nothin'!"

"We shall place Hermione in the next cell," Rhys said. "Then we shall throw away the keys."

Hermione's face turned mulish, though her hands shook. "You ain't got no dungeons."

"No?" Rhys smiled, but his eyes remained cold as ice. "Shall we go see? Lead the way, Lord Ashworth!" He notched his chin at the earl who dragged their former coachman out of the room.

Hermione had gone quiet, her face stolid.

Rhys resumed his seat. "Now, shall it be the dungeons or—"

"I'll tell. Yes, I will, but I don't know nothin'."

Patrick thought of a different tack. "Where is the painting now?"

Silence.

"Where is *Halafair*, Hermione?" Patrick said.

She shrugged.

"And who employed you to steal the painting?"

"A man."

Bollocks! He could strangle the girl with his bare hands. "What man?"

"If I tell, what'll ya do to me?"

Rhys smiled. Patrick was sure he'd use that same chilling smile on the French.

"We will refrain from killing you," Rhys said, tone frigid, eyes unrelenting.

His words must have struck a chord.

"Baron St. Michaels."

TWENTY-FOUR

They again met in the family drawing room, a whole host of them including Banby, whose hand threaded through his hair repeatedly resulting in spikes. All had red-rimmed eyes, shadows haunting them. Two runners awaited, ready to travel any distance in search of Charlotte.

When Rhys offered Patrick a scotch, though it was barely nine in the morning, Patrick declined. Rhys stared at the glass, then thunked it down.

When they announced the perpetrators, all were shocked to learn of St. Michaels', Cadan's, and Hermione's treachery.

"Cadan and Hermione are locked up tight," Patrick said. "Once we have found Lottie, we shall hand them over to the magistrate."

"St. Michaels' main seat is in Cheshire," Rhys said. "Is it not?"

"I believe so," Devonshire replied.

Damnation, the distance was far. On a swift horse, the rider going sleepless, it would take near twenty hours to reach St. Michaels' seat. "Have we any idea what time the painting was stolen?"

"I am afraid *when* the painting was stolen is not precisely known, for we moved it from Ashworth's room to Charlotte's studio around three a.m. It could have been taken any time after that!"

Tears filled Lady Claire's eyes, and she sniffled into her kerchief, then walked to the French doors to face the gloomy day outside. Lady Bea remained in her room, overset by the situation.

Patrick knew Charlotte's mother but little, though he saw her as a brave and stalwart woman. Hell, she had survived the monstrous Lord Fielding. Yet Charlotte's disappearance had crushed her like none other. His heart hardened further against St. Michaels.

"Do you know what more properties the blighter owns?" Banby said.

"Thomasina is researching him in Debrett's," Patrick said. "Once found, she will report back, his properties locked in her mind."

"Locked they will be," Banby said. "I have seen her memory at work. 'Tis uncanny."

Susannah sipped her tea, though her shaking hand did not escape Patrick's notice. Rose drank hot chocolate, eyes alight with fire. If one did not know her, she appeared little affected by Lottie's plight. How wrong they would be. A tall lithe woman, Rosamund never had much meat on her bones. Since Charlotte's disappearance, she had lost weight, appearing near wraith-like, a bump protruding from her belly.

Charlotte's kidnapping had affected them all.

"If Cadan, indeed, stole the painting away," Susannah said, "Hermione helping him, then Cadan must have been on his way to deliver it."

"It was not with him when he was captured," Rhys said.

"Perhaps yet another betrayer in our household?" Rose's cheeks flamed with indignation.

"I think not," Rhys said, resting a hand on her shoulder. "Rather, I suspect Cadan handed the painting off to another flunky before his capture. Either way, we must query the staff once more."

Patrick believed Rhys correct, yet if there were a chance, more would be set on the search. But perhaps... "Let us find Henry, see what he has to say. He is conversant with most of the staff."

"Spider, as well," Banby raised a brow. "Most are in their pockets, they are so charmed by both boys. If another insider lives within Woodbine, we will find him."

"Or her," Rose said.

Banby snapped Patrick a salute and stomped out to find Henry and Spider.

Thomasina returned wearing a smile, but her eyes were sad. She missed Lottie as well, yet her innately cheerful demeanor remained.

"What have you for us, dear sister?" Rhys said.

Thomasina listed the properties under St. Michaels' banner, and they were far more numerous than Patrick had expected for an unexceptional baron. Too numerous, for they ranged from Scotland's lowlands to the Cornish coast to Yorkshire's East Riding.

With too few runners to thoroughly investigate each property, they would marshal men from both the Woodbine and Devonshire estates. But St. Michaels' properties were far distant, particularly the ones in the lowlands and East Riding.

Patrick was as tense as a strung bow. Charlotte remained in peril with each moment that passed.

Thomasina slipped an arm around Claire's waist, both staring at the fox hunt the runner had purchased, set on an easel in the family salon.

Thomasina pointed. "That man was at the auction last night."

Patrick wheeled over, nearly rolling across Rhys' foot, all moving like a herd to the painting.

"That is St. Michaels, or it could be," Ashworth said. "For the baron has a reddened scar on his chin. In her painting, Lady Charlotte could be pointing to St. Michaels."

"Do you think?" Claire said.

"Indeed," Ashworth said in an acerbic tone. "Or I would not have stated thus."

Christ, Ashworth's plain speaking could put a person off. The scarred man helped, now they knew St. Michaels was the thief. Canny of Thomasina to pick that out. Would that they also knew where he had taken Charlotte.

Claire raised her chin and sniffed, basically telling Ashworth he was an ass. "If Lottie painted that scar as an identifier, perhaps she worked more clues into the painting."

Rose tapped a finger against her lips, her foot keeping time, as well. "Something...Something..."

"What is it, love?" Rhys said, smoothing circles over her back.

"Something in the fox hunt is snagging my attention. But...*Drat!* I cannot pinpoint it!"

"Oh!" Claire gasped. "The tree. That big old tree."

"What?" Patrick shouted, not meaning to sound so put out.

"That." Claire stabbed at the painting's immense tree. "It is the Darley Oak. I would swear it."

"Of course!" Rose said. "That is it." She looked at Rhys a huge grin on her face. "Years ago, I was in Cornwall for a horse sale, and I saw it, said to be the oldest living tree in Cornwall, perhaps one thousand years! It is quite distinctive."

Rhys' eyes blazed. "I have seen it."

"Thomasina!" Patrick barked.

His sister jumped, eyes filling with tears.

"Forgive me, sister." Devil it, he was out of control. He managed to modulate his voice. "Did you not say that St. Michaels has property in Cornwall."

"In Padstow." Thomasina nodded, her smile creeping out. "It is called Penrhyn Creigiog."

Patrick glanced at the painting. His clever girl. His clever, clever Lottie. "We leave for Cornwall!"

It was time. Charlotte peeked out the window once more. The wind blustered, rain dripping from the sky, typical Cornish weather, though the storm had eased from the previous two days.

After these many weeks imprisoned, Charlotte had thought she understood fear, her ever-present companion. How wrong she was. Now, fear climbed like a many-limbed monster clutching her throat, her limbs, her mind as she stared into the black, black night.

She took a deep breath, then donned her split skirt, wishing it didn't billow, but was tighter, like men's pantaloons.

If wishes were shillings…

She risked much by taking Mercy into her confidence, yet the girl thought her plan a fine idea, for she despised Charlotte's captor near as much as Charlotte did. Tonight, Mercy insisted on wandering the third floor to guard against attempts to enter Charlotte's room. Charlotte smiled. Were anyone to come near her bedroom, the tea tray Mercy carried would crash to the floor, causing a commotion.

Her course set, Charlotte gathered her rope and made a slipknot around a thick slat on the bed's footboard, then dragged the heavy knotted sheets to the window. She unlatched the casement, always a struggle, and the window flew wide on a gust of wind and rain. Charlotte foolishly peered down into the blackness that swallowed the ground below.

Was she really going to climb outside and crawl down a bunch of knotted sheets?

She scraped a shaking hand across her scalp. She *must*.

Charlotte buttoned her jacket tight, bound a scarf around her hair, then hefted the pouch she had made from a skirt's heavy fabric. Rose had noted the knapsack she'd worn for her escape, explaining how the straps left both hands free for the climb.

Charlotte hadn't much to bring along—her brush, some hair pins, her toothbrush and powder, the pilfered food, and an extra chemise. Last, she slid in a few shillings and swung the knapsack across her back.

With a great heave, Charlotte lifted the rope onto the window sill.

Her teeth began to chatter.

A man's voice in the hall, followed by Mercy's giggle.

Charlotte froze.

She could not do this.

Mercy giggled again.

She stuck a shaking hand out the window, the rain cool and soothing.

Was she a pudding heart? A coward?

No, she was *not*. Peering down, she heard a guard and saw what must be the tip of his burning cheroot. She waited until the guard walked from beneath her window to amble around the manor, as he did each night. She would have a good ten minutes until his return.

She pushed the knotted sheets outside and took a final glance at the loathsome room that was her jail for endless weeks.

Gripping the rope, Charlotte sat sideways on the sill, swung one leg over, then the other. Moments passed as she sat there, her breath coming in quick pants. She turned, awkward to say the least, clutching tight to the rope, her foot pointed until she found the first knot.

Go!

Clinging to the rope, she lowered her left leg to the first knot, and bracing herself on the sill, followed with her right. Both feet now rested on the knot. She pointed a toe and slid it downward, finding the second knot, then moved her hands downward on the rope, followed by her other foot.

Only a thousand knots to go.

A miserable drizzle leaked from the sky, any light hidden by a scrim of thick clouds. Fatigue numbed Patrick's hands and arms, his face stiff. A familiar feeling from the war, exhaustion a constant comrade.

Beside him rode a dozen men, all heavily armed, as they raced to St. Michaels' Cornwall lair. They'd been forced to stop, to eat, and to change horses, and Patrick had fretted though the delays were necessary. Far behind, a dog cart followed carrying a traveling gown and sundries Claire had packed for Charlotte, including medicinals and bandages if needed, and his wheeled chair.

His desperation to find Charlotte had reached new heights, a living creature that urged him to grasp the fabric of time and be with her *now*.

Rhys led them, with Devonshire, Ashworth, Banby, and others from both estates as they charged toward Penrhyn Creigiog prepared for battle. During the Peninsula campaign, Rhys had commanded a regiment of Light Dragoons. Now, he assumed that same duty with the surety of a hardened veteran.

If they continued at this pace, they were two hours out if Patrick's calculations were correct. Sweat greased his face and neck and down his spine, and his second horse—no Diablo—was flagging. He drew near his brother and shouted, "My horse needs a rest."

Rhys nodded, signaling the others, and their troop trotted to a small copse as the night skies unleashed a torrent. The Cornish coastal wind, always miserable, beat at them constantly, and Patrick imagined Charlotte, what she might be doing, how she was faring, his nerves afire at the needful stop.

"Over here!" Ashworth shouted.

He turned his horse toward Ashworth, his mount standing beneath a large oak.

"Good we stopped," Ashworth shouted above the wind's howl.

Devonshire nodded, swiping a handkerchief across his face. "As am I. With the change of horses...This one has not the stamina of my Perseus."

Their company dismounted, many staggering from their mounts, though it was too laborious for Patrick to do the same. Though his crutches were tied to the saddle, they were awkward at best.

Rhys neared with water and grain for Patrick's horse.

"Thank you. My rig does not make for easy dismounting or mounting."

Rhys grinned. "You amaze me in the saddle. Strapped in or not, it is as if you were born on horseback. Like Rosie. I might be an accomplished rider, but I cannot hold a candle to either of you."

"Bollocks." Patrick accepted the biscuit Rhys offered, and his brother moved to check on the other men. The grueling ride offered more to come, including a confrontation, something Patrick anticipated with glee.

Billy Broad rode with them. Patrick had seen the one-armed sharpshooter in action, and he was an asset for tonight's adventure. Rhys and Devonshire were excellent shots, as well, though he had no idea about Ashworth or the other men in their company. That mattered little, for together they were a powerful force.

After thirty minutes or so, the horses rested and fed, they remounted to head for the crags of the Cornish coast.

Oh god, oh god, oh god! Charlotte's fear had escalated on her descent, her shivers increasing with each knot she attained. At times, the wind would slam her against the wall, weakening her grip. She would tremble and squeeze her legs tight around the rope, fighting the fear.

It felt as if she had been descending for hours.

Her scarf was long gone, as were the pins that bound it. Now, wet hair periodically slapped her face, blinding her momentarily. Then, she must clutch the rope with but one hand to wipe the hair from her eyes.

The wind paused, and Charlotte continued downward, though she had yet to look in that direction, for the black pit went on and on. She had no idea if the ground was but a few feet away or hundreds.

Sounds above the wind's hiss.

Charlotte dangled, frozen.

Two guards, chattering away, coming near to where she hung, the white sheets a damned beacon.

No matter her fear, she could not risk them seeing her or the rope. She scrambled faster, trusting neither her hands nor feet slipped, praying she reached the bottom and made it to the screen of trees before the guards turned the corner.

Faster, faster still, hands sliding, the rope eel slick, feet scrabbling, the soles of her boots failing to make purchase.

Go go go.

The men's voices grew louder.

Now or...

Charlotte released the rope.

The ground rose up and thumped her, mere feet away. She teetered, dropped to all fours, then scrabbled like a crab. Laughter, bursting burst close, just around a bend. Charlotte pushed to a stand and flew. She tripped. Flat on her face. Standing again, she raced toward the trees and leapt into the wood. She held her breath.

The two guards ambled around the corner, both tipping flasks to their lips. She scrambled behind a maple and plastered herself against the wet bark.

The taller of the men spotted the rope and blew a whistle from a chain around his neck.

Pushing from the tree, Charlotte ran deeper into the woods. The rain pounded—she could barely see, but she kept on, though branches slapped her and stumps rose from the earth to trip her. She scurried onward, a map of the Cornish coast in her head, and moved eastward, away from the sea and its treacherous cliffs.

Away. She must get far away.

Patrick's cohort thundered toward the manor house, and as they closed the distance, gunfire erupted, flashes of light illuminating each burst of sound.

Whatever was happening could not be good. Patrick leaned forward and pressed his horse faster.

Lottie. The gunfire must be about Lottie. And she was in peril.

Charlotte bent in half, heaving from her run, while shots peppered the air. The guards were nowhere near, making her wonder what was happening. She wished to sneak closer to see, which would be the stupidest possible move.

Rather, she ran toward a cluster of Sitka spruce, and then on and on until a tree root grabbed her foot. She flew, landing hard on a bed of leaves, a stick poking her side. She rolled away, thankful for the tree cover, and pushed to her knees. Before her stood an ancient spruce, a huge hole in its trunk.

Perfect.

Charlotte dragged herself to the tree, her soaking skirts a lead weight. Once reached, she put her hands on the hole's rim and hoisted herself up into the wet, mossy hole that was likely teeming with bugs and other unpleasant creatures.

Nonetheless...

Crouching, she twisted into a position where she faced forward, staying far enough back from the hole to remain unseen. Muck and dead needles lined the base, and she shivered in distaste. No matter, for she smeared the dark mixture across her hands, face, and neck to hide her further.

The rain subsided to drips, forest sounds increasing, and in the distance, the rumble of galloping horses. Some guards must have saddled up to search for her on horseback.

Comforting though her hidey hole might be, she must not stay long.

A *whomp*. Flames shot into the air!

Shouts, screams, a riderless horse running nearby.

More shouts, these far too close.

Charlotte dug her nails into the wood, her forehead pressed to the trunk, praying so hard for safety tears leaked from her eyes.

Shrieks pierced the air.

She *must* move on.

But how could she leave and expose herself?

Fire brightened the night as Patrick and the others arrived at the manor. Someone had pushed a straw-filled wagon against the manor and set it alight beside a pair of open French doors, flames now climbing the drapery.

Men ran every which way, some firing rifles, others screaming for help as the wagon's flames consumed the wall hangings and inched toward the wood doorframe. Yet no one appeared to douse them. Left unchecked, the fire would burn the place down.

The scene could have been from Dante or the *commedia dell'arte*.

In the light of the blaze, Rhys directed half their company to proceed inside on foot. Patrick cradled his rifle, his handgun holstered, a knife strapped to his chest, and his sword on his back in its scabbard. He scanned the chaos for Lottie.

Penrhyn Creigiog's men were ruffians, burly harsh-visaged all. One by one, they were picked off, either knocked unconscious or winged. All who fell were tied to trees.

A woman slipped from a side door. *Charlotte!*

Hugging the manor house, she peered this way and that. When she spied him atop his horse, though shadowed by the screen of trees, she ran toward him.

Patrick deflated as the woman neared. Not Charlotte. Still, she was in obvious distress. He walked his mount forward, lifted the woman into the saddle, and returned to the trees.

"Are you all right, miss?" he said.

"Yer that Patrick," she said. "The one Lady Charlotte—"

"What do you know of Charlotte?" he barked.

Her eyes widened and she licked her lips. "Ye are?"

"Yes, I am Charlotte's Patrick."

"I be Mercy. I be Lady Charlotte's friend."

Hard though it was, he modulated his voice. "Do you know where Lady Charlotte is?"

"She escaped out the window." The girl shook her head, pointing to a window high above the ground. Patrick pictured Lottie's climb down from that height, feeling faintly nauseated.

"I suspect she entered the woods," he said, voice calm when he wanted to howl.

"Ifen she made it without breaking 'er neck."

"Will you be safe if I put you down, Mercy?"

"A 'course." She gave him a saucy smile. "Who da ya think set that wagon a fire?"

"How industrious of you. To help Lady Charlotte escape?"

"That's right. My sweetheart Jemmy helped me ta get the wagon up ta the house. We let the fenced horses loose, too. It weren't right what the baron were doing to Lady Charlotte."

Hideous thoughts swam through Patrick's head. *God's breath.*

"You be a good looking one," Mercy said. "I sees why her ladyship is so fond a you."

A young man ran up to them and raised his arms and Mercy slid into them.

Her Jemmy, he presumed.

Patrick leaned down. "Thank you both for helping Lady Charlotte." Patrick headed into the woods.

Charlotte crouched in her hole, soggy and chilled, as the screams of men and horses and shots fired filled the air, flames and smoke billowing upward.

She should run.

No, she should stay put.

Her indecisiveness felt like a second skin over her own. She *wanted* to run, but she could not get her legs to move from the safety of the tree.

The chaos must be the result of her escape, the tumult a distraction. For that she was thankful.

Few of the manor folk had been kind, though several such as Mercy had, indeed, helped her. She worried for them.

Heaven forefend, she was acting the coward.

She pressed her hands against the tree's sides and lifted a leg onto the rim of the hole, preparing to jump.

"Get yerself outta there."

Failure flushed her body, making her woozy. She had been so close. The guard stood just beyond the hole cradling his gun.

"One moment," she said in a thready voice.

"*Now!*" the cruel voice said.

"I am trying, but I am stiff."

"Bloody hell!" the guard screeched. "Ye get out or I'll haul ye out myself. You'll not like that one bit."

He stepped close, eyes gleaming, lips a snarl of a smile. She recognized him, a nasty brute. Then again, all the guards were loathsome, not a drop of kindness amongst them.

Charlotte got her second leg onto the rim and jumped—a mere three feet—yet her legs buckled, flopping to the ground.

The guard gripped her arm in a punishing hold and hauled her to a stand. She wobbled, but remained upright, and shrugged him off.

He swung his rifle in the direction of the manor house. "Get goin'."

Weary as she was, she would nonetheless delay the inevitable. Charlotte slammed her hands to her hips and if she swayed a bit, so what. "I am not going anywhere with you, sir."

The man snorted, then poked her with his gun barrel. "Get!"

"I believe the lady refused."

Bright stars winked amongst the blackness crowding Charlotte's vision. *Patrick.*

She pinched herself hard so as not to faint, bracing a hand on the tree. Finding a trace of control, she lifted her eyes to Patrick atop a large bay. My God, he was beautiful, like a hero of old—hair windblown, seat in the saddle deceptively relaxed, eyes lit with fire.

Her legs became jelly and she slid down the trunk to her knees.

"Patrick," she said, so soft she doubted he heard her. It mattered not, for he was here, had come for her, not forgotten her. She knuckled her eyes, the pressure of tears fierce.

The guard swung his rifle around, but Patrick's pistol never wavered. He cocked it.

"I would not, sir," he said. "I am accorded a fair shot. And at this distance...? But you are more than welcome to try your luck."

"Bloody hell." The guard spit then lay down his rifle.

"Charlotte," Patrick said, "can you stand?"

She nodded, pulling herself up using the tree to lean against it, panting.

"Well done." Patrick brought his horse near, pistol steadfast on the guard's face, then switched the gun from his right hand to his left. "Now jump, Lottie."

Charlotte pushed off from the tree and leapt.

Patrick caught her waist and hefted her onto the saddle before him, and she wrapped her arms around his waist, resting her head on his chest.

"All right, darling?" he said.

"I am *perfect*."

"As am I." He unwound his cravat, his pistol still targeting the guard. "Sweetheart, I must ask you dismount, to tie his hands with my cravat. Can you do that?"

"I can." Patrick eased her down, ordering the guard to lie on his stomach, and Charlotte completed the procedure.

"Can you remove his bootlaces and tie his ankles?"

"Yes." She struggled, strength ebbing, but fastened the guard's ankles with a solid knot. Straightening, she peered up at the glorious sight of her husband astride a horse. He leaned down, opened his arms, and raised Charlotte to the saddle.

"I will send someone back for the guard." He signaled the horse to walk on, and she clasped his face, that dear face. All her longing and pent-up fear dissolved as she kissed him with all the hope, the faith, and the love stored in her heart.

His lips on hers were warm and welcoming until all that remained was Patrick. She was home. At last.

Early on their return trip to Woodbine, Charlotte's world constantly shifted, blurring with phantasmagoric imaginings—St. Michaels racing after them, a murder of crows circling the coach, trees coming alive in the wind's rage to chase them.

Within Penrhyn Creigiog's purloined coach, Charlotte leaned her head on Patrick's shoulder, his warm arms about her. They had stored his chair in the wagon's covered bed, Mercy and Jemmy seated on the bench beside the wagon master. Charlotte was pleased the pair would be joining their household, Mercy as her personal maid, the former having resigned after the Floating Duck dust up.

Across from them on the seat sat *Halafair,* the painting covered and secured.

While St. Michaels had been nowhere to be found, they had discovered *Halafair* in the cellars, on its face in the floor's muck. To Charlotte's horror, the painting had been smeared with feces. They speculated it was too large and cumbersome to take with him, hence St. Michaels' parting gift. The work could be restored, but Mama would be aghast at the baron's final two-fingered salute.

She slept, awakening as they neared home and family, Charlotte's mind clear.

"How do you feel, love?" Patrick said, offering her a flask. "Only water."

Drinking it down, she gathered her composure for their arrival.

As Charlotte saw it, she had two choices, the easiest to wallow in her fears, reanimating horrid scenes from her captivity over and over. Or, she could paste on a smile, lock those moments away, and get on with her life.

She was no fool. Her family would think she was hiding her distress, and to an extent, she would be doing just that. But if she gave her fears a voice, they would grow, gobbling her whole.

"Love?" he said again.

"I am well," she said. "My aches are wearying, but nothing more."

His lips thinned, his eyes skeptical.

"Let us put this horrid episode behind us, shall we?" she said, her voice chipper, her smile wide.

His ominous pause led to a profound sigh. He nodded. "I shall follow your lead."

Upon arrival, Charlotte stood in Woodbine's entryway

surrounded by her loved ones. As expected, all was chaos—loud voices, bright colors, flickering candles, hugs and kisses. Too much.

Her discomposure must have been evident to Patrick. "Give the woman some air!"

Charlotte laughed, wearing the face of someone with few cares. "I am well, darlings, now that I am home."

Unlike the stone walls of Penrhyn Creigiog, Woodbine's plastered ones felt alien, yet she found comfort in the grand portraits of horses by Stubbs lining the walls. As if they were old friends who needed reacquaintance.

She kissed cheeks, offered smiles, perhaps chuckled a time or two, all to reassure those who loved her she was well.

The throng parted for Patrick, who wheeled closer. "What is it you wish to do, Lottie? Anything you want, darling girl."

Anything...But she did not *know*. She moved down the hall, leaving behind her well-wishing throng, the carpet springy as she enjoyed the portraits of Lansdowne forebears by Reynolds, Gainsborough, and others.

Charlotte stood in the entryway to their rooms, which appeared the same as when she had gone to deliver the painting. She then peeked into her studio, her easels, canvases, and paints standing as she had left them. Back in their rooms, she drifted through the parlor into their dressing room, a glint of crystal stealing her attention. A flagon of perfume, its bottle faceted. Light gilded the liquid gold. Beautiful, until a distant voice drew her like none other.

"Patrick?"

"Would you prefer to be alone, Lottie?" Patrick wheeled across the threshold.

"I would not." She whirled, and she must have looked fearsome, for his face stiffened.

"Apologies, love." Patrick rolled close, his hand grasping hers. "Is this all too much?"

Charlotte shook her head, squeezing his hand.

They stared at each other as if stunned to be in one another's presence, a frisson of energy arcing between them.

It didn't last, the monster taking possession of her thoughts. She had known her cheerful demeanor would be a challenge to maintain, and it was. What she hadn't anticipated was her rising anger. But one thing would assuage these feelings.

"I must paint," she said, her fury a molten volcano.

She hastened to her studio, flung off her gloves, and began mixing paints. Then she lifted a fresh canvas onto an easel and went to work.

Blinded by hatred, Charlotte slashed paint across the canvas—Naples yellow; crimson lake, carmine red, and vermillion; ultramarine and Prussian blue; Scheele's green and black. Yes, she needed *black* to mirror the monster's heart. Dipping her brush, whipping it again and again until a sound penetrated her haze.

Pounding at the door. "May I come in?"

"Of course!" she hollered back. But she wasn't finished. Not yet. Not by *half*!

More colors, and more for the deluge of anger consuming her. Charlotte's chest heaved, and still, there was more to do.

"Stop!"

Charlotte rounded on Patrick. "*Why?*"

"I am concerned, is all, Lottie." Patrick's eyes shifted from herself to her painting. "You are covered in paint, dearest."

She peered at her hands, her dress, her arms. "Indeed, I am!" Shame on her, for she was usually far neater when inspiration took her. Her senses pricked in the aftermath of her rage, and she laughed. In truth, she cared little for the mess.

"Let us clean you up, shall we?" Patrick said.

Charlotte nodded, and he rolled close, his worry obvious.

She sat on her painter's stool, and Patrick gathered a cloth and linseed oil, then began wiping her face and hands.

"Can you finish this later?" he said, his voice calm and measured.

Staring at the painting, she shuddered, for she had indeed

painted the monster, her bold too-colorful strokes depicting him in his physician's mask, the work disorganized and strange, like no work she had executed before. Yet, when she stepped back from the canvas, a charge of energy bristled from the painting, pleasing her.

"I am done, Patrick." And she felt the better for it.

Now, Patrick was her surcease, his presence promising safety and care.

"What do you need, love?" he said, putting aside the cloth.

She dropped to her knees, wrapping her arms around his waist, and laying her head on his lap, soothed by his scent and touch. "I wish for you, Patrick. Only for you."

"I wish for you as well, Lottie," Patrick said. "Rather desperately, in fact."

His wife's eyes glimmered, a cerulean sea of desire and anxiety.

"Come," he said. "Let me fetch something." She unwound and followed him to the bedroom, where he moved to the wardrobe and pulled out a large box. He waved her to the upholstered *klismos* chair.

"I collected these whilst you were gone." He set the box on her lap.

Lottie raised the lid, her hand flying to her mouth.

"Courting gifts, you see." He chuckled. "A bit late, but nonetheless..."

Eyes wide, a smile trembling her lips, she lifted each one, opened the poetry book, popped a chocolate into her mouth, and was charmed by the miniature dingy he'd crafted with "Lottie" on its stern. "Thank you. These are indeed treasures."

"You deserve to be courted," he continued. "You deserve much, my dearest girl."

"As do you, my husband." She began unbuttoning her gown, slipped the sleeves off, then scooched it over her bum, dropping the heavy thing to the floor. "We shall burn it."

Her near-transparent chemise revealed every curve, and he was undone. Lottie was exquisite.

She took his hand, and he rolled beside her to their bedroom. She drew back the covers.

A hullabaloo ensued when the baths he'd ordered arrived with tubs and a procession of maids and footmen carrying buckets to fill them. Clean at last, he donned fresh pantaloons and shirt, to discover Lottie standing beside their bed in a new chemise, her hair freshly washed, dried, and unbound.

Patrick was incredulous, feelings run riot, as she slipped onto the bed, then slid to the far position, peering at him with owl eyes.

A pleasure was before him, and a responsibility. His pride pinched at the thought of exposing his legs.

Folly. For he ached for Charlotte, his wife, this brave, wondrous woman who had survived captivity and devised her own escape. He hoped he was up to the task.

Climbing into bed, he slid close to twine his arms around his Lottie, her hair glorious, her lips parted, her eyes the deepest sapphire. She was *everything*.

Yet reservations for her well-being pinched his joy. "Are you very sure, my dear? You have just experienced trauma. Perhaps waiting would be—"

"Did you know," she said, "St. Michaels wished to marry me?"

"He did not find our wedded state an impediment?"

"As with much, the man ignored that which he disliked. He questioned whether we had consummated our marriage."

"Dear Christ, did he really?"

"I lied and..." Her cheeks pinked. "Well, I reassured him we had done so. I have thought much on this, and I wish to make my lie truth, Patrick, to be your wife in full."

It took but moments for Patrick to shrug off his shirt, revealing a bronzed chest sprinkled with black hair that knifed beneath his pantaloons. His stiffened erection strained beneath the cloth.

Charlotte had never seen such, but Rose's talk eons ago had explained much about the act of making love. *All would be well.* She repeated the phrase in her head again and again.

Facing her, Patrick propped his head on an elbow, his bicep bulging. The urge to touch him, to feel that bronzed skin beneath her fingers compelled her to do just that. She smoothed her fingers over his shoulder and down his arm. His face tightened in a way that said...what? Perhaps he liked her attentions, for his blue eyes burned.

In a daring move, she traced her hand across his chest, the sensations of smooth flesh and springy hair causing bubbles of need to fizz through her, need for what she was unsure, though her private place ached.

He draped his torso over her and dipped his head for a kiss. Then another. And another. The first, soft tantalizing ones urged more until Charlotte could do nothing but deepen their kisses, touching his tongue, licking it, dancing with it as that fizzy urge rose.

When he touched her breasts, she gasped, and he dipped his head to lave her nipple.

"Oh!" Her fingers threaded through his hair, longer than she remembered, while he smoothed a hand across her waist, then delved downward until he brushed her very core.

He kissed her belly whilst his busy fingers moved to that most intimate spot. She grew frantic, the sensations he drew from her intense with pleasure. She touched his shoulders, his back, but that was not enough.

She moaned, knowing not what to do, but wanting...wanting...

His skin grew slick, his brow dotted with sweat, when he reared back, his breath harsh. "I would see all of you, Charlotte. Will you remove your chemise?"

The desperation in his words shocked her. No one had laid eyes upon her since childhood, and now she must expose herself and her flaws to a husband she admired. She steeled herself, for she very much wished to please him. Charlotte lifted her chemise up and over her head. Except the process proved to be rather comical, giggling when the garment proved somewhat intractable.

Patrick chuckled, as well, helping her with the last bit, and then she was naked. If possible, the hunger in his eyes grew more fierce before he dipped to suckle her breast.

Heaven help her, how could she think when his hands and mouth whispered across her flesh? Her breasts ached, as did her private place, escalating Charlotte's desire, wishing to assuage it, but not knowing how.

She wanted to touch him *there*. Yet how could she? Too embarrassing. And yet she must, her hands gliding over that hard ridge beneath his pantaloons. His moan when she did so only served to heighten her want.

In a moment between their kisses and pets, amidst sweaty bodies, their hips met and moved in a rhythm both alien and natural.

Charlotte pulled back, dizzy. The next bit was hard, harder than she had imagined. But she pressed on. "I wish to know *all* of you, my husband. My feelings go far beyond the physical, but I need that, too. To see, to touch, to love, and whilst I am naked, you are half-clothed."

CHAPTER

TWENTY-SIX

Patrick's jaw bunched, but he nodded, rolled to his back, and began to unbutton his falls.

Charlotte's breath held, for she was well aware of how he loathed exposing his infirmity to her. Yet she needed all of him on this, their delayed wedding night.

They must continue in this marriage with honesty, essential after the burden of lies and fraudulent paintings was lifted. Charlotte's rational mind knew what to expect. Yet her desire for him was a strange, overpowering thing that had built over time for she found him glorious, beautiful in feature and form, no matter how that form might differ from other men. He was hers, her very own Patrick. How she loved him.

Once his falls were unbuttoned, he pushed to a seated position, though he refused to look at her, appearing much as a man headed for the gallows.

In a swift move, he lifted his rump and pushed down his pantaloons, then bent at the waist, grabbed the leg hems, and pulled them off, his muscles straining. God in heaven how she wished to touch him. She forced herself to wait.

He tossed the pantaloons to the floor, then slid to face her once more. But his erection had wilted, his face now tight with masked indifference.

Charlotte stared. Patrick's once mighty legs were thin, though not as stick-like as she had anticipated, his thighs showing a bit of muscle. But his right leg was twisted enough to reveal how walking remained an impossibility.

Now, it was her turn.

She brushed her hand across his face. "You are, and will always be, magnificent." She ran a hand down his left leg, and then his right, moving to where she could kiss his limbs. For, in truth, rather than feeling revulsion, she felt joy at kissing them, for they belonged to Patrick. She adored them as much as she did the rest of him. She sat up wearing a smile. "As I said, magnificent."

"Christ, Lottie, you have unmanned me with your warm words and kisses."

Unmanned? Not entirely, for the part of him that was the strangest to her had stiffened again.

On their sides, face to face. "Bend your leg and lift it atop mine, darling girl."

She did as asked and he took her in a powerful embrace, and soon she was lost to all but sensation—his appreciative murmurs, his sandalwood scent, his wondrous expression, and the delicious feelings that frothed through her.

His cock entered her slowly, cautiously. The pinch, nasty, and they stilled as her pain dissolved to a mere ache.

"All right, love?" he said.

"I...Yes."

Rather than proceed, Patrick clasped her face, his eyes afire. "I love you, Lottie. Pure and simple. I have loved you for many months, long before you were taken. Yet I hesitated saying the words, foolish man that I am. For my pride, my hubris, my—"

"Stop." She reached up and kissed him with all the love she held inside. "I am madly in love with you, Patrick Lansdowne. Insanely, crazily, totally. You nestle in my heart, part of my lifeblood. Everywhere there is you. For always."

Patrick began to move inside her, elation lighting his face, increasing her pleasure, and soon words dissolved into heady delight as they rose higher with touches and murmured love words, their slick bodies moving faster and faster.

He slid his hand between them, his fingers seeking her most private place, and touched her there, rocketing her over a peak she had not known existed on joy so intense, she laughed aloud, his groan of pleasure only increasing hers.

Moments passed, the room's silence only interrupted by their heavy breaths and gentle caresses. Charlotte wanted to say things, tell Patrick how much she adored him, how making love was even more thrilling than Rose described.

But exhaustion stole her words, then her thoughts as they both fell asleep.

Patrick awakened before his luscious wife, and he cupped his hands to her cheeks, peppering kisses across her face.

She moaned, her eyes flew open, then warmed. "What has awakened you, husband?"

"Nothing. Everything." He chuckled. "You, for it seems I can not go a minute without touching you."

She nuzzled his chin. "Likewise, my love."

The morning dissolved to afternoon before they left their bed.

Three days after Charlotte's return, she awakened in a panic, rain pounding the windows, the late autumn blow whipping trees to a frenzy. The downpour was torrential.

She must escape and get free of the monster!

Charlotte tossed away the covers, her feet sliding to the floor, the feel of warm carpet rather than chilly boards startling her. She reached for the bell pull to call Mercy, but there was no bell pull, not where it always hung at Penrhyn Creigiog. Why...

Tucking her feet back onto the bed, she drew up the coverlet to her chin. She was at Woodbine, safe and free. She poured a glass of water from the jug on the side table.

Tomorrow, she and Patrick would journey to Hawthorne Hall, though the storm made the trip questionable.

Where was Patrick? He loved storms. For all she knew he might be out on Diablo, perhaps recalling his days at sea. Charlotte had never been to sea, though she had painted many a seascape and knew how a storm made the deck heave, the sails whip, and the boards slick.

That was how she felt at Woodbine, amongst her loved ones, for the ground tilted this way and that, invisible winds knocking the sense from her.

Much of her disquiet was of her own doing—she was *safe*. But her cheerful demeanor proved hard to maintain, her beloved family worsening her irrational feelings either by their conciliation or rigid discomfort, walking daintily around Charlotte as if she were an egg that would crack.

Perhaps they were not wrong.

All had asked about her time at Penrhyn Creigiog and she told them she was fine, that captivity had not changed her. Yet she jumped at shadows or small sounds, her nighttime terrors insisting she sleep with a lamp lit.

God's teeth! She would not yield to fears both irrational and debilitating.

While her and Patrick's accord was a beautiful thing, the world remained a fearful place. Why, at any moment, terror lurking in a corner might pounce.

Charlotte sat on the edge of the bed facing the bank of windows that marched along the far wall, the sky roiling. Unable to tear her gaze away, the trees transfixed her—ballet dancers swirling and twirling to the storm's rhythms.

Charlotte began to hum and sway to the music from the *The Creatures of Prometheus*, the ballet she'd seen by Beethoven.

A shoulder tap, and she leapt to her feet twirling into a wide fighting stance, arms raised as if to punch her attacker only to peer up at a very pregnant Rosamund wearing a troubled smile.

The room focused.

"I did not hear you enter," Charlotte said.

"I realize, and I apologize for startling you. I have brought along our ladies—Susannah, Claire, your mama, Thomasina, and Lucy." She held up two bottles of scotch, while Susannah peered into the bedroom holding a raised a tray holding seven crystal glasses. "Might we come in?"

Did she really wish for a gaggle of women peering at her? Not especially, but she was even more loathe to hurt their feelings.

"Of course."

"We must talk," Rose said.

Whiskey might send her to oblivion, which appealed, and she and Rose repaired to the sitting room, her family's females, all silent and breathless with anticipation.

Mama, Susannah, and Rose took the three chairs as Charlotte brought over her dressing room's stool, Thomasina and Claire arranging themselves on the floor. Rose poured a scotch for each, excepting herself, filling her glass with water. "The little Lord or Lady within me objects to spirits of any kind, much to my dismay." She shrugged, then raised her glass in a toast.

"To safe homecomings!" Rose said.

They all clinked, Charlotte's detachment wrapping her in fuzzy cotton.

"Lottie," Rose said. "We thought you might wish to speak without the gentlemen present on what occurred whilst you were away."

Away. The sip of whiskey burned her throat, then sent a welcome warmth to her belly. Their kind faces bore expectant expressions, their eyes bright with love and understanding.

"Do tell us how you are feeling, Lottie," Mama said.

"We love you," Sina said with a nod.

She sipped her fiery scotch.

"Is it something you wish to discuss," Claire said. "Or would you rather send us all to perdition?"

"The inn," Charlotte said. Another sip and another, relaxing her further.

Thomasina scooched closer and took her hand, Sina's warm, comforting presence grounding her.

"When I entered the taproom, the inn reeked of smoke and stale beer." As Charlotte told her tale, each word easier than the last, until she could no longer contain the torrent.

Many oohs and ahhs as she spoke, along with numerous sips of whiskey, until she came to the climax when Patrick had found her.

"And then I came home." She swallowed another sip, her second glass, and she peered into its empty bottom. "Perhaps, just a wee bit more?"

"A fine idea!" chirped Claire, who refilled the others' glasses as well.

"I believe I may be tipsy!" Mama said.

"No!" Susannah replied, swaying to a silent rhythm. "I am not."

"Of course you are not, dear sister." A giggle followed Rose's words.

"I should very much like to torture that man, Lottie," Claire said.

"*How*?" Susannah's outburst shocked them all.

"What about the rack?" Rose said.

Thomasina shook her head. "My horses! They would scare him."

"They would, Sina!" Charlotte said.

"The Brazen bull," Claire said, her beautiful face wearing a serene smile. "It was a device of torture in ancient Greece where the condemned was placed inside the hollow statue of a bull and—"

"No." Susannah belched. "No more."

Claire's laughter rang around the room. "As you will!"

Mama sniffed. "What about—"

"Enough torture!" Charlotte laughed, noting how her chest had eased, how she was enjoying her family. "He is a horrid man, and once caught, that will be the end of him!"

"Huzzah!" Rose said, clinking her glass.

They all toasted the future demise of the wretched St. Michaels.

Hours later, Charlotte sat in her studio, the wing chair perfect for ruminations. How wonderful her circle of ladies, how extraordinary. For all Patrick soothed her soul, time with her band of females had loosened her captor's grip on her mind. Laughing at their tipsy words and outrageous ideas for St. Michaels' demise had weakened his hold.

Her gaze fell to her knitting bag beside the chair, her work rudimentary at best. But the urge to practice eluded her. Opposite where she sat, three of her easels stood sentinel, two bare and one covered in muslin, beneath which rested the unsold painting for the Scottish gentleman. After that first frenzied day, she had little urge to paint.

St. Michaels remained free. Needless to say, murder and kidnapping were abhorred by the *ton*, the baron a hunted man. Rhys and Patrick assured her he would give Woodbine a wide berth.

Charlotte was not so sanguine, doubting the baron's pursuit of her ended.

The way the moldering paintings contrasted with his obsession... That maniacal glitter when speaking of marriage...His desecration of *Halafair*...She had tried to explain his mania to her husband, yet doubted she had captured the extent of the baron's peculiarity.

St. Michaels' plots had once been calculating and skillful, but she feared he had devolved, his reasoning diminished, his fixation on Charlotte and her art driving his erratic actions.

Heaven forfend, would she ever dispel this fog of fear surrounding her? Would the man ever be caught?

A knock, her musings disturbed. A good thing, for their circularity wearied her. She opened the door to find Thomasina eager as a school girl, hands clasped behind her back.

"I have something to cheer you, Lottie!" Sina's enthusiastic words came on a whisper.

"Come in, come in."

She led her to a sitting room chair and took the one opposite. "And what is it you have brought?"

Thomasina held up a watercolor lovingly rendered. Patrick sat in his chair, his visage proud and unyielding but for the warmth in his eyes as he gazed at his wife. Charlotte sat beside him, her face turned to Patrick, looking at him as if he hung the stars, which she supposed he did. Banby stood beside Patrick, whilst Henry flanked Charlotte, Stella by his side. Behind them reared Hawthorne Hall, not dilapidated, but in grand repair.

"How you have lightened my heart, Sina!" she said. "The beauty of my place, my loved ones, rings with a truth I shall keep close. Thank you, dear sister."

Thomasina winked. "I knew you would like it! Capturing that bouncy Stella was no easy task!"

Laughter bounced around the room, her fear forgotten.

TWENTY-SEVEN

The dining room's fire roared as the family finished their meal, autumn veering toward winter. Patrick looked forward to the snow, though their southerly setting would offer mere dustings. The women retreated to a drawing room to play whist, and Henry and Banby vanished to work on a mechanical project, while Rhys handed him a snifter of brandy, pouring one for himself as well.

"Let us repair to the terrace," Patrick said.

"Winter is near," Rhys said.

Patrick ignored him to fling open a French door and wheel onto the stone. Stars blanketed the sky, the air crisp, while behind him, the door closed and footsteps approached.

"The night is invigorating," Rhys said. "I will give you that."

"I find it quite delightful," Patrick said.

"Delightful?" Rhys said. "I would agree...as long as you wish to freeze your bollocks off."

Patrick laughed, sobering when he thought of the morrow. "I leave for Hawthorne Hall in the morning for an inspection."

"Charlotte will accompany you?"

"Of course."

Rhys paced in a circle. "How does your ladyship fare?"

"You always did get to the point. I fear, not well. She startles at the least noise, looks behind her frequently in fear of being followed, while she awakens on a scream from nightmares."

"I have noticed," Rhys said. "She carries a pocket pistol. Just as Rosie once took her knife everywhere. I saw Charlotte draw it when a maid shrieked at a mouse."

"I am aware," Patrick said. "My deepest hope is that once we reside at Hawthorne Hall and take on the daily rhythms of life, her mind will ease."

"Perhaps they will."

His wife's pain shredded his heart. "What will settle Lottie's mind is St. Michaels' capture. Have you news?"

Rhys shook his head, his pacing about chafing Patrick's nerves, though he knew his brother's steps focused him, much as the model building did for Patrick.

"The man has not appeared at any of his estates," Rhys said. "He must have another bolthole we are unaware of."

Patrick's frustration burst. "Christ, if I could only walk and fight like I once did. If I could be the man—"

Rhys flung himself onto the bench across from Patrick. "You would be but one of many hunting the baron, for we have sent runners to the four corners of England and beyond. The man is part Irish and we search that isle as well."

"I am well aware." Patrick swiped a hand across his face. "Yet I feel impotent."

"As do I," Rhys said. "As does Banby and Devonshire. Men more capable than us search for the baron whilst I sit here in comfort, my focus constantly disturbed by thoughts of his capture."

Patrick knocked back the brandy. "My feelings exactly. I am hoping tomorrow's journey to Hawthorne will prove a distraction for both Lottie and myself. Much progress has been made on the manor and cottages, which I know will cheer her."

"What of the stables?"

"They need work, but less than the manor, and I have men working on them."

"You will, of course, take Diablo. I would like to gift you Beauty and Dante."

Patrick squeezed Rhys' shoulder. "How generous, brother. Charlotte and Henry will be in transports. I thank you."

"Charlotte has a great fondness for the mare," Rhys said.

"She does." Patrick turned his chair toward the house. "Come, I could use another brandy."

"As could I," Rhys said.

In Rhys' study, Patrick poured, the drink warming him from the outdoor chill. "Beauty is a lovely little mare, though Lottie has surpassed her in her riding skills. I have an eye on purchasing another of your horses for her."

Rhys raised a brow. "And who might that be?"

"Ardent. He is a calm gelding, yet can take small jumps and is steadier on rough ground."

"Let me ask Rose," Rhys said. "For he is one of her Norwegian fjords, and she is quite attached to them."

"Early days yet," Patrick said. "First, we needs be settled at Hawthorne. Henry will be over the moon to have Dante with him."

Rhys rose to stoke the fire. "The boy has become a competent rider. I expect he will enjoy the pony very much."

"*Horse,*" Patrick said with a smile. "Henry insists Dante is a horse, and he has convinced me the right of it."

Rhys' laugh boomed. "The boy has tried to persuade all of us to that way of thinking. Do you know, the other day I watched Henry with Thomasina, practicing riding tricks. Worrisome that. He is quite the daredevil."

"God's breath," Patrick said. "I pray he does not break his neck."

"Quite the opposite," Rhys said. "I have seen him lean off to the side, with but one leg across Dante's saddle as well as mount Dante at a run, stand atop the saddle, and stretch out his arms. All while holding steady."

"Henry has not shared this with me." That bothered Patrick, which was rather silly.

"I suspect, brother, that he is merely practicing his tricks to present them in a performance for *you*."

"Perhaps," Patrick said. "If he survives."

The day damp but clear, bucolic fields and pitted roads accompanied their journey to Hawthorne Hall. Though Banby had refined Patrick's carriage, adjusting the springs, none invented could counteract the large potholes. Lottie sat across from him barely speaking a word. Patrick let her be, hoping Hawthorne would be a fine distraction, for he suspected she was frightened much of the time.

The horses trotted down the aisle of trees to the manor courtyard, now a hive of industry. Men hammered and sawed, while the buzz of conversations and periodic shouts filled the air.

The priest's home stood to the left of the manor, screened by a cluster of silver birch. From the reports Patrick had received, Charlotte should be pleased with the home, a charming one large enough to fit them as well as Henry. The first priority had been to repair their cottage and another for Banby, which would suit until the manor's repairs were complete.

They ground to a halt, and Banby lowered the rear gate, then went to assist Charlotte from the carriage. The air had gone from soggy to crisp, the industry that infused the place invigorating. Lottie came to his side and he took her hand. Banby took her other side, with Henry running with Stella this way and that with excitement.

"I am very much looking forward to seeing our new home," Charlotte said.

"As I am to show you." She looked pale and kept fingering that damned pocket where her pistol rested. "Shall we first inspect our temporary home?"

He led the way, the paths smoothed by workmen, to reveal the one-story stone cottage. Fall flowers sprang from beds by the cottage walls, blooms he hoped would cheer his wife. He'd had the door painted the blue of a pellucid sea, and Lottie stood before it, her hands threaded tight before her, knuckles white.

Patrick looked to Banby. "Do enter, Lieutenant."

Banby opened the door, revealing a large main room that incorporated both a dining and sitting areas. Charlotte followed the lieutenant, and Patrick wheeled inside to survey their new home.

Charlotte had chosen the furniture after he'd described the rooms and drew a simple schematic. An oak dining table with its six chairs sat to the left on an exquisite Oriental. Across the room, a teal sofa faced the hearth, a burnt umber wing chair to its left, the space to the right reserved for Patrick and his chair. All rested on another splendid Oriental carpet.

Lottie's furniture choices were both unfussy and comfortable, as were all the fixtures she had acquired for the room. Patrick was pleased.

Charlotte examined the furniture, the rugs, and the fixtures. "I like it very much, Patrick. The room has turned out well. Most pleasing is your ability to amble outside on your own with no steps to impede you."

"A salient point, dear wife. Life shall be more manageable for all of you as you won't have to haul me about."

She peered down at him, eyes bright. "I insist we build ramps down several of the stairways to the manor itself, which will offer you the same access. What do you think?"

Her thoughtfulness pierced him and his lips quirked. "Great minds think alike, love. I have instructed the workmen to do just that, giving me access to the house and world beyond without aid. So, what do you think?" He swept his arm across the room. "Will our cottage suit for a month or so?"

But Lottie had not heard him, having vanished down the hall that held two bedrooms, and a third room for her studio. He trailed along, thankful the wide hall allowed his chair access, and noted her shoulders loosen, her hands no longer clasped in a death grip.

She peeked into their bedroom with its handsome bed, side tables, and an exceptional armoire she planned to move into the manor. The cottage's roof had been reshingled, the walls remortared, his workmen doing a fine job.

"The stone is beautiful and dry as bone." Charlotte ran her hand down the wall beside the bed, and he recalled her tales of Penrhyn Creigiog's drips and damp.

"Shall we see your studio, love?" he said.

"Oh, yes! Have you set up a workshop for your shipbuilding?"

"I have."

He swiveled his chair and led the way to a good-sized room facing north, the light ideal. Patrick had set up the room in secret, purchasing several easels, a desk, and a sofa where she could read or rest.

Charlotte entered and beamed. "What an exceptional space." She walked to the easels. "These are outstanding. I have been using Papa's old ones, but these delight me." Lottie whirled to face him with a smile, which vanished, her eyes fixed on the wall.

He turned to see a sketch by her father, one he had not hung, nor did he believe Lottie had, either. A surprise from Rose and Rhys? Doubtful, as this sketch was a trifle.

St. Michaels, a man who fed off the twisted games he crafted. The baron had done this, and Patrick thirsted for that man's neck beneath his hands.

Charlotte stared at the painting, shivers racing through her at the reminder of her incarceration, only to be superseded by a burst of anger. Fury fisted her hands. How dare he invade their home?

The perfidy! His cruelty! Death would be his...or hers...did he try taking her again.

"We will choose another cottage," Patrick said, face stark with anger.

Charlotte walked to the sketch depicting the Bath seaside. "No, Patrick, we will *not* move. He will not make me flee my new home."

"If you say so, my love." He had hired two Bow Street Runners as

Lottie's guards and had alerted the staffs at Ravenscroft, Woodbine, and the workmen at Hawthorne to be vigilant. Yet the blackguard had somehow snuck onto their property. He'd have Rhys send a few of Woodbine's former soldiers to bolster the runners' presence.

Looking maniacal, Lottie clapped her hands. "A mistake!"

"Love?"

"This sketch," she said. "I have not seen it in years. The last time was in Bath. I was eleven, and father and I sketched side-by-side on the sand, a favorite memory."

"A lovely one."

"But you see, a man came upon us to stare at the sketches. I remember particularly for he was not dressed for the seaside, but rather town. He purchased Papa's, and I was deeply disappointed he had not bought mine, which I thought was quite fine. And then he did!"

"St. Michaels?"

"I suspect so, which is when he discovered my talents. I would bet on it."

"Perhaps the beginnings of his obsession with you."

"Not only that, but he watched me draw, saw the similarities between mine and Papa's work. In later years, and in possession of both sketches, that may have led him to see some Pheland's as my work."

"That is indeed possible."

"You know," Charlotte said, "I never saw his face while captive."

Patrick nodded.

"That hideous doctor's mask...I cannot stop seeing it." She squared her shoulders. "Well, come along, Patrick! We have much to see and I am most eager."

Once their procession arrived at the manor house, Patrick found the new roof nearly complete and the rotted floors replaced in the main salon and the kitchens.

Charlotte and Banby climbed the once derelict staircase, now replaced with new oaken treads, the banister gleaming in the light streaming through the cleaned windows. He and Henry explored the main floor, finding those rooms taking shape as well.

"The second floor is lovely," Charlotte said as she descended the staircase. "Even the attic has become warm and cozy now that the roof is mended and the drafts sealed. The manor is all I had hoped for." Lottie smiled, eyes clear and bright. "We shall make it a home filled with laughter and love. I am eager to settle, to explore the hills and dales on Beauty. What a grand gift from Rhys!"

"That she is. When I received the king's gift of the Hawthorne title, I rode our land, its surrounds green and lush with many over-looks to the sea."

"And you did not take me along?" she said in a playful voice.

His lips quirked. "As you know, that was well before our... contretemps in the library." He grinned. "The minute we are in resi-dence, we shall take Diablo and Beauty on a jaunt."

"Can I come too?" Henry boomed. "On Dante!"

"Of course!" Charlotte said, leaning close. "We must get Banby a horse, too. We can afford that?"

"That, and much more, wife," he whispered.

The lieutenant cleared his throat. "Lady Hawthorne, I am appre-ciative, but I am more a man of the sea."

"Do you not enjoy riding?" she said.

Banby looked askance. "I prefer to sail or take a gig."

Lottie nodded. "Perhaps, one of these days you will ride out with us if we find you a mount you enjoy."

"It is not a matter of enjoyment, my lady," Banby said, running a hand across his head. "But rather a preference."

"Ah. Then a gig it is, one that will be yours."

"My lady, I cannot—"

"You can, given our friendship and your invaluable service to us all."

At Woodbine the next morning, Charlotte saw her husband off on his early morning ride.

The man had been fixed to her like a limpet ever since they viewed the sketch at the priest's cottage, all consideration and kindness. Yet she was pleased to be alone for she must think.

The sketch had deeply shaken her. How could it not? St. Michaels intention had achieved his aim.

Yet it also accomplished something as well—burning more cobwebs of fear to ash. Not all, perhaps, but enough for her think with more surety than she had in weeks.

She hastened to their rooms, her pocket pistol flopping this way and that. A rather foolish thing to carry, considering her shooting skills were abysmal. Since the gun made her feel more secure, she would become a marksman...markswoman. She was sick to death of fearing the baron's next move, a prey response, rather than taking the initiative. She would not be prey.

She walked to the studio's secretary to compose a letter. Each day, she would send St. Michaels a letter, whether they reached him or not. She suspected they would, for he had sycophants to fetch and carry for him. If he remained obsessed with her, and it appeared he did, he would find the letters torturous.

Visions of him approaching, of his boozy breath, the mask's glassy eyes, him reaching for her, his malevolent smile.

Charlotte gripped the desk, fear choking her.

No. She would *not* have it.

She sat, then lifted her writing case from its drawer. Made by Papa for one of her birthdays, Charlotte smoothed her hand across its inlaid top. A memory of his love.

Love. A bouquet of diverse flowers, all wondrous. The thought bolstered her resolve, as did Patrick's love, which was incomparable. Mama, Claire, Rose, Rhys, so many others loved her. Henry, too, and perhaps even Banby. Even Beauty and Stella loved her, particularly when she gave them treats. She loved them all, as well.

With so much love swirling around her, how could she not have the courage to do what she must?

Charlotte's heart fortified, she lifted the lid and drew out two pens, ink, a tin for sanding, and her knife, then pulled out a sheet of foolscap from the secretary. Her pens in good order, she dipped one into the inkwell and began.

Dear St. Michaels—

How I have missed you, missed our chats and discussions on art. Sadly, no one here shares our enthusiasm for my father's work or even mine, for that matter.

I do hope you will contact me again, for once I saw the painting hanging in the priest's cottage, I knew it had to be you who had left it there. A sign.

That particular work is a favorite of mine. How did you know? I thank you.

I miss you.

Warmly,

Lady Hawthorne

With a deep breath, Charlotte sanded the ink, took care folding the letter, and sealed it with wax. She addressed it to St. Michaels' main seat in East Riding.

"How fare you today, my love?" Patrick entered windblown and red-cheeked, hands smoothing hair in wild disarray.

Charlotte slipped the letter into a drawer, turned, and smiled, feeling lighter than she had in days. "Quite well, husband. And you?"

"Exceptional." He wheeled closer and took her lips in a kiss, deepening it until their tongues tangled in a now-familiar dance.

When they drew apart, he said, "Shocking."

The cloud of desire still haloed her. "What?"

He grinned, clasping her hand and rubbing his thumb over its back. "What, what?"

She flicked his shoulder. "What was shocking?"

He leaned back, lips quirked. "Rather than tire of your kisses, I seem to always want more."

"Tire? A good thing you do not, for we are leg shackled."

"There is that." He burst out laughing, then sobered.

"I have a request," she said.

"And what might that be, wife?"

Charlotte rang the bell pull. "I shall order us some tea and biscuits. I am starved and you look rather peaked." Of course he wasn't, but was instead tanned, dashing, and much too touchable.

"Peaked, am I?" He patted his lap. "Come, Lottie. Have a seat."

She complied, fixing herself atop his lap and making sure her bottom tweaked his...person.

He raised a brow. "I know what you are doing, wife. Deflecting."

"Am I?" She leaned into him, running her fingers across his cheek, his brow, his lips. Ah, those lips that did such wondrous things.

"Wait, wait, dear one," Patrick said. "What was your request?"

"Hummm?"

He cupped her cheeks. "Your request?"

Though her face remained serious, her eyes danced. "You must teach me to shoot a pistol."

CHAPTER
TWENTY-EIGHT

Lottie was terrible, a simply awful marksman...markswoman. Patrick was silently appalled. Oh, she hit the targets, all right, but *always* missed what she aimed at by a good six to twelve inches.

Desiring to shoot came from Lottie's fear of that blasted baron. Yet did she take up a gun in defense, she would either miss or seize up, both frequent occurrences during their practice.

Patrick had given Lottie a variety of pistols, hoping a better fit might increase her accuracy. None had done so. How the woman could paint the tiniest ship on canvas with incredible precision and make it appear real, yet failed to hit a sizable target with any sort of accuracy confounded him.

She stood before him in a navy riding habit with white piping, its jacket topped with bright brass buttons. A fetching navy hat with a white plume tilted at a jaunty angle topped the confection. Elegant. Yes, but also adorable. He wished to gobble her up.

"I am improving, am I not?" Lottie said.

Her shot had landed a good foot from her target. "Making progress!" he said in a cheerful voice.

Lottie peeled a laugh. "You are bamming me, Patrick! I am truly dreadful at this."

He could not disagree.

"Not to worry. I shall practice!"

Heaven help them all.

Days later, the letter to St. Michaels weighed on her, for Charlotte had been in a flurry of moving preparations and had failed to write more. One letter would not do. She would bide her time until settled at Hawthorne when the letter writing would begin in earnest.

That chilly day in November, she was all aflutter, and who could blame her? She, Patrick, and their band of merry men, horses, one dog, and accoutrements were journeying to Hawthorne Hall to move in.

Charlotte and Patrick traveled in his specially built coach and much of the family and staff saw them off, with Rose, Rhys, and Claire accompanying them in another coach. Banby sat atop the block beside the coachman, whilst Henry rode Dante, a smile never far from the boy's face, with Stella trotting alongside. She wore a grin, too.

Several wagons and another coach carried their goods. As Rose's babe would arrive in a month or so, she'd had to fight Rhys to join them.

When their caravan arrived at Hawthorne Hall, Charlotte leapt from the carriage, eager to see all the changes. She was amazed. Though hammer and saw still pounded and buzzed and the vast gardens remained rather wan, the path to the entrance had been improved, with mauve Michaelmas daisies, red-hot pokers, and delicate Hesperantha adding a cheerful note lining the walk. Progress abounded—the path swept, the yellow door repainted, and the windows gleaming. The front steps were narrowed by a sturdy ramp for Patrick's ease of entry.

"At present, the carpenters are working on the kitchens," Patrick said as he unlocked the front door, and they trooped inside. A gleaming central hall greeted them. Tapestried window hangings had replaced moth-eaten ones in the small salon to their left, the oak panels now shining from the light pouring from the cleaned windows. Not a cobweb to be found.

"I say," Devonshire said, pointing toward the sea beyond, "that is a grand prospect."

Out the window, beyond the bluff, waves lapped the shore, a few boats bobbing in the distance.

"That it is," Rhys said, squeezing Patrick's shoulder. "I could not be happier for you and Lottie, brother."

"As am I," Rose said examining the oak beams. "I believe the manor itself was built around the time of Woodbine."

"That it was," Patrick said and waved. "Go. Explore."

Charlotte stayed with Patrick as their group dispersed to various corners of the manor house.

"Come aboard?" Patrick patted his lap.

She smiled as she did so, and they wheeled through the foyer into the great hall.

The hearth blazed, the room warm and inviting. Charlotte slid from Patrick's lap, eyes focused on the large painting hung above the mantle. A seascape by her father, a large one she'd last seen at Penrhyn Creigiog on that horrid fourth floor. She shivered, recalling the moldering paintings in that strange room and St. Michaels hovering.

No blight darkened the canvas now, the work restored. Ice shot through her veins.

"Did you have this hung here?" she said, a hot ball of anger in her belly.

"I have never see it before," Patrick said.

She dragged a wing chair close, unlaced her half-boots, and climbed atop the seat.

"What are you about, Lottie?"

Charlotte steadied herself on the hearth's stone, for she must see the painting up close.

"The mold has somewhat been cleaned," she said. "But it was done in haste."

Patrick wheeled close, raising a hand to steady her as she descended. "You have seen this painting recently?"

"I have. It is one of my father's." She sat to retie her boots. "At the manor in Cornwall. This is but another game St. Michaels delights in playing."

"So it seems." His mild words belied his stony expression.

"In any case, I am glad to have the painting returned to us." Charlotte pushed the man, his games from her mind. "While the others are wandering the manor, shall we check out our temporary home?"

"Lottie," Patrick said. "Are you well?"

"Perfectly! His infuriating games grow tedious."

Though Patrick gave her a skeptical look, she squeezed his hand, and they proceeded to the priest's house. Upon arrival, their stoop held a gentleman moving from foot to foot to keep himself warm. He stepped forward as they approached.

Dressed in fine clothes, the stranger doffed his hat to bow, revealing a shiny pate. "My Lord and Lady Hawthorne."

"How may we be of assistance, sir?" Patrick said.

"I have business to discuss and prefer we do so inside, my lord."

Business? Charlotte kept her council as Patrick directed the man into their home.

A cheery fire burned in the hearth, a new footman taking Patrick's hat, the stranger's hat and cane, and Charlotte's pelisse. She requested tea, gestured the man to the sofa, then took a wing chair before the hearth, Patrick setting his chair opposite hers.

Once seated, the man pulled a sheaf of papers from his satchel and placed them on the table before him. "I am Sir Joffrey Reynolds from the Royal Academy of Arts. I have been tasked with revealing to Lady Hawthorne allegations laid against her to both the academicians at the academy and the trustees of the British Museum. These represent..."

Their staff was thin, at present, and Mercy appeared bearing a tea tray and biscuits, and they remained silent until the girl left the room.

"Allegations, Sir Joffrey?" Patrick said.

A volcano raged within Charlotte, her hands clammy, her heart thumping a tattoo loud enough for the men to hear.

She reached for several of the papers, while Patrick read the others. "These allegations say a piece by Reginald Pheland in the British Museum is a forgery, yet they do not identify the work."

Charlotte held up another paper. "These say that two Phelands in the academy's permanent collection are forged as well, again without noting the works. *I* am supposed to have painted these alleged forgeries?" Charlotte was pleased how steady her voice sounded.

She forced eye contact with Sir Joffrey, the man related to an original founder of the academy, the famed Joshua Reynolds.

Reynolds' face pinked. "I am afraid so, my lady."

Here it was. After all these many years.

Patrick smiled, his soft chuckle oddly reassuring. "My lady wife a forger? How amusing."

"*We* are not amused, sir," Reynolds said.

"I would suppose you are not," Patrick said.

She sipped her tea, eyeing both men. "Which works are in question, and how and when did I supposedly paint them?"

"And whom, I might ask," Patrick said, "laid these allegations?"

"For the sake of a fair investigation," Reynolds said, "we are not at liberty to release the gentleman's name who claimed thus. Nor are we allowed to inform you regarding the works in question."

Charlotte daren't look at her husband, but was sure he knew, as well as she, who had laid the charges.

"I admit," she said. "As well as inane, I find these allegations quite flattering."

Charlotte was not stupid. When forging her father's work, she had applied *his* palette of paints, rather than her mentor Turner's more experimental colors, which she used in her own works. She mixed her father's pigments with refined linseed or walnut oil and used his sable brushes, though she owned equally fine ones. The same held true for her canvases and gesso primer, both from her father's stores, and she fastened each canvas to a wood frame constructed by him.

Reynolds cleared his throat. "I do not know when the committee of academicians and trustees will meet, m'lady. But experts on your father's oeuvre are studying the paintings in question."

"You are aware, Sir Joffrey, that this accusation is offensive." Patrick's relaxed pose belied a face fierce with that small, dangerous smile. Rather terrifying. "Are you not?"

More throat clearing. "I am merely the messenger."

"Have you any instructions for us?" He gave Reynolds teeth.

"Not at present."

"Having delivered your papers and message, we thank you," she said. "Do tell all involved that we find these allegations both laughable and offensive. We will be contacting our solicitor regarding the matter."

Mercy magically reappeared with Reynolds' hat and cane. He bowed to both of them.

Charlotte nodded. "Mercy will show you out, sir."

Once the door closed behind Reynolds, Patrick took both her hands in his. "Lottie, do not be concerned."

"I can't help but be so."

"These accusations must terrify you. They do not me. For they shall be impossible to prove."

Charlotte saw not Patrick, but the Royal Academy's great hall, pictured it filled with observers, them all staring at her with accusatory eyes. "Difficult, yes. Not impossible."

"Nearly so, then."

She lifted her eyes to take him in, all concern and care. "Either

way, it will cause a fuss, make the Royal Academy wary of us...of me."
Even as they spoke, her large piece for the academy's Summer Exhibition was on its way to Hawthorne, where she would complete it for
submission.

"I do not give a rat's ass about the Royal Academy," Patrick said.
"I care little for how they act, and less for how they think. The same
is true for those stuffed shirts at the British Museum. But I know you
care, my darling."

She slapped her lap intending to rise, but he kept hold of her
hands. "Let us address the situation as matters unfold. I have a
friend, a trustee on the museum's board. I shall write him, see if I
cannot discover which paintings are in question and who laid the
charges." He ran a hand down her cheek.

"Yes, I shall write Mr. Turner to see if he has any knowledge of
these events."

"We are in accord," he said.

"Are we not always?" She tapped a finger to his lips, eyes
mischievous. "Except when I am right and you are wrong."

He bellowed a laugh as Lottie grinned.

That night, the wee hours upon them, a cry awakened Patrick
from the woman in his arms, who tossed fitfully as she repeated the
word "no" again and again. Wishing to soothe her, he began kissing
her brow and cheeks in hopes of waking her with gentle caresses.
Her eyes blinked wide, then she reached for him as if he were a buoy
to keep her from drowning. They made sweet, silent love, and upon
completion, his Lottie fell into a dreamless sleep nestled against his
chest.

Unlike his lovely wife, his mind was now busy within a maze of
frustration, with that lackwit St. Michaels, not to mention the situation with Saumarez. Dawn soon creased the sky, and he tugged the
bell pull. He needed a bracing cup of tea.

Bees were less busy during the following week, with workmen, staff, and their band of four bustling around the estate setting things to rights. Banby aided their cooper and woodworkers at the outbuildings, while Charlotte oversaw the household improvements, and Patrick, with his trusty helpers, Henry and Spider, the latter moving from Woodbine to Hawthorne, headed up the stable contingent.

He had set men checking the pasture fences and gates, while he examined the tack alongside their new stable master. He would have brought on Arjuna, the man incredibly competent, but Lucy would never leave Rosamund, and Arjuna would never leave Lucy. On several recommendations, he had hired a local man, and so far, Patrick was impressed.

A month to six weeks would see the manor complete enough to move in, Charlotte presiding over the household improvements, while they'd hired groundsmen to bring the many gardens back to life. Patrick found the work kept her from dwelling on the forgery charges, though he feared it crouched, ever-present, in the back of her mind.

Overall, the week had been pleasant, with much accomplished on the day Rhys rode up to their dooryard.

Charlotte stood in the entryway, hand shading her eyes, the sun was bright on this clear November day. "Hello, brother!"

Rhys handed his reins to a stablehand, then embraced Charlotte with a hug and a kiss to the cheek. "Sister! How fare you?"

"Well! Much has been accomplished since you and Rose were here."

"Excellent!"

"I am enchanted by the place and the sounds and scents of the nearby sea. To what do we owe the honor of a visit?"

"I received a letter and wished for Patrick to read it."

"Ah. He is with the horses." The letter must be important for Rhys to personally deliver it. Not another worry, she fervently hoped. "I shall bring you to him."

"You need not. I can—"

"I am most happy to do so, as I shall get a kiss from my husband."

"Ah, newlyweds." Rhys chuckled, extending his arm.

Charlotte took it. "Not so new!" she said with mock anger.

He raised a brow, chuckling as they made for the carriage house and stables, abuzz with activity. Rhys leaned close. "I still love kissing my Rosie, and we are old married folks."

"Ancient."

Patrick spotted them and waved, wheeling to greet them. Charlotte bent for a kiss, and once the men's back slaps were done with, Rhys bent to whisper in Patrick's ear.

They exchanged dark looks, ones that presaged difficulties. Charlotte wished to stay, but bid them farewell rather than intrude on their private conversation. She would learn the contents from Patrick later, these new concerns added to her bundle of worries.

Patrick led Rhys to his study, free of dust and done up in hunter green leather wing chairs, with an imposing cherry desk constructed at a perfect height for Patrick's chair. A sofa in the same leather sat before the hearth, the fire taking the chill from the crisp air. Charlotte had placed several of his ship models around the room, while one of her seascapes hung above the mantle. His midshipmen's dirk, his captain's sword, and the sword given him by the Prince of Wales after Trafalgar graced the far wall, though Lottie talked of moving them to the great hall.

Rhys peered at the painting, hands clasped behind his back, remaining silent for long minutes. "This is *exceptional*."

"It is."

"I knew Lottie was skilled, but this work is beyond my imaginings."

"Far better than her father's, in my estimation, though I would never say so to Lottie. She would take offense for her father's sake. The letter?"

"Indeed." Rhys flung himself onto the sofa.

Patrick rolled closer. "You appear frustrated."

"I am."

"Perhaps will be less terse if I ply you with drink? Do hand me the letter, brother."

Rhys nodded, and Patrick moved to the sideboard, reaching for the glasses to pour them each a Scotch whisky. He handed Rhys his, who knocked it back and held out the glass for another.

"That bad," Patrick said as he poured.

This time Rhys sipped, then reached into his pocket and withdrew a crumpled letter. "I have sent out feelers to the Admiralty, as you know. This arrived today." Rhys waved the missive. "Farley sent it. You remember him?"

"Of course."

"In essence, Admiral Saumarez is waging a feverish campaign to deny your return to duty."

Patrick swiped the letter and read. "Of course he is, that prick."

"As you can see, he alleges your infirmity makes you unfit for desk duty."

"I cannot say I am surprised." Patrick tossed the letter into the flames. "Nor can I imagine *not* being a part of the Royal Navy. *Christ!*"

"Does this concern the slaver incident?"

"I believe so. At the musicale, Saumarez tempted me to drop it by aiding in my return and elevating my rank. More interesting, Henry recognized Saumarez at the auction as having boarded the *Despoina* whilst the slaves were being loaded. The boy said the admiral talked with the captain and first mate for a long while."

"As you know," Rhys said. "I have set two powerful friends to investigate the *Despoina*."

"A first-class idea," Patrick said. "If we can prove Saumarez had ownership of the ship and slaves, his career would be destroyed. The drowned slaves have already cost him a pretty penny."

"Slaves are no longer insurable as cargo, are they?" Rhys said.

"They are not. I confess I long for the day slavery is not merely

prohibited from our shores, but made illegal in all British territories."
The practice was despicable.

"The ownership of human beings is an abomination." Rhys began to pace and stopped abruptly, his eyes narrowed on Patrick. "A crusade for you to undertake. Perhaps seated in the House of Lords?"

CHAPTER

TWENTY-NINE

Patrick eyed his brother, whose face shone with care and hope. Abolishing slavery was dear to Patrick's heart, and not merely due to his friendship with Banby, who was half black. Yet he could not picture himself in the Lords expounding before hundreds from a wheeled chair. And yet...His mind was fit, as was his conviction.

"A humble suggestion, brother," Rhys said.

"Humble?" Patrick chuckled.

Rhys grinned. "Talk to Charlotte about this matter and about joining the Lords."

"She knows my sentiments on slavery. The Lords?" Lottie's insights always interested him.

As time had passed, he had shared much with his wife, including many of his weaknesses, though he found humbling himself before Lottie an arduous task. Yet he had done so. In fact, they had recently talked about such disclosures, about being forthright with one another. Patrick shook his head, for he was torn. St. Michaels. The alleged forgeries.

""Perhaps I shall, though Lottie has burdens enough," he said, his words sounding flimsy.

"Listen to me," Rhys said. "Withholding things from Rosie only ends poorly. I suspect the same is true with your Charlotte. Do you not love her?"

"What has that—"

"Rose says she loves my frailties, including my fears, as well as my strengths. I suspect Charlotte is of the same mind."

Patrick wheeled from the sofa, frustrated he could no longer pace. "I shall think on your words."

"Good."

"Saumarez holds much sway with the Admiralty."

"Of that I am aware."

Bloody hell. Patrick failed to imagine the life he would lead could he no longer serve.

Nearly a month had gone by at Hawthorne when Patrick sat atop Diablo, ruminating, as he watched Henry practice the Passage, a measured, collected trot.

Lottie had set up her studio, and her Summer Exhibition work had arrived from Halafair, while Patrick had a splendid new room for his model building. As winter approached, he valued the room's warmth over Woodbine's drafty workshop.

Shocking them all, the prince regent had come to call at Hawthorne accompanied by Rhys, as Prinny—awful nickname—had been visiting Rhys' stables. Lottie was pleased, though she missed seeing Mrs. Fitzherbert, a woman she'd enjoyed during an exuberant country weekend at Woodbine.

But the baron, Saumarez and his career, and the Royal Academy, were never far from his thoughts. St. Michaels' pursuers were dogged, yet none had located him. Patrick was certain it was he who had leveled the forgery charges against Lottie.

Oh, damn. Henry had fallen apart at the end of the Passage, consequently Dante did as well. "Again, Henry!" he hollered with a smile, uncommonly pleased. "You and Dante almost have it!"

The boy complied with a grin, and Patrick's heart warmed,

finding joy in teaching Henry, the boy a blotter who absorbed every drop of information.

Both he and Banby had proved boon companions, ones he would not have known—not as he did now—had that mast not taken his legs. In all likelihood, minus his injury, he and Lottie would not have wed, either. These fresh insights offered a perspective on his accident he had not considered.

Once Henry completed the exercise with precision, Patrick called the boy over. "Very good, Henry."

"Won't Lady Charlotte be gobsmacked when I shows her!" Henry tossed him a jaunty smile.

Patrick was thankful Henry's governess had arrived. "Language, Henry! I will be excited or I am excited to show Lady Charlotte."

"I *am* excited to show Lady Charlotte," the boy parroted.

"Well said. Shall we go for a jaunt?"

Henry's eyes lit, then dimmed. "I want to, really bad, Captain. But..."

"But what?" Patrick said.

"I got to tell Banby something first."

"And what might that be?" Patrick said.

"Banby's woolie is near done, the one with the frigate and the slaves." Henry steered Dante to the gate, leaned to open it, and rode through.

Once Saumarez was revealed as the villain he truly was, Patrick anticipated the embroidered woolie's conflagration, along with his miniature frigate. He closed the gate behind them. "What are you about, Henry?"

Henry frowned. "Them tossing them men overboard. That were the most awful thing I ever seen."

"That *was* one of the most—"

"It was!"

Even with Akiko, Henry's efficient new governess, a battle raged over Henry's proper speech. One they were losing.

"I was lookin' at the woolie," Henry said. "And by accident, I spilled tea on a corner. Banby din't see me, but I should tell him I did it. Don't you think?"

Patrick had yet to tell Lottie of Saumarez's campaign to oust him. "That would be best, Henry."

Time to take his own advice.

He found Charlotte in her dressing room sorting through her chemises.

"Oh!" She beamed him a warm smile.

"What are you up to?" he said.

She slid onto his lap, wrapping her arms around him and offering a deep kiss, one that prompted other ideas.

"A housemaid collected a favorite chemise to launder," Charlotte said. "I am digging for its twin."

He kissed her neck, taking in her scent. To him, she smelled of joy, pure joy.

"I thought you were giving Henry a riding lesson." She wove her hands through his hair.

"I was, and he did very well," Patrick said. "But I must tell you of a situation."

She tucked her head to the curve of his shoulder. "Continue."

He detailed Saumarez's campaign to oust him from the navy.

"That swag-bellied pig!"

He laughed. "Where did you acquire that expression?"

"Where else?" Charlotte rolled her eyes. "Henry."

"I worry for the boy, that Saumarez will figure out the role he plays and what he saw aboard ship. He witnessed Saumarez's treachery. I have posted extra men around the estate, but nonetheless..."

"He is well protected, then," Charlotte said. "But you worry."

"I do. Saumarez is lethal, well-respected, and has the ear of the Admiralty."

"You doubt your success in returning to duty."

"That is the essence of it." He hesitated, then... "Without the navy, I have no purpose. For this past year, I resolved to heal as much as possible. That done, it now appears my naval career is done as well. What is my purpose?"

"A purpose is a funny thing, I think. For years, mine was forging paintings. Now, I have the honor of being your wife, no need to craft forgeries. I can paint what I wish. A beautiful thing, though my drive, my *need* to protect my family remains. What purpose can I turn that energy to now?"

Lottie's point did not elude him. "You will find another. Perhaps children?" He waggled his brows.

"Yes," she said, eyes filled with warmth. "They will be yours, too, you know. And, perhaps, becoming a member of the Royal Academy? My thought is you shall discover a new purpose, as well."

"Rhys suggested I join the House of Lords to fight these slavers." He laughed, as if it were a joke.

Charlotte frowned. "How dare you laugh. You would be exceptional in the Lords and they fortunate to have you."

What was there to say? He could not see it.

"I know you wish to resume your naval career," she continued. "For that is where your heart lies and what you have always known. But if fate or Saumarez wills it otherwise, the Lords is a fine place to put that fury to work. You are a commanding and talented speaker."

"Only aboard ship," he grumped.

"Then think of the Lords as your ship!" she said.

How odd, for he could see that, see the members as his crew. Interesting.

"Patrick, my love." She kissed his cheeks, his brow, his chin. "In addition, have you considered purchasing your own ship? A pleasure craft? I could be your crew! We could race it in the Vauxhall sailing match!"

He reared back. "Getting a bit ahead of yourself, Lottie. Have you ever been on a ship."

"Well, no." Lottie's flush made her particularly lovely. "But I have been studying. As I should, since my husband is a sea captain. I shall be your first mate!"

Sailing with Lottie, bringing Banby and Henry along, too, even Stella. Not the same as commanding a ship of the line, but owning a ship, perhaps a schooner, could prove pleasurable. "Let us hope Rhys and I succeed in reinstating me to duty."

"Let us hope," Charlotte said.

But her eyes told a different tale, and he took that into account as well. "That issue is for our future." He nuzzled her. "I have a different concern at the moment."

"Do you?"

"Indeed, I do." Soon, talk of purpose, sailing, and the navy were forgotten.

Joffrey Reynolds returned, and Charlotte supposed she should be grateful the man personally brought news of when the Royal Academy and the British Museum would convene regarding the alleged forgeries.

The meeting would occur at the academy in two weeks, such a brief time, and they sent messengers to their supporters, including Rhys and Rose, Claire and Lady Fielding, Devonshire and several others who owned Reginald Pheland paintings.

Three days prior to their departure for London, Rose and Rhys arrived at Hawthorne to discuss strategy, gathering in the newly appointed library. The room was filled with books, comfy wing chairs, and a blazing hearth, its blues and greens complementing the view of the evolving gardens and the sea.

Once the tea tray arrived, they dug into the sandwiches and drinks, the atmosphere heavy with the impending trial, as Charlotte deemed it.

The idea of the committee's interrogation chilled her. Not that she had a choice. Thus, she must rise to the occasion.

Rhys sipped his tea. "Have we any experts who will assure the assembly of the veracity of the works in question?"

"We do not know which works *are* in question," Patrick said.

"How could they refuse to name them?" Rose said with indignation.

"Because they *can*," Patrick said, a bite to his words.

Rose took Charlotte's hand. "What do you know, Lottie?"

"Very little." She bit the side of her cheek. "Neither the person putting forward the allegations nor the works themselves have been revealed to us."

"We believe St. Michaels brought the charges," Patrick said.

"It seems likely," Rhys said. "Is the man that much of an idiot to bring charges against the woman he held captive for weeks?"

Charlotte's stomach squeezed. "Oh, he would. He is arrogant, and not the most rational of men. He insisted we would marry!"

"How odd, given you already were," Rose said.

Patrick poured a finger of scotch for himself and Rhys. "Ladies?"

Charlotte accepted, while Rose shook her head.

"The sprog objects to spirits most emphatically," Rose said.

"I can inform the assembly of my captivity," Charlotte said.

Rhys squeezed the bridge of his nose, a sharp look passing between the two men. "That is a possibility."

"What are you not saying?" Charlotte said.

"The *ton*," Rose said on a sigh. "There would be much speculation about what occurred during those three weeks, Lottie. Unpleasant speculation."

"The caricaturists would have a field day," Rhys said. "The papers, too."

A flush rose, this time one of anger. "I am aware, though nothing untoward occurred. But you are right, the *ton* will vilify me. Let us pray revealing my captivity will be unnecessary."

"Will Turner attend?" Patrick asked.

"One never knows with Mr. Turner, for he is both eccentric and fickle. I did write to him about the meeting."

"He will be in our corner," Rhys said, pouring himself another scotch. Patrick lifted his glass and Rhys complied, adding a good two inches. Rhys looked to his wife and Charlotte.

"None for me, love," Rose said. "But do refill Lottie's glass. I suspect she needs it."

The scotch spread a much-desired warmth from Charlotte's belly outward, and she relaxed a fraction.

"How certain are you," Rose said, "that the academy will be unable to detect the ones you painted?"

Charlotte took a sip. "Quite sure. I used all my father's materials, including the canvases he stretched before he died, though recently I have begun to stretch my own. When I do so, I use old wood for that purpose. The brushstrokes themselves mimic my father's style, the composition is similar or a mirror of my father's original works. I am confident of this."

Rhys nodded. "Is the girl, Mercy, coming?"

"Why would she?" Patrick said.

"I think she should, Patrick." Charlotte nodded. "As support and confirmation of my imprisonment. Jemmy, too, as he is now a Hawthorne footman. Both were with me at Penrhyn Creigiog."

"But they saw you forge—"

"Only the fox hunt," she said. "I painted nothing else whilst there. Mercy witnessed how St. Michaels demanded I paint that scene over and over and they can attest to that and my confinement, if needs be. Which I hope it will not!"

Patrick chuffed. "You are right, Lottie."

"We shall attend, of course," Rhys said. "Your mother and sister will come, and I am certain Devonshire and Ashworth will, given they were in your rescue party. Both have expressed interest."

"Our family has weathered worse storms, m'lady." Patrick reached over and kissed her palm.

"We shall weather this one, as well." Rose nodded.

Charlotte fervently hoped so.

After a flurry of preparations, their band of four, along with Mercy and Jemmy left for London, the trip giving them several days in town before the forum convened. Beauty and Diablo came along, Patrick riding while Charlotte switched between their carriage and Beauty, too restless to remain in one spot for long.

They arrived at the Ravenscroft townhouse with little fanfare, thankful neither the papers nor the caricaturists had been alerted to the news of the committee.

All changed the following day when a small crowd clustered outside the townhouse, their faces hungry for the latest news. Visitors, including Ashworth and Devonshire, had to fight their way through the daily expanding crowd, a man daring to pelt the duke with questions.

Rhys, Rose, her sister, and Mama arrived the following day, with Devonshire and Ashworth visiting yet again. Charlotte found the noise from the crowd, the comings and goings, the constant focus on the imminent meeting unsettling.

Two days later their un-merry troupe set off for Somerset House, home to the academy. Patrick and Rhys had hired five plainclothes

Bow Street Runners to accompany them on the chance St. Michaels showed. Once at the academy, they would station themselves by the exhibition room doors to capture the miscreant.

Stepping outside, shouts and cries of newspapermen assaulted Charlotte, while the caricaturists madly sketched. Thankfully, tall brawny men surrounded her, Patrick, and the others, as they made their way to the carriages stationed before the townhouse. When she slipped inside, the crowd's focus changed to Patrick, like a murmuration of starlings, as he wheeled up the ramp into the vehicle.

Once arrived at the Royal Academy, they met their hired solicitors and barrister, though this was not a legal court. Both brothers believed their minds would slice through any deceit or obfuscation by the parties involved.

The crowd thickened as they approached the Exhibition Room, Charlotte's heart a-thunder. This was St. Michaels' final gambit, one in which she was loathe to participate.

A side door revealed Sir Joffrey Reynolds, who waved their group forward. Once inside, they proceeded down a short hall, Reynolds hesitating before opening the door to the room.

"Are you ready for this, my lady?" Reynolds said.

She produced a smile, noting the cluster of dear family and friends around her. "We most certainly are, Sir Joffrey."

His eyes twinkled. "Good!" He swung open the door, and they moved into the great hall hung with painting upon painting, one atop the other all the way to the graceful arched window where the day's soft light bled inside. On the exhibit floor sat a semi-circle of chairs flanking an empty podium, the seats occupied by Royal Academy academicians and museum trustees, along with the museum's director.

Chills trilled up her spine.

A current academician headed their way, but Sir Joffrey held him off while escorting them to their seats. Patrick in his chair sat in the aisle beside Charlotte, and she reached for his hand. He gave hers a firm squeeze. So very soothing to have him here with her. To have him at all, in fact.

The scents of oil paint and wood hung heavy in the air, while murmurs and whispers mimicked busy bees. She searched for Turner and failed to find him, though she spotted the portraitist William Owen, artists Samuel Woodforde and Thomas Phillips, and John Soane, a professor of architecture. Charlotte recognized others, as well, all eager to view the proceedings. The hall was filled with a preponderance of men. A spurt of anger at the lack of women members, as two of the academy's founders were women. Yet only men were now accepted into the fold. But there was Lady Ablethorp, writing away and moving her mouth simultaneously, with a few other women sprinkled about the room. Thank the stars Lady Ablethorp was a good distance from Charlotte's front row seat, yet she'd swear a hungry gleam shone from the gossip's beady eyes.

Henry Howard, the Royal Academy's secretary and acting chairman for the proceedings, stepped to the podium and pounded the gavel. Several minutes passed before the crowd quieted. Once satisfied, Howard explained the purpose of the "gathering." His term.

Fustian. This was no gathering, but a mock court, meant to expose her malfeasance.

No matter what came, Charlotte had the love and support of her family. Were she to be found culpable, she would be shunned, as would her mother and her sister, even perhaps Patrick. Her father's paintings would plummet in value, though some quirky collectors would want a forged Pheland. The horror struck her hard.

This could not be.

And yet...it was.

"Remember, we have a strategy, love," Patrick said.

"I do."

"Fear not."

"Fear? Me?" She tinkled a laugh knowing full well Patrick did not believe a bit of it.

Charlotte schooled her face as they read the charges, but

inwardly she cringed, the unpleasant trait learned from their time with Lord Fielding. *Heaven forfend*, best to avoid thoughts of that horrid man.

A door opened, and her heart sped. St. Michaels entered the room.

Charlotte gasped, her eyes searching for the runners. Once found, she returned her attention to the baron, resplendent in formal wear, while three men walked behind him, one holding a thick sheaf of papers.

The monster took a seat in the first row, across the aisle, thankfully far from her. More murmurs arose, increasing with much chatter and several oohs and ahhs from the fine figure St. Michaels commanded. Objectively, the man *was* striking, but all Charlotte saw was that grotesque doctor's mask, a far more accurate reflection of his twisted self than his handsome visage.

A whisper in her ear. "That cretin was always filled with self-importance." Her mama's words appeased her somewhat. "His father was the same. Little men with big heads and small..."

A bubble of laughter rose, and Charlotte clamped her jaw tight.

Howard introduced the baron and gestured him to the podium. St. Michaels shook his head, motioning to the man beside him. The stern-faced older man struggling with his bundle of papers moved to the stand beside Howard.

Charlotte wished to scream. She did not, of course, but oh how she wanted to.

In a sonorous voice, Howard referenced the three paintings and their provenance, two of which hung in the Royal Academy of Arts' permanent collection and one belonging to the British Museum.

Howard waved a hand at two men standing before a closed door, then detailed to the crowd the three paintings' provenance, whilst the men retrieved a large painting, a seascape hung at British Museum.

Charlotte recognized the painting, of course, a work her father had done just before his death, his second to last, the final depicting

Halafair Hall. The memory made her weepy, her emotions on high alert.

St. Michaels' representative, Abbot, tall and thin with a mighty beard, began to expound using Jonathan Richardson's system of art criticism to find inconsistencies with her father's style in the work. Given Richardson's utilitarian bent and weak arguments, art historians and critics now discounted his ideas for judging works of art. Yet here they were.

Abbot ripped the painting apart, claiming how such an adept artist as Pheland would never have painted the seascape before them. The man's sonorous conclusion rang around the hall in a resonant baritone.

Charlotte rubbed her forefinger and thumb over and over, pinpricks of fear pinching her nerves.

Behind her, a flurry of movement.

Good Heavens! Mama had stood.

Howard lifted his gavel, but paused, for he seemed to recognize her mother and laid the gavel back on the podium. The room was silent as Mama began to speak.

"I am Countess Fielding, formerly Lady Halafair, wife of Reginald Pheland, Lord Halafair. I watched my late husband execute that work. It was his second to last painting, and was sold to the Earl of Cholmondeley, who is now the Marquess of Cholmondeley. From there I cannot tell you where the painting traveled before its arrival at the British Museum. But I can attest that my late husband, Reginald Pheland, painted the seascape in question." Her mama waved over Secretary Howard and handed him a piece of paper. "A copy of the receipt given to the Earl of Cholmondeley for the painting." Her mama sat.

Patrick chuffed, and Charlotte was tempted to join him, for the commission had a choice of calling her mama a liar or of accepting her words. How ironic that the first painting in question was, indeed, executed by her father.

The men flanking the podium rose to confer, heads bobbing like chickens pecking at seeds. Her hands grew damp beneath her thin leather gloves.

The men consulted, and how tired was she of seeing *men* decide everything. At last, they returned to their seats, and one of the committee whispered in Howard's ear.

The chairman nodded and banged his gavel. "The committee has concluded Lady Fielding's testimony and receipt assures the authenticity of the work."

Charlotte melted with relief. Two to go, and with each murmur and cough and shuffle around the room, Charlotte's apprehension rose. She wished she'd worn a veil to hide her expression, for her face had begun to feel as if it were a plaster mold.

Patrick leaned close. "Fear not, Lottie. We shall win the day." He bussed her cheek, tickling it with his tongue. Shameful man. She must not smile at his antics.

A second large work draped in muslin was presented next. Once the bearers reached the easel, they set the painting upon it and lifted the cloth.

A bucolic landscape stared back at her, one painted by Charlotte. Lord Wrexum had purchased the piece perhaps five years earlier during the time she studied with Turner. It seemed forever ago and she noted subtle issues with the painting, ones that reflected *her* style rather than her father's, inconsistencies few would recognize. Nonetheless...

"Do illuminate us, sir," Howard said to Abbot. St. Michaels stood for no apparent reason. "Why do you and Lord St. Michaels claim this to be a forgery by Viscountess Hawthorne?"

St. Michaels jabbed a finger toward Abbot. "He knows!"

Murmurs at St. Michaels' odd behavior.

Abbot stroked his beard as he neared the work, his pointer gesturing to a sheep, a haystack, and an outbuilding.

"The great artist and collector, Jonathan Richardson, comes to mind, for I shall use his exceptional "An Essay on the Theory of Painting" to critique the work. I find these three elements unfailingly weak. Is that a sheep or a blob of white? The outbuilding seems to be out of harmony with the piece as a whole, while the haystack lacks grace. These elements caused the baron and myself to question the work's authenticity, given Pheland's mastery."

Abbot took his seat beside St. Michaels with an air of self-satisfaction.

Charlotte wanted to retch.

A well-dressed rotund man rose from a seat at the back of the room, and the committee chairman waved him forward.

He stood before the painting. "I am Sir Robert Smirke, as most of you know."

Murmurs flew, and Charlotte leaned toward Patrick to whisper. "He is one of the academicians. I have met him, but I do not know him well."

"Might he be in league with St. Michaels?" Patrick whispered back.

"Perhaps," she said. "Though he is an esteemed professor of architecture."

"I possess two Reginald Pheland paintings," Sir Robert continued. "One of which is quite similar to this one in question. I cannot agree with Lord St. Michaels or his representative." He bowed to the baron and the committee as well.

"I see the haystack," Sir Robert continued, "as a buttress for the pair frolicking beneath it, its color congruous with their clothing. In reference to the outbuilding—while appearing ramshackle, and I do not disagree with this—note how it leans toward the mighty oak that towers above it. I see this as a sign of a harmonious coupling. Finally, the sheep."

Voices rose amongst the crowd to near cacophonous levels, arguments bursting forth like shooting stars, only to dissipate, wherein others began.

"I agree!" shouted one man.

"Ridiculous!" hollered another.

"Excellent work!" screamed a third.

Howard's gavel pounded with no change in volume.

"Quiet!" Patrick boomed in his captain's voice. "Now!"

The room went silent.

"Thank you, my Lord Hawthorne," Sir Robert said. "As I noted, the sheep is merely a marker, pointing the way to the frolicking couple, to enhance the artist's message."

"And what message might that be?" barked St. Michaels, flailing his arms as he rose from his seat.

Sir Robert seemed taken aback by the baron's hostility, and he brushed invisible specks of dust from his waistcoat. "The message, my lord, references the delights of the countryside, how it assuages the heart and soul, as is evidenced by the light pouring through the clouds to beam onto the joyful couple. Can you not see this?"

"Of course I see it, you idiot!" St. Michaels' said.

Murmurs of shock wafted around the room.

Abbot stood. "The painting is all wrong for Pheland. It is a fake pretending to be what it is not."

Sir Robert shook his head. "I fear I must disagree, sir, for I see this work as a hallmark of Pheland's mastery and style."

Abbot threw up his hands and sat, but the baron began to gesticulate, waving his arms, and though Abbot tried to calm him, he failed.

Howard ignored the fracas and thanked Sir Robert, who returned to his seat. "Does anyone else wish to speak?"

Met with silence, Howard gestured to the committee, their heads bobbing again until a member rose and whispered to Howard.

The secretary stood before the painting. "The committee verifies the work entitled *Harvest Time* is by late Reginald Pheland."

Charlotte released a breath as murmurs and whispers ensued whilst Howard signaled for the third painting, which was set on the huge easel, where the much smaller work looked rather silly.

Howard flipped back the muslin. "This work is entitled *Fox Caught*."

Charlotte froze, her hands clamped tight.

Disgruntled murmurs wove through the room, for it must be difficult to see the painting from the farthest rows.

Charlotte saw it clearly—a hunting scene where dogs ripped apart a fox—the painting Charlotte loathed. Memories crowded in, where St. Michaels demanded she repeatedly paint the hunt, and she had done so, this one of three, the third purchased by a runner at Rhys and Patrick's behest.

St. Michaels stood, but Abbot pulled him down again, whispering in his ear. Abbot approached the painting, pointing that damned stick at several portions of the work.

The chatter continued until, to her surprise, Mr. Turner rose from his seat. "Sirs." He bowed to Abbot, then the baron. "Lord St. Michaels, is this not one of the two paintings you recently donated to the Royal Academy? Might I ask how you acquired it?"

"Why, directly from Lady Hawthorne, Mr. Turner," Abbot said.

"It looks to be Lord Halafair's work," Turner said. "And I have had the privilege of viewing numerous Pheland paintings."

"Lord St. Michaels believed it an original, as well," Abbot said. "At the time."

St. Michaels bounded from his seat, across the hall, to the painting. "Can you not see? It is a fake!"

He lifted the painting, eyes lit with mania, turning it to the audience. He moved in a circle, the audience and the committee wearing shocked expressions. "*She* painted it!" He pointed to Charlotte. "It is a fake! A fake!"

He walked toward Charlotte, painting thrust forward. She reared back.

"I watched you paint it, did I not!" he screamed at her before Howard's gavel pounded and Abbot corralled the baron. St. Michaels went silent, blinking rapidly, as if seeing the audience for the first time.

The cat had fled the bag.

THIRTY-ONE

Many were horrified at the baron's antics, yet some stared at Charlotte, their eyes questioning, while the committee whispered amongst themselves.

St. Michaels' ravings appeared mad. Yet no matter the committee's decision regarding the fox hunt, many in the audience would wonder about the truth of St. Michaels' words.

Charlotte knew she would suffer for her forthcoming revelation, yet she must act.

Before she did so, she observed those around her. Her family. Her friends. Her supporters.

Her breathing deepened as she contemplated the result of her words to come. Her dear husband—Patrick would survive, for he cared little for the *ton*. Rhys and Rose, given their elevated station, would survive as well, her taint affecting them little. The same was true for Thomasina and Susannah.

But Mama and Claire. Her heart wrenched—they would be the most affected. Darling Claire's amber eyes peered at her, warm and serene. She nodded, as if she knew Charlotte's intention. Mama, on the other hand, surveyed the hall, vertical brackets of worry scoring the bridge of her nose.

She leaned close. "I must speak, Mama."

Much to her surprise, her mother's smile appeared. "Of course you must. We shall weather this storm as we have all the others." Her mother waved a hand toward the committee. "Compared to Lord Fielding, this contretemps is child's play. Give that blackguard St. Michaels *hell*."

Charlotte smiled inwardly and rose. "I wish to speak to the assembly regarding this painting."

Patrick quirked a brow, but he tipped her a small nod. The knowledge that he would support her meant everything. She smiled down at him and he winked, which made her startle.

"Of course, Lady Hawthorne," Howard said.

"The painting is indeed in the style of my father."

St. Michaels raised his fist. "It is yours!" he screeched, as Abbot wrangled him away from the painting.

That released the wolves amongst the chickens. The ensuing din near made her laugh, and if her hands clasped any tighter, she would break a bone.

Much gavel banging ensued until the room stilled.

"Pray continue, Lady Hawthorne," Howard said.

She surveyed the crowd, making eye contact with as many as possible. Mr. Turner appeared particularly bilious. Her family was wide-eyed, all except for Patrick whose eyes streamed warmth and support. He'd sussed out her plan.

She focused on the committee, and only them, and after a deep breath, she spoke. "I painted this as Lord St. Michaels watched me work. You see, Lord St. Michaels held me captive at his manor house, Penrhyn Creigiog, in Cornwall, forcing me to paint in the style of my father, Reginald Pheland."

That did it. If the previous din was loud, it now reached cacophonous levels. Charlotte focused on Patrick, and only him.

"Do proceed, Lady Hawthorne," Howard said after settling the crowd.

"Lord St. Michaels kidnapped me as I was delivering a painting of my father's to a client. Said 'client' was a ruse, for it was St. Michaels himself who took me. Lieutenant Banby here," Charlotte gestured to the lieutenant seated in the third row, "accompanied me and was incapacitated by St. Michaels' ruffians, who used ether to render him unconscious. I was then taken under duress to his manor in Cornwall and forced to paint in the style of my father. He did thus so he could sell the forgeries to raise money. He kept me under lock and key for three long weeks, and I have witnesses who can attest to that fact."

"How did you escape, my lady?" A voice hollered from the crowd.

The audience hushed.

"With the help of a maid, Mercy, I fled out my third-floor window using bedsheets. Simultaneously, Lords Hawthorne, Raven-scroft, Ashworth, the Duke of Devonshire, and others rode to my rescue. They, too, can attest to the truth of what I say."

Silence absolute. Then the committee began to whisper amongst themselves.

Charlotte had discussed her possible revelation with the family. They knew what would occur—in a blink she went from reputable viscountess to tarnished woman, the implied intimacy with St. Michaels under speculation. Lady Ablethorp was scribbling away.

But Charlotte had given her confession great thought. She sat, and Patrick winged out an arm, and she slipped her hand through it, holding on for dear life.

Howard addressed the baron, who remained standing with Abbot. "What say you to this allegation of Lady Hawthorne's, my lord?"

St. Michaels threw up his hands. "The absurdity astonishes me. These proceedings are a mockery of justice. I am done!" He stalked from the room, Abbot following red-faced.

Charlotte panicked, then watched the runners slip from the

doors they guarded, while Ashworth and Rhys moved from their seats to follow the baron.

"Lady Hawthorne," Howard bowed. "The assembly would hear your witnesses."

She remained seated, too discomposed to rise. "I believe His Grace of Devonshire has a few words."

Devonshire told of racing to Penrhyn Creigiog, of her escape, and of the ensuing fire. He noted the many guards, her bedsheet rope, and more. Mercy followed, and then her Jemmy spoke.

"We were accompanied by many," Patrick said. "And we would be pleased to present them at another time if needed."

"That is not necessary, my lord." Howard walked to the assembled committee, addressing them in quiet tones. When he returned to the podium, all in the room leaned forward in their seats.

"We understand," Howard said, "the reason Lady Hawthorne forged *Fox Caught*. These extenuating circumstances lead us to dismiss any charges of forgery against Lady Hawthorne, the two previous paintings already verified. We apologize to her ladyship for these proceedings and hope she fares well in all future endeavors."

The infernal St. Michaels had escaped their net. Again. No one could say the man wasn't clever for how he had done so eluded them.

The papers were riotous with the news, speculation and innuendo running rife. Caricatures in windows depicted Charlotte in various postures of incarceration, humiliating, yet they did not distort her face or make her look the fool. St. Michaels, on the other hand, was drawn with numerous monstrous expressions, more gargoyle than man.

Even anticipating the brouhaha, Charlotte found the gossip and maligners bruised her soul. All whilst her captor remained at large.

A week after the inquiry on a crisp, sunny November day, Charlotte rode to Woodbine accompanied by Banby, her riding stamina and skills increasing with daily practice. For all his protestations, the lieutenant proved a fine rider.

The previous week, she had sent notes to the ladies, for she had a plan, one she hoped would erase St. Michaels from her life forever.

Today, Patrick was overseeing his workshop's refurbishment, and Charlotte was confident he would be engaged for hours, perhaps into the evening. She and Banby would spend the night at Woodbine, and Patrick was pleased with her visit.

Arriving at the manor, Susannah and Thomasina flew down the steps, while Rose toddled out the door with Lucy to stand on the landing. Rose was the size of a medicine ball, looking like she would drop the babe any minute. She could not get any bigger, could she?

Mama and Claire were coming from Halafair Hall with a special package, and Charlotte longed to see them.

"Lottie!" Thomasina exclaimed, wrapping her in a hug, Susannah not far behind.

"Stay on the landing, Rose!" Charlotte hollered. "I will come up."

Banby headed to the stables with their mounts. He would visit with Arjuna for they'd formed a friendship. Perhaps Banby would speak of Akiko, Henry's governess, for she'd spotted their interest in one another. Then Arjuna would tell Lucy, who would tell Charlotte.

Charlotte raced up the stairs to Rose and Lucy, hugging both. She doffed her hat and pelisse as she entered the hall, and handed them to the butler with thanks. She was bursting with energy and excitement, eager to explain her idea, but would wait for Mama and Claire's arrival.

"You are in a dither, Lottie," Rose said entering the salon. "You mentioned a plan in your note. What is it about?"

"Yes! Do tell!" Thomasina bounced with excitement.

"We must wait for my family's arrival," Charlotte said. "And the package they bring."

Beside Rose, Lucy sat ramrod straight, her face dour, whilst it was obvious Susannah was dying to know, too.

All began to talk at once, words folding over words held in check since their last gathering when sounds of a carriage interrupted their chatter. Susannah and Sina followed Charlotte outside just as the carriage came to a halt.

Her mother descended the steps aided by a footman. Next came Claire, who paused and spoke to the man assisting her. He, in turn, waved over a second footman and once Claire was on the ground, both men entered the carriage.

"What are they doing?" Susannah said.

"Retrieving a package," Claire said "A rather strange one."

"Strange?" Susannah said.

Her mother's lips twitched. "Unexpected."

The footmen reappeared carrying a huge, narrow wooden box.

"Bring that to my studio, if you would," Charlotte said to the footman, then collected Rose and Lucy. They proceeded to the family dining room where luncheon sat on the sideboard—a tower of fresh fruit, along with meat pies, cold meats, breads, cheeses, and triangular sandwiches eaten with a knife and fork. Cakes and other desserts perched at the end of the table.

Charlotte's mouth watered. Once they made their plates and poured their drinks, the staff vanished and they dug in.

"Do you know what is happening?" Rose said to Claire as she cut a sandwich.

"I do not." Claire slipped a grape into her mouth.

Susannah reached for a meat pie. "I suspect our conversation shall prove interesting."

Rose lifted a forkful of meat pie. "The babe and I are starving."

"I smell trouble." Lucy crossed her arms.

"You would be right, Miss Lucy," Charlotte said buttering a slice of warm bread.

All eyes swiveled Charlotte's way.

"St. Michaels has haunted Patrick and me for months."

"But you defeated him at the inquiry!" Thomasina said.

Charlotte nodded. "That we did, but he eluded capture when he left the exhibition room and remains on the loose, his threats hovering over us like a poisonous spider."

"You know how I hate spiders." Susannah shivered.

"Not near as much as I loathe St. Michaels," Charlotte said. "We shall pounce on *him*!" She held the eyes of every woman at the table. "I propose we set a trap."

Thomasina clapped. At least one of the family was onboard.

Rose laid a hand on her belly. "I doubt I could trap much these days."

Charlotte smiled. "Oh, you will play a part, dear sister."

"Ah!" Claire said, waving her fork. "I know your plan, well, at least part of it."

"Do tell, Claire!" Rose said.

Mama's eyes gleamed. "We brought *Halafair*, as you requested, Lottie."

"How did you bring a house with you?" Thomasina said.

"Not the house itself, Sina," Charlotte smiled. "The painting."

"The same as was here for the auction?" Thomasina lifted a wedge of apple and nibbled.

"Yes." Charlotte reached for the lemonade. "An irresistible lure to St. Michaels."

"And how, exactly," Lucy said, "shall you bring the two together?"

"That is what we are here to discuss," Charlotte said. "After I returned from Cornwall, I began writing him letters. I wrote one, but life grew frantic, the Royal Academy and all, and I never sent them. A good thing given the inquiry. But letters might prove useful."

Claire smirked. "This should be interesting."

She winked. "I believe, now that he has lost the inquiry, my letter will push him to respond. I hope so. I shall write how I miss him, how we could be together and I could paint for him again. I would apologize for my actions at the inquiry, but that I now have finally realized his passion for Papa's work harmonizes with my own. I could add something about Patrick's disinterest in my painting, too.

A lie, of course, one of many I hope to feed him. Our plan can work. You see, I will gift him *Halafair* as proof of my devotion."

"What makes you think he will fall for this ruse?" Rose said.

Charlotte frowned. "The baron is mentally unwell, desperate for me to paint for him, day in, day out. *Halafair* would be the crown jewel in his collection. As I see it, we have two challenges."

Lucy snorted. "Only two?"

"One, we must find a way for the letter to reach him. And heaven only knows where he is situated at this moment. Two, we must find a clever way to trap him, the location and timing being equal of importance."

Skeptical faces stared back at Charlotte as she peered around the table.

"Should we not bring the men into your plan?" Susannah said. "They will be furious if we do not."

"No," Charlotte said. "Patrick would forbid me to use myself as bait, and I would find it a challenge to oppose him. They would watch us like hawks and interfere. Now that St. Michaels is in the wind, I desperately want him locked away. He crouches in my mind, an ever-present threat."

Claire hugged her. "I understand, dear one. I am so sorry."

"I agree with Lottie," Rose said. "Our men will commandeer the whole operation and squeeze us out. Rhys and Patrick are especially watchful."

"I agree!" Thomasina said. "They are always trying to protect us."

"But how will you keep this a secret from them?" Susannah said.

"Not a problem," Rose said. "Not only are they busy with the estates and projects, but they are racing around the countryside hunting for the very man we hope to trap. I must think on this, Lottie."

"I will do it!" Thomasina said.

"Thank you, Sina!" Charlotte said. "St. Michaels will never suspect that a group of women could defeat him. He is far too arrogant and misogynistic."

"He will surely bring guards," Rose said. "Those awful men you described."

"I expect so." Charlotte thoughts became threads weaving a plan. "While you cannot use your *kalari*, Miss Lucy is most able."

Lucy nodded.

"You are clever with a gun, Susannah, yes?" Charlotte said.

Susannah ducked her head. "So the family claim."

"Humph," Rose said. "Dear sister, you hide your light under a bushel. Susannah's skills near match Billy Broad's. She has uncanny aim."

Susannah's fingers threaded together. "Billy is a true sharpshooter. I do well, though."

"We can practice our *kalari* forms," Clare said to Charlotte. "They will serve us well."

"We must build our strength," Charlotte said. "I did so when imprisoned." She turned to Thomasina. "Perhaps one of your horses may help. They can be frightening."

Sina grinned. "I will bring Dancer! He can charge the guards or strike out, plus any number other tricks." A fast clap of the hands. "Dancer already rears with my whistles. I can teach him new tricks. Dancer is very smart."

"Excellent, Sina," Charlotte said.

Claire reached for a sugared plum, a sly smile tipping her lips. "And my knives, of course."

"She has been instructing me." Lucy nodded. "Lady Claire has much expertise."

Rose was frowning.

"What is it, Rosie?" Thomasina said.

"I hate this." She rubbed her belly. "I love the babe, but I *hate* missing out on the action and—"

"I believe you should orchestrate, Rose," Charlotte said. "Watch us practice, coordinate our timing and moves, along with keeping Rhys away."

Rose chuckled. "That, I can do. What of Patrick, and you must consider Banby for he sticks to you like a tick when you venture out."

"I have yet to devise a ruse for them," Charlotte said. "But I shall."

"Daughter?" Her mother cleared her throat. "You have conspicuously left me without an assignment."

"I am working on that." She tapped a finger to her lips. "I know, you shall come for a visit to Hawthorne."

"Lady Fielding...Humm." Susannah said. "You can be Patrick's and Lieutenant Banby's diversion!"

"I like that idea immensely," Mama said.

"Miss Lucy," Charlotte said, "your martial arts expertise is unparalleled."

The Indian woman remained contemplative.

"You may join us, Lucy," Rose said. "Or recuse yourself."

"Of course," Charlotte said. "There is no conscription here."

Lucy's mysterious eyes rested on Charlotte. "If all the ladies participate, I will consider it as well." Power resonated behind her soft words.

"Thank you," Charlotte said, fervently hoping she would take part.

"Your scheme sounds dangerous, Charlotte," Mama said with obvious concern.

"We women are a mighty force," Claire said. "But I, too, must think on the idea. Much could go wrong."

"It could," Charlotte said. "We all must ponder the plan before committing to it, for it is, indeed, dangerous."

Lucy's lips tipped into a slow smile. "For us to defeat St. Michaels would be a coup. My Arjuna would be most impressed."

The tension snapped with their laughter.

"When we catch him, shall we feed him to the dogs?" Sina said with laughing eyes.

Charlotte chuckled, shaking her head. "Much as I would like to,

Sina, a magistrates writ exists for his arrest. We will turn him over to the Bow Street constables I will hire to assist us."

"Excellent," Claire said.

"As I am spending the night here," Charlotte said. "Shall we convene in the morning?"

Rose burped. "Apologies. The morning will be good for now my babe demands a nap." She stood.

"I cannot wait to meet him," Charlotte said. "Or her!"

"Not nearly as much as I." Rose shook her head. "In truth, I am quite eager to have this little one out of me."

THIRTY-TWO

The next morning, they gathered around the table once again.

"I have thought on your words, Lady Charlotte," Lucy said. "Are you determined on this plan?"

Charlotte's hands worried her serviette. "Until the baron is caught, a part of me lives in constant fear. I am resolved."

"I will join you," Lucy said.

"I am very pleased." Charlotte smiled with relief.

"Me too!" Thomasina said.

"I will, of course," Rose said. "Even though I'll be stuck here."

"You will come to Hawthorne while we practice," Charlotte said. "We need you to watch and coordinate us."

"Of course I will join." Claire laughed. "How could I pass up a fun adventure such as this?"

"I shall take part, as well," Susannah said.

Rhys strode into the dining room. "And what are you participating in, dear sister?" He bussed Susannah's cheek, then rounded the table to kiss Rose on the lips.

Much joking ensued. "You are doling out kisses, brother?" Claire said. "Where is mine?"

"And mine!" Charlotte said.

"I need one, too!" Thomasina joined in with a grin.

Rhys conceded defeat. "I love you all quite dearly, but I am deuced hungry." He moved to the sideboard to make his plate.

Fortune had smiled on them. Charlotte prayed it continued.

The following days were filled with refining their plan, one that would keep all of them safe and yet trap St. Michaels. Charlotte posted her letter to the baron's seat and mailed a second to Penrhyn Creigiog. Perhaps the monster lurked in Cornwall.

With *Halafair* at Hawthorne Hall restored from its abuse, Charlotte began replicating it. Never again would she allow the baron's foul hands on her mother's most treasured possession. She also worked on a smaller *Halafair* for Claire to take on her trip, and miniatures of Patrick, herself, and others she intended for Christmas gifts as the holiday was nearing.

Her work went swiftly and well, a boon, for upon her return from Cornwall her passion for painting, her desire to create, had been extinguished. But like a green seedling striving through the dirt of memory and fear, her creative urges began to trickle. Gradually, they began to flow, then stream with renewed vigor. She thanked God, Krishna, and any other deity she could think of for its return.

Today, while she painted, she imagined scenarios for setting their trap.

It took three days for their group to settle on a locale where they would meet the baron, choosing the Floating Duck from where St. Michaels' had kidnapped her. The barkeep, unsavory and open to bribery, could work in their favor. An ideal setting.

Claire and Mama moved to Hawthorne Hall, much to Charlotte's delight. Their group gave themselves two weeks to prepare, during which she mailed letters of longing to the baron, drilled her *kalari* forms, and painted like a demon, heady with her renewed joy for the work. Earlier, her large Royal Academy Summer Exhibition entry had traveled to Hawthorne, and she worked on it and her Christmas gifts, along with the replica of *Halafair*.

The Woodbine contingent came daily for practice, telling their men they were rehearsing a Christmas pantomime and for several days, Patrick, Rhys, and Devonshire had ridden out for some winter pheasant hunting. A godsend.

They trained, each woman practicing her specialties, while Thomasina brought Dancer, intending to work with the horse. Mercy, in and out of the great hall, overheard their plans and insisted on joining in. She would brandish her cudgel, her weapon of choice.

"He will do all that I ask and more." Thomasina patted Dancer's neck, his tricks refining daily. He could bow, charge, and even pirouette, and had learned the *croupade*, the *ballotade*, and the *capriole* when a trainer from Vienna's Spanish Riding School had visited Woodbine to teach Thomasina the movements. An impressive sight.

Charlotte's mother, Lucy, and Rose observed, insisting they must watch the practice sessions. Her mother, not a bad shot, worked with Susannah, while Rose gave corrections on Charlotte and Claire's *kalari* forms, though neither her mother nor Rose would accompany them to the Floating Duck. Lucy stayed above the fray, but those enigmatic eyes took it all in, much as a raptor's would.

Time flew, and they had yet to hear from the baron. Worrisome, as they would travel to the Duck in a mere five days.

They ate an early luncheon, as darkness came far too soon these days. Afterward, they observed Thomasina's achievements with Dancer. The bay's looks were unexceptional both in coloring and conformation, and he would draw no unwanted attention to their group when arriving at the Duck. Little did anyone know his talents.

Now, Spider, whom Charlotte had sworn to secrecy, led Dancer a good distance from the manor house.

"Are ye sure ye wants me to release 'em?" Spider hollered.

"Quite sure, sir," Thomasina said in a calm voice.

When he freed Dancer, Thomasina raised her left arm, palm facing forward. The bay froze, eyes on Sina.

She whistled. The horse gathered himself and charged.

Charlotte near took flight, standing close enough to Claire to feel her tremble. Rose, on the other hand, appeared relaxed in the extreme. Charlotte tried to do the same, and failing, she nonetheless stood her ground.

The bay galloped toward them.

He neared, so close Charlotte could see the gelding's rolling eyes when he performed a *courbette,* rearing high, all four legs leaving the ground.

Astonishing. She inhaled a shocked breath, fear squeezing her tight, as Dancer flew into the air.

Thomasina raised her right arm, palm inward.

Dust billowed as the bay landed mere inches from the women.

"Well done, Thomasina!" Claire said in a breathless voice. "I have never seen such!"

"Sina's talents with Woodbine's herd are even more astonishing," Rose said.

"Ain't never seen that! Never!" Spider collected Dancer, snapping his lead onto the halter, and led him back to the sables, their group filing into the hall to practice scenarios.

Patrick had ridden to Devonshire's estate with Banby, allegedly to hunt. But Rhys had heard back from the Admiralty and Patrick was eager for news.

On his return trip home, he signaled Banby go ahead of him and halted beneath a wide oak. How to tell Lottie the outcome of his discussion with the men?

A glance at the sky said the rain would hold off for a while.

Patrick stared, but rather than seeing pastures and hills, he pictured the sea, the roiling waves, the blazing sunsets, the gulls that often accompanied his ship. He could almost feel the sway of the boards beneath his feet and taste the brine on his lips. The navy was all he knew.

Poof.

Though he had expected it, anticipated it, yet even so, Patrick was unprepared for the yawning black hole within, where his purpose since he had been nine once lived.

Seated in the saddle, Diablo chomping grass, the air thick with the promise of rain, he stared at...nothing. The future offered a wilderness of empty years, one after the other, scrolling before him.

With a sigh, Patrick gathered his resolve and would focus on the practical.

He cared not how Saumarez had accomplished his treachery, for it mattered little as the admiral had convinced Patrick's superiors that he was unfit for duty at sea, on land, or anywhere else. The deed was done.

He pictured Billy Broad, a former army "lifer." War had stolen one of his arms, yet upon release from service, he had thrived at Woodbine, a man of value and worth. Did the loss of his arm eat at Billy? Wish he were back in the army? Make him feel less?

Perhaps. Patrick oft imagined his legs as functional, fantasizing about striding across the deck. Yet his inability ground him down, though pondering his loss was a fruitless endeavor. The past was gone. Forever. Yet Billy had thrived. He *must* learn to do so as well.

Rhys and Devonshire would continue to hunt down the slaver frigate, Patrick pursuing the frigate's captain. Once he learned the man's name and rank...So far, the deeper he probed, the more rank it became.

He may no longer be an active naval captain, he could still learn the truth and bring to justice the men who had murdered those slaves.

. . .

Their housekeeper preceded Charlotte into the great hall and began throwing back the curtains.

"Will that be all, my lady?" the housekeeper said.

"Yes. You and the staff may begin your dinner, as we will be occupied here for hours."

The housekeeper smiled. "Thank you, my lady. We shall do just that."

After she left, Charlotte used chalk to set up a large portion of the hall to mirror the Floating Duck's private room, marking the room's entryway and setting table and chairs as they had been that long-ago day in Dartmouth. Outside the chalk line, they had arranged comfy chairs for Mama and Rose, who massaged her belly. They'd also piled up baled straw as tall as men to practice on, her mother's brilliant idea.

Now, they went to work, imagining St. Michaels arriving with a crew holding guns on them. Lucy had brought her short sticks called *muchaanvadi*, her *thala*, a piece of cloth, and a small knife, the name of which Charlotte forgot. In truth, Lucy herself was the weapon.

"I wish we had real people to practice on," Susannah said.

"As do I," Charlotte said. "The staff knows we are up to something, but I would rather they not learn any details. The less they chatter, the better."

Two hours later, perspiration dotted Charlotte's brow, dampened her arms, and trickled down her back, the others equally sweaty. Earlier, Susannah had practiced her shooting outdoors, but now was working with Claire, who threw her knives with unnerving accuracy.

Sina stood beside Mama, while Lucy flanked Rose, observing, though every so often, Lucy would call out corrections.

Charlotte staggered to a halt, panting, and took a few calming breaths. "Since we have practiced with the baron's ruffians entering first, let us vary it to where St. Michaels leads the charge."

"A good idea," Claire said.

"Move to your positions." Charlotte took the seat designated for her to greet the monster, the one where *he* had sat when she entered the inn's parlor.

"Wot's that?" Mercy lowered her cudgel.

"Did you hear something?" Susannah said.

Charlotte peered out a French door. Twilight was upon them, the world darkening to opaque shadows.

Which was when Charlotte heard wheels cross the stone floor.

Heavens above, Patrick!

Glass tinkled at the hall's far end, wood splitting, a crash.

The women turned as one, goggle-eyed.

Men poured inside, half a dozen bristling with guns to form a semi-circle, their weapons aimed at Charlotte and her family.

Charlotte knew two from Cornwall—St. Michaels' ruffians.

The baron stepped through the broken door, pistol in hand, kicking glass and wood aside as he took his place before his men. "I have come for you, my Charlotte!"

The man smiled, a child eager to regain his toy, though his face bore a haggard cast, his skin, pasty.

The world slowed.

Someone gasped.

Lucy stepped forward, her stick on her back in its sheath.

"Do not move!" the baron barked, aiming his pistol at her.

Everyone froze, Charlotte glancing over her shoulder to see Rose drawing Thomasina and her mother further into the shadows.

Again, she heard those wheels. Did no one else? Terror choked her. Patrick was here and unarmed, helpless before these foul men.

How had the baron gotten onto Hawthorne land and breached the house? Had they killed the manor's guards? Her anger grew.

That he *dared* to invade her home...

The baron's hand beckoned her. Charlotte could decline, or she could get close to the man and throw him with a *kalari* move.

A foolish idea that could get someone killed.

Oddly, Charlotte felt little fear. Rather, a calm fury bubbled within for this addlebrain who had stolen three weeks of her life. Had terrorized her. Had made her feel small.

"Why are you here?" she said.

"Your letters, my dear," St. Michaels said. "Of course I would come."

"I proposed we meet at the Floating Duck. You have invaded my home!"

He bowed. "Forgive me, my love, but I suspected a trap."

"I see." She waved her arms. "So you break in with these ruffians?"

Susannah held her pistol behind her back, but Mercy's cudgel had fallen when the men entered the room. Claire's knife lay on the floor, as well. A good thing she had three more secreted about her person.

If needs be, Charlotte would accompany the monster. She had survived him once and could do so again, for no one must be hurt.

She stepped toward St. Michaels.

"Stop!" Patrick boomed.

Charlotte did, for her husband having wheeled into the room, aimed a pistol at St. Michaels' heart.

St. Michaels' men cocked their triggers.

Patrick wheeled closer to the baron, all attention focused on the two men holding guns on each other.

Gods above, St. Michaels' men would shoot him.

A thunk on the stone floor.

The room exploded.

Lucy raised her stick to take out St. Michaels.

"He is *mine*, Lucy!" Patrick shouted, who charged.

Lucy's stick whirled through the air, knocking the gun from St. Michaels' hand.

The ruffians attacked the women.

"Do not fire!" screamed St. Michaels.

Susannah shot a ruffian in the shoulder.

Claire's knife dove into another's neck.

Another shot rang, and Claire staggered, her face gone white, while red bloomed on her arm.

Charlotte leapt in front of Claire, ducking low to clutch the man who had shot her sister, tossing him over her shoulder.

Lucy took out two ruffians simultaneously, her moves blindingly fast, while Mama headed for Claire, who clutched her upper arm, whirling, knife in hand.

St. Michaels drew his sword to swing at Patrick who leaned forward, the baron's blade missing by inches. He punched St. Michaels in the gut.

The man pitched onto the floor.

"Halt!" Patrick hollered, both hands pointing pistols at their enemies.

The room became motionless and quiet, St. Michaels staggering to his feet, pistol aimed at Charlotte.

One other ruffian remained standing, but where...

Charlotte bit her cheek so as not to scream, her heart exploding with fear.

The remaining ruffian hovered beside Rose, his pistol's barrel pressed to her pregnant belly.

THIRTY-THREE

"You move, Hawthorne, and your wife dies." The baron's eyes narrowed. "So will Lady Ravenscroft and her unborn child."

Patrick's face hardened, but he placed his gun on the floor.

"Move." The baron waved Charlotte to stand beside Rose.

She complied and reached for Rose's hand, which trembled. Yet her sister's face remained stolid.

"Good," St. Michaels said, gesturing at his man. "Stand by, Hawthorne, and point your gun between his eyes."

He moved as Patrick leaned down to scratch his leg.

"I said do not move!" St. Michaels barked.

Patrick shrugged. "I had an itch."

Mania stared from St. Michaels' eyes as they skipped from person to person, his tongue flicking the corners of his mouth. If he had ever been rational, he was no longer.

The ruffian reached Patrick, pistol aimed at Patrick's head while the baron approached Rose. He raised his sword to her belly, his smile diabolic. "When are you due, m'lady?"

Charlotte rubbed her fingers together again and again. Would the baron order Patrick killed? Would he stab Rose? What to do?

Patrick had scratched his leg. An itch, he said. Interesting, as he had no feeling in them. Her husband was up to something.

She must distract St. Michaels.

"You are ridiculous, my lord." She approached St. Michaels, walking with swagger. "You must realize that."

"Shut up," he said.

"Why?" she continued. "You lost at the Royal Academy, and now you are acting out a violent scheme that will only end in—"

He slapped her. "We are leaving *now*, Lady Hawthorne." He grabbed her upper arm and pulled her close, his eyes shifting from Patrick to Rose to Charlotte.

Patrick bellowed, "Now!"

A gunshot, and down went Patrick's guard as a knife flew from his hand to lodge itself in St. Michaels' shoulder.

The baron screamed.

Charlotte breathed in energy preparing her side lunge, *neeki theruthu*. But before she took action, a whirlwind flew atop the baron's back, the pair tumbling to the floor.

Henry!

All the women moved. Charlotte and Henry subdued the baron, then both sat on his rump. Lucy hovered over the two she had dropped, while Susannah and Claire stood beside the pair they had felled, pistol and knife drawn, blood dripping from Claire's wound onto the floor. The final ruffian sprawled on the floor, unmoving.

Banby strode into the hall, lengths of rope looped over his shoulder. "Apologies for my late arrival. One of the baron's sentries held me up."

Was it over? Charlotte felt dizzy.

The lieutenant tied St. Michaels' hands and feet, performing the same for his men. Henry had disappeared, returning with a dozen footmen and other servants who hauled away St. Michaels and his cohorts.

"Lock them in the ice house," Patrick said to their butler.

Those last few minutes of terror…Charlotte braced her hand on a wall, sparks of relief needling through her.

They were safe, no one seriously harmed, with Mama now tending Claire's minor injury.

Yet frissons of fear continued to ripple. She stumbled to Patrick and sank onto his lap. He hugged her tight. "All is well."

She couldn't reply. Patrick smelled of gunpowder and sandalwood and his own musk. She breathed deep.

"How fare our outdoor guards?" Patrick said to Banby.

"Alive," the lieutenant replied. "Though all will have serious headaches on the morrow."

Alive. Thank all that was holy. Yet she could not settle, reliving the gunfire, the shouts, the gun pointed at Rose. She closed her eyes just for a moment. She whispered in Patrick's ear. "I cannot believe you said your leg itched."

"Why ever not?" he said.

She hissed. "Because you have no feeling in your legs. If he had realized—"

"I know that, Lottie mine, but I was thinking in the moment, my knife strapped to my calf, and an itchy leg seemed a fine solution."

"Harrumph."

"Do not be angry, darling," he crooned.

Charlotte's eyes began to well. "I am not. Merely overset."

Boots rat-a-tatted down the hall.

Charlotte startled.

Everyone froze, as if posing, while Patrick raised his gun toward the entrance.

Rhys halted there, gaping. "What the hell?"

Rose waddled to him, arms outstretched.

It was too much. All too much. Charlotte started to laugh just as the skies opened to unleash a torrential downpour.

In the following weeks, life settled as they prepared for

Christmas celebrations at Woodbine, always a merry time, and this year particularly so.

Nonetheless, Patrick was out of sorts and pensive in the extreme. Ruminating, Charlotte expected, though he had not shared on what. Charlotte would probe, but she would let it be for now.

Since Hawthorne's grand hullabaloo, St. Michaels and his cronies had been held by the constabulary, then transported to London. His ruffians now sailed the seas bound for Australia, while St. Michaels' new home was a suite in Bethlem Royal Hospital, more commonly known as Bedlam.

Charlotte peered out a studio window, looked beyond the gardens to the pastures beyond. The leaden skies failed to dim the pleasure of watching Henry ride Dante over poles set on the ground. For days the boy had lunged the horse over them, but this was Dante's first time with Henry in the saddle. Snow began to drift down, the pair seeming dusted by magic.

A knock, then the door opened. "His Lordship has asked you meet him in the study, m'lady."

"Thank you, Jemmy. Please tell him I must clean my hands and will be with him shortly."

She moistened a rag with linseed oil and began to massage her hands free of paint, walking to the window to watch Henry's doings. The snow was flying harder, and though Dante was white, she saw him standing in the middle of the pasture, reins dropped to the ground. She pressed her hands to the glass, looking this way and that, but Henry was nowhere in sight.

Charlotte ran through the house hollering for Patrick, then flew out a side door toward Dante, twirling as she yelled Henry's name.

No one appeared, and she was about to fetch Patrick when a pair of their burly groundskeepers emerged from beyond the fence line, hauling two men who resisted mightily. A sorry-looking Henry trudged beside them.

Thank all the stars! "Patrick!" she yelled, her heart pounding near out of her chest.

Henry ran toward her, and she was about to meet him when a hand brushed her waist. She whirled. "Patrick."

"Henry is fine, Lottie," he said. "Stay here. I have business to conduct."

The boy thumped into her, arms flung around her waist, squeezing tight. "They tried to take me, m'lady. Take me away! But the captain had a watch out. Runners!"

Charlotte stared down at the boy, not quite believing he was real. Henry's face was bruised, with a bloodied lip, and dirt smearing his forehead. But when he peered up at her, his eyes sparked with humor. "They didn't get me!"

"No, they did not!"

"Lady Charlotte." Banby walked toward them, Akiko at his side.

"Someone tried to steal Henry!" Charlotte said. Patrick had noted his fears for the boy regarding Saumarez. But would an admiral abduct a child?

Charlotte turned to speak with Patrick, but he and the others had vanished.

Patrick observed as his men, both Bow Street Runners, bound the kidnappers, then stowed them in the wood shop guarded by two additional runners. Now, their trio trotted a woodland path in silence beneath a cloud of falling snow, the horses' breaths puffing the air.

The road wasn't far, which was where they headed, for an hour earlier his lookout had reported the arrival of a post chaise, one stationed well beyond the entrance to Hawthorne in shadow beneath two large oaks. His men had watched as the two postillions dismounted and entered Hawthorne's wood. The runners riding beside him had tracked the postillions, observing as they sprung on Henry, which was when they had captured them.

Sensing Patrick's anticipation, Diablo pranced, but he brought him down to a walk. Snow swirled around the horses' hooves, which crunched on the blanket of white, the quiet intense.

Would the coming confrontation truly be the end of it?

They neared the road, and the man to his left widened the distance between them, for he would hold the carriage horses at bay. Patrick held up a hand, and they paused.

He prayed the chaise held a man he had long wished to apprehend, unable to erase the horror of those slaves' faces and cries as they sank without hope of rescue.

Patrick seized the eye of each runner, then nodded.

They galloped from the trees, one man containing the chaise's horses, Patrick aiming his pistol at the driver's head, while the second runner leapt from his mount to fling open the carriage door.

"What is the meaning of this?" barked Admiral Saumarez from within.

A thrill roiled through Patrick. The man himself had come. "You have failed, Admiral. Time to end the charade."

Patrick ducked, seeing the glint of a gun barrel in the wan light.

A boom shattered the silence, followed by the runner manhandling Saumarez from the carriage.

"How dare you, Captain?" Saumarez scowled as the runner released him and the admiral straightened his clothes, civilian ones.

"Kidnapping my ward?" Patrick said. "You failed, and your men have given you up. A sad end to a mighty career."

Saumarez straightened, shoulders thrown back, chin notched. "Your ward?" The admiral scoffed. "He is nothing but a lowbred guttersnipe of no importance." He offered Patrick a smile. "Let us speak privately."

The admiral was unaware Patrick's men were runners, constables who would haul him to the magistrate for the attempted abduction.

He nodded, the man beside Saumarez mounting the box to tie the driver, while Patrick walked Diablo to the rear of the carriage. "Back here if you wish to speak in private."

Saumarez planted his feet. "Come inside, man!"

"I cannot dismount, Admiral." He could, but no point telling the bloody prick that.

Saumarez swanned to where Patrick sat on Diablo and leaned against a carriage wheel, crossing a leg. "Now see here, Lansdowne—"

"I am afraid it is you who must see, Admiral."

Saumarez's smile was slow, his eyes aglitter. "Think of what I can offer you, man. A position at the Admiralty, and, in future, an elevation in rank."

"Exactly what rank?" Patrick said, feigning curiosity.

Saumarez appeared to think for a moment. "I see, perhaps, admiral. Certainly commander would be in your future. Is this not what you wished for?"

"At one time, it was indeed." Patrick grinned. "But I shall request to resign my commission. I do not doubt it will be granted."

"Think on it!" Saumarez said. "You could have the many benefits of an elevated position! The advantages would be immense."

A sudden exhaustion drained Patrick. He wanted this over. "You recognized Henry at the auction, the boy having been on the *Despoina* when you brought the slaves aboard, which puts you aboard that frigate that transported those murdered slaves. After you noted the boy, you were patient, bided your time through the Royal Academy committee meetings and our return to Hawthorne before making your move."

"I know nothing of any of this!"

"Take him!"

Two mounted men bled from the trees, one leading a horse for Saumarez, the other binding the admiral's hands.

"You dare restrain me!"

"Ah," Patrick said. "You see, Bow Street has a magistrate's writ to apprehend you on suspicion of trading in slaves. All it needed was for you to move against me or mine."

With little ceremony, the men hauled him onto the back of the horse, a third standing at its head. Patrick was thankful all three were heavily muscled for Saumarez was large, a powerful man who dug his heels into the dirt, refusing to move.

The snow paused, night fallen, with moonlight glimmering down on them, Saumarez's face reddened with fury. And fear. An image Patrick would long remember.

Saumarez and his attendants rode away, four men surrounding the admiral, the fifth driving the chaise that followed.

Patrick closed his eyes and tilted his face to the once-again falling snow, cooling his ire and soothing his soul.

Christmas at Woodbine approached, and it was magical, for Rose insisted upon it. Food with all the trimmings, carols sung, and church attended. Gifts given and parlor games played with family and friends around the hearth. Charlotte could not wait.

They had decorated Hawthorne early, rather than the traditional Christmas Eve, with evergreen wreaths, kissing balls, and mistletoe throughout the manor, along with a large Yule log from Hawthorne's home wood resting in the great hall's hearth, which the staff would light on Christmas Eve. All decorations would be removed on Twelfth Day, the manor would be thoroughly cleaned, for it was said every stray leaf that remained, a ghost lingered behind.

Charlotte did not wish to welcome any ghostly inhabitants, though she toyed with the idea. What an adventure that would be.

Patrick wheeled beside her as she directed him to a spot in the room. Charlotte slipped onto Patrick's lap and pointed upward to a kissing ball hung from a rafter. "Well?"

His face transformed, turning desirous, and he took her in a wild kiss.

Finally. *Finally,* they were safe.

Their carriage jounced along the road to Woodbine, Charlotte bubbling with excitement. The air was crisp, the sky a blue as intense as Patrick's eyes. Charlotte hoped for snow.

They were full to bursting with Banby, Henry, Spider, and Akiko accompanying them, the beautiful Asian scholar a treasure of a find. After two months, she had become a quiet and calm presence at Hawthorne Hall. *Most* interesting was the friendship forming between Akiko and Lieutenant Banby.

A crowd greeted them upon arrival, which included Ashworth and Devonshire, and once the rumpus settled, they dined, then disappeared to their rooms, exhausted.

Patrick's odd musings had not lifted. That he hadn't shared his thoughts concerned Charlotte, yet when asked, he claimed nothing of substance troubled him. She didn't believe him.

After church Christmas morning, they reconvened late afternoon for an exceptional Christmas feast, including mince pies, as tradition demanded. They would eat the pies daily for the Twelve Days of Christmas, ensuring good fortune the following year. Charlotte only accepted a sliver, as by the tenth day, she would be sick of them.

Rose appeared discomforted during the meal, and the men had formed a betting pool as to when the new Lansdowne would appear. The talk turned to other Christmases, and Ashworth regaled the company with the ones he and his father spent exploring Greece. In a few days, Claire was off to those fabled isles, accompanying Louis-François-Sébastien Fauvel, Lord Elgin's renowned competitor.

After the meal, they reassembled before the Christmas tree, a tradition taken up by Rose after reading of Queen Charlotte's tree. Rose adored anything festive, for her life before marriage to Rhys had been anything but.

Presents sat on a sideboard, while lit candles glowed on the tree, with holly and other decorations dotting the family salon. The room sparkled. Everyone milled about including the dogs, except Rose, enthroned in a wing chair. They drank sherried eggnog or wassail and exchanged hugs and kisses, jokes and tall tales, which added to the merriment.

"Rhys, would you bring a pillow for my back?" Rose said.

He moved like lightning to place one behind Rose.

Patrick raised a brow. "You have become quite the empress, pest."

Rose snorted. "If the babe does not appear soon..." She growled. "I shall take a good long ride on Ace. Yes, I will!"

Amidst much laughter, the gifts were dispensed.

Charlotte gave painted miniatures to Rhys and Rose, and had miniatures of Patrick and herself as well, but those were for later, in private.

During a moment of quiet, Patrick wheeled to Henry and handed him a packet of papers. Charlotte's heart pounded. They had other gifts for Henry, fun ones, but this was the most precious of all.

Henry opened the packet and paused, glancing at Akiko. She nodded wearing a small smile. "Our Henry's reading has progressed, but I suggest these should be read by you, Lord Hawthorne."

Patrick began to read, and when finished, he looked at Henry. Stars shone in the boy's eyes. "Is this real, Captain? Am I to be your and Lady Charlotte's ward?"

"Aye," Patrick said. "'Tis real and true as can be. If you wish it so."

Henry wrapped his arms around Patrick's neck, her husband holding the boy close, eyes closed, face sublime.

Then Henry dashed to Charlotte and repeated the hug, shaking with emotion. As was she. Now he was theirs in truth.

Henry straightened, slapping his hands to his hips. "Then what's my name now?"

Patrick chuckled. "Henry Lansdowne, if you wish."

"I does!"

Akiko cleared her throat.

"I *do*. Yes, I do very much." He walked to Patrick. "And what shall I call you both—Captain and Lady Charlotte?"

"If you wish," Patrick said. "Or you—"

"Can I call you Mum and Da?"

Patrick smiled. "You can, indeed. I would like that, and I expect her ladyship feels the same."

Too overcome, Charlotte nodded.

Patrick slid his hand into Charlotte's, then raised his glass to Banby. "You shall be Henry's uncle. What say you?"

Banby's eyes shone bright gold. "I say, that is quite excellent. Perhaps with 'uncle' attached, he will finally heed my words!"

Charlotte privately doubted that.

"I'm gonna go tell Spider!"

After the boy raced off, Rhys and Rose excused themselves. She and Patrick did the same, returning to their suite. They slipped off their party clothes and began to exchange their gifts, yet Patrick's distraction remained.

She gave him the miniature of her, and he grew quiet, running a finger down the glass that hovered above her ivory-painted portrait. "It is exquisite, as are you, my beloved wife."

Her eyes burned as he handed her his gift. Lifting the lid revealed a gold linked bracelet dangling with charms—an artist's palette and paintbrush, a carnelian inscribed with their entwined initials, a locket with a curl of Patrick's hair beneath glass, and a gold charm of an open window.

"This is beyond anything, Patrick. Fasten it on me?" Utterly entranced, she held out her wrist. "An open window?"

"Your escape, course!"

Soon they were in bed, making slow languorous love. Time was theirs. Safety was theirs. The world flowed over and through them as Patrick moved inside her, with bliss bursting like a shooting star accompanied by Patrick's groan when he spent inside her. That was bliss, too.

He moved to her side, his arms still surrounding her, and she rested her head in the dip of his shoulder, utterly content.

"Making love only gets better, does it not?" Charlotte said.

He kissed her shoulder, then chuckled. "Yes. I confess it is startling how these feelings continue to grow. I love you today more than I loved you yesterday. How is that possible? Yet I do."

"We are lucky. Blessed."

"That we are," he said, his warm eyes darkening to serious. "I have news."

Finally. She leaned back to study his expression. "Your tone sounds rather dire."

"I shall resign my commission, Lottie, and soon will be officially retired." His eyes were shadowed, his face tight.

Platitudes bit at her lips, ones she did not voice. "If I could not paint, I would be crushed. I suspect you feel the same."

His eyes cut from hers. "The press of the thing weighed me down, but I have come to terms with it."

She cupped his chin, and turned his face to hers. "We shall buy that boat!"

He leaned in, warmed by his love's suggestion, then nuzzled her neck. "To race in the Vauxhall sailing match. What made you so wise, Lady Hawthorne?"

"I suspect it is my husband's influence." Her smile was shy.

"Ha! I doubt that." He grinned.

"Banby and Henry can help crew!" An awful thought occurred. "Will Banby be leaving us?"

"Banby will resign as well, much to my surprise. Once assured his decision was freely made, I asked him to stay on as our steward. He has accepted."

"That is brilliant. Have you noticed the shine he has taken to Akiko?"

"Hard *not* to notice," Patrick said, his grin roguish. "There is more. Saumarez is gone."

"Rotting in a cell, I hope!" Charlotte said. "Or hung!"

Patrick chuckled. "Not exactly. As his treachery would reflect poorly on the Admiralty, it must stay hushed."

Irate, she went to speak, but Patrick put a finger on her lips. "They have stationed Saumarez in Canada's far north by the North-western Passages, a permanent posting. He will not fare well."

"I expect not." She was both relieved and pleased, though she wished he'd been hung. "Given his love of women and creature comforts, both few and far between in that frigid land."

"Tomorrow, Banby and I burn his woolie and my frigate in a victory celebration. You are welcome to join us." Patrick wore a piratical grin. "One thing more."

"What? Another scheme?"

"I will join the Lords next January, as I intend to effect the end of slavery throughout the Empire. I have written William Wilberforce of my intention."

"The abolitionist?"

He nodded. "Along with several Quakers and other abolitionists such as Buxton and Lushington. Did you know slave-grown products comprise about eighty percent of Britain's foreign income? Early days yet, but I have also begun drafting my first speech."

Charlotte had no words.

"Your thoughts?" he said. "I confess I am a bit nervous about the prospect."

"Nervous? Bah. Will it be the Tories or the Whigs who welcome you with open arms?"

"The Whigs." Patrick winked.

"I confess my surprise, yet I suspect a good fit."

"Indeed." He grinned. "I imagine politics will keep me out of your hair."

"I like it when you are in my hair, silly man. I like it when you are...Everywhere." Her smile was sultry.

Patrick barked a laugh.

"Hush!" Charlotte said. "You will awaken half the house. Rose needs her sleep."

He moved to hover above her once again. "I can think of one way to keep us quiet, my dearest girl."

On a grin, Charlotte reached up and pulled him close. "I believe I can, as well."

EPILOGUE

Days later, Patrick and Charlotte crawled into bed at five in the morning, having celebrated Hogmanay. Rose adored the idea of the Scottish tradition on New Year's Eve, as it was ancient, purportedly from the Norse era. The party had been festive, the bonfire exuberant, the high-spirited dancing continuing on into the wee hours.

Lord Ashworth was the first-foot—having arrived just after midnight—the first person to cross the threshold in the new year, who was proclaimed as a bringer of good luck and prosperity.

After Rose's effusive greeting and many toasts, Rhys and Rose said their good-nights, Rose weary in the extreme. Charlotte was done in as well, but as she and Patrick made to leave, cries from Devonshire, Claire, and even Mama insisted they remain. So they stayed...and stayed.

On the morrow, they would leave and though the holiday celebrations had abounded joy, love, and merriment, Charlotte was eager to return to Hawthorne Hall. To home.

Too weary to make love, they held each other as they fell asleep until a pounding jerked them awake.

Charlotte leapt from the bed, wrapping her dressing gown around her, while Patrick pulled on his nightshirt and slipped into his chair. A glance at the clock said six a.m.

Patrick wheeled to find Banby at the door, half-dressed in a shirt and pantaloons.

"Lady Rose is having her babe," Banby said.

They made it to the grand staircase when Henry appeared at the top. "Wait! Lady Bea said Lady Rose had her baby! It is a big fat boy! A lot of people were crying. I think even Lord Rhys. Which was odd."

A boy. Rose had given Rhys a boy. No Hogmanay gift was more precious than that.

Perhaps an hour later, they met their new nephew, little Gareth, bundled and asleep on the bed between a bleary-eyed Rose and Rhys. Charlotte pressed the lightest of kisses to his forehead, as did Patrick, and they chatted for long moments before returning to bed.

Much, *much* later that morning, Charlotte and Claire oohed and cooed at the bright-eyed child, Gareth staring at them in that intense way newborns had about them. They remained as Rose put the babe to her own breast, having disdained a milk nurse. Gareth proceeded to eat with greedy slurps, the women beaming.

Moments later, a knock, then her mother's whispered, "Patrick wishes to speak with you, Lottie."

With a kiss to the babe's and Rose's cheeks, Charlotte left to find her husband awaiting her outside the door.

She clasped his hand as they progressed down the hall. "Rose is feeding Gareth."

"Feeding him *herself?*" Patrick said. "Will you do the same?"

Charlotte started. Imagining her own child, their child. *Oh, my.* She took a seat on a nearby chair. "I...I do not know."

He grinned. "You will when the time comes."

Charlotte flushed. *When the time comes...*As they could not keep their hands off each other, it should not take long. "What is it you wished to see me about?"

Patrick held up a letter. "This came earlier. I suspect you shall enjoy reading it."

She unfolded the foolscap already unsealed.

Dear Lord Hawthorne—

The Royal Academy of Arts is pleased to inform you that Lady Hawthorne's painting, The Sea Dance, *has been accepted for the Royal Academy's Summer Exhibition.*

Sincerely,

Benjamin West

President, RAA

"No!" Incredulous, her heart fluttered with excitement. She read the missive again. "Really truly?"

"Really truly, darling." Patrick kissed her palm, then looked up, his face mischievous. "I snuck an academician into Hawthorne to view your work in progress. He was quite taken with *The Sea Dance* and shared his thoughts with the Royal Academy's exhibition committee. Hence your acceptance. My darling wife, you deserve this and much more."

Her beautiful, thoughtful husband. How she had been so lucky, so blessed that long-ago day in the library? "I have all I desire and deserve, Patrick. I have you."

Acknowledgments

My readers are so special, and I thank you all for your support, enthusiasm, and daily inspiration! You're the best!

Many thanks to those who helped shepherd *THE DECEPTION* through to the finish line. Yet again, my matchless editor, Aria Jones, worked her wizardry. No matter the genre, Aria is superb at what she does!

To the extraordinary Camille Cotton—this book wouldn't exist without you. To the amazing Rosemary Hill, whose friendship, aid, and insights are both invaluable and inspirational. To Monica—for your fabulous assistance.

To my much-loved Betas: Ro, Camille, Joanie, Wayne, Meri, and Vivi for their invaluable critiques and, most of all, their friendship. To Lorelai—who brings me joy through the sweat and tears.

To my exceptional cover artist, Blake Ricciardi, aided by Mike Le —my dream cover was turned into reality by you. Thank you!

To Eleanor, for your sharp mind and quick pen.

To the Illuterati and my Facebook pals who inspire me with warmth, humor, and truth-telling. To the Warrioresses, who soothe my heart, and to Parris Afton Bonds, who hugs my soul. To my yoga pals, Ren, Chris, Sheri, Franny, Annette, Edie, and Emma, who support me in so many ways. To my Trivia pals, Robin, Amy, Franny, Laura, Abby, Deborah, and Kresse — you keep me laughing.

To Let's Ride, and all its denizens both two- and four-hooved. To Andrea Urban, Suzanne Hendrich, Pat Murphy, Donna Cautilli, CJ Williams, Linda Windels—love you. To Cindy's Knitters for the many stitches we wove together. To Betsy Bair, Georgi Mueller, Alison Hall, and Karen Waxman for your love and friendship. To Cynthia Michaels, for your friendship and giving Cranberry love.

To Peter, Kathleen, Summer and George—your love and support make my world turn. Love you! Finally, to my beloved boys, Blake and Ben—for all that you are, for all that you have gifted me, and for all your abiding love. I'm the luckiest mom in the world.

Any errors or screw-ups are mine alone.

THANK YOU! AND NEWSLETTER

Thank you for reading *The Deception*!

Reviews mean everything—they're an author's lifeblood as readers find us through your reviews. If you enjoyed Charlotte's and Patrick's tale, leaving an honest review would be a kindness.

Would you like a free book? Do sign up for Vicki's newsletter (Sanna doesn't have one) and receive her bonus novel, *Body Parts*. Her monthly newsletter contains info on The Secret Tales, The Made Ones Saga, the Afterworld Chronicles, life in L.A., and lots more yummy stuff.

Come visit with me... VickiStiefel.net & SannaBrand.com
Facebook • Instagram • Twitter • BookBub

THE SEER
THE SECRET TALES, BOOK 3

CHAPTER 1, 1819

Claire Cassandra Pheland wished to discard her skin, her nerves were *that* prickly.

What was she doing here, about to present a paper to London's Society of Antiquaries? She must be mad or foxed. Sadly, she was neither as she surveyed the audience of Fellows and attendees from her seat. All male.

She had wrangled her presentation with the help of the Marquess of Ravenscroft, her brother-in-law, along with aid from Viscount Hawthorne, another brother-in-law. She sat between them in the audience, their expressions stolid.

No fool, Claire had made her request to the society using the initials, CC Pheland, avoiding any hint of gender.

As she listened to a clever paper on Roman coins, her palms turned greasy with sweat beneath her gloves. Her foot jiggled, too, an altogether inappropriate activity. Yet she could not seem to stop.

A trustee called her name. *God help her*. She rose, then moved between legs and chair backs to reach the aisle, thankful eighteenth century voluminous skirts were not in fashion.

Murmurs began, then voices rose, a shout or two, bursts of laughter, while several men pointed fingers as Claire approached the dais a line of trustees and presenters staring daggers at her.

Eyes forward, spine stiff, Claire endured the catcalls. Why shouldn't there be? After all, she was a *woman*. Claire tried to encase herself in iron, but as she reached the podium, she almost tripped on her cursed skirt. Women's clothes were so very inconvenient.

The room's din rose, as did her fury at their disrespect. Nonetheless, she lay her notes on the podium, staring at her written words as if they might leap off the page and attack.

With a deep breath, she raised her head and perused the crowd. Claire smiled.

"My paper will illuminate and substantiate my hypothesis that the ancient Greek statues, busts, and other marbles we so admire were colorfully painted. Few were pure white."

Raucous laughter bounced off the walls, and Claire didn't know whether it was due to her hypothesis or her gender. Or, perhaps, both. It mattered little, as the cacophony was drowning out her words.

She slipped on her glasses for a more scholarly look, though it appeared they made little difference to the discordant crowd.

Trustees quieted the audience, and Claire proceeded. "From my examination of numerous statues, stele, and plinths during my time in Greece, along with my studies here, I have come to the conclusion that the Greeks, rather than being admirers of austere white sculptures, painted patterns and bright colors on the majority of their figurative works. I would even to go so far as—

"Shut up!" hollered a man in the audience.

"What is this woman talking about?" Another hollered.

"She is deranged!"

Claire tightened her grip on the podium and continued to speak. Whether she must shout over the crowd or not, she would *finish*.

Theseus Ashworth was disgusted with the behavior of his esteemed colleagues. No matter a woman expounded at the podium, members of the Society had read her paper and deemed it worthy of discussion.

He could barely hear her above the shouts and laughter. Unconscionable.

No dialogue was to be found here, but rather jeers, swearing, and fists raised in protest. All due to her gender, which was absurd. Though he admitted Lady Claire's premise was ludicrous.

Along with Ravenscroft and Hawthorne, both acquaintances, his good friend, the Duke of Devonshire, appeared as furious as he. But there sat the offensive Lord Elgin, arms crossed, lobbing jeers along with the rest of them.

He was acquainted with Claire Pheland, daughter of the famous artist, Reginald Pheland, Baron Halafair. He didn't particularly like her, for her tongue was sharp. Nonetheless, she was Devonshire's friend, thus she must have some redeemable qualities. That was neither here nor there. The Fellows behavior was inexcusable.

Theseus rose, and given his height, bulk, and respect as an antiquarian, the audience took notice. "Hush, you cretans!"

His booming baritone succeeded...for a moment. For the catcalls, laughter, and lewd comments soon recommenced.

Ravenscroft ascended the dais to whisper in Lady Claire's ear. She nodded, then faced the crowd.

"Gentlemen, my work stands on its own! If you are too blind to see it, then I am too mute to speak. You should be ashamed of your unwillingness to listen to a point of view that differs from your own. Ashamed!"

Devil it, the woman was impressive.

With that, she took Ravenscroft's winged arm, fisted her notes, and stepped from the dais.

Four months after Lady Claire's debacle at the Society of Antiquaries, Theseus received a letter from the woman herself. On that day he'd observed an appalling demonstration of men's prejudice. Fools. He had left the symposium shortly after she.

Lady Claire's letter thanked him for his attempt to quell the audience, then she made a request to study his father's extensive collection of marbles from Greece.

Damnation. To examine the works, Lady Claire would want time, more time than he could afford, given his departure for the Greek isles.

His plan to return his father's collection of marbles, "appropriated" in Greece, was fraught with dissenters. The Crown pressured him to keep them, as did the British Museum, and that cursed Lord Elgin, the mawworm who stole the friezes from Athens' Parthenon.

He cared not one whit for any of them. His father's marbles did not belong in England, but rather deserved to be repatriated to Greece.

Many antiquaries wished to examine his busts, statues, and stela. On a good day he had little patience for any of them. And still the requests poured in. Vultures all.

The concept disgusted Theseus. Not the discoveries themselves, of course, but his father's thievery for his own personal gain. That was how Theseus saw it, for he equated the appropriation to rape, Unsurprisingly, few shared his viewpoint.

He would soon leave for Greece accompanied by the entire collection of marbles, hundreds of them, which he would return to their home country, where they *belonged*, rather than resting in some British country manor.

His blood boiled thinking on what his father had done.

The British Museum and the king himself placed enormous pressure on him to keep the marbles in England. He would not.

He set Lady Claire's letter aside beneath a shard of marble on his desk. Physically, Claire Pheland was exquisite—blonde, amber-eyed, with a fine figure and proud carriage. Yet she seemed oblivious to her own beauty. An act? He wondered.

How much *did* the woman know about the ancients? Where had

she studied? Women had no access to British universities. Another absurdity. The Italian, Laura Bassi, earned a Ph.D. at the University of Bologna, and began teaching physics, of all things, at that same university. Another Italian, he failed to recall her name, also received a Ph.D from Bologna. He knew of women attending universities in Germany and Sweden, as well. But they were outliers. No woman could attain a university degree in England.

Yet men persisted in seeing women as less intelligent. Astounding. He knew numerous bright-minded women equal to or surpassing men's acuity.

Given Lady Claire's history, a titled and entitled daughter of a baron, she pursued her unique subject with uncommon fervor. She may have failed to finish reading her paper, but what little he heard had given him pause. Yet he remained incredulous. Colored statues? He could not fathom it.

Lady Claire was on some wild goose chase. Nonetheless, given her courage at the gathering, he would consider admitting her to the marbles' room.

The Seer, Coming June 2025!

About the Author

BY VICKI STIEFEL

A fable~

Once upon a time...

When my great grandmother came to America from England, she carried only two items—her Bible and her great-grandmother's diaries. Great-nana Susannah (Sanna) Brand was an inveterate diarist and wrote daily. For years, I've been pouring through her journals, fascinated. Much she wrote was mundane—about family, fashion, food, and her beaus (until she met my great, great etc. grandfather). I read and read until I came upon a peculiar journal—which turned out to be Sanna's novel!

~In truth, that is how I imagine Sanna, my alter ego.~

Award-winning author Vicki Stiefel's romantic science-fantasy series, The Made Ones Saga, concluded with *Ascendant*. Vicki continues work on her Afterworld Chronicles, a five-book series begun with *Chest of Bone*. Her mystery/thrillers feature homicide counselor Tally Whyte, and Vicki's knitting love produced *Chest of Bone The Knit Collection* and *10 Secrets of the LaidBack Knitters*.

Having grown up in professional theater, Vicki planned to become an actress. Instead, she slung hamburgers, managed a scuba shop, and taught at Clark U. She's a mom to two wonderful humans and is currently playing with her pups, Penny and Sebastian, and her kitties, Sammy and Odin, while pounding the keys on *The Seer*, the third book in The Secret Tales.

Come visit with me...
vickistiefel.net

facebook.com/vicki.stiefel.5
x.com/vickistiefel
instagram.com/vickistiefel
pinterest.com/vickistiefel
bookbub.com/profile/vicki-stiefel

ALSO BY VICKI STIEFEL & SANNA BRAND

The Secret Tales

The Bond

The Deception

The Seer (coming June 2025)

The Made Ones Saga

Altered

Changed

Ascendant

The Afterworld Chronicles

Chest of Bone

Chest of Stone

Chest of Time

Chest of Fire (to come)

Tally Whyte/Homicide Counselor Series

Body Parts • *The Dead Stone* • *The Grief Shop* (Daphne duMaurier Award winner) • *The Bone Man* (Daphne duMaurier Award finalist)

Nonfiction

10 Secrets of the LaidBack Knitters

Chest of Bone The Knit Collection

Visit with Vicki:

Website • Facebook • Instagram • BookBub

9 798987 023266